THE SUNLESS COUNTRIES

KARL SCHROEDER

THE
SUNLESS
COUNTRIES

Virga | BOOK FOUR

A TOM DOHERTY ASSOCIATES BOOK ▲ NEW YORK
TOR®

This is a work of fiction. All of the characters, organizations, and events portrayed in this novel are either products of the author's imagination or are used fictitiously.

THE SUNLESS COUNTRIES: BOOK FOUR OF VIRGA

Copyright © 2009 by Karl Schroeder

A Tor Book
Published by Tom Doherty Associates, LLC
175 Fifth Avenue
New York, NY 10010

www.tor-forge.com

Tor® is a registered trademark of Tom Doherty Associates, LLC.

Library of Congress Cataloging-in-Publication Data

Schroeder, Karl, 1962–
    The sunless countries / Karl Schroeder. — 1st ed.
        p. cm. — (Virga ; bk. 4)
    "A Tom Doherty Associates book."
    ISBN-13: 978-0-7653-2076-6
    ISBN-10: 0-7653-2076-2
    I. Title.
    PR9199.3.s269s865   2009
    823'.54—dc22

                        2009013881

First Edition: August 2009

Printed in the United States of America

0 9 8 7 6 5 4 3 2 1

To the Temagami gang

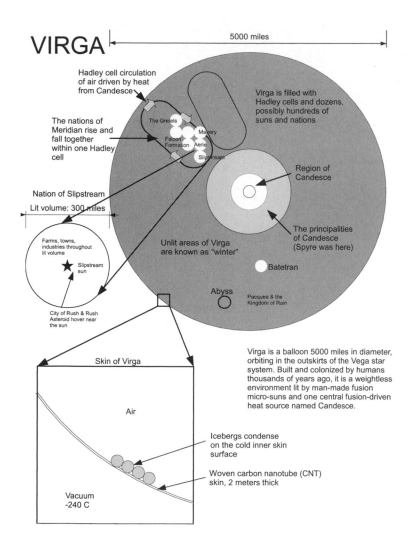

VIRGA

5000 miles

Hadley cell circulation of air driven by heat from Candesce

The nations of Meridian rise and fall together within one Hadley cell

Virga is filled with Hadley cells and dozens, possibly hundreds of suns and nations

The Gretels

Mavery

Falcon Formation

Aerie

Slipstream

Region of Candesce

The principalities of Candesce (Spyre was here)

Nation of Slipstream

Lit volume: 300 miles

Unlit areas of Virga are known as "winter"

Batetran

Farms, towns, industries throughout lit volume

Slipstream sun

Abyss

Pacquea & the Kingdom of Rain

City of Rush & Rush Asteroid hover near the sun

Skin of Virga

Air

Virga is a balloon 5000 miles in diameter, orbiting in the outskirts of the Vega star system. Built and colonized by humans thousands of years ago, it is a weightless environment lit by man-made fusion micro-suns and one central fusion-driven heat source named Candesce.

Icebergs condense on the cold inner skin surface

Woven carbon nanotube (CNT) skin, 2 meters thick

Vacuum
-240 C

WHEN LEAL SHUT off the engine the whole world went away. Sight, sound, and touch fled into darkness, leaving only the sighing of her own breath. The touch of the pilot's seat faded as her weightless body drifted away from it. Leal kept her long fingers on the starter key for a few seconds, as if she might never find it again once she let go.

She glanced down at the reassuring radium glow of the instrument panel. Then, hesitantly, she reached out to unseal the pilot's canopy. Straining, she swung it up and back, letting in a puff of cold air scented with ice. There was barely a breeze against her face.

That was not good. According to the gyrocompass, her little cutter should have been making a good twenty knots. She should have felt as much breeze on her face. That she didn't meant either that she had entered a mass of air that was moving that fast itself; or her instruments were wrong.

"Come on," she muttered, leaning out of the canopy and craning her neck for any hint of light. The headlight might be piercing the air for hundreds of feet, yet she saw absolutely nothing—not even a mote of dust sparkling in the dark. "Where are you?"

Her city, Sere, should have appeared by now. Even if its glittering wheel-of-wheels wasn't directly visible, Leal should at least be seeing a red and blue brightening in the air every three seconds or so, as the outlier beacons flashed in their turning. She should hear distant ringing and honking, the grumbling of industry. If the whole city were embedded in cloud, she should at least hear foghorns.

"Damn." It wasn't a long journey from her hometown to the capital—three hours—and she made the round-trip every weekend. This wouldn't be the first journey where Leal had let her eyes drift away from the endless wavering length of rope that stretched between town to city; always in the past, she had come upon the city by sheer inertia and sloppy dead reckoning. It was hard to miss the biggest, noisiest, smelliest mass of humanity for four hundred miles.

Of course, if you did miss it you were, as the dock-boys would say, royally screwed.

The absolute darkness was familiar but unnerving. Leal fished around under her seat and found a gas lantern. She brought it out and the key said *zick-zick* as she wound it with steady fingers; this was the only sound except for the faint *ping* of the engine's metal parts cooling. She thumbed the striker plate and the little cascade of sparks lit the wick. The sudden white light was intolerable; she shielded her eyes as she held it out and away from herself.

Leal clipped it to a ring on the open canopy and turned to look at her passenger. "It's okay," she told her. "Just a snag, that's all."

The doll's porcelain features reflected back arcs of highlight from the lantern. Two huge seat belts crisscrossed its torso, pressing it against the cutter's passenger seat.

You're so full of it, she imagined the doll saying. "Yeah, maybe," she muttered, turning back to the empty view.

The cutter was dart-shaped. Leal sat in a fuselage shaped like a seedpod, with a spar sticking out behind that ended in the jet and four big vanes she could turn to steer the vessel. You could tie baggage and extra fuel to the spar, but right now Leal had nothing but a couple of suitcases back there. The cutter had maybe two hours of fuel left. She was quite unprepared for being lost.

She was getting angry—not at herself for her inattention, but at her mother, for obstinately refusing to spend her last days in the city, where she could have gotten decent care. "It's not that I like it *here*," Mother had said during their last conversation—impossibly, already six months ago. "It's just that that city, with all its sophistication, is what wrecked your father's scavenging business. After all those years of work, he ended with nothing to show for it. And it was that awful man, Eustace Loll, and his policies that did it to Langdon. I couldn't live in Sere knowing I shared the same streets with that man."

Rather than look out upon the expansive parks of the city with their expensive electric lights, Mother preferred to waste money that could have gone to subdue her constant pain on gas for the lanterns that glowed over her little garden box. A substantial amount of Leal's salary went for upkeep on this cutter and for travel costs to and from Taura Two. It hadn't been practical to sell the cutter because the estate still needed settling.

It was done now, though. This might be the last time Leal ever took this route.

Mom would be furious if I told her that. And the darkness weighed heavily today, despite the promise of finally getting things over with. It was as if some new element had been added to the air, an extra cloak of black lowered behind the mere absence of light that prevailed here in the outer precincts of Virga.

No one raised in Abyss should be afraid of the dark, for there were no suns to light this nation. The giant sphere of Virga, a balloon thousands of miles in diameter, could not be lit entirely by any single source, despite the presence of blazing man-made infernos such as Candesce, which itself lit the skies for hundreds of miles in every direction. Even the modest little nuclear-fusion suns of the smallest nation could carve out a sphere of brightness fifty to a hundred miles in diameter.

Leal had never seen sunlight. Out here, those great infernos were long since reddened and dimmed with distance. Clouds absorbed the light; so did the dust in the air and, finally, the air itself.

Candesce's heat kept Abyss from freezing, but the so-called sun of suns would never be seen here. Abyss had no sun; and so, it had made friends with the dark.

Leal slammed the canopy with a muttered curse. She stretched her legs down to find the bike pedals below the cockpit saddle, and started pedaling. After a few seconds she yanked on the sparker cord and, fifteen feet behind her, the cutter's little jet engine whined into life.

The gyrocompass told her she was on course, so Leal opened the throttle. Nothing changed outside to indicate that she was moving at all, but she was pressed back into the seat for a few seconds, and the instruments estimated that she had accelerated by sixty miles per hour. But how fast had she been going prior to that? Velocity was relative in a weightless world like Virga. Go too fast, and she might come upon Sere at a differential speed of hundreds of miles per hour. She would splat like a bug on the underside of one of its great iron wheels. So after reassuring herself that she was actually moving, she eased back and let the engine idle.

This was the last straw. She was going to sell this damned cutter as soon as she could, and pay other people to pilot her from now on. She gnawed at a fingernail, running through arguments and anticipating what Mother would say in reply. This took her mind off her situation for a little while, but it was starting to get noticeably colder in the cockpit. Colder than it should be near the city.

Leal unstrapped herself and fished around in the cargo netting behind the backseat. She brought one of her current books back to the pilot's saddle and opened it under the lantern. *Oral Traditions of the Winter Wraiths* had been written a hundred years ago by a little-known scholar who just happened to also have the last name of Maspeth. They might even be related. She tried to focus on the words, but her possible ancestor turned out to be a terrible writer, one of those with a fatal aversion to coming to the point about anything.

What should happen at this point was that the ghost of Langdon Maspeth should appear and extend its hand, effecting mysterious repairs before topping up her tanks and pointing her in the right direction. Or some handsome airman in a flashy yacht would sweep in and politely ask if she needed help. She'd demure and he would insist, and thus would start an initially adversarial banter that would end with . . .

Blinding light blossomed directly ahead. Leal fumbled the book and it hit her in the nose. She batted it aside and hit the brakes.

Twenty feet behind her, the four vanes all flipped sideways. The shuttlecock configuration caught a great chunk of air and Leal was slammed against the instrument panel; she'd forgotten to strap herself in again after getting the book. Pushing back, she looked out the canopy in time to see a dark spindle shape shoot past the cutter.

No, she mustn't stop here. Desperately Leal hauled on the controls and the cutter yawed then banked, barely missing another spindle shape as it swept past. Now she could make out the ropes rising off its back, and she was able to steer to avoid them. Gradually, the cutter came to a stop relative to the giant, silent pendulum.

The pendulum was one of two ships, each the classic finned-rocket shape of most Virgan vessels—but huge, two hundred feet long at least, and joined to its partner by a thousand feet of rope rigging. The ships were facing opposite directions and spinning like a bolo, a common enough maneuver that would provide artificial gravity in them. Leal's cutter had just missed them.

Now she could see curving glimmers in the dark—the faint running lights of other ships, how many she couldn't tell, all lashed together and turning silently in the dark.

Goose bumps were rising on Leal's arms, but not because of the cold. Strangely coincidental, she thought, that she'd been reading about the winter wraiths to pass the time—and here they were in the flesh.

She glanced down; the fuel gauge wasn't reassuring. In braking she'd overwhelmed her little gyrocompass. She had no idea which direction she was facing now, and an encounter with winter wraiths could only mean that she was very, very far from home.

Within the vista of wheeling running lights, faint flickering dots ducked and dove, swirled and turned: a flock of fish or school of birds eating a bounty thrown from the ships. The wraiths supported a whole ecosystem of dependent species, just as Leal's people did. Hidden in the darkness around her would be aerial fungi and shrimp, anemones and tube worms writhing their way through the air; mites hopping between widely separated strands of mold; misty spiderwebs and darting fireflies; fish to snap up these, and bats to snap up those. The winter wraiths were nomadic and secretive, but their economics, at least, weren't entirely alien.

Leal knew a lot more about wraiths than most of her people. Telen Argyre, from the wraith nation of Pacquaea, had been her roommate in college. The good news was that unlike many of her countrymen, she knew these people wouldn't be pirates. She and her ship were not about to be captured or boarded. The bad news was, they were unlikely to help her. They were unlikely to even speak to her.

Why, then, did she seem to be hearing voices?

Leal frowned and cocked her head. —No, not voices, but *a* voice. She heard someone calling out, a cry whose words, vast and resonant, were nonetheless too faint to understand.

She killed the engine and popped the canopy, letting in chilly air that stank of decay and rust. Echoes from the cutter's engine slapped off the other ships for a few seconds, then dissipated. What was left was a silence so absolute that she shuddered and went to close it again.

But there it was! Someone had spoken. It wasn't a shout, and there was no seeming urgency in the sound. Echoes from it barked faintly from the ships of the wraiths, but whatever it was, it didn't seem to be coming from them. Rather, Leal was drawn to look away from the hypnotic running lights, into a region of air so black that it felt like she had forgotten how to see.

She could not make out the meaning of the words but they were not, she felt, an appeal for help. Rather, it seemed a voice gigantic and cold proclaimed something—an annunciation aimed at no one living, issuing from the very heart of emptiness.

Leal shuddered again, slammed the canopy, and started her engine. As she did she saw that hundreds of windows were coming alight along the wraith ships. Surely that wasn't her fault? It couldn't be, she realized, as the ships began to turn as one, gliding in pairs away from her—and away from that black depth from which had issued the strange voice.

Fish flashed past as she accelerated, then a cloud of bats. They were following the ships, and she debated whether to do so as well. They might be her only safe port in this desert of air. As she turned the cutter's nose in that direction, though, she saw that one wraith ship had hung back. This vessel was not tied to another one, so was not pinwheeling like the rest. Now a hatch on its back opened and a tiny, dark figure swung out onto the gleaming, water-beaded hull.

The man clicked on a bull's-eye lantern and waved it. Leal yawed the cutter to make her own headlight waver. Satisfied, the tiny figure swept the lantern in a series of arcs, always ending with it pointing in one particular direction—away from both the speaking blackness, and the way that the wraith ships had taken. When Leal realized what he was doing she swore under her breath. She lined up the cutter and eased it through the air, past the great dark hull and the half-seen man atop its back. He now held the lantern steady; the air was dirtier here so she could see its shaft of light in the form of faint specks of fungal matter and dust. Leal slid the cutter into the beam and reset her gyrocompass. Then she popped the canopy, leaned out to wave, and started her engine. In seconds she had left the wraith ship behind.

She listened as she cranked the canopy shut again, but the strange distant voice did not speak again, and the engines of the wraith ships were drowned out by her own jet. She slumped back in her seat, breathing a heavy sigh.

After a few minutes she spotted a flash of light in the distance. Leal held her breath: it flashed again.

This was where the winter wraith had directed her: a light-house of her own people.

It was all anticlimax from there. Leal brought the cutter up to the little blockhouse and spotted the rope that looped away from it into the distance. That rope was the weightless version of a road; it led (provided it hadn't snapped at some point) to the nearest town. From there she could take her bearing on Sere and, if she tended her engine carefully and didn't let her eyes stray from the rope, she could be home in a couple of hours.

She was not about to let her eyes drift from the rope again.

WHEN THE CITY appeared it did so all at once. The darkness parted, revealing itself to be at least partly due to dense cloud, and light burst upon Leal. She blew out a sigh of relief and actually grinned at the beauty of the place.

Sere was a wheel made of wheels. Each "town" making it up was an iron ring a half-mile in diameter. These town wheels spun in lockstep at exactly one rotation per minute. Their inner surfaces were festooned with the glittering lights of city towers, houses, floodlit greenhouses, and Industry's red tongues of flame. She couldn't see all sixteen of the wheels, just an arc of six or seven of them jabbing into banks of deep gray cloud. They formed a great circle, their positions stabilized by cables and massive jet engines. Hovering around them in attendant swarms were hundreds of lesser lights—buildings, fungus farms, and giant storage nets, foundries and the houses of the rich that twirled in pairs, roped together in bolo configuration.

The whole glittering nebula of shapes was framed by midnight colors—black, bruised blue, indigo, all textured into intricacy by clouds and the reachless vaults between them. Here, darkness was not simple; it hinted at structures and meanings, hidden activity and watchful eyes. Beacons flickered, miles away, then disappeared behind fog banks. Half-glimpsed ropes twisted and contorted their way up, down, and to every side, synapses reaching to contact the outlier towns and factories of Sere's hinterland. One or two of those ropes, if you followed them far enough, would emerge into sunlight at other nations' borders.

She could hear the city foghorns even through the closed canopy. Deep sonorous voices, they sang out one after another, in a rising cadence: *brooom, brauum, braaaam*, then fell silent for ten seconds before repeating. Their horns faced away from the city wheels, into the endless night, but some sound leaked back. Leal associated their voices with being outside, with streets and markets, with the docks and flea cars. She associated them with home; and so, she now began to relax.

She wound up her running lights (*zick-zick-zick*) and lit them off her lantern. Then she leaned back to snap them into their little domes on the side of the cutter, just behind the passenger seat. "Almost home," she said to the doll, which was flopped forward as though asleep.

Very tired, she steered the cutter between flashing marker buoys and under the curving bellies of the town wheels. Floodlights hovered in the air, their broad beams aimed at the undersides of the wide, open-ended cylinders, upon which huge municipally funded murals were painted. She passed Whale Cylinder, Fireball Cylinder, and the cross-shape of the giant tree painted on the next cylinder rose over Fireball's tiny horizon. She aimed the cutter up a channel loosely defined by several long, fluorescent ropes that disappeared around the edge of the cylinder.

One of the kids she tutored worked a shift keeping the floodlights in place. He described it as mind-bogglingly boring work that consisted of jetting from one floodlight to the next, making some minor adjustment, then moving on in an endless round. He was one of her best students.

The ropes ran up beside Rowan Wheel; Leal tried to ignore the doubled sensation of movement as the towers and houses on the inside of the rotating habitat flashed past. The ropes converged at the axle of the wheel, a giant metal cylinder open on both ends. The countless cable spokes of the town wheel were fastened to this cylinder, and gantries, jetties, and diving boards jutted out from its two ends.

Leal cursed, a new flush of adrenaline waking her out of the trance that had started to come over her. Her way was blocked by a huge fish-shaped ship that was just being hauled into berth at the axis. If they fit it into the docking cylinder it would take up the whole width of the thing.

Normally the space here was open and easy to navigate, with one or two ships docked at a time. As Leal deployed the brakes she saw that the air around the docks was dotted with people, some of whom had drifted into the channel she was using. She blew her horn and saw heads turn; but nobody moved. It looked like a mob of ordinary citizens, not dockworkers. Sightseers? But why?

She throttled her engine way back, risking a stall. As the cutter drifted past a couple who clung to a channel rope Leal pushed back the canopy and shouted, "Hey! What *is* that?"

The man turned his head. "It's the sun lighter!" he yelled. "He's back!"

The sun lighter. Startled, Leal turned to look at the giant ship. It was built on exotic lines, and did have far more windows than the usual Abyssal design. Those windows blazed with light, providing tantalizing glimpses of galleries and red-carpeted walls, the sort of accouterments fit for a prince; yet next to the wide windows were rocket ports and the snub-noses of machine gun nacelles, as you might expect on the hull of an adventurer.

Hayden Griffin, the sun lighter of Aerie, was a bit of both.

Leal suddenly realized how she would look to someone gazing out those windows—with one leg crooked up, her foot on the hull, and two hands holding the canopy open while she stared. She wore a brocaded jacket with ruffles at the wrists, and tight trousers; from a distance, she must look like some gawking boy. She sat back, slamming the canopy, and steered the cutter away from the foreign ship.

She refrained from glancing at it again until she reached a jetty. The jetty was a long platform that extended out from the docking cylinder; since it was attached to the cylinder and the cylinder turned with the city wheel, the jetty swept up and around in a closing loop that took one minute to complete. Normally Leal would dock with it by bringing the cutter to a stop right where it had swept past, and waiting for it to come around again. Nets on its trailing edge would gently catch the cutter and centrifugal gravity would ease the vessel down onto the jetty's surface. Except that, today, the jetty thronged with people.

Leal popped the canopy again. "Come on!" she yelled. "What are you doing? Out of the way there!" Whatever the burly man balanced there on one toe shouted back was carried away by the air as the jetty rotated up and away. Well, she'd warned them, and she was too tired for this nonsense. Leal maneuvered the cutter into position and waited for the jetty to come round again.

It did, but nobody was paying attention to her. Leal glanced up and saw why: the monstrous ship had opened a grand set of hatches and people were emerging from it into the long proboscis of an enclosed gangway. Leal blared her horn and screamed, "Get out of the way!" and the crowd on the jetty noticed her and began to disperse.

She waited one more revolution, then let the jetty slide under the cutter's hull like a silent sword. The net caught the ship and jolted it gently into motion. As the jetty swept up the cutter settled onto it with a faint thud. Leal weighed all of five pounds now—but to have any gravity under her at all was a relief. Suddenly crushingly tired, she rummaged in the back, pulling out the doll and a few other items, then climbed out to retrieve her suitcase. The dock-boys would know where to put the cutter; she'd pay them later. Right now, she needed nothing more than to get home, curl up, and sleep.

People were shouting and pointing past her. A silhouetted figure had appeared at the door of the ship. There could be no doubt who it was—or at least, who the crowd *thought* it was. Despite herself, Leal paused in wrestling her suitcase out of the cutter's cargo net. She had never seen Griffin in the flesh, and had often wondered what he might be like.

He was a lean man, surprisingly young, dressed in an ordinary russet-colored tunic and gray trousers. He had practical, toeless flight boots on his feet, and even from here she could see how battered those were. The only way she could tell that this was Griffin was because he was the focus of everyone's attention.

"He's supposed to be the best pilot in Virga," somebody said. Leal didn't hide her skeptical smile—but that and other stories she'd heard pulled at her. It was a guilty pleasure of hers to imagine that a man might exist who really was a pilot, adventurer, and former pirate, an engineer and the savior of an entire nation.

"It was Slipstream," somebody else was saying. "They invaded and blew up Aerie's only sun. Plunged the whole nation into darkness, except for the zone their own sun could light. As ruthless a way of conquering a people as you could imagine."

"And Griffin gave them back their sun?" It was a little boy asking the question.

"He flew all the way to Candesce and stole the pieces he needed from the sun of suns itself! And then he built Aerie a new sun."

Griffin had done exactly what they said he'd done. Leal even felt she had a connection to him, however distant, because Antaea Argyre, the sister of Leal's college roommate, had apparently been involved in the recent revolution in Slipstream.

. . . And yet, heroes were not to be trusted. After all, what had Griffin done lately? She felt like this crowd should have been waiting for *her*, not him; that it should sigh and hang on *her* words as she related her adventure; that *she* should be the one welcomed home—

"Hey!" Someone pushed her. Leal staggered and dropped the books and doll. For a long second she was stranded in midair; when she touched down again she used her toe to turn her and opened her mouth to snap at whoever had been so rude.

It was a policeman. "You endangered these people with that stunt," he said. Belatedly she realized he was the burly man who had yelled something at her earlier.

"But nobody's supposed to be on the landing slip," she said, flailing her arms to keep her balance. "I waited until they were out of the way. It's just—I've been flying for—I got lost—"

"Nearly took my head off!" He put his hand above her breasts and pushed her; Leal staggered against the side of the cutter.

He reached down to pluck the slowly tumbling *Oral Traditions of the Winter Wraiths* out of the air. With an air of disgust, he held it up by one corner. "What, are you reading the enemy's stories?"

"I-I'm a tutor at the university," she said, dismayed that the pride she should take in saying that didn't come out in her voice.

The policeman sneered at her. "An apologist, then. We'll see how high and mighty you are after the referendum."

"W-what?"

"No decent citizen has any reason to be learning about *them*," he said. Casually, he tossed the book off the platform. Leal watched it curve away, disappearing into the darkness like a slowly flapping bird. "Now get out of here," he said, "before I arrest you for endangering the public."

Humiliated, furious, barely suppressing her tears, Leal stumbled away. Her suitcase might only weigh a pound up here, but its mass hadn't changed and it was hard for her to maneuver it and herself through the crowd. Her feet couldn't find purchase on the planks of jetty because gravity was too low.

As she approached the elevators that led down to the city below, Leal glanced back at the floodlit Aerie ship. Griffin still stood in the hatchway, and he was speaking, in a tone too low for her (or, probably, anybody else down here) to hear. He looked serene and confident, just like the hero he was supposed to be.

He said something, turned, and gestured for another man to come forward. As the other moved into the light, Leal hissed.

The Minister of the Interior, Eustace Loll, took Griffin's wrist and raised the sun lighter's hand with his own in a grinning salute to the crowd. Leal's diaphragm clenched and she looked away quickly.

She stepped into the cage and turned away from the rest of the passengers. The car began to drop; they all reached up to brace their hands on the ceiling, and Leal felt her face twist, of its own accord, into a rictus of misery and disappointment.

They fell past taut cables, copper decks, and cast-iron stanchions toward the smoking, night-lit city, where no one waited for her.

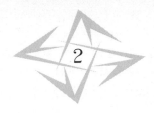

2

"LET'S SAY YOU see somebody pinwheeling in freefall," said the instructor. "Can anyone tell me how you know whether it's a man or a woman?"

"Tits!" shouted Barthol, the youngest of the annoying clique of young men who attended class. Leal exchanged a long-suffering glance with Uthor, the leverage arts instructor. Uthor said, "Nooooo," and then, "Anybody else?"

Leal put up her hand. "A woman's axis of rotation is her hips. A man's is his solar plexus."

"Correct," said Uthor with a grateful smile. The clique were nodding to one another as if they'd actually learned something. "In today's class," Uthor continued, "we're going to learn how to use awareness of your own center of gravity to maximize the force and leverage you can bring on objects in weightless situations."

He kept glancing at her as he spoke, which was flattering but surely not a sign of actual interest; Leal knew she was merely today's star pupil. An inconvenience, that, because she was tired enough that she kept losing the thread of Uthor's explanations.

The class was in ball formation above one of Match Wheel's gymnasia. Black sky was visible to her left and her right, past a slowly turning jumble of buildings, nets, and latticework gantries. Match's axis had only a minimal docking structure, unlike Rowan, and so the entire open area above the cable ring was crowded with buildings and open, rope-latticed spaces—courts, they were called—like the one where the leverage arts class met.

Uthor had set himself into a slow spin and was making eye contact with everybody as he spoke, occasionally flipping over somehow in a remarkably fluid movement. Leal had no idea how he did it; without something to push against, she couldn't turn herself around in freefall. It was almost like Uthor had invisible wings, or as if he had an invisible ring around him that he could grab with hand or foot. Leal tried to focus on his words: she wanted to learn how he did that.

He was just a cook—and Leal had sworn on the ashes of her father never to marry a cook, or day laborer, or mechanic—but somehow he'd found the time and dedication to become a master of Leverage. If he could do it, so could she.

Uthor demonstrated some moves and then the class practiced them. Just as Leal thought she was getting the hang of turning, the three foghorns sounded—followed by a fourth. Shift-change already? Lucky thing she didn't have any—

Leal cursed lividly, causing heads to turn up and down the ball. Uthor grabbed a rope and swung over. "Problems?"

"I just remembered an appointment," she said shamefacedly. "I have to go." Quickly she wrapped her toes around the rope and—to prove to Uthor that she took his class seriously—exited the formation in the hand-over-foot-over-hand cartwheel he'd demonstrated last week. She even made six revolutions before she missed a grab and ended up clutching the rope with all four limbs. By that time Uthor had politely turned his attention back to the other students.

"Damn, damn damn," she muttered as she hopped from rope to ledge to pipe, down into the microgravity of the city's upper reaches. In her fuzzy state she'd completely forgotten the two new students she'd agreed to tutor. She couldn't afford to miss the few bills they would pay her for reviewing their work.

At the level of the cable joists she began to bounce along in the direction of the elevators, but stopped when she saw how far she was from any of the university-bound ones. They were moving altogether too slowly, as well. She had maybe ten minutes before the students decided she was a no-show and went elsewhere. Luckily, the solution to this problem was adjusting his footwear not twenty feet away.

"Hey! Are you free?" The spokesman looked up at her call, and grinned. He was young, with a buzz cut and large hoop earrings. He had a wicker chair mounted facing backward on his back, and his profession's long asbestos strap wrapped six times around his waist.

"Always free for a pretty lady like yourself," he said in the city's gutter accent.

Leal smiled. "I need to get to the university library in . . . oh, about five minutes ago," she said.

He nodded calmly. "Then climb aboard." She put one hand on the seat of the chair and boosted herself the five feet into it. As she fastened her seat belt her spokesman began moving, at first in a long horizontal loping stride, then as he built up momentum, great leaps that took him thirty feet or more. Leal hung on and grinned; it had been a long time since she'd used a spokesman—they weren't for reputable folk and she was trying to look reputable—and she'd forgotten how much fun they could be.

He reached a broad opening in the cylinder deck and without preamble turned and let himself fall through it. Now he and his passenger were half a mile above city towers and streets that curved up and away to either side. Hundreds of spoke-cables were mounted to the cylinder that was now above their heads; these dwindled and disappeared into the haze of light and street detail below. With casual grace he grabbed one of the smaller ones (they called these "tuning cables" for some reason) and then let go again. He and Leal began to slowly fall beside it.

"You a student?" he asked; she felt his shoulder shift in what was probably a glance back at her.

"Senior tutor, actually," she said. "Hoping to make full instructor this term. I've put my application in and . . . well, we'll see."

"Good for you," he said. Then: "What do you think of the referendum?"

"It's a disgrace," she said bravely. That kind of opinion could get you beaten up in any of the common pubs, she knew—but he just laughed.

"I was hoping to go to school," he said as he kicked off from the cable again; he'd positioned himself so that Coriolis force from the city's turning pushed him toward it. They were starting to pick up speed and a bit of a breeze; Leal felt her hair belling upward. "Hoping," said the spokesman again, "to take classical literature. But the Eternists are talking about banning it."

"I know," she said bitterly. "I teach history."

"Ah, yeah. They'll ban that, too, I guess."

"Only if they win. You've got to get everybody out to vote," she said.

"Oh believe me, I'm working on it. You wouldn't believe some of the things I've been called in the past couple of days for telling people to vote no."

"It's very . . ." Leal remembered *Oral Traditions of the Winter Wraiths* fluttering away into endless dark. "Sad."

They were now plummeting down at frightening speed. Leal braced her hands on the seat of the chair. The spokesman unwound his asbestos strap, got a good grip on one end, and then whipped it at the cable where it wrapped once. He grabbed the free end and, planting his asbestos-shod shoes against the cable, pulled hard. With an escalating hiss he began to slow their fall.

By now a stiff gale was blowing them against the cable. Leal's hair flipped forward making it difficult to see—but it was hard to miss the spires of the university as they rose up to all sides. Tall stained-glass windows shone endlessly into the night, their permanent pools of light and shade as effective as walls in channeling the movement of students and faculty in the quads and galleries below. Gargoyles pretended to vomit on Leal and her ride as they skidded past; and then a rooftop was coming up fast from below.

"Brace yourself." He'd only just said it when they hit the green copper slope. The spokesman unwound his strap with a flourish (the cable continued down to the ground about a foot outside the building) and slid down the roof to the crenelated stone gutter. There, a broad flat walkway led to an iron-bound door in the corner tower.

The spokesman knelt down and Leal climbed off his back. He puffed for a few seconds then nodded at the door. "I use that one all the time. Library's straight across the avenue."

Leal laughed in delight. "That was wonderful! You're my spokesman from now on."

He bowed. "The fee's ten dites. Sorry it's a bit steeper than usual, I've got, uh, extra expenses to take care of."

She paid up without complaint and they walked to the door together. From there it was an anticlimactic stroll down to street level. The spokesman tipped an imaginary hat at her and went the other way. Leal grinned again and headed for her office.

Sere's streets were shod in copper except under the streetlights where grasses and boxed trees had been planted. The campus pathways were scuffed clean by countless walking feet, so they gleamed amber and red under the streetlights; toward their edges, they faded into the pale green of verdigris. The university buildings were built around steel skeletons but sheathed in asteroidal stone; they all had sprawling buttresses reaching out from their bases like root systems, an extra measure of support for those times when the wheel was spun up or slowed, and "down" tilted one way or the other for a while.

It was the beginning of cultural shift, which followed labor shift and preceded maintenance shift. Throughout the wheel-of-wheels, restaurants, pubs, and theaters were opening; the university's class-rooms were swelling with students. Weary workers flooded the streets looking for distraction. Leal slept through labor shift (a privilege of her class) and for her, maintenance shift was the time to be out and about. That was when the bohemian artists' salons opened and the vibrant, seductive off-shift street life flourished. Lamptenders sang as they walked from pole to pole; street polishers pedaled their contraptions around the plazas of the rich and powerful, making the copper gleam; lovers murmured in shadowed doorways; and spokesmen knelt on the rooftops, coats flapping as they hunted for potential customers. The air was quiet. You could be yourself.

But, right now, Leal ducked between bicycles and hurrying students, across the gleaming street, and into the fluted stone Fine Arts building. Down a pillared hallway whose central line was carpeted in rich but fading red, she came to a tall doorway flanked with gargoyles. The office beyond was high-ceilinged, well lit, and lined with books. Several staff members looked up and nodded as Leal entered. "They're waiting," said one, nodding toward a corner of the room.

"Leal!" Gereld Hackner loomed out of nowhere and smiled down his nose at her. "Good paper on systematic errors in pre-Ombian translations. Worthy of anyone in the faculty, if I do say so myself."

"Why, thank you, Gereld." He nodded in satisfaction and continued on, humming, his august brows wrinkled in an imitation of deep thought. Leal glared at his retreating back. *Condescending old bat*, she thought. Hackner had gone into academia after a long career in the civil service. He knew nothing about anything, but could talk a good line, and for two years now he'd been a fixture around the office. As far as she knew he never spoke with the students, only the staff and faculty—but he was careful to speak to all of them on a regular basis.

Leal skirted around several desks and approached an unobtrusive door hidden between the jutting woodwork of two bookshelves. She opened it to reveal a space that was as small and cramped as a closet—that being because it *was* a closet, or had been until she took it over.

Two students were crammed into the little space, their shoulders pressed together and knees touching. They held sheafs of paper in their hands and looked simultaneously grateful and annoyed as she shuffled past them to sit at the little desk she'd managed (by dint of disassembly) to fit in here. Seated, Leal's head was framed by the spines of dozens of books that jutted out of her makeshift shelves, their titles hovering inches from her ears as though cryptically labeling her thoughts. "Sorry I'm late," she said. "I'm taking a leverage class and, well . . ." The two boys (they weren't really old enough to be called young men) smiled woodenly. "Ah," she continued gamely. "Let's see what you've been working on."

"Well, I don't have much to show right now—really, nothing," stammered the first student. "You see, I wanted to write something about the time before the Great Refusal . . ."

She laughed. "What a grand ambition! But you know there's almost no records from the building of the world. Just legend."

"But what about after?"

She mused for a second. "It would certainly get you noticed. What do you know about the Refusal?"

He shrugged awkwardly. Leal smiled encouragingly. "We know the world was built by the original colonists who arrived at Vega. The environment near the sun is too chaotic—dangerous, full of coursing meteoroids and debris from the sun's creation. Vega is a young star. So, the builders decided to place Virga here, on the outskirts of the system. They were humans only, at first; but those humans made their own allies, machine-intelligences, engineered organisms, even the gigantic, ambiguous monsters like the capital bugs and, uh . . . worldwasps."

They were both gazing at her intently, though the other boy had a skeptical look on his face. Leal continued, trying unsuccessfully to avoid a lecturing tone.

"But as the finishing touches were being put on Virga, and people began moving into it, something arrived from *outside*. A new power, which may have come from our ancient origin, Earth, or could have existed in the galaxy for millions, maybe billions of years. We don't know. For lack of a better name, we called it *artificial nature*, and it changed everything."

"The Eternists say that's a myth," said the second boy boldly. "That there's nothing outside of Virga."

"They're wrong," Leal replied confidently. "Else why do we sometimes get visitors from that outside world? Humans, from the civilization that has made its accommodation with A.N.?"

They both frowned, one in thought, the other doubtfully. "Virga is the only place we know of in the whole galaxy," she told them, "that is free of artificial nature. A.N. isn't a political system, it's a technology. You see, once you have an accurate physical model and fast enough calculating engines, you can use natural selection to *evolve* designs and processes in what they call 'virtual environments.' This process is faster and more efficient than what we call thinking . . . and once you've got the technology, you don't need to know anything about how it works. You just use it. In fact, anybody—or *anything*—can use it. There are plenty of nonsentient powers in the realm of A.N."

"So what does that have to do with the Refusal?" asked the student.

"The Refusal was our refusal to accept A.N. into Virga. The Refusal was our turning on Candesce and its protective field, which keeps A.N. out of Virga. —Or so a casual reading of the records indicates." He looked puzzled and she grinned. "Here's where you can score some extra marks, maybe, if you follow a particular thread that dangles from this story." He scribbled hectically in his notebook as she rattled off a set of titles he could refer to. "There's another interpretation of the Refusal," she said. "Some records indicate that it was an internal division between the humans of Virga, that happened *after* we cut ourselves off from A.N." She leaned forward dramatically. "These sources say that the schism was between those who thought we should ally with those humans who had elected to remain outside, in A.N.'s territory, and others who believed we should ally with . . ."

"What?" asked the student.

"We don't know," she admitted, "which is a big hole in that version of things. But they say that the people who won the dispute went on to become the Virga Home Guard!"

The other lad laughed derisively. He was dressed in fireproofed canvas that reeked of homemade rocket fuel. "The Guard's a myth!" he proclaimed confidently.

"Is it?" She smiled at him. "Then how is it that I know two people who joined it?"

The first student gazed unhappily at his notes. "This could be hard," he admitted.

"Don't try to reach conclusions," she said. "Document the conflict over the stories: that's a history in and of itself."

As he chewed his pencil and squinted at his pages, Leal turned to the other lad. "How about you?" she asked. "What are you working on?"

He handed her a half-finished paper on Demarian history—a mundane subject after what she'd just talked about—and she flipped through it. Leal started this process with a polite and hopeful smile on her face; as she went, her brow furrowed; her nose wrinkled once or twice; and her mouth slowly formed itself into a faint moue. The amateur rocketeer watched this gradual transformation with mounting concern. At last Leal put down the pages and looked at him quizzically. "This is very interesting," she said. "Where did you get the idea that the Demarians fought a war with Slipstream?"

"It's true, in't it?"

"Well, in point of fact, it's not true. The records show—"

"But I aksed ten people and they all said it was true." He gave her a sly smile. "And truth's owned by the people now, in't it? That's what they say."

She shook her head. "Either something happened or it didn't. You—"

"—But how do you know? You gotta go with the majority. That's democracy, right?"

He was challenging her! Leal just sat there for a second, gaping at him, then handed back the paper.

"Every man's entitled to his own opinion," she said. "But not his own facts."

The rocketeer scowled. "So I guess I should wait until after the referendum to hand this in."

Leal smiled as sweetly as she could at him. "No. That won't change anything."

"It'll change how I get marked."

"But not what's true."

"I don't care 'bout that."

"Clearly."

"I gotta go." He pushed past the first youth and stormed quite dramatically out of the office.

Leal poked her head around the door frame. The staff were all staring in her direction. "It's okay," she called, "just another free thinker." There were nods of comprehension and sympathy all around, and they turned back to their work.

"Now," she said to the more ambitious student, "let's talk about the Great Refusal." He clutched his papers to his chest.

"Is she in? Leal! There you are." She recognized the voice, but he was bumbling through the shoals of desk, wastebasket, and file cabinet in an uncharacteristically excited way. "Hang on," she said to her student, then leaned out around the door again. "Easley, what's up?"

The dean's secretary clattered to a stop just outside. "Leal, I've been looking for you since start of shift! I told you this was coming, but you pooh-poohed it. You're far too cynical for one so young, haven't I told you that?"

Easley Fencher had a hatchet-shaped face, outthrusting eyebrows, and curiously mobile mustaches that led him around like whiskers. His clothes were all angles, as though made of origami rather than fabric—a style prevalent twenty years ago. Leal liked him but could only stand ten minutes in his company at a time before his numerous tics crushed her patience. Still, he was harmless, and useful, and probably did need a friend, or at least some connection to a generation other than his own.

"Excuse me." She squeezed out past the student, who leered at her, and straightened her clothes with what dignity she could find. "What are you talking about, Easley?"

"You are summoned! Summoned, I tell you. Can you guess what this means?"

Leal felt a flush of excitement, but refused to let the secretaries see it. "I wouldn't have to guess if you told me." Easley looked crestfallen, and Leal cocked her head. "You mean you don't know? You're getting my hopes up without knowing what this is really about?"

"Oh, Leal, but it's time, it's high time," he said, hands darting about to punctuate his words as he followed her between the desks. "You've been passed over too many times for it not to happen now. Just think! A full-time teaching position. Why, you'll have to throw another party."

She eyed him sidelong as they pattered down the corridor. "Easley, I've never thrown a party."

"Which is why you must."

"Have you *seen* my apartment?"

"No, because you've never invited me over."

"And if you'd seen my apartment, you'd know why that is."

He said something further, but she was no longer listening. Since Leal first set foot in this building as a bright-eyed undergraduate, a shift hadn't passed when she didn't imagine what her name would look like embossed on a brass plate beside one of the faculty doors. Once, she had dreamed of being worthy of such an honor, and the agony of not knowing if she could achieve such heights of scholarship and knowledge was terrible and wonderful. She'd never imagined then that the agony of knowing she was worthy would be worse.

But she wouldn't give in to Easley's pressure, and start to hope. He so wanted to see her face light up right now! It would validate his faith that the world rewarded patience and modesty; but that was his need, not hers. Leal crossed her arms and fell silent as she walked, footsteps staccato and uneven, in the direction of the dean's office. She glanced neither left nor right. After a few more lame attempts at levity, Easley shut up, and as they neared the stairs he fell behind. "Well . . . good luck," he said, half-raising his hand to wave as she trod down the creaking, well-worn steps.

She heard wind whistling beyond the walls of the stairwell. Leal knew if she touched her fingertips to the wood paneling, she would feel the faint tremble and cold of the town wheel's rotation. She was underneath it now.

Some university official, name now lost in time, had discovered that no office in the Fine Arts building was big enough to hold his ego. Local ordinances forbade him building any annex around or above the edifice, so he went down. There was ample real estate on the streamlined under-surface of the wheel, after all. There, his only neighbors would be cooling fins and sewage-flinging pipes. He commissioned a vast, octagonal room, with windows on four of the outward-slanting walls; and he bolted his massive iron desk in the prow of this mighty chamber. Since the windows faced the direction that the town wheel spun, everything in the black sky behind him appeared to be plummeting downward. Or (and perhaps this was his intention) he and his desk seemed to be eternally rising through the midnight-bruised air, outpacing lights and ships and clouds. This ascent was framed in the lintels by carved cherubs.

Dean Porril could not live up to the standards of the room. He hunched under those fantastical windows, a single banker's lamp painting his crumpled, disconsolate features onto a canvas of dark air. The cherubs were vague shapes framing him, contorted curves that appeared to be trying to escape the weight of his disappointment. The windows rattled ominously in the fierce headwind caused by the wheel's rotation. Porril's pen scratched inaudibly against the resistant paper of some memo or requisition; aside from it and the lamp, the acres of black iron tabletop were utterly empty.

Porril saw Leal approaching, and *diminished* somehow, as if he'd found a way to fold his shoulders further into his body. "Leal," he husked. "Good of you to show up."

She glanced around, but there was no one else in the room. A bad sign. She drew up one of the heavy oak chairs and sat opposite Porril, waiting alertly as he finished whatever it was he was writing.

Finally he put down the pen, looked up at her, and sighed. "Leal, you've done some outstanding work since joining our little team."

"Why, thank you, sir. I love the subject."

"As you know, finances are tight lately. The government's not exactly sympathetic to education in anything 'impractical.' " Leal suppressed a laugh at Porril's sarcasm; the current regime's hostility to learning of any kind was legendary.

"And yet they've passed the Age law, stating that Virga is infinitely old," she said, to agree and encourage him further. "On the one hand they balk at funding half the curriculum, and on the other they want to legislate truth itself."

"Despite which," said Porril, showing some energy by straightening a bit in his chair, "we have persevered, replacing Professors Ardosty and Garrul after their retirements last year. History is still on the curriculum, Leal; I consider that a small triumph, all things considered."

"Absolutely, sir."

"Which brings me to you. You have been passed over time and again for an appointment you are more than qualified for. The board and I have discussed this and we agreed that it's grossly unfair. You deserve a full professorship, not just to be languishing as a teaching assistant and part-time instructor. 'The situation is intolerable,' I told them. 'Leal is one of our best and brightest!'"

"It means a lot to hear you say that, sir." Leal allowed herself to hope. Maybe Easley did know what was coming, but hadn't been allowed to confirm or deny it to her.

"You'd be starting in the Downturn," he said, "when the bulk of the new students are arriving from the outer provinces—as a full professor, with your own office, tenure track, the lot."

Leal felt faint. *This moment,* she thought, *I will always remember.*

". . . That is, you would be starting, if the board had agreed," continued Porril. "They didn't."

It took a few seconds for her to realize what he was saying. "I-I'm not—you mean y-you're not going to—?"

He shook his head sadly. "The decision had nothing to do with the quality of your work. The issue is purely political. The whole department is hanging by a thread; we could have our funding pulled at any moment. The board was unanimous that we should appoint a new professor of Middle History studies, to prove our independence and continuing commitment to historical research. But . . . they also agreed that it should be someone with the age and . . . gravitas . . . to not cause any public resentment or skepticism. Someone who, well, looks the part."

"Not—" Leal could barely speak. "You don't mean Hackner!"

Porril withered some more. "I thought you should know before we made a general announcement. Leal, he knows his way around the government bureaucracy. He was an insider. His experience could prove very useful in securing appropriations . . ."

He stared at her. Leal was sitting absolutely still, but her whole stance was the opposite of stillness. A shock seemed to reverberate down her body; her hands and feet had taken the whole weight of her body so that while she seemed to be sitting in her chair, in reality she hovered a fraction of an inch above it. For long seconds she sat, paralyzed in midflight or midattack by a decade of self-taught lessons in how to play along, when to remain silent, when to smile and agree with the boss. A thousand words were caught in her throat along with her breath.

Then she let go and, while she hadn't moved, she was now sitting again. "I'm sure the board has made the right decision," she said, only a little shakily.

Porril shrank back as though she'd hit him. "Leal, I'm so—"

She stood up. "I appreciate your telling me in person, sir. And when the time is right, I hope you'll consider my candidacy for a position on the faculty."

She turned like an automaton and stalked through the velvet-hung blackness, finding the door next to the only other visible object in the room: a lamplit portrait of Porril's late wife that gazed at him, forever silent, as he worked. Leal imagined slamming the door and dislodging the painting, but she closed it softly. Better that Porril should have to look into his wife's eyes for the rest of the afternoon.

Easley was waiting at the top of the steps. "So?" he said over intertwined hands. "How'd it—" Leal broke into a run. She made it through the front hall and down the steps without anyone seeing the expression on her face. She didn't slow to a panting walk, or burst into tears, until she was a quarter mile from the campus.

SHE TOOK TROLLEYS and flea cars randomly around the city, afraid to go home to an empty apartment. Somehow she ended up on Steam Wheel, standing with a small crowd of indigents who were pointing up at the spokework far above, where a diffuse amber light glowed. It looked as though there were a gigantic paper lantern up there, suspended a quarter mile above the streets, but she couldn't make out any details.

That, somebody said, was the sun lighter's workshop. Who knew what he was doing there? If they expected bolts of lightning there were none, but Leal found herself indulging a wistful fantasy while gazing up with them; and then, felt even sadder as she walked away.

Late in the shift she found a telephone that only had a small lineup, and after shifting from foot to foot for a few minutes she reached it just as it rang. Leal snatched her hand back and a twelve-year-old phone-runner who'd been loitering nearby with his friends sprinted over to pick up the receiver. "I can hear you!" he yelled. "Okay! The Krant building?" He fell silent for a second, squinting in concentration as he tried to make out the voice on the other end. "Will do." He hung up the receiver and set off at a sprint.

Leal picked it up; a roar of static—interference from distant Candesce—assaulted her ear. She shouted until she heard an operator's voice, the thin words sounding like the murmur of a dying man in a windstorm. She yelled out the street corner she wanted to hail and, after a pause, heard a faint ring. The ringing went on for a long time, then a very young voice shouted, "Yeah?"

"Message to Seana Aerosian. She works at the clothiers in the Pillard Mall. Tall, black hair, long nose—"

"Whatever, I can find her, lady."

"Okay. Tell her: they chose Hackner over me." Her voice shook as she said this.

"Hacker?" The voice was fading behind a fluttering noise like the approach of some gigantic bird.

"Hackner! Hackner! She'd understand."

"Got it."

"Tell her I'll be at the caravansary—caravansary!—in half an hour or so."

"Hey, posh. Yeah, I got it. See ya." Whoever it was hung up.

Leal hung up the phone (which immediately rang) and set off up the gaslit avenue, which curved up ahead of her, reaching the vertical many blocks away. The buildings likewise curled upward, those close by showing her their facades and windows, the distant ones their rooftops and chimneys. Leal paid no attention to this vision, since it was the only kind of cityscape she had ever known. She strode head-down through the hustle and hubbub of cultural shift, past Coriolis jugglers and gesturing street orators, crowded sidewalk cafes and parked jitneys whose drivers' flanks shone with sweat. Above the rooftops, past the spokes with their flying men and shuttling elevators, spotlit ships were queuing up to deliver their cargoes during maintenance shift.

The caravansary was an open storefront, its windows gulled upward during cultural shift, its tables and chairs spilled out into the street. Musicians and laborers from outlier towns like Taura Two converged here to sing, tell stories, and drink. The place had no regular staff; instead, the patrons themselves helped out. Right now the boisterous crew of a trash carrier were acting as bartenders and cooks. In respect of the place's unwritten rules, Leal donned an apron as soon as she arrived. She ferried drinks to the outer tables for a while; it was just like when she was a girl helping at the spontaneous caravansary events that sprang up whenever two or more ships made port at Taura.

A couple of unshaven louts with dueling scars and calloused

knuckles began tuning up their sitars, and soon people were dancing. Leal abandoned her waitress role and joined in. For a while,
the familiar keening music, the swirling bodies, drove all thoughts
of academic performance and political one-upmanship out of her
mind.

Her father had taught her these same dances. She vividly remembered practicing the moves atop the curved hull of his ship,
which was lashed to another scavenger by long ropes. The two
ships had spun around one another—like the wraith vessels she'd
seen the other day—and in the spin-gale atop her father's, she had
twirled and taken his hand.

Father's cargo was discarded scrap and items lost to winter by
people in the sunlit countries. He found it and sold it; but he also
studied it, and he'd taught her how to as well. By the time Leal was
ten she could tell the difference between engine parts made in the
Gretels and those from the principalities of Candesce. From the
patina on a piece of metal, she could judge how long it had been
tumbling through the air. She had helped her father log all their
finds in the great book where he puzzled out the existence of distant
wars, economic trends, even the passions of individuals—evidenced
by a necklace someone had thrown angrily into the sky or the man-
gle of a shattered pistol.

The air carried tiny fragments of a vast puzzle, and Father and
the other scavengers put that puzzle together. "The air's a book,
and you can learn to read it," he'd told Leal. She'd wanted to; but
Mother had insisted she get a proper education in a real school, so
they'd bought a place in Taura Two.

And then Eustace Loll and his cronies had made scavenging il-
legal. "It reinforces Abyss's reputation as a parasite nation," he'd de-
clared. "Besides, we don't need to scrabble through other people's
trash. We have Industry now." Her father had been unable to sell
the business or, for any decent price, his ship. Leal had never again
been able to dance on its hull.

She was seated and working on her second pint of Sargasso Pale Ale by the time Seana showed up. Leal had picked a spot by the low wrought-iron fence that separated the chaos of the caravansary from street traffic. All sorts of people had streamed past while the euphoria of the dance faded and her practical nature dragged her mind back to the present; if the passersby had been on fire she still wouldn't have seen them. Yet she knew instantly that Seana was approaching: the subtle metallic snicking of her silver exoskeleton was unmistakable.

Seana was, indeed, a study in flesh and silver: she had spent too much of her childhood in freefall, and now was extraordinarily tall and willowy. The curving whorls of her supports sported semiprecious stones and lacquer inlays; they were quite beautiful even though their purpose was obvious. Even her chin was cupped by filigree and faience, yet she carried herself with dignity despite the frequent headaches and backaches that could ground her for days at a time. She was too proud of living under gravity to give it up.

She was also proud to have Leal as her friend—especially since they had come from similar backgrounds.

She sat, cupped her chin in her hands, and said, "Tell me."

Leal told her. She told her past tears and around a mouth girded in anger; she told her with broad gestures and contemptuous parodies of Hackner and the dean. She told her by silently glaring at the tabletop while her hands, with malice of their own, slowly tore up a paper napkin, rolled up the bits between white fingers, and tossed them at the ground with sharp jabs.

After a while the traffic thinned. Maintenance shift was approaching, but the rotisserie was one of the better places to remain open to serve the Maintenance shift workers. Seana had just returned from quickly closing up her shop, and Leal was leaning exhausted in her chair, when: "Look who's here!" said a richly male voice.

Leal blinked, turned to see a flashing gold belt buckle and the fluorescent green of a naval officer's jacket leaning over the black fence. She tilted her gaze up, and found the affable, nicely chiseled face of Lieutenant Brun Mafin smiling down at her. "Wow, you ladies are giving a whole new meaning to the term 'liquid lunch.' "

Leal glanced down at the devastated battlefield between herself and Seana. Shredded napkins, emptied plates, and pint glasses clustered there in stunned little groups, obvious testament to an intense heart-to-heart.

"Leal needs cheering up," said Seana. "Join us?"

"Don't mind if I do." Brun hopped the fence then dragged an empty chair from a nearby table. He twirled it and sat, folding his arms across the back. "What seems to be the trouble?"

Brun was so clearly too-good-to-be-true that Leal never fantasized about him, only about someday meeting someone who might be like him. He was handsome, dashing and clever, honest and brave.

She wasn't about to admit her humiliation to him. "Just a bad day at work," she said with a smile.

"I get those," he said. "They usually end in scars."

"This one may well do that."

"Badges of honor," he said, waving a hand loftily. "Wear 'em with pride." He turned to Seana. "What're you drinking?"

They kibitzed for a while and Leal's mood improved. Brun was attached to the *Hammerhead*, one of Abyss's most prestigious ships of the line, but he wasn't happy with the posting. "The problem with big ships is they only bring 'em out for major confrontations," he said. "It's hardly economical to patrol your borders with a dreadnought. We spend all our time in port, or doing parades. How's that any fun?"

"I could have used a friendly dreadnought—or any patrol ship at all, yesterday," confessed Leal. "I got lost on my way back from Taura Two."

He spared her a sharp glance. "You were flying alone?"

"I had to. My mother lived at Taura, she died last year. I've been going back and forth every weekend, settling the estate. Got my own cutter up the docks." She nodded upward, proud to surprise him with this little fact.

"What happened?"

She told her story and Brun listened intently. Having heard the tale already, Seana smiled at the points where Leal embellished it for his benefit. When she finished he frowned, shaking his head.

"I'm surprised the wraiths let you get away, after what they've been up to."

"What do you mean, 'up to'? The wraiths are never 'up to' anything."

"No, the clever bastards have learned their lessons about meeting us directly." He smiled wryly. "They're sneaking about on the skinward borders, where there's next to no shipping. It's such slim pickings out there that they're being forced deeper in. I wouldn't be surprised if they'd gotten as far as the Aracen Graves."

"Wait a minute." Leal was confused. "Are you saying the winter wraiths are engaged in . . . what? Smuggling?" He shook his head. "*Piracy?*"

"It's hard to believe, I know. But there've been raids—attacks on ships and towns. And yet," he added regretfully, "it's small-time stuff, still no job for a ship the size of mine. We stay in port while the other lads have all the fun."

Leal and Seana made suitably sympathetic noises. Brun lapped it up; but then he scowled at his massive wristwatch. "Speaking of which, I have to get back. Back to painting whatever moves, and saluting whatever doesn't. —Or is it the other way around . . ."

He sauntered away, serene in the absolute knowledge of who he was and of his place in the world. Seana sighed, then said, "I'll have to open early tomorrow to make up for closing today . . ."

"All right, I can take a hint." Leal signaled the waiter and, a few minutes later, she and Seana parted in the middle of the brass avenue. "You just hold on tight," Seana said as she tick-ticked away. "Your time will come, Leal."

That small reminder of the day's events was enough to plunge Leal back into a state of gloom. She had been about to head home, but couldn't bring herself to do it. Instead, she wandered the closed markets, watching mushroom-laden jitneys and crate-laden trucks arrive to drop off wares newly arrived from the ships crowding the town's axis.

The usual ambiance of clashing machines and swearing labor-ers reigned here—at least it did until she came around one corner and found a delivery man arguing with a group of shopkeepers. The smell told her that this was a fish market. Trucks mounted with steam-powered shovels were scooping up offal and broken boxes, dumping them noisily into wheeled hoppers; she could hear the argument over this din.

"—Nothing to bring you," the delivery man was shouting. " 'Cause they're still late."

"Five ships?" The lead shopkeeper was incredulous. "How can all five of them be tardy? One or two, maybe, for a day, if they strayed from the rope roads or found an unusually big school they wanted to pursue . . . But this is the third day . . ."

The delivery man shrugged. "Listen, this costs me money as much as you. I've lost customers, too—by the look of things, I'm going to lose you. What am I supposed to do? Conjure the ships out of thin air?"

The shopkeeper swore and turning, walked back to his store-front. The others stood talking among themselves, one or two ar-guing with the delivery man, while Leal loitered under an awning to watch. The first shopkeeper meanwhile was writing something on a placard which he then hung on his door: CLOSED DUE TO LACK OF STOCK.

Leal frowned, and walked on—and now that she had seen this little drama, she spotted several similar ones playing out across the market quarter. Now that she knew to look, she saw that there were fewer delivery vessels than usual in the streets.

Wraith pirates? she thought; it seemed hugely unlikely, granted the Pacquaeans she'd known. She shook her head and, finally feeling her exhaustion, she turned toward home.

3

THE KETTLE BEGAN to sing just as, somewhere in the distance, Rowan's gravity bells rang. Out of habit, Leal glanced over to make sure the kettle was firmly seated on the stove; then she went back to whisking her breakfast eggs. Faint shudders trembled through the building a moment later, as the town wheel's massive jet engines began the thrice-daily ritual of spinning the town back up to speed.

When her breakfast was ready Leal went to curl up in her flat's one window, which looked out on a vista of shingled roofs and glittering windows, with black sky a constant beyond them. It was Leal's habit to sit in the window niche and watch as the lighted windows of office and guild towers went dark while the more brightly colored marquees of theaters and restaurants came alive in the streets below. It was as though the light were draining from the towers into the street. And of course in a sense it was; it went where the people went.

The doorbell tinkled as she was sitting there with her knees near her chin and the plate balanced on them. "Damn." She wormed her way out of the niche and skated the plate onto the table before running to the door. "Are you early?" she asked as she opened it.

Easley Fencher was wearing a new suit; his hair was freshly cut and he held a bouquet of delicate pink anemones. Leal blinked at him for a few seconds while various emotions darted over his face: anxiety, happiness, and a kind of horror that Leal knew meant *Oh no, I've overdone it.*

"You look great," she said with her own mixture of heartfelt sincerity and embarrassment. This was never supposed to be a date, and Easley knew that—should have known that. Except that she had misjudged the depth of his middle-aged desperation, and the fundamental guilelessness of his personality. "Come in," she said shortly. "Don't mind the mess."

She took the anemones from him and hurried to find a vase for them. They strained to keep their little eyeless heads up under gravity and their filigreed feeding threads were drooping; unless she transferred them to her cutter they'd be dead before the end of the day.

"I remembered you've got a boat," stammered Easley from the doorway. "I figured you could use the little guys to keep it clean."

"That's very thoughtful of you, Easley." Of course Leal already had some coral in the cockpit, but he didn't need to know that. There was an awkward pause while they regarded one another. "Well, come in," she said again. "The others will be here any minute."

"O-others?"

Leal refrained from wincing. She'd told him that Seana and Mafin and several friends were coming on today's wine tour.

That she'd felt she had to was a testament to Leal's own desperation. Just walking into the office had become a nerve-wracking experience, for while she did everything she could to avoid running into Hackner, it was bound to happen sooner or later. Leal had no idea what she'd do when they did meet. Murder him, maybe—or worse, break down into bitter sobs.

In order to fend off complete despair, she'd devised a plan. If Hackner could play departmental politics to his advantage, so could she. One cornerstone of that plan was increasing her social time with her peers—while, of course, never crossing the line into any emotional relationships. It had seemed safe and prudent to practice with somebody she already knew.

So, what part of "wine tour with friends" hadn't he understood?

"You remember," she prompted brightly, "we talked about whether we should all meet up there, or take a flea car together."

"Oh. Yes," he said in disappointment. He finally stepped inside, and once there, looked around wide-eyed. It was as though he'd never seen a single woman's apartment before. Her main room, which was also the kitchen and dining area, was well lit by three gaslights. Her mother had given Leal some hardy green plants and she gamely tried to keep them alive by hanging them right next to the lamps. They cast leafy shadows across the walls and floor. Gas costing what it did, her bedroom and the bathroom were almost always kept dark; she did her hair and makeup at the kitchen sink.

"You have, ah, a pretty large place," Easley said as he sat at the dining room table. Leal thought he was being ironic, then noticed him looking at the door to the second bedroom.

"I'm a researcher, I need an office," she said, trying to sound indifferent.

Easley perked up. "Can I see it?"

"Uh . . ." At that moment there was a knock on the door. Grateful for the interruption, Leal opened it to find Seana and Brun Mafin lounging outside. "Ready?" asked Seana. "I hope so, otherwise we'll be late."

"Yes, let's go. Oh, Brun, Seana, this is Easley Fencher. We work together." She very slightly emphasized the word *work*, which Seana noticed. It was hard as always to tell whether Brun perceived any social nuances; he just stepped forward with a grin and stuck out his hand for Easley to shake.

Out of deference to Seana's frailty, they took the elevator down to the street, then a crosstown trolley to the edge of the town wheel. Here, three of Seana's clothier friends joined them. All looked casually stylish, which made Easley stand out even more. He had lapsed into sullen politeness, but regained a bit of energy when one of the young ladies expressed some awe at his academic credentials.

"I've never seen it like this," Seana said as she gazed at the crowds. "Are all these people here for the referendum?"

Leal nodded. "If you think this is crowded, just imagine what the lower-gee streets are like." She pointed straight up.

For days now, every kind of ship, boat, cutter, and catamaran had been queuing up at the docks. Small-town citizens emerged from the elevators to blink at the city's radiance and gawk at the distant lamplike glow of Hayden Griffin's workshop. The hotels were all full so the extra arrivals had started camping in the parks. There, they lined their tents up along the paths because they were afraid to crush the grass; most of them had never seen plants outside of a greenhouse.

Leal felt a swell of pride at her countrymen's democratic passion. The outlying towns had their own voting stations, but Sere so dominated its local airspace that many of its services could only be found here. The city's vote was to be held over the course of four days to permit everyone a chance to come in.

Chatting and weaving in and out of the foot traffic, Leal's party made their way to a flea car stand at the rim of the town. The street and houses here were protected from the hundred mile-per-hour wind of Rowan's rotation by high walls topped by awnings. The awnings flapped so quickly that they buzzed, and the wooden walls trembled, easily transmitting the roar of the spin-gale so that conversation became difficult here. Here, the flea pilots had built a set of doors into the wall. Several dart-shaped cars sat on rails, ready to be rolled through those doors. Mafin stepped up to negotiate a price with the flea pilot, then they all crowded into one car. The plastic canopy swung down as they strapped themselves in. The doorman hauled on a chain and the doors rolled back. Air pressure from inside the city pushed the car outside.

Now their little dart perched on two thin spars above a rushing ocean of dark air. The lights of Rowan Wheel had vanished behind the wall; only if Leal looked straight up could she see the inside surface of the town glittering high above. The lights of hundreds of vehicles twinkled in the eternal night beyond the city, swirls of them like sparks caught in an updraft. Most were headed for the docks at the axis of the cylinder.

The pilot turned. "Which place again?" he asked, ignoring the uneasy sway of the vehicle.

"Phantom Winery," said Mafin with a grin. The pilot grunted and turned back, hunching over his controls to stare out the windshield.

The floodlit underside of Match Wheel was emerging into view as Rowan—and their little taxi stand—turned. Match itself, which was several miles away, turned majestically at the same rate as Rowan. If the pilot had wanted to take them to Match, all he would have to do was wait for some lamps on Match's rim to line up with the crosshairs mounted on his dashboard, then throw the big lever by his right hand. Newtonian physics would take the flea straight to Match's rim.

Match's navigation lights flashed one-two-three, but the pilot ignored them. As Match fell slowly behind them other lights began to twinkle far away in the dark air beyond the city. When the fifth light flickered into brief life, the pilot yanked hard on the lever and the flea car tumbled into the air.

". . . As I was saying," Mafin drawled as they all went weightless, "the rumor mill is working overtime." The car tumbled end over end and the pilot fought for control. City lights spun around them dizzyingly; Leal, like the others, ignored the sensation of falling and focused on Mafin's words.

"People have been talking ever since the wraiths started harassing us." The pilot got the flea straightened out. "But pirates are too boring and ordinary an explanation for the disappearances. Every little town has its story of monsters in the dark." Wisps of cloud shot past as the flea, falling through the air at the same rate Rowan had been rotating, closed on Match.

"Are you saying that every town has had a ship disappear?" asked Seana.

Brun hesitated. "No, not at all. There's only been a couple—but these things get . . . amplified."

"It's anxiety over the referendum," said Easley blithely. He smoothed down the material of his new suit and cleared his throat. "You'd expect an outburst of irrationalism at a time like this."

"And what time is that?" The pilot had turned to look into his crowded cabin.

"A time when science and learning are under assault, sir," said Easley. "When the government believes it can legislate what is real and what is not."

"As opposed to what?" asked the pilot. "Letting a few self-proclaimed 'experts' do it?"

"You see, that's the fallacy . . ." Easley started to say, but the pilot had turned back and was steering the flea in a spiral to find the navigation beacon again.

Their fall drew a perfect tangent from Rowan's circular rim. Propelled by Rowan's rotation, the flea was now knifing into the blackness at over a hundred miles per hour. Every now and then Leal caught a glimpse of a rope road way off to the left, but their pilot was navigating by the beacons, not the road. That was faster, but took more concentration.

The conversation drifted around over the long minutes of the flight. At one point, Seana pointed and said, "Hey! Is that Erdosh's tree?"

Leal looked with the others, catching a glimpse of something like a distant tangle of white hair that quickly fell behind them. "It was indeed," said Brun. "I'm never sure what kind of omen it is."

"Neither is anybody else." Seana laughed.

Erdosh's tree was a ball-shaped oak, its ancient roots clutching a clod of rock and dirt less than ten feet across. It had died centuries ago after drifting into the sunless countries from some warmer home.

Carved on its trunk were the words, "Julette, let this be my gift to you, a living reminder of my love. —Erdosh." Had Erdosh etched those words and then, untangling the tree from whatever grove it was attached to, pushed it in the direction of Julette's home? Had it found her in its drift? Or had it missed, and her message died with the tree as it fell slowly away from its sun of origin, through skies that faded from blue to mauve and indigo?

No one knew; Erdosh's tree had simply shown up one day, many years ago, on the outskirts of Abyss. A romantic movement existed to send it on its way, as if it might finally meet Julette's spirit somewhere out there in the dark. Nobody could decide what to do; but lovers moored there, and left notes to one another among its leafless branches.

The taxi fell onward, and after a time, while Brun argued with Seana's friends over some fine point of etiquette, Easley leaned over to Leal and said, "I'm terribly, terribly sorry about Hackner's appointment."

Leal felt a flutter of anxiety; but she had been hoping to have this conversation. "You didn't have anything to do with it, Easley."

"I did the paperwork!" Easley looked anguished. "And when it came time to write the appointee's name in the blanks, do you know what I did?" She shook her head. "I wrote your name in, just so I could see it in black and white, and then I tore up the sheet and did another one for Hackner."

"Oh, Easley, that's . . ." Sweet? Creepy? Leal truly did not know how to take that admission.

"The question is, what can I do about it?" Pushing like this didn't come naturally to Leal, but she'd learned that it was necessary. Always take the next step.

"Ah!" Easley brightened. "Have you thought of applying for a Principalities grant?"

"Those are grants from foreign governments, right? I'd have to leave Abyss—"

"No, no! That's a popular misconception. Some of the grants are for local work. Historical fieldwork—archaeonomy, for instance—would have to be done here . . ."

They discussed the options as the dart hissed through cloud banks and passed the stabbing lights of ships coming the other way. After about ten minutes a galaxy of colored pinpricks began to expand in the blackness. The navigation beacon flashed past and the pilot deployed the dart's braking ailerons. Now in shuttlecock configuration, the flea twisted and air roared behind it as it slowed. Leal and the others leaned forward against their seat belts. The lights of the Phantom Winery swept past above, below, and to both sides.

Seana was first out of the car. As Brun settled up, she swam through the weightless air like a lithe fish, shouting, "Where shall we start?"

Phantom made three things: wine, beer, and jet fuel. It was easy to tell which division was which, because there were no crowds queuing up to drink the fuel. Mobs of tourists clumped here and there in the air, sampling the other two wares. The winery's owners had set up a number of basket-shaped wicker hutches, each one containing a bartender, lights, and wineglasses. The actual fermentation balls hung in semidarkness outside of these cozy little nests.

"Is that the experiment?" Easley pointed at a faint curving sheen in the distance—the side of a dark liquid planet some hundreds of feet across. Numerous metal pipes jutted out of the thing, and smaller balls of water, bags of hops and barley, and nets full of grapes orbited it at almost imperceptible speed.

"Apparently half the stuff they pull out of it is deadly poison." Brun hand-walked along a guide rope to a sampling basket. "It's been fermenting for fifty years now. Sometimes they pump stuff in, sometimes they pump stuff out, but nobody really knows what's going on in there."

Closer at hand, dozens of smaller gleaming balls sat ranked in the air, each one pinioned by one or two copper pipes that snaked back through the air to central, can-shaped pumping shacks. The spheres were about ten feet in diameter; they gleamed in various colors of rose, deep red, or pale yellow. One beautiful red drop had been towed near to a wicker tasting station, and was surrounded by lanterns. A serving girl was ready with helix glasses for each of them. "What is this?" asked Leal as she held her glass up to the light.

"We're calling it Aere Fourteen," said the server. "The grapes are from Cullen, deep in the principalities. They send them here because, of course, our air is so still . . ." Leal made a swirling motion and surface tension drew wine smoothly to the end of the glass coil. One drop broke off and hovered in midair. She sniffed the floating drop delicately, then took it into her mouth.

"Mmm! Very dry."

The others tasted theirs and commented on it. The room-sized ball glowing outside the tasting station was a single giant drop of aging wine, coated by a thin skin of mineral oil to prevent contamination from drifting dust or spores. The balls were usually stored inside large paper and wicker warehouses; several of those large geodesic structures lurked in the distance. What with the festival atmosphere around the referendum, the winery had brought out selected stock for public display—and consumption.

Leal sampled some cheese made at a nearby farm. Fermented goods were one of Abyss's main exports, since anything that grew in the dark could be raised here by the kiloton. Plankton and algae sprouted within clouds of water and dust as they rose slowly through Virga's microgravity. There was plenty of light in the regions of Candesce, so the air itself turned green with life. Eventually, though, it wafted out of civilized areas and into "winter": the unlit regions of the five-thousand-mile diameter balloon that was Virga. In death, the formerly green clouds turned white as they were eaten from within by fungi and consumed by vast schools of benthic fish and birds. As one life form was transformed into another, the people of the sunless countries harvested them. Those clouds eventually reached the frozen outer skin of the world, to turn and begin a long fall. Thus was dead matter brought back to Candesce to sprout and bloom again.

The cycle seemed almost mystically balanced. Ageless; perfect. Small wonder that so many of Abyss's people believed the world had always been like this.

Easley was discussing the referendum with Brun right now, as a matter of fact. ". . . Gloss over the fact that humans have *legs*, and never wonder why that should be," he was saying.

"Oh, they know why," said Brun laconically. "We were given legs as punishment, remember? Made to rely on gravity in a gravity-free world because of our past sins."

"Surely no one believes that!"

Brun raised an eyebrow. "What country do you live in, again?"

Leal turned away, letting her eyes rest on the hypnotic well of darkness that presided outside the tasting station. Maybe, she thought, the world was really a vast ball of wine, and she and Easley and Brun and the others merely motes in its long, slow fermentation. . . . And that, she mused, was just how myths began. Generation by generation, tiny fancies and fables snowballed into elaborate stories, while the truth—that this world was artificial, had in fact been made by men in the deep past—dimmed and was forgotten. Here in Abyss, people had come to believe that the world had no beginning. Maybe in some other one of the sunless countries, they really did think they were steeping eternally in a ball of booze. Depressing thought . . .

A tiny ember of light had become visible in the reachless dark. It was literally the only thing in sight, so Leal's eyes drifted to it. Doubtless an incoming ship.

". . . It's worse than that," Easley was saying. "There's talk of closing the department!"

Leal whirled. "What? Where did you hear that?"

Easley wrung his hands. "I shouldn't be telling you this. It's just a rumor. One of, well, Hackner's contacts in the ministry let it drop—"

"And Hackner believed him?"

Easley nodded. Leal was about to sneer something about Hackner's credibility, but stopped herself. She had to play the political game, she reminded herself. Easley had to deal with the faux professor on a daily basis, and so would she if she was to eventually gain her appointment. Besides, Hackner might not know anything about history, but he knew who was who in the ministry.

"If the past is infinite, then progress is impossible," Easley continued. "The most you could hope for is that progress goes in cycles; but even then, nobody wants to know whether we're on the upslope or decline of one of those. So why study history at all?"

"That's why we all have to vote, and have to vote no," said Leal. She turned away again to scowl at the dark—

—Which had filled with red-lit clouds whose banks and pillars were split by endless canyons of black air; and out of this tumult shot a flaming airship.

She screamed and pointed. Everybody turned and yelled or yelped or cursed and then they were all clambering out of the wicker ball because the ship seemed headed straight for it. Leal threw aside her drink and followed. In her panic she kicked off in a random direction, hesitating only long enough to make sure there was a rope in the distance. As she flew she spun—remembering one of Uthor's Leverage moves—and watched as the ship passed at well over a hundred miles per hour. The cockpit area of the wooden fish-shape was bearded with flames and she caught a glimpse of passengers or crewmen clambering along the peeling skin, gamely trying to reach the ailerons at the tail while the headwind whipped flames and smoke at them.

Big chunks of burning wood and canvas flipped end over end as the wind pried the ship's nose off, chunks of debris slapping wine balls in sudden puffs of spray. The bow separated from the stern, which immediately began to spin end over end. Men were tossed off its back to vanish in the dark. Then something vast and mirror-bright flowered into view ahead of the plummeting wreck. It was the *experiment*: the gigantic, ancient ball of fermentation the winery had indulged for decades.

Leal caught one of the winery's outrider ropes and hung on, unable to look away as the blazing prow of the ship struck the experiment a glancing blow. That part of the wreck carried on past the erupting splash, but the tail section shot straight into the giant black ball of liquid.

The spray from the impact caught fire; the finer mists exploded, breaking up more of the sphere and spawning new fireballs. Each fresh blast became stronger and in seconds that whole part of the sky was an inferno.

The heat seemed to peel back the skin of her face. *Now I've seen a real sun.* She threw up an arm to shield herself, but the light and heat were already fading as the blaze consumed all the oxygen in its vicinity. Without gravity there was no convection to bring in more, so even though the blast had ignited many of the smaller wine balls, it couldn't spread. All the fires were extinguished within seconds. The winery's lanterns began to gutter and go out as well, as the exhausted air from the fire reached them. The workers jumped from rope to wicker station to rope, trying to stay ahead of the spreading anoxic cloud.

But her friends might still be in there! Leal looked around for a rescue party—ambulances, anything—but the whole disaster had taken less than a minute. Nobody had even had time to ring the winery's alarm bell.

Phantom Winery's "experiment" was now a spreading smudge against the night, eating light in all the ways that were possible. It was only by sheer luck that something silver turned the right way as it drifted inward, and caught Leal's eye. She followed the glimpse to one of Seana's bracers. Tiny as a doll at this distance, Leal's friend was climbing hand over hand along a rope, shaking her head to drive away the exhaust that was coiling around her. But both she and the rope were slumping into the miasma of airless heat; Seana's hand reached out one more time for the line, missed, and curled limply back into the air. She was unconscious.

"No!" Leal braced against her own rope, about to jump—but if Seana's line wasn't attached to anything then Leal would have nothing to push against after catching her. The momentum from her own jump would carry them even farther into the deadly cloud.

"Seana! Somebody help her!"

"Leal! Grab an end!" Of all people, it was Easley who came to her aid now. He had another loose rope, a good hundred feet of it tangling and coiling behind him as he sailed to her position.

"What are we going to do?" She fumbled her way into a good grip on the rope.

"Tie it around my feet," he said. "Then I'll jump and catch her and you pull me back."

"Yes!" She found the end and he turned over to present his feet. Easley looked scared, but determined.

"Wait!" They turned to see Brun hand-walking up the rope to meet them. "It's a great idea, Fencher, but I might just have more experience in free-jumping than you. Are you sure you could reach her on your first try?"

Easley hesitated, then, looking crestfallen, said, "Tie it to his feet, Leal."

She did, and Brun planted his feet against the rope, frowning in concentration, and jumped.

FOUR HOURS LATER, Leal drifted listlessly out the admittance entrance of Rowan's freefall hospital. Easley was gallantly holding her arm, but she hadn't spoken to him in many minutes. She felt like she'd been awake for days.

After pulling Seana out of the anoxic cloud, Brun had given her mouth-to-mouth and revived her almost immediately. He had then left the friends to find the rest of their party, as he went back to help the winery staff. His manner made it clear that Leal and her friends were rescued, not rescuers; and Leal couldn't decide whether to resent him for that, or admire his military efficiency. She did make sure to heap praise on Easley for his good idea.

Brun returned after just a few minutes, shaking his head. "Everyone from the winery's accounted for," he said. "Some burns, some smoke inhalation. We need to get them, and Seana, to a hospital."

"I'm fine," Seana whispered huskily. She had taken a few lungfulls of smoke and was coughing dryly. Brun just shook his head again and flew off to commandeer an aircar.

He was silent as they led a convoy of vehicles along the rope road. Leal knew what he was thinking: the burning wreck had been heading for the city. If it hit one of the town wheels . . .

In fact, by the time the tumbling wreck arrived at Sere, the fire was out and the few crewmen who had stuck with it had managed to rig a makeshift parachute from some lengths of spare canvas in the forward stores. Hauling on the ropes, shouting orders back and forth across the severed heart of the ship, they had somehow steered it to the docks at Rowan Wheel. Just a coincidence, surely, that it should come straight to Leal's home . . .

Now she let herself drift through the jumbled buildings of Rowan's axial docks. The great wheel still spun majestically around her; the wreck had not damaged anything. Leal had glimpsed it, crumpled into the jetties alarmingly close to the boathouse where she kept her cutter. It had been swarming with emergency workers and surrounded by a cloud of spectators; but she didn't really know what had happened.

Seana would be okay. She would be breathing oxygen for the next day just in case. Leal had been allowed to see her briefly, but she was asleep by then, so after some hesitation Leal had left the others to stay with her. Easley had quickly followed her out.

"I will see you home, Leal," he said. "You've been through a lot today."

"So have you," she pointed out. "I'm fine, really. —Look, my elevator's right over there, I'm just going to ride it down and go straight home. If you come along you'll have to retrace your steps, or take a trolley all the way around the city."

"That's of no account," he said. "It's no trouble, really."

"Please, Easley, I—" She sighed. "Actually, I need to be alone right now."

"Oh." He bit his lip and looked away. "I . . . understand. Listen, I'll tell the dean not to expect you tomorrow—"

"Don't you dare! I'll be there at my usual time, Eas." She squeezed his hands. "It—it really was fun, I mean right up until that ship exploded and all. We'll have to do it again sometime, maybe after the craziness of the referendum."

"Yes." He nodded briskly. "Too many people coming to the city. That must be why . . . I, I'll see you tomorrow then." He ducked his head and retreated. With a sigh, Leal turned and headed for the elevators.

Balls and knots of people were crowding around the wrought-iron stanchions that framed the brass elevator doors; once again it looked like she was in for a long wait, and this time there were no spokesmen in sight. They'd be doing a roaring business with all the tourists, she was sure.

Leal hated waiting. Above her, gaslight wavered on the angles and cornices of towers and warehouses similarly balanced on tip-toe, their shapes jumbled together like dice in a bag. Windows shone out at all angles; behind one, a tired man with his sleeves rolled up yanked the levers of a calculating machine. The chatter of a typing pool drifted across the air, mixing with revving engines, rattling chains, shouts, and the regular foghorns ringing the city. Leal loved these sounds. They soothed her, so maybe a stroll would be a better idea than returning to her apartment.

She walked away from the elevators. Each step covered fifteen feet, only her toes touching down. Despite her better instincts, she let her feet and gaze drift to where the docks were framed by the triangles and trapezoids of surrounding buildings. There it was: hundreds of people were swarming around the collapsed nose of the wreck, covering it like flies.

She shouldn't go there—and yet, she found herself resentful of those spectators. She, Leal, had a true connection to that thing, she had seen it come apart. In an obscure way, she felt like it was hers.

Closer in, she saw that there was a lot of order to the hovering and darting crowds. The men actually touching the wreck wore the sashes of accident investigators; they were vigorously tossing away the hovering souvenir-hunters who flapped their spring-powered wings just overhead. The fires were long since out, the bodies carried away or modestly shrouded in white. Several press photographers were standing around talking shop, but they had obviously finished their work a while ago.

Leal detoured first one way, then the other to avoid knots of people. She didn't approve of their laughter and prurient curiosity. Soon she found herself near open air, where a loose weave of jetties and diving boards extended, like fraying cloth, into the turning skies. There were fewer people here—none, in fact, except for a serious-looking young man who was frowning at the gutted backside of the wreck. To match his expression, he was dressed somberly in a dark airman's jacket, suede trousers, and stout open-toed boots. Leal guessed he was a pilot.

A particularly loud laugh drifted over from the spectators. Leal glanced at the youth, and found him glancing back. On impulse she said, "They shouldn't do that. It must have taken great courage and skill to bring it in here."

He nodded, murmured something that might be assent as he raised one hand to brush at his hair. She noticed that he was missing the tips of several fingers. Frostbite?

Encouraged, she said, "I saw it break in two. We were at the winery when it came past."

He thought about that, then asked, "Was anybody hurt?"

"My friend Seana, smoke inhalation . . ." Leal looked away, suddenly feeling all the things she should have felt at the time they were happening. "I was so scared."

"Yet you came to look at it." He didn't step closer; this wasn't Easley.

"I just wondered . . . what happened?"

He was silent so long that she looked over to see whether he was still there. He was examining the wreck with a pensive look.

"They panicked," he said at last. "I was in unloading some supplies from my ship when they came in. We had to pry one man's fingers off the parachute strap he was holding. As if he couldn't bring himself to believe he'd made it to the city. They said they had met something in the dark."

"*Something?* Pacquaeans?"

He shook his head. "Not men. —Though, they thought it was at first. Followed a voice they thought was some stranded airman calling for help."

"V-voice?"

"It got louder and louder, they said. Inhumanly loud. They couldn't make out the words. And then—something came . . ."

He glanced at her, and now he cracked a lopsided grin. "Nonsense, of course. If you stare long enough into the dark, you will definitely start seeing things there." He had an accent, she realized, not Abyssal. "They scared themselves."

"Yes, of course. But what did they think they were seeing?"

He shrugged. "Have you ever heard of something called a *worldwasp?*"

Startled, she said, "Why, yes. It's an obscure reference—"

"An old story?" he asked. "Something to scare children?"

"Yes, and no." She smiled. "They were real, once. Back when the world was young, and humanity made the decision to wall itself into Virga. We call that time the *Great Refusal.*"

"So you believe Virga was built?" His smile was ironic now. "I take it you'll be voting no in the referendum?"

"The referendum is a joke!" She folded her arms and glared at the wreck. "I'm a historian, I work at the university. And yes, Virga was built by us long long ago, and yes, we fought the worldwasps not long after."

He laughed. "Next you'll be telling me that the Virga Home Guard are real, too."

"As a matter of—" She stopped herself. Leal knew the Guard was real; the Argyre sisters, one of whom she knew, had joined that legendary order. She refused to be baited by this stranger, though; and the mention of worldwasps had gotten her thinking. *A mighty voice from the darkness, proclaiming words no one can understand.* Where had she read something about that?

"I don't trade in rumors and legends," she said. "I'm just glad some of these airmen made it home safely." She made a shallow bow to the young man. "Now if you'll excuse me, I should go."

"I'm sorry if I offended you."

"It's not that. It's been a long and hard day, is all. Good-bye." Weighing as little as she did, she couldn't exactly stride away, but Leal made her exit as gracefully as she could.

On her way back to the elevators she tried to place his accent; it didn't remind her of any of the other sunless countries. His skin, in fact, had been dark by Abyssal standards. Could he be from farther afield?

"Oh!" She almost tripped as she realized where she'd heard his voice before. She'd already walked away in disgust, on that occasion, and couldn't make out the words he'd said. But she remembered the voice of the man who'd spoken warmly with Eustace Loll on the gangplank of an exotic ship that now nestled in the heart of the docks.

She had just been speaking with Hayden Griffin.

The sun lighter.

QUESTION 4: *Should the government of Abyss extend the System of Decision by referendum to include all matters of fact not immediately determinable by simple observation or experiment? That is, should it be admitted that there is no mechanism superior to public opinion to determine any contentious matter of truth?*

LEAL STARED AT the words as if they were the barrels of a firing squad pointed at her. There it was, in black and white: the unthinkable made real.

Even last week, she'd been confident in the wisdom, if not the education, of the common people. Leal spent her days disguised as city-born and middle-class—she even practiced the local accent, and woe to her if she'd slipped up and used *that* around Mother. But none of this elaborate posing meant she rejected her scavenger background. She just wanted to avoid her father's mistakes. He'd stood out, became too successful in the wrong line of business. In fact, Leal often felt like her class's secret agent, sent behind the barricades of the shopkeepers and academics to prove that her own people were as capable as those who'd inherited their privileges.

But even her students—her *students!*—had told Leal they'd be voting yes to Question Four. Just listening to trolley passengers on the way to the polling station, she'd had to admit to herself that she'd been naïve. People would jump at any chance for self-empowerment, even if it was illusory.

She gnawed her lip and stared at the questions under #4. Granted that the proposition was likely to pass anyway, she now faced a terrible decision.

QUESTION 5: IF YOU *VOTED YES TO QUESTION* 4, *should newspaper recycling be brought under the jurisdiction of the National Referendum Division; and, should all popular press outlets be required to include true/false tick boxes beside all new statements of fact in news items?*
QUESTION 6: IF YOU *VOTED YES TO QUESTION* 4, *should the People immediately declare as a matter of fact, and to resolve a source of recent popular unrest and religious schism, that our World of Virga is the ONLY world, that there is NOTHING beyond the walls, and that the AGE of Virga and its future duration are both infinite?*

. . . And this was beyond unthinkable. Leal was standing at the polling booth; she landed in the helpfully-provided chair with a thud. The damned Eternists had wormed their way far enough into the government that they'd actually been successful in getting their proposition put on the ballot!

Abyss was, as her father would have put it, screwed.

The Eternists continued to exhibit the sort of low cunning that had gotten them this far. They'd set up a little mind game with voters like Leal and they must be laughing themselves silly right now imagining her thinking, *if I vote no to Question Four, I'm not allowed to vote against Questions Five and Six. So if Four passes, as it looks like it will, I'll have lost my vote against Six. But if I say yes to Four so that I can say no to Six, I'll be guaranteeing that Four passes and raising the odds that Six will pass, too.*

"What's taking her so long?" She glanced up; there was a lengthening queue at her polling station, and one of the invigilators at the table was frowning back at Leal. Her pencil trembled over the paper.

"Fuck it." She put a big X in the No box next to Question Four.

Then she stalked back to the ballot box, feeling hollow, and stuffed her ballot into the slot. Not meeting the gazes of the impatient voters in the lineup, she hurried for the exit. She felt defeated already.

THE CITY'S GREAT foghorns roared out their warnings, and in ones and twos and by the dozen, the ships that had come for the referendum departed. For two days they made traffic jams in the sky, blaring their horns and waving spotlights. Most had come singly, but they left in one another's company. Nobody would admit to why; but if their trajectory took them past Rowan Wheel, every passenger and crewman craned their heads to see the burnt-out wreck of the ferry *Porphyry*.

The parks were emptying of squatters, who had not disturbed a single blade of grass in those well-lit expanses; they'd been too much in awe of the greenery, such a rare thing in Abyss, and had walked on tiptoe lest they accidentally bend the stalk of a flower. Those who'd camped in alleys or plazas were not so kind to the city. A stink of garbage and human waste followed Leal for days, and she was constantly coming around one corner or another only to find her way blocked by work crews that were artistically sluicing away the crap. They skidded it into opened manholes using high-pressure hoses, and woe-betide anyone who might be flying under the wheel at that moment.

The shopkeepers were reluctant to let their visitors leave, but the visitors themselves seemed to be dawdling. They were used to boarding friable little vessels made of imported wood and canvas; used to plying their way slowly along a rope road with only intermittent and unreliable beacons, and the guttering flames in their own headlights to show the way. For the most part they lived on small, creaking wood-and-rope towns that were seldom more than a few hundred feet across. In the farthest reaches of the country, mold farmers lashed two or more houseboats together by rope and spun them like bolos, once or twice a day, to get a few hours of gravity. They lived out their days with black and empty skies right at hand, those depths relieved only by a few tentative lights that flickered in the constant wind of their home's rotation. The wind sighed constantly; or, oppressive silence reigned if home was motionless today or if they were out at work in the vast cloudlike fields of fungi they tended. You could hear clapped hands a mile away in air like that.

The newspapers were full of poll results, voting irregularities, and the outrageous proclamations of various politicians. There was nothing there about it, but the citizens queuing at the elevators for the ride back to the docks knew that the five missing ships had not been found.

They were afraid of journeying today. They were afraid of being home. They dreaded to hear, in a quiet broken only by the groan of the ropes and creaking of planks underfoot, a distant voice.

"THAT'S THE THIRD one today and it's only an hour into shift," commented one of the faculty secretaries. Leal poked her head around the doorjamb, something she could do without leaving her desk. A man dressed in a stained farmer's jumpsuit was just leaving, a frown on his face.

"Who was that?" she called.

The secretary shrugged. "Another question about worldwasps. Should we send the next one to you?"

"Gods, no. Keep doing what you're doing." She retreated back into her tiny domain, but laid a hand protectively on a stack of cards from the library card catalog that sat on one corner of her desk. She'd swung by the library on her way to work this morning and pilfered these (intending to look through them then return them at end-of-shift). The cards listed books on worldwasps.

They were all fantasies—kids' stories, for the most part, or old romances. Historical references to the ancient beasts were much harder to find.

Leal turned her attention back to the assignments she was marking, but she couldn't concentrate. The cards faced her like accusations of amateurism. Her original impulse to take them had revolved around a fantasy of her own, anyway: that she might be the only expert in worldwasp lore when Hayden Griffin (being the hero that he was) came to find out more about them. Well . . . he'd seemed curious about the beasts, hadn't he? —and it was the only point of contact they'd had.

But okay, it was silly, especially in light of how the *Porphyry*'s story was getting around. Its panicked crewmen still claimed they had encountered a monster, but according to the government and the newspapers, this was impossible: there were no ancient creatures in the dark, because the dark was ageless. The world was eternal, so had no history, so could not have once contained anything different.

This idea, once the opinion of a few loopy Eternists, was now official doctrine. The constant knowledge of the referendum's outcome had caused Leal to walk everywhere quickly and with her shoulders hunched since the day of the vote.

The government believed impossible things; but it did not believe in ancient monsters. Leal did—and that was the other reason why she'd sought out these references.

Eventually Leal lost her mighty struggle to concentrate, and gave up on marking for now. She gathered up the cards and slipped out through the outer office, where the secretaries were still joking about the lunatics who'd come to ask about worldwasps; they were probably right to, she conceded to herself as she hurried out the door—

—And collided with someone.

"Oh!" The cards fountained into the air, past the surprised eyes of the department's newest faculty member.

"I'm so sorry, Gereld!" She knelt to pick up the white rectangles; to her mortification, he knelt, too.

"That's Professor Hackner, or hadn't you heard?" His tone was amiable, but Leal got the point all right. She tried to smile.

"Of course, I just—hadn't seen you since the appointment—"

"Quite all right, dear, quite all right." He was holding up one of the cards—damn it, he was reading it! After an upward loft of those magnificent eyebrows and a simultaneous belly laugh, he stood up, fanning more of the cards he'd retrieved. "Shouldn't these be in the library?"

"Of course, G-professor. I was just looking for some stories my, uh, the son of a friend, he'd like. Kids' stuff."

"I should hope so," said Hackner with an audible sniff as he handed back the cards. "But not for long, do you get my drift? This sort of thing really isn't fit to be of any interest to you, or to any children you know. For their sake . . . and yours."

"I see." She clutched the cards to her chest, backing away.

Hackner bellowed another laugh, tilting his head to wink in the direction of the departmental secretaries, who were perfectly visible through the opened door. "Worldwasps! Quite an interest for a legitimate historian, eh?" Still chortling, he sauntered off down the hallway.

Ears burning, Leal stalked out the main doors. The sight of the white spotlit pillar of the library calmed her a bit, but she still jammed her hands in her pockets and stared downward as her footsteps ticked quickly across the burnished copper roadway. She didn't glance at anyone until she reached the library entrance.

There were a lot of students bustling about the card catalogs, but nobody noticed as Leal slid back one long thin drawer and reinserted the cards she'd taken. She scowled at the burnished cabinet as she pushed the drawer in; she felt in no ways satisfied, and Hackner's derision had gotten her back up.

Sure, it might be ridiculous to imagine a worldwasp loose in the world today. Yet they were a historical reality, and all such realities should be treated with equal dignity. And who was he—or anyone—to tell her what was or wasn't a fit subject for inquiry?

Within a few minutes Leal had followed this train of thought into a fine fury, and she began pacing up and down the catalogs, reviewing her mental inventory of their contents. Sure, you could find the traditional descriptions and stories of worldwasps in the encyclopediae, and in standard reference works; she'd already glanced at those. But humanity's written memory was deep, and Sere's library prided itself on having original texts that were unique. Surely one of those would reveal some new insight into the primordial world of the wasps. But which one?

She didn't bother with the card catalog this time, but marched up the stairs, past the sleepy library staff who, long familiar with her visits, simply waved her through. Four floors up was the rare books collection, a hushed, cross-shaped chamber carpeted in crimson and overhung with a domed ceiling upon which was painted an azure-and-gold depiction of the Gates of Virga.

"Leal! So pleased to see you." Old William Peeve, the wizened curator, hobbled over to shake her hand. "It's been at least a season since I saw you up here." He coughed dryly, stepping back to give her an appraising look.

"I've had other duties," she said regretfully. "But I miss this place. I miss browsing."

"Ah, I like to hear that. Oh! Come. I must show you something." Peeve tottered off energetically. "I wouldn't reveal this to just anyone, and I must have your absolute discretion, mind. Some people . . . would not understand the impulse. Some might even find it, well, 'creepy' I believe is the word."

He disappeared down one of the cross-arms. Leal followed,

bemused. When she found him, Peeve was peeling back the carpet at the foot of one of the fluted pillars that held up the room. "I've come to an . . . arrangement . . . with the powers-that-be on campus," he said. "It's only taken me twenty years! Here, look at this."

The floor under the carpet was stone, except where he'd pulled back the carpet. Here was revealed a gleaming copper square about three feet on a side. She could make out no hinges or keyhole, but it was obviously a door.

"My tomb," said Peeve with pride. "The lads from the architect's office installed it in the dead of night, about three weeks ago."

"Oh, William, that's . . ." At a loss, she merely shook her head and smiled.

"Ah, you understand," he said with a smile. "I knew you would."

"But—a tomb?" She knew he wouldn't be offended if she laughed, so she did. "Nobody has *tombs*," she chided. "They're for planets, where you can 'bury' people. Not Virga."

"Bah!" He waved a hand irritably. "Cremation? Even in the fires of Candesce, it would be so . . . banal. But this! I've devoted my life to this place, and now I need never leave! And besides . . ." He seemed to consider whether to say something.

"Leal, how old is Sere, do you think?"

"Think? It's exactly four hundred fifty-seven years since the founding of the city." (How odd, she thought in passing, to be discussing such things while straddling a—what was the word?—a "grave".)

William nodded. "And every day some piece of these great wheels is replaced or renewed. Constant renovation, for four hundred years. And you're right, the city is four hundred fifty-seven. But what of the wheels themselves, Leal? Do you know their age?"

She opened her mouth to say, "Well obviously, they're the same age," then closed it again. The great metal wheels were, as William had said, constantly renewed. There had been wheels since the beginning of the world.

Leal squinted at the librarian. "What secret are you hiding, William?"

William grinned and for a moment he looked like a boy rather than an old man. "Once," he said, "many years ago now, they set out to build a new tower—here, on this very wheel. It was in an area that had not been extensively rebuilt since the founding of the city. The buildings were dilapidated and unsafe."

She shrugged. "Just like my apartment."

"And half the city. Now, I happened to be working in the city planning department at the time. One day I heard that while taking out the buildings—it's a complicated art, you know, you have to bring in temporary ballast of the same mass as you're taking away, or the wheel will become unbalanced in its turning—while doing this dance of weight-shuffling, the workers had opened an ancient vault built into the buttresses of one of the old buildings. It was a structural member, very very old. It was, in fact, older than the city by some centuries. This wheel, it seems, was once part of some other city, or at any rate some of its buildings and streets were.

"And what, do you suppose, was in the vault?"

Leal smelled a trick question. "Bodies?"

William shook his head. "Books, Leal! The vault held books."

Now he had her entire attention. "Of course the workmen were disappointed. They'd kept them as part of the ballast, just tipped them into a rubbish-bag. When I heard that, well, of course I went down during Maintenance shift and opened the bags."

"You found them?"

He looked away sadly. "Not all, I'm afraid. I couldn't shift some of those broken pieces of wall and floor. But I found a few. Enough to know that this city, or part of it at least, dates all the way back to the Great Refusal."

The Refusal? If he was right, then the span of time William was talking about was breathtaking. "This city *predates* the Virga Home Guard?"

"Oh, it's more than that, Leal. Have you ever heard of the *Polyhistoria?*"

The name seemed familiar. She pursed her lips, half-shook her head.

William harrumphed. "If you spent any time in primary texts, girl, you'd have run across references to it. It's legendary, but supposed lost. There was a copy, in this cache."

"No! You kept it?"

"It's here," he said. "Hidden in this collection. But never mind that—the point is that the *Polyhistoria* confirms something. Not only do parts of this city date to the Great Refusal. This is the very city where the Home Guard was created!"

Leal blinked at him. "I've never heard this—"

"—Because I've never told anyone. You know this government's feelings about the Guard—why guard Virga, they say, from an outside world that doesn't exist? Even back then, the Eternists were powerful, and brutal. I couldn't reveal what I'd found. But the *Polyhistoria* is here," he said with a sly smile, "if you know where to look."

"But William, this is amazing! We have to get this book to some outside authority, someone who'll be able to study it properly . . ."

He shrugged. "Well yes, naturally. In time. But you see my point is—it was, before you distracted me—that cities like ours, they're not so temporary as you might think. There are graves, and other things, in wheels like Sere's. I hope my library," he smiled up at it, "will remain a thousand years. And if it does, I can abide here with it."

WILLIAM RESTORED THE carpet, smoothing it over with his foot. "Now, Leal dear, now that I've had my moment of overweening pride, what can I do for you today?"

Leal twined her fingers together, suddenly remembering the impulse that had brought her here. "It seems silly now," she said, "after what you've just shown me . . ."

"Now now."

Irritated both at herself and his suddenly condescending grandfatherly look, she said, "What do you have on worldwasps?"

He barked a laugh as he walked to an overfull book cart. "Can you be a bit more specific?"

She followed him. "What do you mean?"

" 'Worldwasp' is a generic term. Like 'outsider' or 'enemy.' There was never a specific thing called a worldwasp, Leal. Not until the storytellers got hold of the term and embellished it to pieces."

"Oh?" She was sure she'd read differently—that the wasps had been creatures that helped humanity build Virga. But one thing William knew was categorizations. Maybe all manner of creatures had helped build the world.

"Why do you ask?" asked William.

"Haven't you heard?" she said. He cocked his head. "About the monster?" she went on.

He grinned. "Monster? What monster?"

She told him the news. It seemed William had been preoccupied lately, and anyway he had contempt for newspapers. He listened indulgently as she quoted the survivors' descriptions, then shook his head.

"It's a muddle," he said. "Doesn't add up to anything. A great voice, you say? That's a detail from children's fantasies, not anything historical." He smiled, musing, at the wall. "And what does this great voice have to say for itself, anyway?"

"Well, you know the papers aren't going into specifics, because the government line is that there's nothing out there." She hesitated. "The rumors are pretty specific about the words it spoke, but you know how reliable rumors are." He waited. "I think one was . . ." He smiled calmly at her as she tried to remember. "Ah," she said, "one witness claimed it said, 'Just as there was a time before Man, there will be a time after.'"

The smile, and, it seemed, all the blood drained from William's face. He staggered, sitting down suddenly on the carpeted step. Shocked, Leal knelt next to him. "Are you all right?"

"I'm fine." He waved her away irritably. "I . . . I may be able to help you."

"A DISCOURSE ON Ancient Shapes," she called down. "Is this it?"

"No, no," said William from the shadows below. "To your right."

"But what are we looking for?"

"I may be misremembering where I read those words, Leal. I don't want to embarrass myself."

"At least tell me which book I'm after," she muttered to herself. William had shooed her up a narrow rolling ladder, which in turn perched on the gallery; her head was twenty feet above the carpet where they'd been talking five minutes ago. William was displaying a level of slyness she'd never expected of him: as curator of this collection he was naturally protective of his books, but who would have suspected he'd be hiding the best volumes?

Leal gently pried the dusty cover open, shivering for a moment in a puff of cold air from the tall window beside her. William might not want to look at this book, but she did. She kept it in her hand as she turned back to searching.

What exactly she was searching for, William wouldn't say. His whole demeanor had changed when she'd quoted the witness's words, but he refused to elaborate. All would be explained, he insisted, when she'd found what he wanted her to find.

Was it the *Polyhistoria*? Surely not . . .

These top-level shelves were supposedly given over to ancient census records. From the gallery or the lower floor all that was visible was row after row of identical bindings, and if you opened one of these books you'd find nothing but lists of names and dates. But, scattered throughout the mind-numbing specificity of these tomes—generally in positions of permanent shadow—were the spines of a few other books.

She was already holding another one, *Denizens of the World's Skin*, which also looked fascinating. The very fact that the *Ancient Shapes* volume was bound in a waxy kind of plastic she'd never seen before suggested its great age. The words inside—printed on another kind of plastic—were in a dialect so old that only a dozen or so people in Abyss could understand it. Leal had studied that, but she would need to pull out some of her fourth-year texts to help her.

"Up!" said William. "Two shelves up and to the right, I said."

She was weighing the two texts in her hands (momentarily wondering if one was stout enough to withstand being dropped on William's unhelpful head), when she heard bustling footsteps downstairs. Leal grabbed a shelf for support and leaned out, peering downward.

"—Don't you 'good shift' me, young man," William was saying. He appeared almost doll-like among the large men in black coats who surrounded him. "This collection is for students or faculty only."

One of the men laughed. "Haven't you heard? Knowledge belongs to the people now."

"It always did," snapped William. "But the books belong to us."

"Those books that the people decide hold genuine knowledge will be kept," said the man. "The rest are going to have to go."

William said nothing.

"We're just here to change the locks," continued the man in a kindly tone. "You can take a break for a few days while we inventory this stuff. Then there'll be a public vote on what's worthwhile and what's—"

"Out! Out now!" William stepped forward and took a swing at one of the bulky coats. The man danced out of his reach.

Reason told her to stay out of this. The last thing she needed at this delicate point in her career was some official black mark for obstructing the government's thugs.

Leal glanced around quickly. The tall window she'd leaned the ladder next to had a pane that pivoted from its center to bring in air. It was open right now, hence the cold breeze on her neck. She put the two books she'd recovered on the little table formed by the open glass flap and then shouted, "Hey!" at the men below.

Their faces tilted up. "What are you doing to that old man?" She made a big show of bustling down the ladder. "Have you no respect for your elders?"

"It's okay, ma'am. We work for the government."

Leal leaned over the gallery banister. "Really? And here I thought you worked for the people."

"Same thing."

"Then isn't he one of the people?" William was straightening his collar and stepping away from the goons now.

"Could you come down, ma'am? This room's closed until further notice."

She looked around. "We'll still have access to the books, won't we?"

"No," he said, sounding annoyed. "That's the whole point."

"I see. William, I'll just close these windows to keep out the damp. So you don't have to." She stepped back and pushed on the iron rode connected to the window-flap, thumping it closed.

"So tell me," continued Leal as she paced down the steps, "why does it take four of you to change a lock?"

"I'm going to have to ask you to leave, ma'am." One of the big men gestured to the door. "Wait!" he said as she made to slip past. "Let's see your coat." She hesitated, then took it off and handed it over. He patted it down, then eyed her figure. "Turn around."

"I beg your pardon!"

"'sokay," he said. "Just making sure you wasn't hiding no books." He handed back the coat.

Leal reached for Peeve's hand. "Come on, William. Best to take indignity with dignity, as my father used to say."

"But—I have to update the—" William pointed feebly to a cart stacked with tomes.

"I'm sure these men won't touch anything," she said, giving the goons a needle-sharp glare. She led poor William out of the library and to his little office. "It's dark in here," she commented dumbly, fumbling for matches and peering about for a gas lamp.

"Never light the lamps," muttered William. "Just leave the door open." With the door wide, a fan of light illuminated his desk and chair and part of the back wall; but Leal wasn't satisfied and finally found the light fixture, above the desk. She lit a match and touched it to the fixture, which popped into life with a little burst of burning dust.

"What's that sound?" said William peevishly. Leal was just lighting the burner on his little stove to boil some water for tea. She intended to sit with him for a few minutes to make sure he was all right. It was true, though—a strange murmur, like thousands of voices, had begun to permeate the walls of the library.

She turned away from the stove and blinked in surprise. The office was fully lit now, and it may have been the first time in thirty years. The paint on the walls was a teal blue, but lighter in a fuzzy parallelogram shape that exactly matched the fan of light from outside. In fact, now that Leal looked closer, she could see the faint imprint of the desk's shadow against the floor and rising up the wall—and a fainter, fuzzy outline of someone sitting at the desk. It was as if a brilliant flash had burnt William's shadow onto the floor and wall, except that it had just been ordinary light over thousands upon thousands of days that had done it.

He sat there now, waiting, as if this chair were his natural home, maybe even his bed. "Listen," she said gently, "I've put the kettle on for you. I'm just going to see what it is."

She hurried down the stairs, and the sound grew louder. It *was* a crowd, and over it she heard the smooth, resonant tones of a practiced speaker. She couldn't make out what he was saying, but the voice had a kind of syrupy self-confidence to it that she associated with politicians. At the library's front doors she ran into another group of dark-coated goons, who were standing in a tight knot there looking out. When Leal said, "Excuse me," meekly, one of them turned and cursed.

"Where were you hiding?"

"I—"

"Get out of 'ere!" He shoved her roughly onto the front steps.

Leal found herself standing a couple of heads higher than a vast throng of people that filled the street and the quadrangle beyond. Halfway down the street a parade float was inching along behind a puttering steam car.

"—Newest reforms are to education," proclaimed a broad-waisted man on the float. He held a megaphone but wasn't using it, trusting to the power of his unaided voice to carry. Leal recognized Abyss's prime minister from photos.

"Transparency and equal access to all were not just election platitudes!" He gestured around grandly. "From now on, the artificial barriers to an equal and open education for all are removed. This university is now a university for all people!"

The crowd roared enthusiastically. Leal shuddered.

A couple of dozen other officials stood on the float with the prime minister. She recognized the mayor and the head of the university, as well as a couple of uncomfortable-looking deans. And there—oh, it was inevitable—there was Hackner, smiling genially at the crowd.

Quite unexpected, though, was the presence of Hayden Griffin a few feet away from the newly minted professor. He looked even more uncomfortable than the deans. Surrounding him was a small team of men with similar faces and dress, as well as similar expressions. Members of his sun-lighting team?

As she stared he suddenly raised his eyes, and they met hers. Involuntarily, Leal raised a hand to her mouth. Griffin looked surprised, then something else . . . she couldn't make out the expression. He turned and spoke to one of the men at his side.

Embarrassed and profoundly uneasy, Leal hopped down the steps and pushed her way through the fringes of the crowd. She felt his eyes on the back of her head as she slipped around one of the library's big buttresses. In the chill shadow of the grand building, she paused for a second to let out her breath. Then she started walking again, this time craning her neck to look straight up.

She'd just found the right set of windows high up the side of the building, when Leal noticed a crouching silhouette perched on the lip of the first roof, fifteen feet overhead. Was it a gargoyle? No— the figure shuffled to one side, into a beam of streetlight. She recognized the earrings, caught a glimpse of a coiled strap around his waist—then realized that what he was holding up to the faint light was a book.

"Hey! Hey you!" He looked down. "Where'd you get that?"

The spokesman laughed. "You ask as if you already know the answer." He leaned carelessly over the edge of the roof. "If you must know, I was just delivering a passenger to the parade, here, when this piece of weighty knowledge struck me a solid blow on the head. *Somebody*," he tilted his head and squinted at her, "had thrown it out a window!"

"Um." She bit her lip. "You didn't, um, happen to see another one go by, as well?"

Silently, the spokesman brought his other hand into the light. It held *A Discourse on Ancient Shapes*.

"I'm sorry! I didn't know you were out there!" He scowled at her. Desperately, Leal said, "They were closing the library! Who knows what's going to happen to all the books. I had to save something. I—" But he'd disappeared into shadow. A second later she saw his black shape climbing lithely down a drainpipe. He landed with a thump not four feet from her.

He turned and bowed. "Hazards of the profession, ma'am, hazards of the profession. Hey—do I know you?"

Leal blushed. "I think you, um, might have given me a ride a couple weeks back."

"Ha! Never forget a face. Oh, say, look at this." He dug in his jacket pocket. "I've had business cards made up. Relying on chance encounters is a mug's game, I know that now. See?" He handed one to her; Leal had to stand on tiptoe to get it into the light from the street. JAX MILCHER, it said. SPOKESMAN AND GUIDE. RATES REASONABLE. Under that was the address of a post-office box.

"Keep it," said Milcher magnanimously. "And, I take it these are yours?" He held out the books.

"Oh, thank you," she heard herself gush as she took them. "I'm so sorry I hit you, I really had no other choice if I was ever going to get a chance to read—" He held up a hand.

"Say no more. Reading is important. Well, unless you need a ride, I'd best be on my way. If I do enough business from this crowd, I can take tomorrow off!" He tipped his nonexistent hat to her and strolled away.

Leal turned the books over in her hands. They seemed to be in good condition, which was, she decided, pure dumb luck. What had she been thinking, ejecting them out the window like that? If William found out she had endangered his treasures, he'd have a fit . . .

Both books fit into her coat's inside pockets. Even with them invisible like that, she hesitated to return to her office. The crowds had mostly followed the prime minister into the quad, but there were a lot of stragglers in the street—many of them people who looked out of place on a campus. It was unlikely that any useful teaching or studying was going to happen today, so she decided to go the other way, further into the shadows between the library and Sailcloth Hall. The dark here was permanent, like it had been in William's office until today. Leal picked her way between tall mushrooms and under draped fungi like huge cobwebs. She knew that this alley eventually let out onto a city side-street.

She was halfway through the little maze when she heard something behind her. It sounded like a footstep.

Too many people on campus today. Too many strangers. Leal hurried on, her breath quickening, and gave a whoosh of relief when she stumbled out into a well-lit street where several passersby were visible.

"Stupid, stupid," she told herself. Today had been one ridiculous blunder after another. She turned right and hurried to the nearest flea station.

Yet, even when she disembarked on the familiar streets of her own neighborhood, Leal couldn't shake the feeling that she was still being followed. Once or twice, when she glanced back, she caught a glimpse of a tall figure striding well behind her. On one occasion street light gleamed off something on his head—airman's goggles, she realized after a few seconds.

The city was full of airmen, of course. But all kinds of terrible scenarios filled her head as she picked up her pace, feeling the stolen books flapping inside her long coat, its tails swirling around her ankles. Other scenarios flitted through her mind, too—of the spokesman Jax leaping down to rescue her, or Uthor with his well-muscled arms. She deserved to be rescued, at least once. She trotted through swirls of vapor vented from municipal heating units, sidestepping mirror-bright pools of water that reflected an upside-down cityscape. The sounds of street musicians swelled and fell behind; so did the buzzing vibration of the street itself as the

giant jet engines suspended under it coughed into life to spin the
city. Her feet clicked across it all, not running, but ticking faster
than a walk. By the time her building appeared in the distance,
her heart was pounding painfully and her breath came in ratchet-
ing gulps. Still she felt there was someone back there, someone
dogged and sure.

She ran up her steps and mashed her thumb against the elevator button, holding it down until the cage rattled and rang into
view. She leaned against the brass filigree and panted as the cage
rose; she caught a glimpse of the building's front doors opening
just before her view was cut off.

Inside her apartment, Leal flipped all the locks and secured the
windows. She knew this place was secure; still, she dragged over a
chair and jammed it under the doorknob just in case. Then she threw
off her coat and angrily kicked her boots into a dark corner. "Stupid,
stupid, stupid." She put on the kettle with nervous darting movements, then sat down at the table and put her head in her hands.

A while later, she realized that she felt chilled despite the tea. She
pried at the knob on the radiator under the window, but couldn't
tease any more heat out of it. Finally, she went and ran herself a bath.

Her toe was just touching the water—a realm she suddenly
longed to enter, one of tranquility and forgetfulness—when a harsh
knock came at the front door.

She paused, balanced absurdly on the edge of the tub. The
knock came again. Reason and caution told her she should ignore
it. She wasn't expecting anyone. There was no good reason why
anybody would be calling right now; the other residents knew she
should be at work.

Wrapping herself in a towel, she hesitantly crept up on her
door. Just as she reached it, the knock came again, and Leal jumped
in shock.

"Damn it," she hissed at herself. Leaning forward, she placed
her eye at the peephole.

Then she swore and, yanking the chair away she hastily unshot the various bolts and locks, then clutched the towel tightly about her and pulled the door open.

"Hello, I'm looking for—" Hayden Griffin stopped as he saw her state of undress.

"Leal Maspeth," she said. "Yes, we met the other day.

"Come in!"

5

NOTHING ABOUT HAYDEN Griffin suggested privilege, past or present. Having heard the stories, Leal knew he was the son of a pair of engineers from the nation of Aerie. After Aerie was conquered by the pirate nation of Slipstream, they had joined a conspiracy determined to build a new sun for Aerie. He had been educated as an insurgent and, later, had become an actual pirate.

Slouching at her kitchen table, he could easily have been mistaken for a delivery man. He was of medium build and had a compact, wiry frame—not muscular but, she suspected, fast. His face was wide with prominent cheekbones and a strong nose; his eyes were deeply inset. He had the sort of face that would age from the eyes out; indeed, several lines radiated from their corners and another cleft the center of his brow, splitting it in a permanent frown. He wore weatherbeaten canvas flying clothes under a long leather coat.

No flying goggles on his head, though: those had been worn by the other man, the one who waited in the shadows of the corridor outside.

Right now, Griffin seemed a bit tongue-tied. "I'm really sorry," he said finally.

Leal had been dressing in the blackness of her bedroom. "What? Sorry for what?" She finished adjusting her belt and emerged to find him gazing around somewhat distractedly.

For a moment he regarded her—admiringly, she hoped. Leal wore a brocade bolero over a golden tunic, and sky-black trousers. It was her best casually elegant ensemble.

"Mm?" said Hayden, raising his eyes to hers. "Oh. I mean, you must have thought, when you saw me on that float with the prime minister, that . . . well . . ."

"That you were there to support his policies? The thought had crossed my mind."

He grimaced, making an indolent gesture that ended with him leaning his brow on his hand. "It's part of the price I pay for being tolerated here."

Leal paused, teapot in hand. "Price? But you're a . . . a celebrity." She'd almost said *hero*. "You're the sun lighter! Aren't they delighted to have you here?"

He laughed. "A sun-builder in a sunless country? They're terrified that I'll light one here, and cause a revolution."

"Oh." She stood there totally at a loss as to what to say or do. She had the sun lighter himself in her rooms—which were a disaster!—yet this was clearly impossible. What was he doing here? Griffin himself seemed half-awake; was he drunk?

He seemed to finally notice her discomfiture. "When I saw you on the steps I felt ashamed of myself," he said. "You're the woman I met at the docks, right? You said you're a historian."

"That's right," she said, grasping at the connection. "You asked me about worldwasps."

". . . And you said they were real."

She turned to fill the kettle. "I never said the *Porphyry*'s crew saw one."

"Neither did I."

She stared at him, heedless of the tap water overflowing onto her hands. "But you think they saw *something*! Is that what this is about?"

He stood up and paced to the window, swinging his arms at his sides restlessly. Whatever he saw outside didn't satisfy him, so he turned and walked the other way—to the darkened doorway of her second bedroom.

"Considering some other things I've seen," he said, "a world-wasp wouldn't surprise me at all." He frowned into the unlighted room, and Leal suddenly found herself blushing. "What's all this?"

"No no, it's nothing—" But he had already stepped inside, and a moment later emerged holding a beautifully detailed, properly proportioned porcelain doll. Leal watched in horrified embarrassment as he turned it over in his hands. "It's beautiful," he said after a moment. "You collect them?"

"No." Obviously this was a lie, the second bedroom was crammed with the things. "Yes—it's not what you think."

Griffin looked at her curiously. "I don't think anything."

"There's this town," she said quickly, "it's often near where I grew up. Dreamweal. They're craftsmen and so, so poor! There's this one family, they're doll makers, they make the most beautiful pieces. But they sell hardly any. Ever since I moved to Sere, I've been buying them whenever the toy shop gets them in. To . . . to support the family."

His face lit up in comprehension. "It's your charity!" He glanced into the bedroom again. "But some of those dolls look quite ordinary."

"That's because everybody seems to have decided that I love dolls, so I keep getting them as presents. Truth to tell, I never even look at them. It's gotten quite . . ."

". . . Embarrassing." He put the doll back and came to sit down again. "Sorry. I'm imposing on you awfully, I realize. It's just that your government's managing my contact with people so tightly. I only talk to people they've approved. —And they are, without exception, the most deluded pack of idiots I've ever encountered. Not to say dangerous, I mean I can hardly open my mouth without offending some ridiculous fairy tale that they believe fervently." The little exchange about the doll seemed to have awakened him out of the half-trance he'd been in when he showed up. His gaze was piercing and his words clipped and precise. His presence was even a little hypnotic when he got worked up.

"Eternists, I'd bet," she said sympathetically. "There's talk they'll shut down my department."

He shook his head in disgust. "Good thing I ran into you, then."

"So you ducked out on the parade, is that it?"

Griffin nodded, giving her a boyish grin. "It was easy in the confusion. First I sent my man Tarvey to follow you. That's not nearly like it sounds—I expected you to pop into one of the campus buildings, I just had no idea which one was yours. I thought Tarvey'd be gone for two minutes and then I could go meet you in your office."

"He tailed me all the way home!" she said indignantly. Griffin winced.

"Tarvey's a good man, just a bit . . . literal-minded. When he told me he'd done that I was even more embarrassed. So . . . here I am."

"Tea?" she said brightly.

"Thanks," he said in a heartfelt tone. She bustled about domestically for a while, then when he had the tall porcelain cup in front of him, he frowned at it and said, "So tell me about worldwasps."

Leal sat down opposite him and brought out her two stolen library books. "I don't know much. To get to primary sources, you have to go back to books like this. —Which are likely to be banned and—who knows?—destroyed if the government gets its way."

He turned *Denizens of the World's Skin* over in his hand, then opened it to peer at the incomprehensible text. "Here," he said suddenly. "Does this say 'precipice moth'?"

Leal looked at where he was pointing, then nodded dumbly, and Griffin seemed satisfied. "Not complete fiction, then." He laid the book down gently.

"Precipice moths are real," she said. "There's rumors that one attacked the palace at Slipstream last year—"

"Not rumors," he said. "Though I didn't see it. I was busy starting Aerie's new sun at the time." He half-smiled, as though expecting some outburst of admiration from her. Leal was thinking that she could ask him if he really did know Antaea Argyre, adventurer, supposed Home Guard member and her former roommate's sister. To think they shared a connection! Yet it would be so gauche to do so, provincial even, and admitting she knew Antaea would be admitting the stark contrast between her and Leal.

"The moths," she said, acutely aware suddenly of how close he was, just across the table from her. "The moths work for us. That's a very important distinction. Either they allied themselves with us in the distant past or . . . we created them." She waited for disbelieving laughter, but he merely shrugged.

"The worldwasps are something entirely different. Older, bigger, and more intelligent. We built Virga with their help—as well as the help of many other creatures, mind. Some of those are just names, we have no idea what they were or whether they still exist.

"It's possible that the capital bugs are their descendants—"

He swore loudly. "I've seen one of those! It was so big its flanks faded into the air before you could see the edge of it. So loud it nearly killed us, and we were sailing by a dozen miles away."

This was an adventure Leal hadn't heard. "Well," she said, "imagine something that dwarfs even that. The bugs make some kind of noise—"

"A drone," he said. "Enough to unhinge your skull."

"—But the worldwasps, they *spoke*. It's said their voices could shatter forests. Like the capital bugs, they were so big they had whole ecologies inside themselves—whole weather systems. It was nothing for them to hop out of Virga and sail through space itself. They barely felt the cold and vacuum."

"So the wasps built Virga?"

She frowned at him. "Even sensible, worldly-wise people find the idea that humanity built our world just too . . . daunting . . . to believe. But it's true."

"How do you know it's true?"

"Oh, don't you start! There are records. I'll tell you if you want." To her surprise, he nodded.

She eyed him for his reaction as she said, "Human beings aren't native to this part of the universe. We come from a place called Earth—a planet. Heard of it?" He nodded. "You've heard of planets?" He nodded again, impatiently.

She smiled at his studious intensity. "The first people to arrive at the star Vega were expecting a kind of . . . paradise of free building materials. They'd seen, through great telescopes, that the star we circle is young. It's only recently finished forming planets—hundreds of them—and now those hundreds are jockeying for position in the stellar pecking order. Some are being swallowed by Vega itself; some are migrating inward or outward. Some are being ejected into eternal exile between the stars. And some—some collide."

Leal no longer saw Griffin; she was imagining the vision of those ancient times as she related it. "Whole planets'-worth of raw materials—oceans of water, nebulae of iron, you name it— they were all orbiting Vega just waiting to be used. The human colonists planned to use all the free energy and materials to terraform some of Vega's worlds. —Essentially, to green them a billion years early."

"You say they planned to. It didn't work out that way?"

"Well." She made a side-to-side nod of her head, admitting the ambiguities. "Maybe they did—but we don't know. Most scholars think the inner system proved to be just too dangerous. The new planets were getting plastered by infalling debris. Imagine if Candesce were Vega, and one day all the icebergs coating the inner surface of Virga's skin were to crack off and fall in at once. —A rain of destruction on sunlit and sunless countries alike."

He nodded. "I rammed a couple of pirate ships with some ice-bergs on one occasion. I get the picture."

Ignore that, just ignore that, she told herself. If he was going to keep making outrageous claims, she had to remind herself that the story she was telling was much bigger.

"So," she said, "they decided to build somewhere safer: here, in the relatively calm outskirts of the system."

"That's why," he said. "But I'm an engineer, I don't care about the whys. *How?*"

Leal grinned, and poured herself some tea. She stirred it vigorously for a second, then said, "Look, quickly now." A little froth had formed as she stirred the cup. The bubbles rapidly consolidated, popping together until there was only one. Then that one burst.

"You don't build a shell five thousand miles in diameter *manually.* And you certainly don't build it out here so far from Vega, where it's cold and energy is hard to find. You start, though, with some dwarf planets that formed way out here. Using engines like Candesce—yes, the sun of suns started its life as an engine—you nudge them so they converge and, in a cloud, begin to fall at Vega.

"Next, you harvest the carbon from the smallest pieces and you create a kind of half-alive stuff that grows the tough nanotube skin making up Virga's skin. But to begin with, it's not set, it's a loose fog that you shape using pressure. In the cup here, it's air pressure that blows the water into bubbles. But when the world was made, it was Candesce and its sisters that inflated the bubbles."

"How?" He looked puzzled. "By burning off gases?"

She shook her head. "We know a lot more about all this than you might think. No, originally Candesce didn't produce visible light; at least, not much of it. Originally, it and its children were powerful radio sources. That radio inflated giant bubbles made up of microscopic carbon whiskers, into a froth."

Griffin sat back, nodding in comprehension. "And the bubbles just merged under their own power, getting bigger and bigger . . ."

"Until there was only one." She nodded. "But meanwhile, the icy bodies that the froth grew up around were much more massive. Thousands of times more so. Embedded in the froth, they began to boil when the whole conglomerate made its first close pass by Vega. The builders, you see, had nudged it all into a long orbit that came close, then sailed away—" She mimed the motion with one fingertip, bringing it close to her teacup then trailing it far out to the edge of the table and back. "The froth acted like a filter, letting through the gases the builders didn't want, keeping inside the oxygen and nitrogen they needed. So imagine this vast comet flinging its body like fire into the night, trailed by a retinue of human ships and gigantic, huge-voiced worldwasps . . . What a sight it must have been!"

"Radio waves instead of light . . ." He had seized on one detail, as students sometimes did, and was in danger of missing the big picture. Leal hastened to wrap up her little lecture.

"On the last orbit, as the whole assembly passed close by Vega, the carbon bubbles made their ultimate merger into one, and the last of the hydrogen and other gases vented out. As the newly minted Virga sailed back into colder space, the radio generators inside the sphere switched modes, because gas pressure was now sufficient to keep the big bubble inflated. They went from producing radio waves, to producing light, and some came together in the very center of the bubble. Those ones formed Candesce. The rest became the kernels around which the first human nations of Virga would form.

"And lastly," she said, "they used the remainder of the hydrogen and other unwanted gases to nudge Virga out of its cometlike orbit, and into a permanent circle far outside the planetary chaos of the inner system. Here. Where we still reside." She sat back and smiled at him.

Griffin shook his head. "Incredible. But what went wrong? Why did the wasps end up fighting us?"

She shrugged. "Maybe they wanted Virga for themselves. We're not sure. Anyway, there was peace for a century or so. Then it all went to Hell, and we fought. We won, obviously, and it was thought that all the worldwasps either died or fled. But maybe not."

"Right." He sat forward, knitting his fingers together and scowling into a dark corner of the room. "And that's when Candesce was retooled to create its jamming signal. To keep them out, only it also makes it impossible for us to build computing machines and such-like . . ." He noticed that Leal was shaking her head and turned his frown on her. "What?"

"That happened much later," she said. "Centuries later, actually. There's no evidence that Candesce's jamming signal was intended to keep the worldwasps out. It couldn't, in fact."

Strange, but Griffin looked . . . upset. "Why not?" he blurted. "Surely they were a part of it, of this 'artificial nature' that rules outside Virga." Again—regretful that she had to deny him but unsure why it mattered—Leal shook her head.

"Remember, the worldwasps helped us build Candesce. They knew as well as we, what it was capable of. Surely they would know how to counter that force? They're like the precipice moths, who are creatures of Virga and can roam freely anywhere in it. What makes the possibility of a worldwasp so terrifying is that it could go anywhere, from the Gates of Virga all the way into the heart of Candesce itself, and nothing could stop it . . ."

He was looking away, his shoulders slumped. "Is—is something wrong?" Leal asked, suddenly anxious. Griffin didn't respond.

She drew away his empty teacup and, uncertain what to do, stood to take it to the sink. Deliberately, she made a loud clattering noise there. He still didn't move.

Leal returned to the table, almost leaned on it and at the last moment curled her hands closed, withdrawing them to her sides. "Mr. Griffin—"

"I should go," he said abruptly. He stood, his eyes unfocused, and patted the chair back, fingers searching out the coat he'd thrown over it when he first arrived. "I . . . thanks for the tea," he said. "Sorry to have wasted your time, Ms. uh . . . Maspeth."

He moved to the door. Before Leal knew it he was in the corridor—she, still standing at the sink.

"Wait!" She stepped outside and stopped. Griffin was already on the stairs, but the man in the aviator's cap stood between them and he blocked her way. Tarvey, Griffin had called him.

"Interview's over," he said in a thickly accented, deep voice. "Thank you for your time." He had a narrow face with high, wind-burnt cheekbones, and very serious eyes.

"Thank you for—? You *followed* me!"

"Just doing what I was told, ma'am."

"Don't you ma'am me, have you people no common decency?"

A look of comprehension came over his face. "If it's payment for your time that you—"

"Payment?" Leal was almost, but not quite beyond words. "What kind of transaction do you think we're performing here? I'm a teacher, Mr. Griffin came to me for information and I told him what I know. That's what a teacher does."

"All right, then." He backed away, then turned to follow his master.

"Something's wrong with him," she blurted. Tarvey stopped, and looked back.

Leal sighed heavily. "And now you're thinking I'm going to blackmail you."

"You're not?"

"No." Griffin's footsteps were fading down the stairwell. "If you want to pay me for my time, and aggravation," said Leal, "you could tell me what's going on. Why did he come to me in the first place?"

"Because he trusted you." Heavily shadowed as he was at the top of the stairs, she could no longer read Tarvey's expression. "I don't know why."

That was no answer, but at least the man was still here. "He told me the government's surrounded you with spies."

Tarvey barked a short laugh. "The crowds were thick enough today that we could get away, first me, then him. . . . You wouldn't happen to know a good cook, would you? Ours has been jigging the locks on the main office."

"Actually, I may at that."

"Then bring him by sometime." Tarvey stepped all the way into the shadows, and disappeared. She didn't even hear his footsteps on the stairs; but she knew he was gone.

LEAL DIDN'T HAVE to see the headlines; the trolleys and flea cars were buzzing with the news.

A town was missing.

Men crowded together on the streetcar, hats touching as they talked about it. Leal held one hand to the throat of her coat, the other clutching a ceiling strap as the trolley rattled and pounded its way along the metal street. She'd been looking over her shoulder ever since her strange meeting with Griffin the week before. The gloom and shifting beams from the streetlights painting the faces of the seated women and children made it seem like everyone was turning their eyes her way.

Like everyone else, the first thing she'd wanted to know was, which town? Thankfully, it wasn't Taura Two, or Dreamweal or any of the others in her old constellation. Aldglass was some little wobbler of a wheel on the outer rim of the nation, where the air was freezing and adrift with snow, and icebergs cruised.

There had been no official word from the government. Everybody knew it was the winter wraiths, of course, except for the other everybody who knew it was worldwasps (a whole nest of them, apparently). Nobody was talking about the most likely possibility: that a passing shard of ice had snapped Aldglass's spokes or cut its rim cables, and it had come unraveled. It did happen: Leal had heard many stories about houses and inns being shot into the dark from unreeling streets. If it was a small wheel they would disintegrate from the headwind. A bigger one could send dwellings tumbling for hundreds of miles before air resistance slowed them enough for people to bail out.

At any moment some ale house or dormitory might emerge from the eternal clouds, as the *Porphyry* had, and shatter itself against the rooftops of Rowan Wheel. Or, they might never find any pieces at all; but that was unlikely.

The trolley stopped at the theater district. Leal disliked the elbowing mobs that boarded and disembarked along this route, but she'd developed a distaste for walking on her own. Especially at end-of-shift.

A half hour ago, a telephone boy had shown up at Leal's office. He'd pushed his cap back on his head and swaggered into the outer office, but once there had gazed with wide eyes at the evidence of learning surrounding him. "Message for Leela Maspeth," he'd said, and Leal's head had popped up from her work. Nobody sent telephone boys to talk to her; she just didn't know enough people, for one thing. A little fancy had taken her, that Hayden Griffin had summoned her to his laboratory. In some ozone-perfumed office, lit by sparklight, he would confess that he hadn't been able to stop thinking about her . . .

"Seana wants you to meet her at the shop," said the kid. "Where's my half-dite?"

"Did she say why?" Leal hung the coin above his open palm.

"Naw. I even aksed." He squinted at her, daring her to deny him.

"Okay, thanks."

Leal was tired, but still she hurried to Seana's shop through the last crowds of the shift. Still half a block away, she saw that the store's lights were out. She walked up and rapped on the glass. No movement inside.

Then she noticed a sheet of paper lying on the floor of the display window, under a dummy sporting the latest style of freefall blouse. The light was dim but Leal still made out the words, *Leal, had to run. Meet me at navy docks. Urgent!*

The navy docks? They weren't even on this wheel. "This had better be good," Leal muttered to herself; then she turned to trudge to the nearest flea car station.

The flea was crowded with silent, nervous-looking people, so Leal put her nose against the glass and stared into the dark. This gave her the opportunity to get a good look at Hayden Griffin's famous sunlighting workshops as they passed Steam Wheel. There were two of them: a round, geodesic ball hanging in freefall outside the axis of the wheel, and another similar ball three quarters of the way up the spokes and spinning for about one-tenth g of weight. That one looked like a wasp's nest, the way it was lashed to the cables; a network of precarious catwalks splayed away from it at various levels, and stairs, ladders, and even an elevator shaft ran erratically down the cable-ways to become lost among the factories and smokestacks below. Steam Wheel glowed with thousands of worklights and was constantly wreathed in clouds of its namesake. Griffin's workshops loomed over it all, like demonic egg sacks about to burst.

After her most recent Leverage class, Leal had approached Uthor. "You're a cook on-shift, right?" she'd asked him.

He grinned. Uthor had very serious features, but when he smiled an inner impishness was revealed. Now he held up his hands to display a pattern of tiny round white burns across their backs. "Never wok naked," he said. "It's something I've learned."

Leal laughed. "Never wok in freefall."

"And in particular, never wok naked in freefall."

"Under acceleration."

"In the dark . . ."

"Listen, Uthor, I heard about a job. Are you interested?"

He shrugged. "I've got a job. I'm the weekend cook at the Prestan estate. It pays well enough; gives me a good profile among the rich and self-indulgent, too."

"How'd you like to work for Hayden Griffin?"

He looked startled. "What, bring him breakfast in bed?"

"His team needs a cook. It would be more regular work than weekend stuff . . . but I'm betting it'll pay better, too."

Uthor had smiled off into the distance, and said that well, he'd give it some thought, and thanks. But Leal could tell he was hooked.

She wondered if he'd gone to see Tarvey yet. She might just trump up an excuse to visit the workshop herself, and inquire . . .

Steam was falling behind, and the navy wheel emerged from behind a fist of cloud. Constellations of ships were crowding around its axis—far more than usual—and floodlights were waving this way and that. Leal swore in surprise as she caught sight of one ship in particular, that wallowed its slow way through the rest toward the docking gantries.

The flea wasn't allowed to dock at the center of the wheel; the passengers had to make do with a quarter-g platform lashed, like Griffin's workshop, to a spoke high above the admiralty offices. Stairs (more like a tilted ladder with rungs three feet apart) led up to the hubbub overhead. As Leal left the flea she saw numerous other cars docking nearby, passengers spilling out of them hastily and in some confusion. She joined the general rush up the stairs, realizing with a sinking heart that she was surrounded by families: wives with young children, mostly, but some elderly parents as well.

They had all heard the news at the last minute: another town had disappeared. None had been notified officially, but they all knew what was going to happen; so they were here to see off their husbands and sons.

Leal had no idea how she was going to find Seana in the chaos at the top of the stairs. These docks were an open-ended metal cylinder fully six hundred feet in diameter and as wide as the wheel. Dozens of vessels hung weightless in the central space overhead, like ominous clouds bristling with rocket-ports and machine guns. There was just enough gravity for people to stand on the inner surface of the cylinder, but nets had been strung above the pavement to keep civilians from approaching the ships. Some visitors clung one-handed to the netting as they shouted and waved at distant relatives.

Ladders made of stacked hoops led up to the ships. Airmen were swarming up them, some pausing to wave back, but being pushed relentlessly by the press from below. This gave Leal an idea, and in the end it proved easy to find Seana: she was standing under one of the ladders that led up to the massive iron flank of the *Hammerhead*.

Leal put her hand on Seana's arm and they hugged. "He's right there! See him? He's ticking off names on a clipboard as they come past." Leal squinted, and could just make out Brun Mafin's profile. He was braced inside an iron hatch, taking roll call as the crew entered the dreadnought. He, like them, looked grim and businesslike.

"Why won't he just look down? Brun!" Seana hopped up (ten feet into the air) and waved. Brun didn't hear her.

Leal and Seana stood together for a half-hour, watching Brun go about his work. He never once glanced out of the hatch, though he spoke to the incoming men, laughed with a few, shoved one or two roughly, and stopped one or two to interrogate them.

He wasn't wearing his usual uniform; none of them were. They were in utilitarian airmen's garb consisting of fluorescent green overalls with a black coat, more of a cape, that could be wrapped around them to hide them in the dark air. There had been no announcement that they were leaving.

The last stragglers made it up the ladder, and Brun checked off their names and then disappeared. The hatch slammed shut and the dreadnought's hundred engines whined into life.

Seana cried on Leal's shoulder. After, as they bounced slowly back to the stairs, she looked back at the departing fleet and said, "It's not really the wraiths, is it?"

Leal shook her head. "No. It's not." But she couldn't say—nor, she suspected, could anyone—what exactly it was that had mobilized the fleet of Abyss.

6

THERE WAS A strange mood to the city; Leal could sense it as she walked to work. The people on the streetcar were subdued, their words guarded. Ever since the referendum, everybody seemed to think twice about anything they said, as if they were afraid of being caught in a lie. The newspapers were full of multiple-choice quizzes about trivial and mundane details. It was like one of those nightmares where you have to write an exam on a subject you know absolutely nothing about. As if Abyss had been turned into a giant school, but one without teachers where all the students were craning over one another's shoulders, trying to figure out what they were supposed to learn.

Things were no better on campus. The students argued with the professors—in class!—and quibbled over their marks, as though they could fast-talk their way into an exemplary grade. For the first time ever, Leal was actually glad she wasn't a full professor.

Not that she'd ceased trying. Easley remained a fountain of advice, and she'd actually been doing everything he suggested. She'd applied for grants, took her lunches at the faculty club now even though she couldn't afford it, and had even volunteered for extra administrative duties. She'd sworn to her mother that she'd never do that unless more pay was attached.

Now, as she stepped through the university gates at start-of-shift, she noticed that the campus was even more quiet than usual. Leal could hear the hissing of the gas in the streetlamps, and the ring of her own footsteps on the richly burnished street. As she approached the faculty of history all other traffic faded away; alone, she reached the bottom of the steps and looked around, puzzled.

"Hsst!" The sound had come from above, and slightly to the left. Leal looked up to find a silhouetted head poking out of one of the main floor windows.

"Don't come in!"

"Easley? Is that you?" She braced one hand on the wall and stepped up on the balustrade. The dark profile was only ten feet away now.

"Not so loud!" It was definitely Easley Fencher, secretary to the dean, hanging out of the window like a schoolboy.

"They're doing it! They're shutting down the faculty. Listen, Leal, the whole faculty is getting sacked, it's happening right now in the next room. The rest of us are going to be reassigned."

"Oh." The moment was too ridiculous—her balanced over the stairs, Easley skulking about—for her to feel it yet. "What are you doing there?"

"I'm the lookout. The office staff—we decided, well, you and some others weren't here yet. I'm here to make sure you don't come in. Leal, you're not on the government lists, there'll be no black mark next to your name if you keep your head down. I don't know if that's what Porril had in mind when he advanced Hackner over you, but I'd like to think so." He craned his neck to look back inside. "Somebody's coming. Go home, Leal! We'll talk later. Just remember: you're not part of this and if you play your cards right, you won't be."

He slipped back inside and she heard the window closing. Sensibly, Leal hopped off the balustrade. Then, standing in shadow, her hands began to shake.

An impulse to run to the library filled her. It had always been her refuge, but it was closed now, too.

Careful to keep shaded by the knuckled buttresses of the buildings, she made her way back to the university's gates. With a dozen other chattering, careless citizens, she waited for the trolley to take her home.

SHE SPENT THE next few days in her apartment. Leal was afraid to go out; some spirit of malice had taken over the city and she didn't know how big it was or just who it had infected. She could feel it prowling outside her door, though: something awakened from deep inside the collective soul of the people.

Maybe it was that sense of being under siege that brought her back to her stolen books. Maybe it was simple boredom, or a sense of defiance. For whatever reason, Leal began to spend long hours seated at her kitchen table, poring over the texts. She wore a housecoat and slippers, and kept a teapot close at hand. Slowly, she began to translate the ancient words.

Denizens of the World's Skin was particularly revealing. It was crammed with fragmentary tales, unsubstantiated sightings, and baseless speculation. There were definitions and descriptions for creatures that might or might not exist:

EANORS

Of genus animalia, eanors may be related to capital bugs, although in appearance they more favor flattened worms or maggots. Their immense size makes it difficult to see them in their entirety, and they are only to be observed crawling on the inside of the world's hide . . .

Eanors appear to despise icebergs, for they dislodge and cast them forth wherever they meet them. Which, of course, is everywhere since Virga's inner surface is paved with them. Herds of eanors can scour hundreds of square miles free of this choking ice, and it may be that this is their intended function . . .

IMMOLANTS

In appearance immolants are like brass wasps or hornets. They are of similar size, but are not living beings. They are born in the millions in hives attached to Virga's skin, and during their brief existence they fly steadily inward. Ultimately all im-

molants die in the flames of Candesce. It is thought that they harvest certain elements needed by the sun of suns, for instance boron for its fusion lamps . . .

TEGUMEN

The tegumen are silvery spiders, perhaps related to immolants (see Immolants, page 267). Their webs are shipping hazards, as they are spun from the same material as Virga's skin, and are thus stronger than steel by many orders of magnitude. The role of the tegumen is to repair Virga's skin when it is punctured by meteroids or other forces from outside.

As she read it became clear to Leal that *Denizens* had largely been written from memory; its author had once read the *Polyhistoria*, and had lost it or been forbidden to consult it by some authority; his frustration was obvious as he tried to remember all that it had said.

Polyhistoria, *he wrote, is named for the fact that there is not just one history to our world, but many. More than one set of eyes contemplated Virga as it was born; more than one kind of mind had a part in its design. We think of Virga as our home, but it is only that incidentally and accidentally. The Polyhistoria reveals what it really is, and I shudder to remember all that I read there. I shall not relate such terrifying revelations now. Perhaps, when I am older and have less of a stake in my own life, I may commit those recollections to paper.*

But William claimed he had the book! She started systematically hunting for references to the *Polyhistoria*, and soon had a few choice quotes written into her notebooks:

Just as there was a time before Man, there will be a time after. That time has come in all places save one.

Another fragment said,

The laws of civilization apply among beings of a similar kind. Between beings of different kinds—even sentient beings—the laws that apply are those of nature.

These were the sorts of cryptic, oracular hints you'd expect from a prophet with nothing to say. There was, however, one quote that suggested the author of *Denizens* had deliberately chosen to excerpt the most obscure passages of the *Polyhistoria*, for it seemed terrifyingly clear:

The first species to develop eyes must have dominated its environment. There was no defense against sighted creatures, and the animals without vision could not even conceive of how they were being caught. Gradually, though, they adapted, and many of them developed eyes as well. Once most of them could see, the playing field was leveled. Vision became just one more tool in the adaptive tool kit, which a species might or might not rely on as circumstances warranted.

Within Virga, Candesce shelters you from experiencing the same thing, which has now happened with toolmaking intelligence and self-awareness. The first species to develop these talents was irresistible for a time. But now, they are available to anything. Any thing that can desire can use them, even if it is not itself intelligent nor conscious.

Anything that wants, can become a worldwasp.

It was very late as she transcribed this. The apartment building was utterly silent, only the faint hiss of the gas in the lamps connecting her to a world of sounds. Leal shifted in her chair and the grate of its leg against the floor brought her alert with a start. She put down her pen, stood, and walked to the window.

There were times, if she was in a pensive mood, when everything she saw presented itself as an artifact: as evidence of invention and history. The architectural styling of the building across the street was two hundred years old, and owed itself to an architect named Herringer, who had died tragically young. He was present throughout the city, if you knew how to look.

Within the geometric simplicity of Sere's town wheels was a chaos of backstreets, dead-ends, nigh-inaccessible buildings, and mysteriously empty lots. Even to people who'd grown up here, that jumble made little sense. But after William had spun his tall tale about finding the *Polyhistoria*, Leal had remembered a day, years ago, when she'd caught a glimpse of that world. Her father had been planning on opening an office—this was just prior to his business being shut down by Eustace Loll's party—and one day he'd brought home some of the city's original planning maps. The papers were all out of order and Leal had helped him sort them by date. After he'd used them to find a possible site for the office, she had out of curiosity laid out, one after another, the charts, blueprints, and emergency plans of a dozen subsequent generations. The city seemed a jumble, but as she compared the plans, Leal had experienced a wonder that would later impel her into her primary area of study. For what had seemed random was not even complex; it merely had a history.

Every few years, she had a moment when she wondered how far that palimpsest of maps and plans went. What if it was not just the awkward streets of the city whose true nature could be revealed in an overlay of stories? There was the human body, with its appendix, tailbone, and muscles that once had been able to turn the ears any which way. Smudged overlays of old blueprints.

And what of the air, the darkness, the distant suns? There was a certain logic to the world; the Eternists certainly thought God had designed it to be the way it was. But what if all Virga's features—its hospitable atmosphere, its temperature, and even the balance of creatures living within it—were the result of many plans and intentions, dramatic catastrophes and reversals, overlaid one atop the other through the aeons? —Hiding an original purpose not remotely connected to human needs?

She shook her head, set aside her cup, and went to lie down. As she drifted off, she imagined what sort of person had written the *Polyhistoria. Candesce shelters you,* this unknown author had written. Not, *shelters us.*

And: *Anything that* wants, *can become a worldwasp.*

"HEY," SAID UTHOR after class, "thanks for putting me on to that job with the sun lighter."

"You mean you got it?" Leal had been mopping her face with a towel, holding a bracing cable with two toes. The rest of the students were dispersing like the debris from a slow explosion. She grinned as Uthor nodded.

"Some of my richer clients have a taste for Principalities cuisine," he said. "It's similar enough to Aerie and Slipstream food that I was able to fake it in my resume. But what really got me in the door was dropping your name."

"Oh?" She was hugely flattered; certainly, it was good to know she was remembered by— "Who did you talk to?"

"This fellow Tarvey. He scared the hell out of me. First time in my life I think I've actually met a real killer." She nodded. "The rest of them are as bizarre a pack of eccentrics as you could imagine," he went on. "Scientists, engineers, poets, painters, and cranks, all of them working together to build a new sun for this little breakaway province of some country I never even heard of. There's a few of those guys around, too, and they're the worst of the lot—fanatical doesn't even begin to cover it. They'd make the Eternists blush. Probably why the government's not letting them out much."

She narrowed her eyes, tilting her head as she looked at him. "Sounds like you're having fun."

"Absolutely!" Behind his head the sky was an all-devouring black. Normally it would be crowded with ships coming and going, their lights like little fireflies.

"Listen," said Uthor, "would you like to get a drink or something? I know a nice little place where the spokesmen go. Everybody knows the spokesmen are informers for the secret police—so, naturally, they're not. It's the safest place in the city to have a conversation."

Leal hadn't heard that about spokesmen. She pushed off from the bracing cable and she and Uthor fell very slowly toward the curving platform with its teetering, jumbled buildings. "Why would we need to find a 'safe' place to converse?" she asked. She didn't really care; she was delighted that he was asking her to go with him. Uthor shrugged, a bit uncomfortably.

"The secret police did visit me after I got the job," he said. "They wanted to recruit me. Were none too happy that I'd got the job, seems their last cook took ill under suspicious circumstances. Fact is, I've got the cleanest record they'd ever seen, I even attend Eternist services now and then—to meet clients, you know. My clients are the people the secret police work for, so—ha!—they couldn't really do anything. But, you know . . . people are saying another town's disappeared. I'm afraid of what might happen if they get desperate."

"You think they're watching you . . . right now?"

"I think they would be stretched too thin to keep twenty-four-hour tabs on a cook." They reached the elevators, where for once there was no queue.

"Well, let's go then," said Leal suddenly. She'd been sunk in her own misery for days and craved some kind of escape. A spokesman's bar sounded like the perfect place to find that.

That was how she ended up passing a fine afternoon with Uthor. They took a booth in the corner of the spokesman's bar and talked about leverage whenever the waitress came by. The rest of the time they traded stories. Leal was surprised to find how many little adventures she had to relate: her encounter with the burning *Porphyry*, her first and second meetings with Griffin; even her archaeological work at the Aracen Graves proved germane. Uthor said almost nothing about himself, but he had plenty to say about the sun lighter's team.

They had all been outlaws, once. When the pirate nation of Slipstream invaded Aerie, its navy had bombed Aerie's sun, extinguishing it. An entire country, wholly dependent on that single terawatt lantern, was plunged into a twilight relieved only by the glow of Slipstream's own sun. Aerie's people had no choice but to move their farms and cities into formation around Slipstream and its capital city of Rush; the alternative was to wither in the dark.

"This time, Griffin brought an economist who's studying how

we survive without a sun," Uthor told her. "To see if they can survive if it ever happens again."

Griffin had been born into an insurgency dedicated to restoring Aerie's autonomy. His parents were engineers, and his formative years had been spent watching them design and build a new Aerie sun, in the secret twilight on the edge of Slipstream's territory. First his father was killed by Slipstream agents, then, when Slipstream's Pilot learned of the new sun, Griffin's mother died in the holocaust of its destruction. He swore revenge against the murderers.

This much Leal knew. Uthor told her the story of how Griffin had been press-ganged into joining the Slipstream fleet when that country was threatened with invasion by the larger Falcon Formation. Griffin found himself on board the flagship of commodore Chaison Fanning, whom he blamed for his mother's death. Somehow, he stayed his hand long enough to learn that Fanning was not responsible; in fact, the commodore had tried to dissuade his people from destroying Aerie's new sun. Against all odds, the two men became friends.

Griffin had gained the trust of the commodore's wife, Venera, so he became a key player in the Fannings' desperate gambit. As Venera's driver, Griffin was charged with conveying her safely into the heart of the sun of suns itself. There, she would employ the services of a woman who claimed to be from outside Virga itself—Aubrey Mahallan, an engineer and armorer. During the voyage, she and Griffin had become lovers.

"She died inside Candesce," Uthor told Leal. "I think she was his first love; I don't know about 'true love,' but whatever there was between them, Griffin never fully recovered from the loss. He feels responsible."

"I've never heard any of that," Leal mused, gazing at the lamplit, weatherbeaten faces of the spokesmen who lounged in the other booths. "He seemed sort of . . . shattered, is the only way I can put it . . . when I met him. Dazed." Uthor nodded vigorously.

"He's often like that, apparently. Tarvey said that when he pulls himself together, he's absolutely sure of himself, and calm and focused. He was like that the first time, when he gathered those men to himself and they came here to build Aerie's new sun in secret. When he's like that, he's utterly charismatic.

"But there's a darkness that follows him. Tarvey says it's like whispers in the night that wear at him, constantly pull him down. Sometimes, they get the better of him."

"What sort of whispers?"

"Tarvey says Griffin's afraid of something—some force from outside the world itself called 'artificial nature.' He says it sent Aubri Mahallan into Virga to destroy the world; and if it tried it once, it'll try it again."

Leal blinked at Uthor. "Griffin believes the world is going to be *destroyed*?" Uthor nodded again.

Leal sat back, frowning. Griffin had mentioned artificial nature to her. He'd been disappointed that she wouldn't connect the world-wasps with it.

She had floated all sorts of theories to herself as to what that part of their conversation had meant. She realized now that he'd been trying to connect the worldwasps to his own story. "Do you suppose," she said slowly, "that to Griffin, a rogue world-wasp would be just a sideshow . . . next to something much bigger?"

Uthor snorted. "Now there's a frightening thought."

It *was* a frightening thought. After she presented it, her little date with Uthor sort of wound down. They parted happily enough, an hour later, but Leal was distracted and Uthor could obviously tell. He was polite enough, and in a veiled sort of way asked if he might see her again outside of class. She didn't say no; but her mind was elsewhere.

———

AN ENVELOPE HAD been clumsily jammed into her door just above the knob. Leal couldn't make out the writing so she unlocked her apartment and put on the gas lamp before turning it over in her fingers.

From Easley Fencher was written on the outside. *Now what?* she thought, in a resigned sort of way, and opened it.

Dinner with Dean Porril, six o'clock, it said. There was an address inscribed at the bottom of the sheet. Next to that Easley had scrawled, *back entrance.*

Porril lived in a posh neighborhood on Kite Wheel. Was she being summoned to the servants' entrance? For a few minutes Leal was convinced that this was the case, that Porril wouldn't deign to see her socially and, lacking an office now to summon her to, was simply calling her in as the employee she was.

But then again, she wasn't his employee anymore, was she? And there were other reasons why he might not want it to be known that they were associating. Uthor had talked about the secret police and their increasingly hair-trigger assumptions about people. Easley had shooed her away from the campus on the day they closed the department for—he'd said—her own good. Maybe he hadn't been lying.

In which case, what could Porril possibly want to talk to her about?

Nervously, she ransacked her closet for an outfit that could be simultaneously elegant and austere. Scholarly fashion was difficult at the best of times; but what did you wear to a secret assignation with a former dean?

In the end, she swept out of the building in a burgundy suit enfolded by a long, hooded black cloak. She took a flea car to Kite and a cab to Porril's general neighborhood, and then she walked the rest of the way.

The houses here were of ancient design, inherited, she knew, from Earthly forerunners. They had all kinds of projecting windows and details that she knew had ancient names, like *gable* and dormer and bay. Their construction was of stone, with solid wood beams and steep, shingled roofs. The streets were copper; otherwise, Leal might have imagined herself walking down some street on an ancient planet—Mars, maybe, or Earth itself.

Many of the houses had front gardens lit by numerous gas lamps on poles. They were offensively ostentatious, but also fascinating. Naturally, they were inaccessible behind tall wrought-iron fences, but Leal couldn't resist putting her nose to a couple of those to peer in at actual roses, hyacinths, and dahlias. The paths between the flower beds were of grass—actual grass that was intended to be *walked* on. It was shameful.

By contrast, Porril's house was a hulking brick cube that had no yard but took up its entire frontage. There were no windows on the ground floor, and its front entrance was deeply inset, an archway of black shadow. Clearly visible from the end of the street was an ornate steam-car parked directly in front of the house. Leal's steps slowed as she approached it; this vehicle was far above what the dean could have afforded. A driver lounged in the front, reading a newspaper by candlelight. He didn't look up as she sidled past, and around the side of the house to the back.

Leal raised her hand to knock, then hesitated. What a strange moment this was, so utterly unlike any future she might have imagined for herself. She didn't even know why she was here, only that what would have been perfectly innocent six months ago had now somehow become subversive.

She knocked. A few moments later, a pleasant-faced, middle-aged woman opened the door. "Dr. Maspeth, come in." Porril's housekeeper—if that was who she was—led Leal through a maze of teak-lined corridors hushed by green carpeting, to a windowless lounge at the front of the building. Easley and Porril were sitting with someone else at a small table set for four. They all stood as she entered. When the third man turned and held out his hand, Leal nearly stumbled.

She was face-to-face with the one man in Sere she hated the most: Eustace Loll, the Minister of the Interior.

"Minister, may I introduce Leal Hieronyma Maspeth, one of our brightest lights."

Leal stammered something. Loll's hand was slightly moist, his grip tight.

When he let go, Porril also shook her hand vigorously. "So glad you could come, Leal."

Leal had never seen Loll up close, though he'd occasionally had dealings with her father. At the time, he'd been just one more anonymous male face going in and out of her father's office, or chatting with him at the foot of their ship's gangplank. He did not loom large in person as he had taken to doing in her imagination: he had a mop of slick black hair on his white forehead, tiny black pinprick eyes, and a face and jaw that seemed to have been built out progressively in blocky layers: wide cheekbones hammered on over a brick-like jaw quite out of keeping with the softness of his cheeks and his small ears.

"You're Langdon's daughter, aren't you?" said Loll. "Why, the last time I saw you, you were this high." He held out a hand at chest-level. Leal smiled weakly but had no idea what to say. Leal glanced around surreptitiously, taking in a surprisingly comfortable space whose walls were lined with couches and settees—enough seating for twenty or more people. Skyscapes in frames were mounted on the dark wood paneling and lit by gas lamps behind green shades. The ambiance was soothing, but more like a waiting room than a living room. She wondered what the upstairs chambers were like.

They exchanged pleasantries, and the housekeeper brought the food. The four ate together in silence; Leal felt almost too sick to eat—sitting as she was next to this man she despised—and smiled weakly at the jokes and banter, unable to summon her usual political mask of cordiality. Finally, Loll looked at his pocket watch and

said, "Must hurry away. Thank you for the wonderful meal, and,"—
he smiled directly at Leal, "the commendable company."

Leal stood as the others did, and waited silently as Porril and
Loll made pleasantries into the front hall. When the door finally
whispered shut behind him, she burst out, "Why him?"

"Because we may need him," said Porril reasonably. "I understand now that you have a history with him, Leal, and I'm sorry if
that made you uncomfortable tonight. But cultivating allies in the
Ministry is the only way we're going to recover our beloved faculty."

He returned to the table, sat, and got down to business.

"Your next paycheck will arrive on time," he said brusquely.
"You may actually find that there's a bit more there than usual."

This wasn't one of the directions Leal had been imagining the
conversation might take. "What? I thought we were all fired?"

"We were," said Porril, nodding at Easley, "despite our relationship with Loll. But you're still on the books as an employee of the
university, Leal. —Just not . . . as a teacher."

Easley straightened his collar, coughed into one hand and
smoothed his hair, and grinned. "I had sufficient time before they
escorted me from the premises to have your position, um, *redefined.*"

She looked from one to the other. "What do I do now, then?"

"You're a cleaning lady," said Easley.

"Maintenance engineer, second class," corrected Porril. "Safely
out of the sights of the Eternists and their damnable purges."

Leal was bewildered, both by what they were saying, and by
Porril's clear dislike of the man he'd just had an amiable dinner
with. "Am I supposed to show up for work tonight, then, and . . .
what? Clean the toilets?"

Porril frowned at her. "A job is a job, Leal. You should be grateful. But, no, I wouldn't advise it. The maintenance department
wasn't consulted about this, they don't even know you exist. Your
position is entirely a paper thing."

"But I get paid."

"You do get paid."

"Oh. Well. Thank you."

There was a long pause. Easley was still preening, adjusting the cuffs of his suit and staring off into space. Porril took a sip of wine, then peered at Leal.

"Leal, name the nine First Princelings of Abyss's ancestor state."

"The Princes of Bittersnout?" She rattled off the names without hesitation.

"And what is the substance of the third paragraph of the Charter of the Greater Hirats?"

"You know perfectly well there is no third paragraph."

"And what is significant about the Local Year 312?"

She frowned. "Nothing. Only that it lies in between the purges of 305 and the Great Fire of 320."

Easley and Porril exchanged a satisfied look.

"We did not invite you here tonight, or extend your salary out of charity," said Porril. "Loll says that the government intends to reconstitute the history department at some point. They don't want anyone they consider 'tainted' by too much education involved. Well, no one other than Hackner, perhaps."

"Hackner?" *Dean Hackner*, she thought. What a nightmare.

"He's as unhappy as the rest of us about the situation," said Porril. "You were his idea. Someone to hold in reserve. When the Eternists move to open the department again, expect a letter from him. You may make senior faculty yet."

"But that—that's—" She felt sick.

"Leal, with us banned, and in the absence of the library, you are the one free repository of historical knowledge left in Abyss. You *are* the library."

"Ah," she said, sitting back in bewilderment.

"William Peeve is dead," said Porril suddenly.

Leal blinked at him. It took a few seconds for his words to penetrate. "William? The—the rare books collection—" With a deep pang of sorrow, an image flashed into her mind of William's shadow, burnt onto the wall of his office by decades of lamplight. *All that he is now.* That image was immediately replaced by the picture of William standing defiantly looking up at the brown-coated men who'd come to change the library's locks. "What did they do to him?"

Porril looked puzzled. "They? Oh—nothing, nothing except close down his library. That was enough. He died four days ago, and as per his final wishes, has been embalmed. But, there's a problem . . ."

Again, it took Leal a moment to catch up to the drift of the conversation. "His tomb! It's in the rare book collection. He told me about it." Porril nodded.

"William was a good friend," he said. His face, slightly improved by good food and wine, was now declining back into its usual expression of weary grief. "He told me that he'd let you in on his little secret. That's one of the reasons I invited you here tonight. Another is . . . this." He held up a sealed envelope.

She took it from him, saw her own name written on the outside. "Oh. But who—?" Was this from William?

"I found it while going through his desk," said Porril. "So distasteful, riffling another man's private papers. Anyway, this was addressed to you, and sealed recently. Evidently he didn't get around to posting it."

She balanced the white rectangle on her palm as though it were some sort of poisonous insect.

Easley leaned forward, the very picture of fidgety intensity. "About the tomb . . . William lived in the residences. His room has already been cleared out. He's been embalmed, but, well . . ." He and Porril exchanged glances.

"Come," said Porril. He rose from the table and fetching a lantern, led Leal and Easley down one of the dusky side passages to a narrow room near the back of the house. There, lying on a table, was a small elegant coffin. Leal recognized it for what it was, though of course she'd never seen one. The envelope in her left hand was forgotten as she reached out to draw a finger along its lacquered surface, which shimmered like oil in the lamplight.

"Those of us who loved William now have a responsibility to fulfill," said Porril. "We must keep his body safe until such a time as the library is opened again, and we can find a way to move it to his tomb. It has been my honor to host him these past several days—but the Eternists want to send an 'auditor' to investigate my personal library. They're bound to find him . . ."

"They're watching me," interrupted Easley. "Me! A lowly secretary." He shook his head.

"Wait." Leal shook her head in confusion. "What are you asking? Do you want me to take William's coffin? Where?"

"We want you to play host to him, for just a few days, I hope," said Porril. "Until all of this blows over. Once things calm down a bit, I'll gladly take him back."

Of all the things I've had to do to advance myself, Leal thought, *this is surely the strangest.* Then—*No,* she decided. *I don't have to do this.*

She smiled at Porril. "William was a good man and he deserves his resting place. I'll do what I can."

IT WAS DEEP in Maintenance shift, and the streets of Rowan Wheel were deserted as Leal hurried home. William's letter was in an inside pocket of her jacket, but she wasn't about to open it out here in the open. She didn't fear being stalked by another Tarvey— just the usual contingent of criminals and drunken youths who might be out and about.

So she took main streets, though her building was a shortcut from the flea station, down some darkened side streets she'd once proudly walked. With enough traffic around to be reassuring, Leal let her thoughts drift to the politics of her situation.

Once, she'd hated thinking about anything in political terms. It seemed so . . . shallow. That had changed in university, not because of her direct experience, but after she saw her roommate and friend, Telen Argyre, treated with prejudice and shunned. Telen had been brilliant, and stubbornly refused to play political games. She didn't call herself a "winter wraith"—her national origin was *Pacquaean*, she insisted. Her obvious pride and refusal to live up to stereotypes meant she'd been frozen out of any chance at career advancement.

It was a harsh lesson, but one Leal had taken to heart. The secret was to compartmentalize your life, keeping the noisome political stuff *here*, and your true passions protected over *there*.

The well-lighted route she was taking went past a set of axial elevators. Their wired enclosures rose dizzyingly above the office towers, clinging like vines to spoke cables that themselves quickly faded into invisibility in the permanent darkness. At the zenith, framed by a bow-shaped spangle of glittering city lights, the docks were normally bustling with cargo vessels. Not much to see there. For some reason, Leal looked up as she passed by the elevator station, and stopped walking.

Three navy vessels were nosing their way through the usual press of unloading transports. That was odd; why wouldn't they dock at the admiralty?

A commotion drew her eyes down to street level. Three cars careened around the street corner, jockeying for position as they pulled to a stop next to the elevator station. The car doors opened, and a small crowd of newspaper reporters and photographers spilled out. Arguing and jostling, they quickly surrounded the station entrance.

Leal slipped into the shadow of a nearby doorway, curious but unwilling to be drawn into whatever was happening.

When she looked up again, she noticed what the newspapermen had doubtless seen from their offices: a spotlit man perched on the nose of one of the navy vessels. He was waving flags in a semaphore pattern. This was meaningless to Leal, but clearly meant something to the reporters.

It took a few minutes for the ships to dock, and she debated continuing on home. The reporters were excited, though—and what if it were news about Brun's ship? Seana would want to know at once. Finally the elevators shot up and, after another long wait, emerged again in their descent.

Leal gnawed her thumbnail. The elevator cars vanished behind the roofline. The reporters stopped arguing and insulting one another, and formed a ragged semicircle around the station entrance.

The doors opened. Two naval officers emerged and the flashbulbs began popping. The reporters were shouting questions, but Leal was too far away to hear what the officers were saying in reply. Reluctantly, she abandoned her safe doorway and walked slowly up to the back of the scrum.

"Let's see them, then!" a photographer shouted. The officers conferred, then nodded. One disappeared inside the station.

Several soldiers came out, guns at the ready. Leal found a cold feeling settling in her stomach. She did not want to be here, stopping had been a mistake—

Three more soldiers led a line of men and women shuffling into the street. The prisoners were chained together, and hung their heads fearfully. Leal knew them by their bright clothing, though that was now in tatters; she had seen those designs before in books and in magazine articles—once or twice, even in market stalls where Seana had exclaimed at their worksmanship and outrageous price.

"Not enough!" yelled the photographers. "Their faces! Our readers'll want to see what pirates look like!"

Obligingly, a marine stepped forward and grabbed one of the prisoners by the hair. He yanked the man's head back, and a collective shout rose from the crowd. Leal shrank back.

She had seen eyes like those, many times. Leal's roommate, Telen, had been of winter wraith ancestry. She'd had those outsize eyes, the tiny nose, and childlike mouth. It was shocking to see those features on a man, but his resemblance to Telen was even more disturbing. He stood, gazing at nothing, as flashbulbs went off in his face and reporters shouted questions over his head at the brave men who'd captured him.

Shaken, nauseated, Leal turned away and ran, not slowing until she was around the corner and the flickering of the cameras had receded.

In the end, Telen and her sister Antaea had been forced to leave Sere. They'd tried to integrate, tried to make a life for themselves; Telen had always proudly proclaimed herself an Abyssal citizen. Neither had an accent; but it didn't matter. Despite Leal's indignant exhortations—that they should fight for their rights, stand up for themselves—they had fled.

Were these wraiths really behind the attacks in the dark? Maybe Telen and her sister had been right to leave their people. But if so, then Leal had to admit that they'd fled to a place no better than the one they'd left.

SHE SAT IN her window, knees up. Labor shift was half over, yet Leal hadn't slept more than five minutes. It was just that nothing had worked out the way she'd hoped. Leal had come to this dark, unfriendly city hoping to make for herself the name that her father should have had. She had sacrificed everything: old friendships, family ties, economic stability—gods knew, even marriageability! She had become an expert in an area she loved, shown rare talent and played the very political games her father had hated, to get ahead.

Now she was officially classified as a washerwoman, and there was a coffin under her table.

The lights of the city were bright. She seldom saw them in Labor shift, but the wheels were beautiful at this time, and the streets brighter even than during Cultural shift. The sky was crowded with darting flea cars, as they should be; yet there was something different about that sky, if she cared to look. Its backward depths were black, blacker than she'd ever seen. The normal midsized and large-sized ship traffic that swirled around the city was missing.

It was a crisis that could be ignored—at least around here. The city got on with its work, and the government pronounced the skies safe because the navy was out. Yet Seana had made inquiries, and the tense harbormaster had told her that Brun's expedition was overdue. It should have sent back supply ships at the very least, but nobody had come.

On the table, next to *Discourse on Ancient Shapes*, today's newspaper lay open to an article about the Virga Home Guard. The government was warning the people not to believe anyone claiming to be a member of that mythical organization. The polls had confirmed what the Eternists already knew: the Home Guard did not exist. The exotic, heavily armed ship that had arrived at the admiralty last week had actually been a pirate vessel in disguise, and it had been run out of port by the ever-alert militia. Its offers to help investigate the disappearance of the outlier towns had been a ruse. Everyone was to remember that, and the people must remain vigilant against any more foreign spies.

Also lying on the table was William's letter to her. Leal hadn't known what to expect, but in the end she'd been both pleased and disappointed. There was nothing personal in what he'd written—in fact, all he'd done was scribble one line across the middle of the page:

Balcony stack six, shelf fourteen. Polyhistoria.

Tantalizing. But the last thing her career needed right now was for her to own one more seditious book.

She frowned at the well-lit windows, the turning skies. Somebody had to do something. Someone had to step up. It was infuriating: where was Hayden Griffin in all of this? He was a real, tested hero, and yet whatever was hunting Abyss's towns was too small for him to worry about. This wasn't *his* country anyway. He'd already saved that; she supposed he considered his obligations fulfilled.

Her home on the fragile wheel of Taura Two wasn't her home anymore. Her mother was dead and Leal couldn't bring her here now or ever talk to her again. There were no heroes in Abyss to save her.

Maybe there was one thing. If nobody else would act . . .

Leal hopped down from the window and went to her desk. She drew out a fresh sheet of paper and dabbing her pen in the inkwell, began to write.

7

UP CLOSE, GRIFFIN'S workshop no longer looked like a paper lantern. It was more like the monstrous, molting pupa of a capital bug, a roughly egg-shaped vault built of arching ribs of low-grade iron, with ragged and patched canvas stretched over them. The spin-gale was lower up here than at Steam Wheel's rim, but there were no other buildings at this level so the canvas still flapped and buzzed in the breeze.

Leal stood on a narrow catwalk that swayed slightly with the stretching of the cables. A maze of such catwalks zigzagged out from the platforms footing the workshop. Some terminated at shacks or elevator stops; others meandered off between the spokes with no seeming purpose. Wrapped around all of this, Steam Wheel looked like some vast, glittering machine—a city of machines, really—billowing smoke and dark miasmas into the night to the accompaniment of metallic grinding, groaning, shrieking, and the sound of shift-supervisors' horns blaring to coordinate the work. There were no spokesmen here to catch Leal if she fell.

Her heart was pounding—not so much from the height, which as an inhabitant of Virga, did not frighten her—but because she was so obviously out of place here. The usual mob of sightseers had crowded at the foot of the elevators and for a few minutes Leal had been just another of them, until she reminded herself of William and her mother's empty house at Taura Two. She'd taken a deep breath and walked up to the bored security guards lounging by the elevator doors. "Excuse me, I'm here to see a Mr. Tarvey," she'd said.

"Do you have an appointment?"

"Tell him Dr. Maspeth wishes to see him."

"I'm sorry, without an appointment—"

"He knows me. Please."

He'd phoned up, head tilted and a finger in his other ear as he listened to the thin distant voice on the other end. Finally he shrugged. "Go on up."

The trembling, wind-washed catwalk meandered below the great egg-sack of the workshop, and finally terminated in a set of iron doors set into a broad vertical disk of metal. The disk was doubtless intended to prevent you from just cutting a hole in the canvas and slipping in. So much security! She hammered hard with the heavy door knocker, not wanting to spend a second's more time out here than she had to.

Tarvey himself opened the door; he must have been waiting for her. Lacking his aviator's cap, his bald skull gleamed in the industrial glow. "Ms. Maspeth. What can I do for you?"

He hadn't opened the door wide enough for her to enter. Suddenly Leal felt foolish. She reminded herself of how she'd felt much the same way when she'd first applied to the university, and again when she'd asked for a teaching appointment. Mindful of those previous interviews, she carefully smiled and said, "Mr. Tarvey, I'd like to beg a small indulgence from you. It will cost you nothing, rest assured."

He eloquently raised one eyebrow. Evidently she amused Mr. Tarvey a great deal. Then, with his lips half-quirking into an ironic smile, he swung the door back. "Come in, then."

One of Seana's friends was a salesman; he'd once said that if you made it in the front door, the sale was yours to lose. Leal followed Tarvey down a short steel-floored corridor and through another set of doors. *Say something,* she told herself, and just as she emerged into a new, open space she heard herself say, "My, this is homey."

Tarvey's laugh was swallowed by the sheer volume of the chamber they'd come to. They stood on a ring-shaped platform, like the lowest level of a vast stadium whose canvas sides swept up and away. The interior of the egg-shaped space was entirely filled with metal scaffolding that imprisoned a monstrous, mirror-bright thing. Bundles of chrome pipe, each pipe as thick as her waist, swept in along tortured curves defined by some architect's fever-dream, to splay and tangle into half-realized order in an ill-defined core. The assembly dwarfed the dozens of men who were working within it. Other work gangs were swarming over a dozen gigantic shapes, like dragonfly wings made of metal, that were stacked along one side of the chamber. Their stalks were made of the same piping as the bizarre bush-work within the scaffolding. Knife-sharp shadows from the floodlights chopped the whole scene up into complex, geometric shapes of light and dark.

Leal realized she had stopped and was gaping up like an infant. Tarvey grinned. "This is just—"

"Let me guess," she said quickly. "The radiator?"

He looked impressed. "You've seen a sun up close, then?"

Leal shook her head. "I've often wondered how such a thing could shed such fantastic heat without melting. What do you run through those pipes?"

"Various gases," he said. "Ammonia, steam, and something called helium for the reactor itself. This kind of nuclear fusion produces almost nothing but raw electricity, but the tiny fraction that escapes as heat would still vaporize the assembly if we didn't pump it away."

She nodded, musing. "I'm told Candesce needs to employ the whole atmosphere of Virga to do the same thing." She pictured the completed sun: the stalks of those dragonfly wings would likely extend thousands of feet, and the wings themselves would be turned edge-on to the sun's radiance. The whole thing would glow like a fantastical diatom for hours after it was turned off.

"It's beautiful," she said. "I like it."

Now Tarvey was smiling. "There's a room this way where we can talk." He led the way around the ring to a wooden building that must be the size of a respectable home, but looked like a dollhouse in this setting. Inside was not one but a number of offices, and stairs running up to more above. Secretaries were typing in one room, engineers arguing over vast blueprints that drooled over a table in another. Tarvey entered a small cubby at the back, where a single desk and two chairs sat under the light of a single lantern.

"Hmm," said Leal. "This is even bigger than my office."

Tarvey laughed again and sat behind the desk. Then a shadow of a frown crossed his face. "Your former office—am I right? We were given to understand that the history department had been shut down."

"Temporarily." Leal was careful to show nothing but quiet confidence, though her stomach tightened at his words.

"That would make you . . . unemployed?" Tarvey leaned back, steepling his hands.

He's so quick to judge! It was with some satisfaction that she said, "You misunderstand the nature of scholarship, Mr. Tarvey, if you believe it to be something that ceases when the paychecks stop. It is not possible for me to be *unemployed*, although it is possible for me to not be paid for what I do. Thankfully, I am not in need of money—and that's certainly not why I came here today."

Tarvey was doing his best not to look bewildered, but she could tell she had the better of him. "Thank you, by the way," he said (fishing now), "for pointing us to that man Uthor. He's a good cook, and discreet. Hayden was even joking that we should consult with you on all our hires."

Griffin had talked about her? Though secretly thrilled, Leal pressed on. "I'm glad my advice was useful. Perhaps, then, there's a small favor you could do me."

Tarvey tilted his head, narrowing his eyes. "Certainly—within reason, of course."

"Of course." She brought out the letter. "I need to send this letter. It's bound for the principalities, but I'm afraid . . . I don't want the censors to see it. —There's nothing seditious in it," she hurried on when she saw his expression. "I'm no spy, you should know that by now, Mr. Tarvey. It's personal, but it's going to an old friend of mine whom the government may look upon with suspicion." She let him take the letter.

His eyebrows rose. "You know Antaea Argyre?"

"Her sister and I roomed together, and we've kept in touch since then." That last part was a lie, but not an unforgivable one.

"And you think we can post this letter safely, where you cannot?"

"Am I wrong in that assumption?"

He grimaced, and wafted the letter onto the tabletop. "No. Okay, we'll post your letter. But I don't like it."

Leal's hands came together in her lap. "Why?"

"Because it reeks of exactly the sort of skulduggery that we thought you, of all people, wouldn't be a party to."

He'd agreed to send the letter; so Leal felt safe in saying, "You thought me some species of holy fool, then? Incapable of deceit?"

He shrugged in exasperation. "A man can dream. Anyway, didn't you just declare yourself above such base considerations as money? As a scholar, shouldn't you also be above politics?"

"This is not politics." She sat up straight. "Attacking and rounding up innocent winter wraiths as *propaganda*, to prove that you're doing something when you're really not . . . that's politics. What I have is . . . a terrible worry, about what it is that is lurking out in the darkness. Worry that the government is in denial as to the nature of the problem. Surely you know that the return of those cruisers the other day is a smokescreen to hide the fact that the rest of the fleet is overdue? You know that towns have disappeared? Not been raided by winter wraith pirates—the wraiths have *never* been pirates in all history—but simply vanished? And ships as well? Mr. Tarvey, my nation is suffering through a crisis that has nothing to do with the Eternists, the wraiths, or the closing of my department. It may be of little interest to you that my government refuses to admit the nature of the threat; but I assure you it is far from a merely political consideration to me!"

"It's a rare thing," said someone behind her, "to see someone withstand the withering flame of Tarvey's cynicism so well."

She turned to find Hayden Griffin leaning in the doorway. He was very pale, with dark smudges under his eyes and untidy hair. Now he jammed his hands into the pockets of his shabby work clothes and said, "To what do we owe this visit, Dr. Maspeth?"

"She wants us to post a letter," said Tarvey lightly. "To the Home Guard." He held up the object in question while Leal shifted uncomfortably, trying to find some way to keep both men in view at the same time.

Griffin frowned. "The Home Guard? I'm sure they don't need you to tell them about the monster—if it is a monster."

"Clearly you didn't read yesterday's paper," she said. "Or you'd know that our government has rebuffed the Guard's offer of aid."

Griffin exchanged a puzzled glance with Tarvey. "I did read yesterday's *Post*. Cover to cover. There was no mention . . ."

"Oh? And are you sure you read the same paper as I did?"

"Isn't there only one *Abyssal Post*—oh." He scowled at Tarvey. "Is there still a copy somewhere?"

"The cleaning staff are pretty fanatical about removing them . . ." Tarvey smacked his forehead. "But then, they would be, wouldn't they. Let's see." He rose and slipped past Leal and Griffin. A moment later she heard him shouting at people in the front office.

Griffin stared pensively out the door. "I never thought of my-self as a particularly naïve person until I came here."

Tarvey returned with a crumpled newspaper. They spread it on the tabletop—she, Leal, standing with Griffin and his lieutenant in the heart of his workshop. He flipped the pages. "Where was this article?"

"Page four, I think." He turned to it. "Oh!" Leal traced her finger down the columns. "This page is different . . . That article, about the water purification plant. That's old news—months old. And that one . . ." She held it up to the light. "The second sheet is old. They've replaced today's pages with some from an old edition. See? The date's been altered at the top, with . . ." She squinted. "A pen."

Griffin cursed, and Tarvey looked abashed. "Well, once again I'm in your debt," Griffin said. "None of our people noticed this."

She folded the paper. "They weren't like this the last time you were here, were they? You hardly had any reason to suspect all this mistrust." Griffin and Tarvey gazed at one another glumly. "And now you regret coming here at all!" Leal exclaimed. "But that won't do!"

"As you say," said Griffin. "Things are different now. Last time, we were a prestige item—exotic adventurers come to light the flame of civilization in a distant part of the world. Great propaganda value and something to make even the Principalities take notice of Abyss. But now Abyss's on their maps it's another matter. The last thing any country wants is some damned outsider popping a new sun into the neighborhood. It invites emigration, changes in the local balance of power . . . lighting a sun is an act of aggression any way you look at it. Small wonder Abyss's having second thoughts about hosting us."

"You came here the first time because nobody else would take you," she said. "I had no idea . . ." Of course, the government had given totally different reasons at the time.

Griffin grimaced. "You're on the far side of the world from

Slipstream. Nobody'd heard of you there. And you're sunless by choice, so we were pretty sure you wouldn't steal the damned thing out from under us. It worked out well, that time.

"But our problems aren't your concern, Doctor. Thanks again for your help; we'll mail this letter of yours, and," he shot Tarvey a stern look, "we won't even steam it open beforehand. Can I walk you out?"

"Oh, that would be kind, thank you." To her delight he took her arm as they strolled in long low-gravity steps through the outer office. She could tell that heads were turning, and felt a burst of something—pride? Triumph? Outside Griffin let go to better negotiate the circular catwalk; but halfway along it he stopped and smiled at her. "Do you know what this is?" He nodded up at the pipework nightmare.

"Radiator," she said. "I deduced it on my own, thank you."

He shook his head. "This is a country. A sun's mechanisms can't hold much magic for your people, but in most places a visitor to a place like this would fall on their knees in reverence."

She came to stand beside him, and they gazed up together. "You were brought up around these machines," she said. "It must be different for you."

"Different, yes. The lads . . . well, they treat this place like a cathedral. When I was a boy, I used to play in the half-built reactor core at Gavin Town." The smile faded from his face. "This sun will be going to a country called Teleon, about halfway around the world. They have a good sun, but too many people. The idea that they might calve off a whole new country has taken fire with them, it's a national mania. There are other workshops that could give them a sun, but I'm the fabled sun lighter, so they came to me.

"There was a moment, you know—one—when I felt I knew what they're feeling. In the first few minutes after I turned on Aerie's new sun . . . oh, the radiance sprang out . . . It didn't light the sky, it *made* a sky, a whole new sky of perfect blue where everything had been black before. Before you light a sun, you don't know exactly what quality its light will take, and I just stood there amazed at this ethereal, pearly white that flooded everywhere. Nobody could speak. I'm told that the moment that light hit the royal palace at Slipstream was the moment Slipstream's Pilot died.

"For hundreds of miles the air was clear and clean and daylit. In every direction, you could seed cities, and farms, and rope roads, remake the country I once knew, or a new one, something never before seen in Virga's skies . . .

"Only I never really *had* known that former Aerie. I was too young. And born and raised by sun lighters, my next thought was of how well my machine was performing; how I should tune it; who to hire to maintain it. Because, now that I had created a new country, the responsibility for keeping it alive was mine, too. If a million people moved in around it, and then it failed and died . . . unbearable."

He looked at her. "I'm sorry. None of this means anything to you, does it?"

"On the contrary." She smiled sadly. "What you've just described is exactly how I feel about learning, about education and knowledge.

"And the light here is failing."

He blinked in surprise. Then: "I wish there were something I could do for you." He squinted up at the scaffolding, and a slow smile spread over his face. "Are you busy for the next several days? Mouths to feed, plants to water?"

Uncertain, she shook her head.

"Then come." He took her arm again, steering her away from the workshop's entrance.

"We'll go post your letter."

8

ANXIETY DROVE LEAL'S thoughts in a perfect circle over
the next few hours. She couldn't possibly take ship with Griffin
and his roustabouts, even though he claimed that they needed to
make a supply run to Virga's inner nations anyway. It would only
take a couple of days, he insisted; but she knew that the fastest
ship must slow to a crawl when it left civilized air. In the depths of
winter, even Griffin's modified yacht must ply the skies at little
more than thirty miles per hour. And the nearest sunlit nation was
a thousand miles away.

Yet she'd be a fool to turn down an opportunity like this. Griffin
offered to send a man to her apartment to collect clothes and
things, but she refused: "Either I do it or no one does," she insisted.

He'd shaken his head. "You want the government's people to
know you're traveling with us?"

"Don't they already?" She gestured around the vast workshop.
"Even Tarvey admits that you're overrun with spies."

"Actually, your man Uthor is almost the last local-born worker
we have." Griffin smiled with grim satisfaction at the flapping canvas walls. "We undertook a purge. Your discovery that they'd been
censoring our newspapers . . . well, that's a different matter."

In the end he relented, and she spent a frantic ten minutes ran-
sacking her flat for clothes and essentials; and then while Hayden's
bored driver waited outside, she'd hastily scribbled a note to Seana,
and dropped it down the building's mail chute while he struggled
with her suitcases.

The sun lighter had his own boats; after a few minutes of discussion (more like argument) with Tarvey, he gathered up a gang of people and simply flew straight from the workshop to his yacht. Leal sat in the front of one cutter, next to Griffin. She felt like she'd been kidnapped.

This was the kind of adventure she'd always daydreamed about. If Seana were here, she'd be cheering Leal on—hell, even her mother would be.

Thinking of her parents' squandered opportunities led Leal to grasp the guide rope eagerly and haul herself, right behind him, into Hayden's yacht. Men and women were fanning out ahead of them, lighting lanterns and opening portholes. She craned her neck to look at everything, expecting wonders, as they flew down the center of the ship's spinal corridor. She was only mildly disappointed.

Luxury and war had fought over the yacht; it was hard to say which had won. Some of the opulent staterooms had been yanked out, and spartan rocket batteries installed in their place. The unpainted pipes of extra speaking tubes had been unceremoniously stapled to the gold trim along the sides of the corridor. First-aid kits were bolted to the arms of a statue (of a mostly naked woman) just inside the main lounge. The portholes all had heavy metal shutters.

"Yes, we need indium as well as boron-11," Hayden shouted back to someone. "Get ready to leave in ten minutes. I don't want any Abyssal inspectors nosing about."

"Can you do that?" she asked him. He grabbed a guide rope and smiled confidently at her.

"I'm still the sun lighter," he said.

"But can I do it?" She shrugged uncomfortably. "I'm not supposed to travel without a government permit, and . . ."

He held up a hand. "Here—let me show you something." He disappeared down a gangway; unhappy that she was so much in his power, Leal followed.

The hold of the ship was crammed with gigantic crates and burlap sacks. It smelled of machine oil, raw wood, and tarred rope. Hayden grabbed a lantern and bounced his way between boxes to a cleared area, where he stopped next to a hulking, dull-metal sphere that took up nearly the entire ten-foot width of the hold.

"Behold," he said. "A sun."

She shook her head, puzzled but uncertain how to respond to his little joke.

"No, really," he said, slapping the thing's side. His hand brought no hollow echo from it; it seemed solid as a boulder. "This is an inertial electrostatic confinement fusion reactor." He smiled at it fondly. "It's really just a starter engine, meaning it produces just enough power to charge the electromagnets in the bigger unit. Well, it and its five brothers."

Leal had to smile. "Do you show your reactor to all the girls?"

He looked nonplussed, which was far more charming than his attempted sophistication had been. "My point," he said, "is that we're still miracle workers as far as most people are concerned. Your government is intimidated by things like this," he slapped the reactor again, "and by our reputation. We can come and go as we please."

"But not free of scrutiny," she said. "And if this emergency deepens . . ."

"Precisely." He smiled in satisfaction. "As I told Tarvey, if we don't make this supply run now, we may not get another chance for a while."

This may be my only chance to come along. He'd made his point; she nodded, determined not to question his gift again.

There was an awkward silence. "Well," she said, "now that you've shown me your big toy, shouldn't we go back?"

He laughed. "Absolutely. Lead on."

So she had no choice about going. Therefore, she should be happy, because this was a grand adventure, after all. She trusted no harm would come to her at the hands of the sun lighter or his people. She might get a chance to see places she had only heard about, or seen in photos.

Then why did she long for nothing so much as the quiet lamp-light of her little apartment, and the solace of a dusty book? For all her fantasies, Leal had to admit that she wasn't the adventuring type. She'd known that, really, ever since Telen Argyre had left on her own adventure, seeking the semimythical Home Guard with her sister Antaea. Leal had helped Telen pack, and despite her envy, when the door closed she had breathed a sigh of relief at being left behind.

So, no: romantic though this trip might be, she didn't want it. Yet she could not complain, and thus found herself hanging at a porthole with the sun lighter as the yacht eased its way out of the dock and ponderously turned to aim at a patch of sky no less dark and empty than any other.

"Where are we going, again?" she asked him.

"Batetran," he said. "We should be there tomorrow."

"But Batetran is twelve hundred miles away. There's deserts of winter air between us and it. You'd have to fly at, what—"

"A hundred miles per hour?" He smiled.

"Yes—through darkness and cloud that could hide anything, boulders, seas, unexploded bombs from forgotten wars . . ."

He just shrugged. "You'll see. Now, if you'll excuse me, I need to discuss that flight plan with the captain."

"You're not the captain?" But he was already on his way, hand-over-handing his way up the guide ropes to the bridge.

She watched Sere recede, pensive. The thought came to her that there was something other than an adventure that she might get from this little jaunt. As the glittering lights and patterned roofs of Rowan Wheel dwindled to become just another epicycle in the wheel-of-wheels, so did all her cares. For a day or two, maybe the weight of it all would lift from her shoulders. Maybe she'd be granted a little perspective—a silence of mind in which to think.

If that happened, then this interlude would be worth it.

―――――

"I THOUGHT YOU should know," somebody said. Leal started, and turned to find Tarvey hovering nearby. His arms were crossed, his wind-seamed face crinkled into the quizzical look that passed for a smile with him.

"It's been hard for us to gather any reliable intelligence in the city, since our own people are followed whenever they go out," he went on. "But against the odds, we've managed to build ourselves a small spy network." He handed her a photograph.

She recognized the looming facade of Porril's house. In the pool of lamplight by the front door, she made out the unmistakable profile of Eustace Loll. He'd been frozen in midgesture, smoothing back his hair with one hand while the other clutched the lapels of his coat. He was walking out of the house.

"You met with this man and several others," said Tarvey. "He's a prominent Eternist, and—"

"—Therefore of the very party I'm supposed to despise," Leal finished for him. After an initial flush of heated anger, she found herself surprisingly indifferent to the revelation that Tarvey was having her watched. "This was more about Uthor than me, wasn't it?"

He nodded. "I've been considering the possibility that your 'random' meeting with Hayden was anything but random. If you were put in his way to find another way into our organization . . ."

She sighed. "Then you're a vastly sadder individual than I'd begun to think, Mr. Tarvey." She handed back the photo. "The former dean invited me to a little dinner party. He also invited Loll, in hopes that I might make a favorable impression on someone from the ruling party. For my sake, which was really quite kind of him."

"Ah. And this?" Tarvey handed her another photo. This one showed two workmen carrying a long box out of Porril's back door.

She blinked at it. "When did you take this?"

"This box was delivered to your apartment building while you were meeting with Hayden and myself," he said seriously. "Anything you want to tell me about it?"

Leal laughed. "Now this," she waggled the picture at him. "On this there hangs a tale!"

Half an hour later, over a drink in the ship's sumptuous lounge, she had told him everything: from the day she had gotten lost on the way home from Taura Two, to her leverage classes and the wine tour and Hackner's appointment over her, her chance meeting with Hayden Griffin, and William's death. "If your boys were following me yesterday," she said, "they'd have seen me buying spices and garlic. My storage locker isn't big enough for William, and if he's going to be hanging around my apartment, I'll need to cook aggressively to cover the smell of embalming fluid."

She'd said it jokingly, but he didn't laugh. His hand moved, as though he were going to put his palm over the back of hers where it lay on the table. But he didn't complete the gesture, and so an awkward moment passed.

"And what of you, Mr. Tarvey?" she said lightly. "Have you any coffins under your bed?"

He drew his hand back. "Skeletons in the closet, certainly. Well." He smiled ruefully. "I'm sorry I doubted you, and I apologize for having you tailed. It must seem very ungrateful to you, after the help you tendered."

She shrugged. "You had your reasons."

"And old habits die hard." He frowned at nothing.

The lounge was empty other than them; in the ensuing pause Leal glanced around at the décor. The room was built on the conceit that it was under gravity: the tables were all mounted the same way, with lights "above" them and Velcro carpet below. The paintings and other decorations were similarly oriented—a silly affectation, really, and a waste of space.

She eyed Tarvey speculatively. "How is it that you came by such habits in the first place?"

He didn't answer directly, but instead said, "My father gave me a yacht like this once. It was—"

"Sir?" One of the crew was hovering at the door. "We're about to deploy the kite. Should she . . . ?" He nodded at Leal.

"No, it's fine." He sighed, saw her inquiring look, and said, "Another of our secrets—but not one I'm over-worried about keeping anymore." He pushed away from the table. "Would you like to see?"

Leal was bursting with curiosity about Tarvey's yacht, but couldn't think of a suitably witty way to bring the conversation back to that. It was clear he was changing the subject anyway. "O-okay."

Tarvey led her to the yacht's cockpit, a cone-shaped room walled in thick safety glass. The darkness of Abyss's skies opened out before them. The pilot and navigator glanced over as Tarvey and Leal entered, then returned to their controls.

Even with the ship's powerful headlamps probing ahead, the view was uninteresting: blackness and roiling clouds. Then, "Oh!" said Leal involuntarily as three bright shapes shot from behind them. She had time to recognize them as bikes—unmanned jet engines, actually—before they quickly drew ahead and disappeared. But she'd seen something else as well: a net of some kind slung between them. And they were trailing long lines back to a point somewhere behind her on the ship.

"Our answer to radar," said Tarvey with an ironic smile. "We call it the kite. The jets are throttled to pull ahead of us, and we give them about a mile of tether. There's a loose net strung between them. As long as the tethers are taut we know we're okay. If one or more goes slack suddenly . . ."

"You stop the ship." She nodded at the ingenuity of the idea. "Hayden said we'd be able to do a hundred miles an hour in the dark. So this is how." He nodded; after a moment Leal cocked her head at a sudden thought. "Why show me this? Surely it's a secret worth a lot of money."

He shrugged. "We thought so. But it actually doesn't work that well. In fact it's only workable when you're going in a straight line, like we are now. When you turn, the net traces a different course than the ship and we haven't been able to compensate for that. So it's useless in maneuvers."

"Ah. Useless for the military, you mean. But surely merchants . . ."

Again he shrugged. "You can only use it in winter. Use it in civilized airs, you run the risk of slamming an unmanned jet into a town wheel at a hundred miles an hour . . . And for winter travel, accuracy is more important than speed anyway. So it's really amounted to nothing."

"Hmm." This wasn't what she wanted to be talking about, but Leal gave up. Still, as Tarvey turned to leave the cockpit and she followed, she was struck by a sudden thought: Tarvey was less than he had been, Hayden Griffin was not the hero he'd been made out to be, and his company had notable failures among its successes.

From street level, Griffin's lantern-like workshop seemed a romantic fortress, immune to the petty politics of Abyss's runaway democracy. From the inside, though, it seemed more like a threatened lifeboat, buoyed only by reputation and a single past success. For the sun lighter's project to succeed, everything had to go right. It was an enterprise that, like the kite's jets, was driving itself and, like them, it seemed unlikely to be able to survive an encounter with any unforeseen obstacles.

LEAL SLEPT IN a stateroom that must have once been sumptuous. Now it smelled of engine oil; most of the fittings had been ripped out, and the mount for what might be a machine gun was bolted under the porthole. There was no machine gun, but images of darting jets and speeding bullets wove through Leal's dreams. Wind whistled around the porthole and a deep rushing sound signified their rapid flight through winter.

She awoke to light.

At first, Leal muzzily assumed that someone had lit a lantern in the room, or that the door was open. She twitched her nose and turned in her sleeping sack. Eventually, something in her came to realize that this was different. It was the color.

Her eyes opened suddenly; Leal twisted to look at the porthole. The silver circle looked unlike any window she had ever seen—too bright, too dimensionless in that brightness. With a hiss she climbed out of the sleeping sack and sailed over to the window. Tentatively, she reached out to touch her fingers to the glass. It was warm.

The sky shaded from deep blue to her left, to that impossible silver on the right. The porthole was small, but already she had an impression of tremendous scale, a hint that the sky was far, far bigger than she had ever guessed. Tiny puffball clouds drifted miles away, half-silhouettes in white outline.

Leal sighed raggedly. She was wide awake—in fact, her heart was pounding. Quickly she dressed, almost forgot to look at herself in the mirror and just managed to catch her flyaway hair before she opened her stateroom door. Like a sleepwalker, she bounced down the yacht's corridors until she came to the entrance to the lounge.

Wonderfully fresh gusts of air were dancing about the room, which was missing half a wall. Somehow, the ship's hull had opened up clamshell doors ten feet high and twenty long, and so there was nothing between Leal and the new sky but a few grab ropes. The ship had slowed to a leisurely glide, allowing Hayden and Tarvey to sip coffee from helix glasses right on the edge of nothingness. They were speaking in low murmurs. Leal barely saw them, as she was drawn to the open hatchway by the overwhelming majesty that unfolded beyond.

Nothing could be so big. Leal had thought she understood scale; she'd watched the lights of distant ships approach, gaged their distance and speed, oh, many times. She had seen the full round of Sere's town wheels glittering in the dark. These things had been miles and miles in extent.

She clutched a rope and stared down, then up, into infinity. The nearby clouds were recognizable, though brighter and more sharply drawn than she'd ever imagined. But below them—above them— were more and more, tinier and tinier, and farther away in an endless well of detail that made her feel like she was spinning and falling and flying all at once.

And ahead of the ship . . .

She couldn't look directly at it. Even the brightest gas lamps in Sere could be stared into, though they might leave afterimages. This . . . *region*—it wasn't even a thing in any normal sense—simply overwhelmed vision. Leal put up a hand to block it, squinting around her fingers to try to catch some detail. It was impossible. Even more impossibly, it was getting brighter by the second.

"Hey, Leal, you're just in time for day-lighting." Hayden Griffin had come to hang next to her. The radiance surrounded him, seemed to buoy him up; in that moment he became the most solidly real thing Leal had ever seen. Every fold of cloth, every button on his clothing blazed with color and displayed an intricacy of texture she'd never encountered before; she could see the individual threads of his shirt, every one in perfect detail. So great was the shock that she couldn't bring herself to look at his face, lest she see too much there.

"Are you all right?"

She looked into the lounge, but even this seemed only half-familiar. "Fine," she managed to say. "It's just . . . my first sun."

"Too bright? Tarvey, can you fetch the woman some sunglasses?"

Moments later Tarvey was pushing something into Leal's hands. Grateful, she put the glasses on and blinked out at the sky. This didn't help, in fact it made things worse because suddenly she could see so much *more*. Sickly, she said, "Thanks. That's much better."

The whole sky ahead of the ship was disappearing into light. The blue opposite it was lightening; Leal thought she could see a shape to it now, a giant shell of radiance that was expanding through hundreds of miles, driving night and winter before it. She must be imagining that.

"H-how much brighter will it get?"

"Not much in absolute terms," said Hayden in a laconic tone. "But we'll get closer, so from our point of view . . . much brighter. You'll have hours to get used to it, though."

Hours . . . She laughed giddily. "Excuse me. I'll be right back." Heedless of their startled looks, she bolted for the lounge's inner doors. Somehow the light had penetrated even the windowless spinal corridor of the ship; there was no relief there or in her stateroom when she reached that. The porthole was an explosion of radiance in the center of the wall, brighter than any lamp she'd ever seen. With a panicked shout she retreated to the stateroom's little water closet.

Even here, the light sent little fingers through cracks around the door. She could see her hands clearly, lit by a kind of bluish-gray glow she'd never experienced before. She closed her eyes and put her hands over them—and that, finally, gave her relief.

While she floated there, curled up and slowly pinwheeling and aware of how ridiculous she would look, Leal tried to sort out her feelings. This much light was . . . unseemly. Its invasiveness offended her. It was as if the citizens of the sunlit countries went around naked.

Finally she laughed faintly and opened her eyes. Griffin and Tarvey fondly believed that if they lit a sun in Abyss, the people would be grateful. Leal knew better: they'd riot. The idea of the sun lighter was romantic as long as he lit stars for other people—and as long as people didn't realize just how overwhelming that new light would be. Abyss's government had nothing to worry about from Griffin, yet unless they'd visited a place like this, none of them would understand.

She left the water closet and, after giving herself some minutes to get used to the sight of herself in the mirror, she did her hair and makeup. Then, mentally braced against the light, she fixed a smile on her face and threw open the stateroom door.

"I CAN'T BELIEVE I'm doing this."

"You've never ridden a bike before?" Hayden Griffin reached back to pat her calf, which was properly sheathed against the headwind in a leather boot.

"Of course. It's . . . this!" Leal gestured around at the Olympian sky. She was seated behind him in the saddle of a wingless jet engine. Hayden was hunkered down behind the windscreen, testing the throttle on the handlebars. The bike roared and hummed between her knees. Behind them, a hundred yards away and rapidly receding, the yacht was a brilliant spindle-shape wrapped in blue. Ahead, an iron town about the size of Rowan Wheel spun in majestic solitude.

A Batetranian patrol ship had hove to next to Griffin's yacht an hour before, and a small team of inspectors had boarded her. These men were nut-brown products of an actual sun and Leal had watched them surreptitiously as they politely grilled Hayden about his intentions. If they were awed by meeting a sun lighter, they were careful not to show it; but they had no objections to his visiting their country.

"This was my first real job," said Hayden now. He gunned the jet again. "As a pilot." Then without warning he twisted the throttle and with a deep scream, they shot into the clear air.

Terror battled exhilaration as the sensation of weightlessness flipped into the feeling of hanging by her legs from the now-vertical pillar of the bike. Hayden seemed to be above her and she clung to him tightly as they shot, or so it seemed, straight up into the sky.

Objects shot past: water drops, clods of earth bearded by grass, a startled bird. Suddenly the terror gave way and she was laughing in delight.

Hayden leaned back. "Now we can see! Now we can fly!" She'd thought he had the throttle all the way open but no, *now* he did—and the headwind took her breath away. She couldn't hear herself screaming into it.

All too soon they had reached the town wheel and he brought them back to a sedate glide. Leal leaned out to look past him at the approaching curl of rooftops and streets. "No marker buoys," she commented.

"Oh, there are at night. They do have night here, you know."

"Yes, of course." But right now you could see everything, and navigating was easy. Having piloted her cutter into port countless times, Leal appreciated the freedom of picking your own course; why, they could thread the town wheel's hoop, do loops around it if they wanted, without fear of invisible hazards. To live within so much light still seemed scandalous, but now she had an inkling of how much fun it might be.

Hayden landed them on a docking structure that stuck out into the airstream at street level, like the flea stops back home. A big streamlined shield protected the landing pad from the headwind. "This way," said Hayden with a grin as Leal climbed shakily off the vehicle. He set off into the dazzling light, the heat, and the color, as if not really noticing it. Leal struggled to keep up, staring around herself.

The people were dressed scantily, appropriately she supposed for such warm airs. Yet some of them . . . "Hey," she whispered to Hayden, "are those prostitutes?"

He looked where she was pointing, and laughed. "Because

they're wearing skirts? I thought so, too, the first time I visited here. No, in Batetran, women wear skirts as a sign of status. It tells the world that they never have to bother going into freefall."

"Oh." She followed him closely through the crowds, past buildings so fully lit that she could see every cornice and overhang that might fall on her. There were overstreets here, draped above the one she was on; neighborhoods aloft, parks in the sky. And green trees, planted in the boulevards by the hundreds. They were so beautiful. "Where are we going? The post office?" The idea of flying twelve hundred miles to post a letter suddenly seemed absurd to her. Hayden shook his head.

"Tarvey's taking the other boat to buy some supplies—fresh fruit, among other things, in case you're interested. But no, you and I aren't going to the post office. It so happens that I know where the local Home Guard office is. Well, not 'office'. Outpost? Barracks?" He shrugged.

He was acting like a totally different person all of a sudden. Leal had left the yacht with the sun lighter, an awesome hero and commander of men. She'd arrived here with a youth no older than herself—an adult but one who hadn't lost his enthusiasm. He grabbed her arm and pointed out a train that was rising up a steep curving track. As it rose the scaffold supporting the track dwindled, until it was being supported only from overhead cables. The track steepened as the train barreled into lower and lower gravity, until far overhead the rails became vertical. Then they flipped over and began to curve down again, the train roaring down them to the other side of the city. Hayden laughed in delight. "They don't have those in Sere," Leal admitted.

"Nor in Rush."

"But wait a minute," she said suddenly. "If you knew how to contact the Guard all along, why didn't you?"

He pursed his lips, glanced the other way, and said, "I didn't believe your theory, remember?"

"Oh, yes you did. You did believe me. You didn't *care*."

"Nonsense," he said. "Why wouldn't I care?"

"You stopped caring the second you learned that the worldwasps have nothing to do with artificial nature," she accused. "When I told you that, you walked out of my apartment without another word."

"Which was unforgivably rude of me," he said with a conciliatory smile. Leal wasn't having any of that, and gave him her best professorial squint.

"I've chosen to believe that you're not simply indifferent to the fate of my people. That being the case, I'm left with a mystery. Why are you running hot and cold about all this?"

Now he looked away entirely. "The office is up this way," he said, pointing up a long ramp that became a curving overstreet as it rose. Narrow towers clung to the spoke cables that pierced the street, and rich dwellings overflowing with greenery spilled over its side. The house Hayden led her to sat behind a walled court-yard. The building was half-glass, was faced in coral-colored plaster, and thrust several knife-sharp wings into the spin-gale. Palm trees tossed in the perpetual wind. Leal had never seen anything like it.

Hayden rang a bell that hung by the front gate. Nothing happened. After a minute he frowned and rang it again.

Leal reached past him and pushed at the barred gate. It swung inward silently. Hayden grimaced, and stepped through. She followed, trying not to smile.

Nobody was visible through the vast planes of glass that passed for windows here. They strolled around the side of the house and there were four men, sweating in the sun as they loaded crates onto the back of a wood-paneled pedal truck. One noticed the two visitors and snapped, "No trespassing!"

"We're looking for the Home Guard," said Hayden. "This is the address I was given."

"Well, whoever told you that was pulling your leg," said the man. "Now shove off."

"Now wait a—" started Hayden. Leal put a hand on his arm.

"We're sorry to disturb you. It's just that the sun lighter here has news from the sunless countries. We thought the Guard might be interested."

All four stopped in mid-carry. They put down their boxes and stared. "You're Hayden Griffin?" their spokesman asked. "Can you prove it?"

Hayden was looking decidedly annoyed, but he brought out what looked like a business card and handed it to the man. The card flashed in the sunlight; it was iridescent in the manner of some of the butterflies in Sere's little zoo.

"Well." The man shook Hayden's hand. "I'm Oren Paxten, local head of the Guard." He was heavily muscled like his companions, darkly tanned, and the stubble on his closely-cropped head was gray. He looked to Leal like a dockworker; they all did.

"Good to meet you," said Hayden, "but it's not actually me who needs your attention. This is Dr. Leal Maspeth of Sere. She's got a request for the Guard."

The four looked at Leal politely. Her newfound breezy self-confidence dissolved into self-consciousness. "Something . . ." she started to say—and with the words came the memory of all she'd seen and heard in the past weeks. "Something's preying on my country," she said clearly. "Our government is paralyzed and the people are distracted by internal politics. But towns have disappeared. Ships. My researches lead me to believe that it might be . . . something ancient. Maybe even a worldwasp, somehow reawakened in the dark."

She waited for derisive laughter, but instead the four exchanged glances. Paxten cleared his throat. "It seems to me, ma'am, that if you're looking for explanations, the man most likely to be able to tell you what's happening is standing right beside you."

Hayden had crossed his arms, and was glowering at Paxten.

"What does he mean?" she asked him.

"It was Hayden Griffin who let the monsters into Virga," said one of the other men. "When you broke into the sun of suns itself, isn't that right?"

"I was just the pilot," said Hayden.

"Oh, that's right," sneered the man. "It was that alien you were screwing—Aubri Mah—"

Hayden's uppercut lifted him off his feet and he slammed against the side of the truck. A moment later Leal found herself standing with Paxten in between Hayden and the other two men, one of whom had picked up a heavy iron bar.

"We've been cleaning up your mess for more than two years now," Paxten said. "Don't be surprised if we're not happy to see you."

"Stop it! I don't understand what you're talking about," said Leal, "and I don't care. I came to ask for your help. Abyss's in danger—"

Paxten shook his head. "If something had penetrated the world's skin, the precipice moths would have told us."

"But what if—" Leal hated this wild speculation, but she was desperate to be heard. "If . . . whatever Hayden did woke up something that was here all along? Do you know what a world-wasp is?"

The man Hayden had struck was climbing to his feet. He and his friends looked unhappy, but their attention was on her now.

Paxten bent to pick a box off the ground. "I hope you're wrong. Because we're in no position to help you right now."

"What do you mean?"

The box thudded into the back of the truck. "We're moving out," said Paxten. "Pulling up stakes here. The Guard's stretched too thin these days . . . Whether you were just the pilot or not," he said to Hayden, "we're still dealing with the mess you helped cause. You seem to have come off all right—rich *and* famous from the components you stole from Candesce. But us . . . while you were getting rich, friends of mine were dying."

"But where are you going?" asked Leal. She held out her letter. "Will you at least deliver this to your superiors?"

"The Guard is holding a conclave in the Principalities," said Paxten. He took the envelope from her with obvious reluctance. "I can carry your message, Dr. Maspeth, but it's likely to be item ninety on a very long list of issues—not least of which is a backlash against us fomented by one of your own countrymen. Antaea Argyre—heard of her?"

"Ah," said Leal. "Oh?"

"She's left the Guard and published a book revealing some very sensitive secrets. She's calling for Candesce's suppressive field to be dialed back and some of the Guard agree with her. There's a rift . . . we've got to heal it, so we're all coming together.

"So you'll understand when I say that a message from an Abyssal, endorsed by Hayden Griffin, is not going to go down well with the Guard just now. And if your theory's not backed by the moths, we've got little reason to believe in it."

"Thank you anyway," she said. "It's all I can ask to have you deliver this."

"Yes," Paxten said. "It is." He turned to shove the box farther into the truck.

Neither Leal or Hayden spoke until they had left the overstreet and were well on their way back to the dock. Finally the silence got the best of her and Leal said, "You knew they were going to react that way to you."

"I wasn't going to tell them who I was," he retorted. "You did that."

"How was I to—" She composed herself with some effort. "He agreed to take the letter. That's the main thing."

"You think?" He shot her a poisonous look. "Are you just like the rest of them, then? You think your responsibility stops here? You think responsibility *stops*, at all?"

"What do you mean?"

"My whole life I've been picking up after other people," he snapped. "Taking responsibility for things they'd stopped caring for. I remade my country's sun while the rest of my fellow citizens were busy biding their time. I did the dirty work while they argued.

"Do you really think the Guard is going to do anything with your news? —Any more than your government is doing anything?" He shook his head in disgust.

"I appreciate your bringing me here and helping me deliver the message," she said. "It's more than I asked, or had the right to ask. I'm grateful."

"But don't you get it?" He scowled into the exotic cityscape. "More is always asked."

THEY HAD WALKED in silence again, until Leal realized how puerile Hayden's dramatism was. As he strode along, face tight and eyes straight ahead, she burst out laughing.

"More will be asked," she'd said. "You're right there."

"What are you talking about?" His offended look just made her laugh harder.

"Hayden, you've brought me to the most exotic place I've ever seen. I'm standing in sunlight in a foreign city, with time on my hands! Can't you see what this means?"

"No," he said suspiciously. "What does it mean?"

She took his arm. "Since we're here, you could at least let me do some shopping."

She'd said it just to prick his balloon of pretentiousness, yet now, two days later, Leal's stateroom was adrift with bags and packages.

She'd bought some books and clothes for herself, but most of her money had gone to an expensive new gyrocompass for her cutter. As she'd walked, though, Leal had seen so many things that she knew her friends would appreciate. It was fun shopping for Seana, and the wine-party crowd. She even found a paperweight for Easley.

Hayden had accompanied her, and while he'd tried to retain his self-righteousness, she wouldn't let him. Leal had sent an unceasing stream of questions his way, derailing his self-absorption every time he started to get that unfocused look. In the end he was cheerful and carried half her bags on the way back to the bike.

It had been fun, and the little galaxy of packages made a bubble of normalcy every time she entered her stateroom. Yet Leal was uncomfortably aware, even as she'd led Hayden around, that her girlish tactic was costly. It made her look like an empty-headed ingénue at a time when she needed Griffin and the others to take her seriously. It hardly mattered that she'd done it to drag him out of his own childish funk; he wasn't likely to recognize that side of things.

Things were too serious for frivolity. And yet seriousness seemed to be overwhelming Hayden Griffin.

All of these complex considerations explained why Leal was hovering in the ship's lounge by herself when Tarvey entered. She was stabbing a little cloud of soup balls with a straw. The lounge's great doors had been sealed hours ago; they were now deep within the embrace of winter.

"You're going to be wearing that if we have to brake suddenly," he said as he slid his feet into a couple of floor straps opposite her. Leal flushed and began guiding the free-floating soup onto the coils of a large helix glass.

"It was too hot. I was trying to cool it off."

"Mm. That explains why you're sitting alone in the dark."

She grimaced at him. "I appreciate that I looked like a happy consumer the other day, but the particulars of my life won't be changed by one shopping expedition. My department is still closed, I'm officially a washerwoman, and I can't even visit my hometown if I want to." She didn't add that she didn't want to, not anymore.

His eyebrows shot up. "You never mentioned that. Did you ask Hayden?"

"I won't be any more beholden to Hayden Griffin!" If she'd been under gravity she would have smacked the tabletop, but you learned early on not to make grand gestures in freefall. They always ended in unintentional comedy. She just glared at Tarvey.

After a moment he looked away. "I do understand," he said. "I never had to ask for anything when I was growing up. Was never powerless. Not until Slipstream came."

"You think I'm proud?"

He shrugged. "Yes. And that's a compliment."

At that moment the ship gave a lurch and began to slow. Without thinking Leal leaned around the soup spiral and sucked it off the glass helix in one motion, just as little drops began to break off and make for Tarvey's head. He ducked, then grinned at her. "Nice move."

"I've been studying leverage." But he had unhooked his feet and now half-dove, half-fell for the front of the lounge. Unsure what to do, Leal held on to the tabletop and waited; after a few minutes he returned, looking relieved.

"Nothing serious," he said, "but we'll have to slow down for a few hours—might even lose a day."

"Why?"

He nodded at the porthole. "It seems we're crossing a corner of the kingdom of Rain."

She went to look. In the dim light from the portholes, faint rounded shapes glittered in the distance, like eyes looking back at her. "It's dangerous!" She glared back at Tarvey. "Or do you have an invention that lets you fly in water?"

"We use *caution*. It's a well-tested tool." She looked back at the window just as distant lightning flashed. A fantastical skyscape appeared for a second, of millions of undulating crystalline spheres ranging in size from a fraction of an inch, to dozens of yards. Mist wreathed the larger ones and extended tendrils between them. Light shot through the kingdom again, and she saw how the drops moved balletically, merging and breaking apart at the whim of the winds. The yacht was nosing its way through them, knocking the smaller ones aside in bright splashes, and avoiding the larger ones.

"Never underestimate the kingdom," she said darkly as she returned to the table. "We've lost too many ships and towns to it not to respect it."

"Could it be your mysterious monster, then?" He nodded at the porthole. Leal shook her head.

"The kingdom's just water-saturated air from the inner nations that cools and condenses as it approaches the walls of the world. It can be avoided. But it should be avoided."

Voices came from the front of the lounge. Hayden Griffin entered along with several solar engineers he'd picked up in Batetran. The three men and two women were eagerly discussing voltage regulators as one of the crew set up a screen and a slide projector. He lit its magnesium lamp and left. Hayden slapped his shoulder in a comradely way as he passed, and he grinned.

"We can retire somewhere quieter, if you've a mind," said Tarvey.

"Well, what's this about?"

Hayden had heard her. "A little presentation on sun design," he said. "Care to see it?"

"As a matter of fact, yes."

She and Tarvey perched behind the engineers as Hayden fed the first slide into the machine. This showed a big black sphere, perhaps sixty feet across, featureless except for a few riveted ports through which various pipes jutted:

"Ten terawatt Bussard reactor," he said tersely. "Just empty space, except for twelve ring-shaped magnets. The magnets trap an electron cloud at the center of the sphere, and we inject boron ions at the edge. It's a spherical particle accelerator aimed at its own center: when the boron ions collide they fuse into helium-4, which is electrically charged—"

"Do you use liquid helium to cool the magnets?" asked one of the engineers.

Hayden raised an eyebrow. "Straight to the proprietary stuff, huh? No comment on that part."

"But it's the most complicated part of the whole system," said the engineer. "The reactor's easy, a child could design it—"

"A child did design it," said Hayden. "This is the plan I wrote out when I was fourteen. Not that I'm a genius; I was just trying to remember what my parents had shown me of their design. They secretly built the first Aerie reactor after Slipstream destroyed our original sun, and I watched them do it. The cooling system is my mother's, and I won't show you that.

"I got the ion injectors from Candesce; the power ballast as well. There's really nothing else to the reactor itself." The engineers were nodding.

Hayden changed to the next slide. This showed a shape more familiar to Leal, at least from photos: the geodesic curve of a sun's transparent ceramic shell. This one appeared half-built, its background the familiar darkness of Abyssal skies. "Now we come to the hard part," said Hayden wryly. "How to transform ten terawatts into as much light as possible. Even an inefficiency of one percent means an extra hundred gigawatts of heat to dump somehow."

"How big?" asked another engineer.

"The lamp sphere is fifteen hundred feet across," he said. "A nightmare to seal; that's where I'm hoping to tap your skills. We have to sustain a partial vacuum at high temperature—"

"What gas?" asked a third engineer.

"Xenon. The charged particles from the fusion reaction are energetic enough that they go straight through the reactor wall. Outside it, they form a charged shell around the reactor—a virtual cathode. The charge arcs from this through the xenon to the outer shell of the surrounding lamp sphere. A physical cathode would burn out, but this design avoids that. And since the entire lamp sphere is the anode, its shell should be able to absorb the hit . . ." He scowled at the picture.

"I want the purest spectrum I can get for this sun. That's why we're going with xenon. But it's not the most efficient, which leaves us with hundreds of gigawatts of heat and electricity to spend. That's what I was going to ask you about," he said to the engineers. "Do you favor building discharge brushes and creating a lightning field around the sun? Or—" He grabbed at an overhead strap as the ship suddenly braked.

A couple of the engineers tumbled toward the bow; Leal used one of her leverage moves to extend a foot for another to grab. Hayden had jumped to a speaking tube and was shouting, "What the hell's going on?" into it. He put his ear to it and frowned. Then he spun suddenly and grabbed Tarvey's arm. "Open the hatch! And sound general quarters! We need men and survival gear." Slideshow forgotten, he and Tarvey manned the heavy winches that opened the lounge's clamshell wall. It slowly inched apart revealing utter blackness, but now crewmen were arriving with bright hissing lamps. Shafts of white began probing the sky, and once again Leal had the unsettling impression of thousands of eyes glinting there.

"Stop! See it?" One of the crew pointed. Leal and the engineers crowded together at the edge of the doors; she grabbed Tarvey's arm as he passed. "What's everybody looking at?"

He shook his head grimly and broke away from her.

One by one the crewmen found their target, until half a dozen magnesium lamps had it outlined in foggy white. It was a drop of water, about six feet across. The yacht was sliding to a stop next to it. Beyond, dozens more of similar size receded in clusters and lines. Fog wreathed them all in eerie silence.

"I don't understand—" Leal fell silent. There was a shape inside the quivering sphere. Just as she realized what it was, she saw that many of the other drifting spheres had the same kind of shape inside them—a macabre kernel around which the drop must have grown.

In the center of the giant water drop was the body of a man.

9

THERE WERE DOZENS of them. The yacht's shouting sailors roved their spotlights around and as the lights flicked from drop to drop, an unimaginable tragedy became visible. These men had ventured too far inside the kingdom of Rain. All wore foot-fins, but exhausted or helpless from injuries, even the hardiest flier would have had to stop moving sometime. Everyone aboard the yacht knew what would happen next.

A motionless man would attract water.

Small drops would cling at first to hair, shirt, or shoe, and larger ones would join them. You might be able to shake them off for a while, but you had to sleep sometime. Once you were motionless for whatever reason, the drops would begin to accumulate and join together.

The yacht came to a halt, and two airmen with ropes tied to their ankles jumped across the empty air to the nearest dark sphere. They proceeded to kick at it, scattering the water; then one reached in and grabbed the body's limp arm. Two airmen braced next to Leal drew it back in—quickly, but with obvious apprehension on their faces.

The body of a young man, still largely sheathed in water, thumped onto the table where Leal had just been eating soup. She stared at it. The dead airman wore the uniform of the Abyssal navy.

"Oh gods! The expedition!" Leal shrank away from the lifeless gray face. The body was curled into fetal position—a normal sleeping position for freefall—which made this youth look terribly vulnerable. A sleeping boy.

She looked away, but the vista outside was no better. The spotlights had found another giant drop, and for a second Leal thought she was looking at a lost ball of wine from the winery. The sphere was a deep rich red; but then she realized what that must mean: someone had bled out inside that drop. "What happened to them?"

Hayden was standing on the edge of infinity, holding one of the ropes. He shook his head.

"There! That one!" One of the crew was pointing excitedly. Once again the spotlights wove crazily through the dark. This time they alighted on a dark figure only half-covered in water. And was it the unsteady wavering of the light, or was the man moving feebly?

He twisted in midair, batting weakly at the sheath of water sliding slowly up his chest. Leal shuddered. It was as if a monster with infinite patience were devouring him. How long had he been fighting it? —Long enough that he was unable to focus on anything else; the lights in his eyes were mere distractions, not a sign of rescue.

"Got him!" A sailor reeled in quickly, drawing the limp form with him. They all crowded around, shoving away the rest of the water, and someone produced a blanket that they wrapped him in. They spun him in the air to do this, and as he turned he came to face Leal. She screamed.

"Brun! Oh no, what happened?"

Brun Mafin raised his eyes to hers, but there was no recognition in them, only a hollow despair. His lips trembled, as if he wanted to speak; then the light went out of his eyes and his hands turned to bat at the blankets. He seemed to think they were more water.

"Brun, it's me, Leal." The airmen gave her room and Leal cupped his face in her hands. "You're safe, Brun, the water's gone."

"No . . ." He shook his head. He'd begun to shiver violently.

"There's another!" Suddenly she was alone with Brun as all the airmen went back to casting their lines and lights outside.

"Brun, what happened? Tell me."

He shook his head again. "S-stop doing that. Taking those shapes—"

"Brun, I'm real. The real Leal. Tell me what happened to you." As she spoke Leal drew him out of the lounge into the warmer air of the spinal corridor. Not knowing what else to do, she took him to her stateroom.

"Nothing to touch," he muttered. "Grabbing—grabbing for it but it's just out of reach." Tears started at the sides of his eyes.

"It must have been awful," she said. "But how did you get out there? Where's the ship?"

"The ship . . ." His eyes widened. "We were tracking it. Oh, it's easy to find after it's fed, just follow the trail of wreckage. It led us into the kingdom, but we know it's not from here. It nests in the skin of the world."

"What came? What was it?"

His face took on a disturbingly sly expression. "It's not an it. It's a *they*."

His eyes became unfocused, and Leal shook his shoulders gently. "Brun, what do you mean that it's a they? Can you describe it?"

He closed his eyes tightly. "At first there's the voice—you can hear it for miles. But it's not one voice, it's a chorus. And when it comes at you, it's *thousands*. Thousands. And all made of each other . . ."

Stunned, Leal drifted back. Mafin's face was twisted into a horrible grimace now.

"They grab you and they *yell*, and what they say is . . ."

"Hush!" She moved to him again, and stroked his cheeks. His hands had been wiping at himself, but he stopped as she dried his face and hair using the towel from her water closet.

She fully opened the heating vent on the wall; then she peeled off his sodden clothes and dried the rest of him. His skin was cold, and pale as snow.

He sighed deeply. "You need to sleep," she said. "Yes, go to sleep, Brun, you're safe now."

He half-smiled, and his eyes closed as she bundled him into her sleeping bag. He seemed to *let go* then, every part of him going limp. She had to hold her ear to his mouth for a long time to be sure he was still breathing.

There was nothing more she knew to do for him; Leal returned to the lounge. Four more airmen had been rescued by then, and the ship's engines were throbbing slowly as it flew in a search pattern, looking for more. Leal found Hayden and said, "The *Hammerhead* must have gotten stranded somehow. Brun said they left it to find help—"

"Yes, ma'am." It was one of the airmen, a shivering bundle of blankets in midair with a damp mop-head protruding from the top. "We started out on bikes," he said, then paused to cough. "But the damned intakes got clogged almost right away. Carried on with the foot-fins, but I guess we were going in the wrong direction. Just got more and more lost in the kingdom. Two days of it and we started to weaken . . . and the water came . . ."

"But what were you doing in here? And how could a ship like the *Hammerhead* get stranded?"

The airmen glanced at one another. Reluctantly, the one who'd spoken said, "Can't tell you that. It's classified and, minding our respect for the sun lighter here, he's a foreign national and so's this ship . . ."

Hayden shrugged. "I don't need to know unless it'll help us find the *Hammerhead*." Again the men glanced at each other; then all shook their heads.

"But the rest of the crew? Are they all right?"

The looks on their faces told her all she needed to know; their leader simply said, "Ma'am, they are not."

There was a shout from outside. Hayden's men had found another body, and with that the other rescued airmen sighed. "That's the last of them, then," said their leader. ". . . Where's Lieutenant Mafin?"

"Thawing in a stateroom," said Hayden. "Which you'll be in a minute, too."

"Good, I guess. Only—begging your pardon, sir, but we'd prefer if we were together, and that he was with us. He's been talking—"

Leal was offended by the implication. "I'm sure Lieutenant Mafin wouldn't reveal any sensitive information."

"I'm sure he won't, too. It's other things he might be saying, ma'am, sir . . . Things that aren't healthy and it's not just you shouldn't hear them. Nobody should hear him."

"I don't care about your secrets, I care about the safety of my ship," said Hayden tersely. "And the people on her. If you know anything that could put us in danger, or if you can lead us to where the Hammerhead's stranded, you'd better tell me now."

The airmen exchanged another look, then: "We didn't see anything," said their leader sullenly. "We're engine room crows, we was battened down with earplugs in while the battle happened. We heard yelling through the speaking-tube, but—" He glared at his companions. "We don't know who we fought. Or where the ship is."

Leal twisted her hands together impatiently. She didn't want to let Brun out of her sight until she knew he was all right, and Seana would never forgive her if she did. But Hayden was already nodding to two of his men. "Fetch the lieutenant and we'll billet him and his men together."

They were closing the great clamshell doors now, and the ship's engines were changing their tone as it began a final turn. As the survivors were conducted from the lounge, Hayden turned to Leal, frowning. "You'd best keep away from those men for the remainder of the journey."

"But Brun—"

"I understand you know him. But you're not supposed to be traveling with us, remember? I don't want to get you into trouble."

"But they," she nodded to the retreating airmen, "have already seen me."

"They've seen a woman. We'll supply our own explanation for that when we get into port. Or are you sure it will all be fine?"

She bit her lip, but had to shake her head. She cursed her political habits, which were restraining her even now from running after Brun. She was betraying him by so selfishly looking after her own skin. Seana would agree. Yet she didn't move.

"Was the lieutenant unconscious when you left him?" Hayden continued. Leal shook her head.

"No, but . . . those men think he's mad, and clearly they didn't see what he saw."

"Tell me!"

As best she could, Leal repeated Brun's words to Hayden. Tarvey had joined them, and when she finished both men were frowning.

"Is that what a worldwasp looks like?" asked Tarvey. "Like a . . . flock of something?"

She shook her head helplessly. "I don't know. I've only got two primary sources and they're confusing as hell. There's much better material in the rare books collection—William could tell me where to look, but he's dead—"

Hayden had been gazing off into the distance. Suddenly he said, "Excuse me," and without a backward glance he left the lounge. Leal stared after him, puzzled.

"What's he up to?"

Tarvey sighed and shook his head. "Nothing. Why don't we—"

"Hang on." Suddenly she was suspicious. "He's doing it again, isn't he?"

"Leave it alone, Ms. Maspeth."

"That's Dr. Maspeth." She flew to the lounge door; Tarvey followed. He grabbed her arm as she made to leave the room.

"Don't you understand?" he hissed. "He thinks this is all his fault!"

Leal stared at him. She'd gleaned that basic fact from their run-in with the Home Guard; but she wanted to know more. "No, I don't understand at all," she said, looking Tarvey in the eye.

He let go of her arm, suddenly (and for the first time since she'd known him) looking self-conscious. "About two years ago, the commodore of Slipstream hired a woman from outside of Virga, Aubri Mahallan. Her job was to enter the sun of suns itself and shut down its defenses for a night, enabling the commodore to use radar—a kind of device for seeing in the dark that Candesce's radiation usually jams. Radar's like our Kite, only better. The commodore used it to attack an entire fleet at night and make mincemeat of them."

"What does this have to do with—"

"Aubri and Hayden were lovers, and he flew her to the sun of suns. She died in Candesce, and he escaped with enough parts to build two national suns. What nobody knew at the time was that when Candesce's defenses went down, a number of things slipped in from outside the world."

"Things?"

"Call them monsters. One of them trashed Slipstream's royal palace, and may have killed the Pilot of Slipstream himself. That one was on its way to Candesce where it intended to shut down the sun of suns' defenses for good."

"Wait! That battle at the palace—Antaea Argyre was there. I heard about that, but nothing about a monster from outside . . ."

"The Home Guard covered it up."

She looked down the corridor. The door to Hayden's stateroom was closed. "He thinks that because he flew somebody else to Candesce on a third someone else's orders, that he's *responsible?*"

Tarvey grimaced. "Of course it's not that simple. Hayden's no fool, but what a man knows and what he feels are two different things. He spent his youth and early adulthood utterly alone, and now—scarcely two years later—he's got the fate of nations resting on his shoulders. That's a frightening burden, and when you're in that situation, the tiniest hint of additional responsibility feels like you've been accused of a crime."

She eyed him. "You know this firsthand?"

"What I know is that he doesn't need you confronting him at a time like this."

She scowled at Tarvey. "All right then. We have to get Brun and his men to a hospital, but after that—" She'd been about to say *we have to go back and warn the Home Guard that there's a real threat.* But Paxten and his men would be long gone by now. There was no one to appeal to.

Tarvey shrugged. "Your navy is going to have to deal with it. Maybe Hayden will try to help but . . . We'll have to see. Now, if you'll excuse me, I need to make arrangements."

He left her hanging in the entrance to the suddenly empty lounge.

THE YACHT SAILED back into port during Maintenance shift, so luckily, there were only a handful of port inspectors on hand. They were all summoned to help unload the survivors, and while they were distracted at the starboard hatch, Leal slipped out the port side. For once she had an elevator car to herself—well, actually she and her numerous packages and gift bags took up the entire thing—but she hardly noticed, she was consumed with anxiety over what to do next.

Seana had to know about Brun. Leal knew they hadn't been lovers, but things had been going that way. Brun was Seana's great hope just now. If Leal didn't tell her he was back in the city, it would end their friendship when she did find out.

The problem was that Leal knew exactly what Seana would do when she found out: she would stalk straight into the admiralty and demand to see her man. And then they would ask her how she knew he was back—because, Leal was sure, the government was going to keep this disaster a secret for as long as it could.

It wouldn't matter if Seana told them; they'd figure it out. And then the secret policemen would come knocking on Leal's door.

An anonymous letter? Yes, that might even work . . . The doors opened onto rain-slicked streets. She barely managed to get her now-massive cargo onto the sidewalk before the doors closed again. Now that she was under gravity again, it was clear she'd need to hail a cab to get home.

Doing that, and kibitzing with the off-shift driver, who was giddy with fatigue, seemed to take the last of Leal's energy. She barely made it to her building, and would have left a trail of presents to her elevator had she not stumbled at one point and looked back.

She half-fell into the apartment, scattering boxes and bags. With an effort she closed the door. Turning, she nearly tripped over a long wooden box that took up most of the floor.

"William." There was a note from her landlord atop the box. *Too big for your storage locker*, it said. Leal swore and checked the framing of the box, but it didn't look like anybody had forced it open. She wouldn't have put it past her landlord to try.

"I brought you something; well, *me* something, but we can share." She placed a lime-green Batetranian jewel box on his coffin, and imagined him smiling. Then it came to her that she couldn't give any of these gifts out; if the secret police saw any of them, she would be identified as the mystery woman on Hayden's ship just as surely as if she told Seana about Brun.

She sat down on the floor next to the coffin, and draped an arm along it, laying her head on that. "Ah, William," she said. "Who am I to talk to about all this?"

10

PERSISTENT LOUD KNOCKING woke her up. Leal realized she was lying on her stomach, one numb hand trailing off the bed. "J-just a minute!" With an effort she rolled over and stood up. The sleeping arm flopped uselessly at her side. *One hand in the grave,* she thought as it started to tingle.

The knocking came again. "Hang on!" It was a light but insistent *rat-a-tat* sound; somehow she'd always imagined the secret police would have heavier fists. She wasn't surprised when it turned out to be Seana standing in the hallway. She looked gorgeous, her bare arms and throat twined with gold—but her face was twisted with anger and her mascara had run.

"When were you going to tell me!"

Leal stepped back to let her in. "When I woke up." She massaged her pins-and-needles hand while Seana sized her up. Evidently Leal looked as bad as she felt, because Seana's fury seemed to subside a bit—at least until her eyes left Leal and found everything else.

"What is all *this?*" Seana lifted one of the immodestly colored bags.

"I bought it all before we found—hey, how did you hear—" Seana held up a newspaper. SHIPS LOST was the headline.

"So they summoned the courage to actually admit it," muttered Leal as she took the paper. She read two lines of the article but wasn't up to continuing. The rest of Brun's expeditionary force had made it back to port, apparently, but sufficiently damaged to make it clear that those ships that were missing, weren't just on patrol.

Seana threw her arms around Leal. "Oh, Leal! How is he?! A friend of his at the admiralty came by the shop, just an hour ago. The government's not saying anything about survivors from *his* ship. What happened?"

Leal stepped gingerly around her scattered packages. "This one was supposed to be for you," she said, lifting one bag by its little ribbon handle. Clearly at a loss for what to say next, Seana took the package and let gravity drop her into a chair by the table. A *thump* came from underneath as her foot hit something.

"Ah, yes, that would be our William." Leal sat down opposite her, and when Seana leaned down to look under the table, added, "Seana, William. William, Seana."

"*What?*"

She clasped her hands and looked Seana in the eye, and then told her the story, without embellishment or commentary, and without even getting up to make tea. Manners seemed quite beside the point right now. By the time she was finished Seana had calmed down, though she also seemed a bit overwhelmed by the strange turns Leal's tale had taken. Leal ended by asking, "Did your friend at the admiralty say where they'd taken Brun?"

Seana nodded. "Orrery Hospital." She stared glumly at the packages (hers was, of course, still unopened) and the rest of the mess Leal had left when she so suddenly flew off on her adventure. "We'll go see him. They can't deny us that." *Thump*. "Sorry, William."

"Seana, of course they can deny us a visit." Leal discovered she was hungry, and thirsty. She got up to assess the catastrophe of mold in the sink. "There's all kinds of reasons why the government won't want Brun and his men to talk to anybody."

"But we'll find out what they're planning this afternoon." Leal quirked a skeptical eyebrow at her. "It's all there in the paper," said Seana earnestly. "There's going to be a rally this afternoon in Great

Park, and the prime minister himself is going to announce the action plan. Brun's friend said they're out of ideas, they're just planning something flashy to keep the mob at bay while they come up with a real response. Will you come with?"

"You're going?"

"I have to do *something*. I can't stand not being able to see him."

Leal shook her head at the thought of witnessing such crass political theater. "I guess it'll be worth it to see how they eat crow when they admit that there's really something out there."

Seana frowned. "They say it's a fleet of wraith ships. *An incursion,* they're calling it."

Leal shook her head angrily. "It's not the Pacquaeans. It's just one thing. One thing that's thousands of things."

"Leal, that's unusually cryptic even for you." Seana began absentmindedly picking the cluttered packages and envelopes off of Leal's floor.

"I know it's not the wraiths. I used to think it was a worldwasp—well, it could still be. But I don't know enough about the wasps."

"Who does?"

Leal nodded at the coffin. "Ironic, isn't it? William didn't just catalog his books—he read them. And he cunningly hid the rarest and most valuable. If they—" *burn the library,* she almost said, "break up the collection, the books that can tell us whether it is a wasp are likely going to get lost. Filed in somebody's attic along with last century's census records."

"Hey, you've got mail. From the Ministry of Education."

Leal laughed shortly. "That would be a check stub, I expect. From my new position as a washerwoman."

"Can I open it?"

"Sure." She began to run water into the sink as Seana tore open the envelope.

"Who's Gereld Hackner?"

Leal lunged across the room and snatched the letter from Seana's flinching hand. She scanned the page quickly, then swore.

"It's a request that I appear . . . at the office of the minister himself."

"Oh, that can't be good."

"What do you mean?" Leal glared at her. "They've already fired me—no, worse, they *unmade* my job like it never existed! What can they do to me now? Maybe—maybe there's been a change in policy. The Eternists are idiots, everybody sees that—"

Seana half-smiled. "Ah, there's the Leal I came here to see. So what are you going to do?"

Leal tapped the letter against her cheek. "Why, I'll put on my best dress, and show up."

Seana raised an imaginary glass. "Here's to that!"

"Yeah." And then, because they both needed it, Leal broke out a bottle of wine and opened it. If they were going to a government rally, they might as well not go sober.

THEY WERE TRIPPING their way out of the building, feeling significantly elevated, when a young voice shouted, "Hey!"

Leal turned to see one of the phone-runners hurrying out of the door behind them. He was panting. "Hey," he said again, "Is one of you Deelie Maspeth?"

Leal and Seana exchanged a glance. "I'm Maspeth," said Leal.

"Okay. The guys said it was stupid 'cause the line's so bad today, we barely heard anything over the static. But I thought I'd try anyway. Just missed you at the elevator . . . There's a message for you from somebody named Garvey."

"Tarvey?"

"Could have been. It was really hard to make out anything on the line, but I think he said something about 'two days,' and something else about books."

Leal waited, but the boy just stood there. "That's it?"

"Really truly, all I could make out. Well, something that sounded like 'you're cleared' but I got no idea what that might mean."

"Huh." Leal looked up the gloomy facade of her building, wondering. "This could be important," she said to Seana. "Maybe I should . . ."

"Oh, no, don't start that. Once they have you waiting for phone-runners, you're as good as dead. You said you'd go to the rally with me, and we're going."

The phone-runner was obviously bracing himself for disappointment: it hadn't been much of a message. "You worked hard," Leal told him. "Here." She gave him twice the usual number of coins and smiled as his face lit up.

"Thanks, ma'am. Deelie Maspeth—I'll remember that name. I'm your runner from now on." He bolted before she could correct her name, and Seana laughed.

There were no flea cars at the local stop, so they went to the next one down the line. That one was empty, too, but there was no point in trudging any farther. They waited, Leal brooding over the letter from Hackner and the mysterious, garbled message from Tarvey. Eventually a lone flea slammed into its berth and the pilot climbed out to stand dramatically windswept next to it. He didn't bother to winch it out of the Slipstream, so Seana and Leal had to battle the pounding wind to reach its hatch.

"Coin Wheel," Seana shouted as he reached up to close the canopy. "As close as you can get to—"

"—Great Park," he said as the canopy came down, shutting out the wind. "I know, I know. It's where everybody else is going."

And yes, it turned out that Great Park was overflowing. The park was the largest concentration of trees and shrubs under gravity in Sere, an expanse that took up the whole width of Coin Wheel and a quarter of its circumference. There were as many lampposts as trees here, making it the most brightly lit place in the city. At its center was a broad field and bandstand where public plays and musical performances were usually held. The politicians were huddled on this, just above a sea of citizens who were demanding action and information.

Their delay in getting a car had made Leal and Seana late, but it hardly mattered; the men on stage had apparently been speaking steadily for fifteen minutes and so far had said absolutely nothing. The crowd was grumbling and the wine had long since abandoned Leal and Seana by the time the prime minister finally took to the podium. He raised a hand for silence, but by now the crowd was impatient, and he had to shout through a megaphone to be heard.

Even so, Leal was only making out every second word. "—know you're alarmed," she made out, and then, "—situation calls for calm heads, not panic," which only made the crowd mutter louder. Then he shouted, "Today we're calling on special help—an ally no other nation could boast of having." Finally, the crowd shut up and people turned to listen.

"We've been privileged," the prime minister went on, "to have recently welcomed an esteemed visitor to Abyss. He's been here before, and you all know his name and reputation. Today, he's agreed to help us search out the enemy that is pecking at the fringes of our great nation."

"Oh no," said Leal.

"We face a foe who is cunning and elusive," continued the prime minister. "One that is always on the move, one familiar with the most remote, most hostile wastes. They flutter like bats from midden to fungal cloud, and for generations they've stolen the products of our hard work. What we didn't know was that all during that time, the winter wraiths had been building a fleet, somewhere in the black backward hollows where they feel at home.

"They are striking at us now because while the eternal night of winter is our friend, it is our weakness as well. We in Abyss are creatures of both light and darkness, at home in both; but they are children of the dark alone. They want an ultimate triumph for that darkness; they want to build a future where no spark of homey light ever insults their lidless eyes.

"But they struck too soon. They weren't really ready, else they should have overwhelmed us in one bloody day. Clearly, their tactic of hit-and-run is one of desperation, because their spies in the city told them of our visitor, and what he is building. They are attacking now, before they're ready, because they are *afraid*. Afraid of who we might unleash on them."

"You have to hand it to him," Leal muttered to Seana. "He does have a genius for twisting the truth to suit the needs of the moment." She thought of the poor innocent wraiths she'd seen being paraded before the flashbulbs, and hatred for the men on the distant stage boiled up in her.

"They're afraid, and for good reason. For now that we know what they're up to, we're going to stop it. They counted on us being unable to follow them into the absolute darkness that is their home. And it's true, we're not creatures of the backward airs like they are. But their worst fear is about to be realized. We need not fear their darkness, for we can wipe it aside in an instant when we choose. Against their blindness, we can bring *light*!"

And there he was, Hayden Griffin, mounting the podium to stand with the prime minister. The crowd burst spontaneously into the national anthem, and Leal's fury turned to nausea. The only thing that kept her from walking away was the expression on Hayden's face. She'd come to know him a little, and his distaste was obvious to her. To others, his expression might seem neutral, even serene. That was how it would be described, she was sure, in the captions that would accompany the many photos now being taken of him.

He put the megaphone to his lips and said, "I'm just one man."

The crowd went wild, and he hung his head for a few seconds, obviously distressed. Then he raised the metal cone again.

"The prime minister has implied that I might light a sun here in Abyss. I have no intention of doing that, unless it becomes absolutely necessary. For the moment, I've pledged only to help find, and identify," he emphasized the word heavily, "your enemy. I will be equipping my yacht with certain devices that will assist in the search. I remain a foreigner among your boughs, and remain obligated to my clients who have requested a new sun for their own country. But . . . I will do what I can."

He lowered his head and the prime minister snatched the megaphone from him.

"You heard it from the sun lighter himself! A sword of light now protects Abyss! Its mighty shaft shall seek out and pin the damned wraiths wherever they try to hide. We'll catch the bastards, this is my promise!"

"Come on." Leal took Seana's arm and began dragging her out of the shouting crowd.

"But he hasn't said what the navy's going to—"

"Seana, he hasn't said anything, and he's not going to. Let's get out of here before things get ugly." She was terrified that the prime minister would trot out the wraith prisoners. She would rather jump off the wheel than see that.

Seana came, but reluctantly. When they were a block away and things were a bit quieter, Leal took her hands and gazed into her eyes. "Political rallies are not a substitute for Brun. We'll find out how to get you in to see him, I promise."

Leal heard the seriousness in her own voice, and Seana responded to her intensity with wide-eyed surprise. But Leal was only partly determined for Seana's sake. Hearing the prime minister demonizing the winter wraiths had convinced her that they had to hear Brun's full story.

———

"WAIT HERE," SHE told the driver. The sound of the car door closing echoed through the blackness of the alley, and as Leal hesitated the driver stuck his head out the window.

"You sure this is the right place?"

Leal checked the scrap of paper in her hand. "It's the address I've got."

"Obviously you got it wrong." He glanced around uneasily. "What with the curfew and all, things that used to go on in the side streets have been pushed back, you know, kinda . . . squished into the corners. This sure looks like one of them corners to me."

"Yeah. Well, I'll just make sure, then I'll be right back, okay?" He looked nervous, but she knew he wasn't going anywhere. Not with all her luggage piled in the backseat of his taxi.

It was four days since her meeting at the Ministry of Education. Four days of pacing; sitting in her window and staring; drinking too much tea; taking long walks. None of it had brought her an inch closer to a decision. Meanwhile, the tension in the city had grown, and time had ticked down to another deadline—this one introduced by a garbled phone message, only later clarified by letter.

She'd put it all off, and now, literally at the last minute, she had to decide. But she couldn't do it on her own.

A jumble of warehouses and light industries crowded together where the market district abutted the edge of the town wheel. Casual pedestrians had no reason to be back here since it was as close to a cul de sac as you could get in a wheel. The building Leal stood outside was a fine example of industrial pragmatism, built of ribbed concrete slabs that wept rust stains from the iron bars holding it together. Tall windows parodied the ones in the rare books collection; there were none on the ground floor and the ones above were opaque with dust.

Long ago, Easley Fencher had scribbled his address on this scrap of paper, and Leal had kept it out of respect and some dim sense that it might be of use someday. Clearly, she couldn't decipher Easley's handwriting.

Maintenance shift was beginning; stocky silhouettes moved through the alleys, climbing up metal fire escapes and slamming open the creaking iron doors of the other buildings. During her own off-shift walks Leal had always stopped short of entering this district. She turned now to leave, trying not to seem too nervous to the departing workers. Then she stopped, surprised.

Faint piano music wafted from a canted window ten feet above the ground. Dim light glowed there, and not the white of gaslight but the softer amber of an oil lamp.

Leal glanced around, squared her shoulders, and walked up to rap on the iron-bound door. The piano stopped. A minute later a little window in the door slid aside; she heard an exclamation of surprise and the door was thrown open.

"Leal! What are you doing here?" It was Easley, wearing a flannel nightshirt that hung to his knees, and yellow slippers. His mustache drooped as if it had gone to sleep before him. He held a lantern in one hand.

"I'm sorry to bother you so late, Easley. I—I need some advice."

Without comment he ushered her in and the door thundered shut behind her. She was reminded of her visit to Hayden Griffin's workshop—and looking around, realized that the parallels went deeper than their similar entranceways.

"Easley, what is this place?"

It smelled of dust, mold, and oil in here. The building must be fifty by a hundred feet, and at least thirty feet tall. Most of the space was open up to the girdered ceiling, but about thirty feet of the length—just inside the door—had a second floor to it. The only light came from a door at the top of a flight of stairs. From it and the distant windows she could see that all of the floorspace on this level was taken up with wooden racks. Dusty, white-shrouded shapes were stacked on most of them. Oddly, the ground-level pallets were all empty; it was only shelves starting six feet off the floor that held anything.

"This," said Easley, staring glumly into the dimness, "is the collection. My grandfather's, initially, then my father's, and now me and my brother own it."

"But what—?"

A loud bump sounded from overhead, followed by an incoherent noise that sounded like cursing. Easley winced. "I'd better look into that."

"Oh, I'm sorry, I didn't realize you had—"

"It's my brother," Easley said quickly. "He won't hurt you."

Puzzling over that odd statement, Leal followed him up the cement steps and into the building's loft. But she had to stop, head just above the level of the floor, and look twice at what she was seeing, before continuing up to stand with Easley.

The floor was strewn with finely patterned carpets from the Principalities of Candesce. Tall portrait paintings hung on the walls between windows that looked out on the street on one side, and into the warehouse space on the other. Warm lamplight from sconces on the iron pillars lit a vista of sumptuous divans draped in silk, elegantly carved tables, home to many open books; and throughout it all stood many glass display cases, some as tall as Easley. Bright highlights of chrome and ruby shone from the nearest.

In the center of the space stood a large man in a housecoat. His brows were beetled in ferocious concentration, and he was sucking loudly on the knuckles of his right hand. "Hurt," he said in a croaking voice as Easley gently pried his hand away from his mouth.

"You rapped your knuckles on one of the cases, that's all. You'll be fine." Easley turned to Leal and, with an odd and touching mixture of resignation and pride, said, "Byron, I'd like you to meet Leal. She's a friend."

Byron tilted his head back and looked down his nose at Leal. "Hmmm," he said, a quick smile twitching across his face. Then he grabbed Easley's arm. "Whe' you yesteday?"

"Let's not start that again, Byron. I told you I have to look for work."

"Whe' you yesteday?"

"You should be in bed. Just a minute," he said apologetically to Leal. Murmuring in a low voice, he led his brother away.

Lacking any idea of what to do, Leal found herself examining one of the display cases. This one held a softly contoured object, like a melted book, whose top was a square of milky glass. Little buttons were lined up along its sides, just where your fingers could reach them if you held it in both hands. Under the patina of scratches and dents, it was the most delicious shade of fuchsia. It practically radiated age, and yet it was a surprisingly playful-looking object. She had no idea what it might be.

The other cases held similar things. Leal went from case to case with a sense of mounting excitement. She recognized some of these objects! Not by style, but by function, as in the case of the pistols that lay on black velvet in a particularly strong-looking case.

Easley came back from behind a wide partition that separated a third of the space. He'd dressed in his usual natty, but out-of-style clothes. His rapier-like mustaches were still askew.

"Easley, these are treasures! How in the world did you—"

He grimaced. "Not me. I'd be more than happy to drop the whole mess into the sun of suns."

Pacing from one case to another, he said, "I grew up around these . . . treasures. I know each nick and scuff on every one of them. They're my curse."

"But this collection must be worth a fortune. Downstairs—those racks—"

"Hold bigger objects. And yes, most of them predate Virga. But none of them work, you see. Their core technology is the one

Candesce's energies suppress. So they're all curiosities, at best—junk, really."

"But they should be in a museum!"

"They were." He gazed at her levelly. "Leal, this country's slide into barbarism didn't start with the Eternists winning the government. Forty years ago they were just a terrorist group—but they had powerful friends. They were protected. And all of this," he waved at the displays, "was once part of the Abyssal Museum of History and Art. Until they blew it up."

Leal examined a glittering chrome thing in another case. She was puzzled. "There was more than this?"

Easley shook his head, smiling slightly. "My grandfather caught wind of a plot to place mines under the wheel, right below the rooms containing the collection. He was curator and he saw which way the wind was blowing; the Eternists were determined to destroy the collection. It's the ultimate refutation of their theory, after all. If they didn't succeed that time, they would keep trying. So, he spirited away the entire collection during Maintenance shift—with a lot of help, obviously!—and let the bombing happen. One whole wing of the museum collapsed—surely you heard of the incident?" He shook his head. "All that was left was a big hole in the wheel and everybody assumed the collection had fallen through it to be scattered to the ends of the world. But it was here. Grandfather had his own allies, after all. And they kept it safe."

He gave a deep sigh. "And after he died, it fell to my father to keep it, and after him . . . Well, it's as you see."

She examined the glittering thing. "There are no labels on the cases."

"That's because nobody knows what any of these things are. They're products of the technological maximum, so each one is unique."

The historian in her had completely overwhelmed Leal's sense of purpose in coming here. She walked around the case, fascinated.

"And nobody knows what the technological maximum is. Or was."

Easley shrugged. "Oh, I know. But Leal, you said you wanted some advice. Is it about William? Because, as you see, I have ample room. The problem is Byron. He gets upset if anything changes, and he, well, he *patrols* downstairs. I'm afraid if we brought William's coffin in here that he would fly into a rage—"

"It's not about William. Or maybe it is, in a way." She blew out a breath, thinking of all the bombshells she could land on him—not least where she was going after this visit.

"Easley, they're rebuilding the department."

She could tell from his expression that he'd heard nothing about it. "I—really? That's . . . surprising."

"It gets a lot more surprising, believe me. They want me to run it."

"Y-you?"

"Me and Hackner."

Easley sat down; or, more accurately, he crumpled onto a golden armchair. Leal sat down across from him, and haltingly told him of her meeting at the Ministry of Education.

"My first clue should have been the building itself," she began. The Ministry had once been housed in a modest, boxy edifice four stories tall that was tucked between two streamlined office towers. It was apparently undergoing a face-lift. Leal had stepped gingerly over coils of rope and into the primitive colonnade formed by the bamboo scaffolding that now sheathed the building. A workman was having his lunch seated atop a freshly carved stone head, his knee up and booted foot resting on an ear of gray asteroidal stone. He gave Leal a casual once-over as she passed.

"Another fellow was plastering the knee of some Eternist saint. They're putting them up to flank the entrance! Can you believe it?"

Easley smirked. "I know. We've seen this sort of institutional art before—but notice how the original carvings have always been replaced by something bland and nondenominational? Or chipped away altogether. In twenty years these saints would be redone as professors, or abstract spirits of enterprise or something . . . Times change, Leal. That was what my grandfather taught me."

And yet, she thought, *here you are.*

Inside, the ministry was hopping; people sped to and fro, held discussions in corners, staggered past carrying huge stacks of paper. Some staffers had the hungover, shocked look Leal had begun to see at the university after the prime minister's visit. Despite the chaos, she was briskly conducted into the minister's office, which was a refreshingly modest little room spoiled only by the religious paintings on its walls.

"Leal, it's good to see you." Gereld Hackner had risen to shake her hand. He'd been seated in one of two eelskin armchairs this side of the minister's desk. Berner Breckian, Minister of Education, popped up from his chair and leaned over (he was a very tall man) to shake her hand as well. Breckian was strikingly handsome, with the sort of cleft in his chin usually reserved for romantic statuary. His hair and suit were perfect. He and Hackner were almost mirror images of one another.

Leal was instantly intimidated by the man. *He's an Eternist idiot,* she reminded herself. *Don't take him seriously.*

He sat and looked from Hackner to Leal briskly. "Well," he said, "this is an exciting time!"

Leal glanced at Hackner, who was smiling effusively.

"Gereld's been talking about you for, oh, ages," continued the minister, turning his smile on Leal. "And when the Interior Minister himself suggested you . . . well. You're one of the best, I hear. That's good, because we need to start off with a bang."

The *Interior Minister* had "suggested her"? Leal sat there with her mouth open for a moment. The sound of hammering came from somewhere nearby. "Excuse me, Minister," she said finally, "just what are we starting?"

Breckian's eyebrows canted toward Hackner. "Gereld, you've kept her in the dark, haven't you?"

Hackner shrugged. "The decision hadn't been made yet."

Breckian clasped his hands on the desktop and fixed Leal with an intent gaze. "We're rebuilding the history department. Sooner than expected, I might add, but there's a need. Leal, we want you on board for it."

"On board . . . in what capacity?" *And what about Porril and the others?*—but she knew she couldn't even mention them right now.

"We need someone to lead the department who's not, um, shall we say, tainted by association with the previous administration," said Breckian. "I offered Gereld here the role, but as he pointed out, he's much more effective behind the scenes. Plus, you had Eustace Loll's recommendation. Of course, Gereld will be your number-one man; you'd rely on him to grease the wheels, keep things on track, you know."

His words were piling up against one another in Leal's brain, defying understanding. "I'd rely on him? F-for what?"

Hackner laughed. "Leal, we want to make you dean of the new department!"

She just stared at him.

"Oh my," said Breckian sympathetically. "We probably should have laid the groundwork for this a bit better than we have. Leal, Gereld's told me about your previous status at the faculty. You should have been offered an appointment years ago. I'm sympathetic with the former dean's attempt to insulate you from recent events— I understand you're even on the payroll, still?" She nodded dumbly. "Porril's a good man." Hackner nodded sanctimoniously. "The fact is," Breckian continued, "that Eternism has triumphed nationally. We can't escape its influence. But those of us with liberal educations . . ." he bent forward slightly, "may have other views."

He sat back, apparently satisfied with his own daring. "History is a vital part of a well-rounded education. I know it, you know it—and in their own dim way, the rest of my cabinet colleagues know it, too. The government's orthodoxy is . . . a bit too strict. We need countervailing views. We need a forum, in fact, where unorthodox views can be aired without fear of reprisal or condemnation. Your department could give us that."

Leal met his eye. "I always thought my job was to learn the truth as accurately as I could, and to communicate that to people."

Breckian and Hackner both laughed as though she'd uttered some witticism. "We need someone who understands the department," Breckian went on briskly, "and who can reconstruct it. Not an administrator—Gereld here can take care of day-to-day business—but a visionary. Someone with a thorough knowledge of the subject we propose to teach. And should you wish to push the curriculum in . . . certain directions . . . we would be happy to look the other way."

Her head was spinning. They were offering her a chance she believed would always remain out of her reach: the chance to run—no to shape—the department itself. "But why . . ." No, she couldn't ask *why me*, she knew why; everybody else with qualifications had been blacklisted. "Why would you give me so much latitude?"

"We believe in academic freedom," said Breckian, "and how would it look if our best and brightest educators abandoned us? We want to raise a generation of gifted and skilled historians, or professionals in other areas who have a sound historical sense. We want them to understand the truth; therefore the core of the curriculum will be Eternism and its view of history. But we'd be short-changing their education if we didn't give them the chance to study countervailing points of view. As long as the core curriculum is there, you can constellate—is that a word?—anything else that you want around it. Even heresies."

"You mean, like the idea that Virga was built by human beings not much more than a thousand years ago?"

Breckian's mouth twisted in refined distaste. "If you feel you must."

"But Eternism is taught as the accepted truth."

"That's right." He grinned at Hackner. "We're on the verge of an exciting new era. I can feel it."

"Do—do I have to give my answer now?"

Breckian waved a hand indulgently. "Take all the time you want. We won't be starting up the department until next term anyway. Just bear in mind that the sooner you're on board, the greater the say you'll have in framing the new curriculum."

"You mean that it's being designed now?"

"I mean that, yes."

"Th-thank you. It's a lot to take in, you see . . . I'll get back to you as soon as I can . . . ?"

"—And there you see," she said now to Easley, "there's the crux of it! All the way home on the damnable crowded trolley, and in the flea car and even as I was walking up to my door it just kept rolling round and round in my head: *Why didn't I say no?*" She buried her face in her hands.

"Ah." Easley had shrunk into the chair as she'd spoken—much as Porril had done in an earlier meeting that she still vividly remembered. He leaned forward, clasped his hands, and to her surprise said, "You didn't say no, Leal, because you care about history."

"W-what do you mean?"

He perched his chin on his hand and contemplated the glass cases surrounding them. "Did you ever consider that history can only happen in a certain kind of, well, frame? There was no history before people moved into towns, started creating nations and such . . . each person, each family had their own private history, unrecorded and free of the weight of theory and calculation. Agriculture and industry standardize people, they make it possible to talk about the actions of large homogeneous groups. We had history for as long as we had those things—oh, about three thousand years. And nowhere in the universe do we have it anymore, except here in Virga. Because once a civilization reaches the technological maximum, there's no standardization anymore. Every single artificial object is unique and custom-made for its particular use. People aren't made to be the same, either, so the only history out there," he nodded at the invisible distant shell of Virga, "is once again the private history of individuals and families. And therefore, Leal, the knowledge we have here of our past and the grand sweep of our nation's life is infinitely precious, because it is not something that can be found anywhere else in today's world. I *revere* it. I believe you do, too."

She stared at him in astonishment. He adopted a sly look. "You were expecting some sort of outburst from me, weren't you? That I would just say no, to Hell with all of them, stand by your principles and let some other quisling sell their soul to the government?"

She looked down. "Well, something like that."

"History is unfair to collaborators," he said; Leal winced at the word. "I think people collaborate because they're trying to make the most of a bad situation," he went on. "I think you are, too. You're too smart to think that what they're asking you to do is any kind of honor. There's no honor in caving in to them. But if you're trying to place yourself so as to act when the Eternists' self-serving world falls apart—then what you're doing is honorable."

Leal looked up at him. "Is it?"

"It is. If you get that chance to act. If not . . . then you go down in history as one of *them*."

Suddenly dizzy, Leal gulped for air. "Yes, that's—that's it, isn't it?"

The prospect of being forever linked with the Eternist cause made her sick with panic. But balancing that was a memory she couldn't ignore—of *Oral Traditions of the Winter Wraiths* fluttering past her grasping fingers and into the blankness of Abyss's sky.

"I have to do it," she said. "Easley, they'll appoint some hatchet man. They'll gut the curriculum, burn the textbooks . . . William's library—oh, the library . . ."

Neither spoke, then, for a very long time. Each was preoccupied, gazing in their separate directions while somewhere behind the partition, Byron snorted and mumbled in his sleep.

"This is an outrageous burden to have to pick up," Easley said at last. Leal blushed, because she now knew that the weight he bore was at least as great, and he had carried it in silence, uncomplaining, for as long as she'd known him. She was sure she never would have learned his secret if she hadn't come here today.

"We all have to do our part," she said, and now her sympathy was with him. "I'll try, Easley, I really will. All I need, to try, is to believe I can save some tiny piece of what we had before."

He rose, nodding somberly. "Good. Now don't forget you have allies. There's me, and I'm sure Porril—he saw this coming—and a few other members of the former faculty. You'll have to be discreet, but you do have us. We'll do what we can."

He led her down the cement steps to the darkened, musty vastness of the lower chamber. As his silhouette unlocked the iron-bound front door, he said, "Now about William. Leal, I'm sorry I haven't been able to take him off your hands yet. I'll arrange the movers to come tomorrow, if you'd like . . ."

"You know what, Easley? This is going to sound morbid, but I've sort of grown used to having him to come home to. It's not like he keeps me up talking or anything . . . You take care of Byron, and don't worry about adding William to your list of worries."

The door was open; she could see her car waiting at the end of the block. In the gray outside light Easley looked at her, then back at the racked, shrouded shapes he was sworn to keep against some future day. His expression was eloquent and, impulsively, she leaned up to kiss him on the cheek.

"Someday, Easley," she said, "all our burdens will be lifted."

He didn't answer right away; but as she reached the street, and just before he closed the door, he quietly said, "It's okay, you know, to admit that's not true."

She turned in surprise; but the door was closed, and she was alone.

TARVEY MET HER at the yacht's hatch with the words, "Did you bring your books?"

Leal ducked out of the way as one of Hayden's trusted workmen jostled some boxes past her. Shouting and the sound of hammering came from deeper inside. "Yes, I brought the damned books," she said. "Now are you going to tell me what this is all about?"

The note he'd sent her had been nearly as cryptic as his first, failed telephone call. *Need a week of your time,* it had said, *starting tomorrow at beginning of Maintenance shift. Job pays well; bring your books and traveling kit.*

Tarvey shot her one of his superior smiles. "We're going hunting. You can help."

"Hunting?" She gaped at him. Over the past couple of days she'd speculated about this possibility but it still seemed insane now he'd put words to it. "You're going out *there*? After the thing?"

"It's kind of . . . expected of us," he said, "after Hayden's little speech the other day. No, it's not his fault," he went on quickly. "The prime minister cornered us, said, 'if you want to stay here, you'll have to pay your rent' or words to that effect. He gets to use us as cannon fodder. Officially, we're off to visit the winter wraiths. As neutrals, we might be able to talk to them; but everybody really knows it's something else causing these attacks, not the wraiths.

"Anyway, we look like heroes if we come back with something, even if it's just a palaver with the wraiths; and nobody mourns us if we get eaten in the dark, 'cause we're just foreigners. A neat solution."

He didn't sound unhappy. Somehow this situation must play to Hayden's current needs, though Leal couldn't imagine how. She started to tell Tarvey how lunatic the whole scheme sounded, but the hatch was choking on more boxes, so she moved out of the way—deeper into the ship, which was opposite to the direction she wanted to go. "But you don't need *me*," she said sweetly as they entered the lounge. "I'm no expert on the wraiths, and all my speculations about worldwasps are just that, speculation."

"Which is more than we've come up with on our own," he said with a shrug.

Leal looked around herself in despair. The yacht's lounge was almost unrecognizable. All the space had been given over to equipment: a dozen or so box cameras hung from straps, their ornately carved sides in stark contrast to the plain metal boxes strapped to the wall opposite the clamshell doors. Leal recognized these as heavy-duty batteries and capacitors from Hayden's workshop. They were the source of numerous thick cables that snaked all through the space to finally end in huge glass bulbs mantled with reflective cones.

Her heart sank. She had dreamed about working with Hayden and his men. Well, now she was.

It would be a simple matter to refuse this offer and leave. Yet right at the moment, her alliance with Hayden was just too valuable to abandon. The whole of the rest of her life seemed precariously balanced to Leal. She needed friends.

She hated being placed in this position.

"Do I bunk with the capacitors, then?"

Tarvey laughed. "Same stateroom as last time, actually. If that's all right with you."

She almost said no, because she remembered Brun there, shuddering under a towel, wild-eyed and unmanned. Reluctantly, she nodded. "A week? Where are we going?"

"That's up to you." Hayden Griffin had entered the lounge from the far end. He grinned at her, and despite herself Leal had to smile back.

He looked good, far better, in fact, than he'd been since she'd met him. Hayden's face was a bit drawn, he looked tired, true, but he also seemed *renewed*, somehow, as though he'd recently come out the other side of some personal storm. He came up now and shook her hand. "I know it's a huge imposition, Leal, but you're one of the few locals we've come to trust. And you know more than professional caution lets you admit."

"What do you mean?"

"Without compelling evidence, you refuse to speculate. But that doesn't mean you don't have *opinions*, does it? Guesses?"

"Well, maybe," she admitted, "but—"

"The problem is we have to act," he said. "Whether or not we have enough evidence to draw conclusions. Which means that *your* guesses are the best thing to go on, right now."

"I can't be responsible for—" Even as she said it Leal realized what such words would mean to Hayden Griffin, who judged the whole of humanity for its sense of obligation, and found it wanting. His eyes narrowed now, and she looked down. He didn't have to say it. *Somebody has to take responsibility.*

"I can suggest more qualified people," she said. "That's all."

"You're the one we trust."

"Would you trust my judgment on who else you should trust?"

"Maybe," he said coldly. "But we're out of time. When we get back, we can discuss who might replace you."

She said nothing.

"I want to visit the winter wraiths, to start with," he said. "The military told us where they think they'd be hiding. I want your opinion."

Damn it! This was far from fair.

She looked him in the eye. "I have not the faintest idea," she said. "The wraiths are not my area of study. But . . . I suppose if you want a place to start, you should try the midden."

He nodded, and seemed to shake off the tension that had held him a moment ago. "Good—and thank you. As it happens, the navy boys said the same thing. Hearing you agree reassures me that they might not be lying."

"Get us under way," he said to Tarvey. "I'll show Dr. Maspeth to her quarters."

"I REALLY AM sorry," he said from the doorway. Leal was shoving her bags under the cargo netting that lined the stateroom's ceiling.

She cocked an eyebrow at him, waiting for him to follow through.

"I'm placing you in an impossible situation," he continued. "It's the same impossible situation the prime minister's put me in."

"So this is payback? An Abyssal puts responsibility on you, so you shove it back onto another Abyssal?"

"That's crude," he said, "and not fair. You're practically the only person in this country who's been brave enough to face some of the more dire possibilities."

She gazed at the dark porthole, thinking. "The airmen at the docks just waved me through," she said after a while. "They'd been expecting me."

"We identified you to the government," he said. "You're cleared to travel with us—actually, to travel anywhere and by yourself if you need to. I thought you might want to drop by your hometown on the way back."

"Oh!" That was genuinely thoughtful; Leal didn't know what to say. "Maybe you should come along," she said, suddenly wishing with a wounded heart that her mother could be there to greet them.

His smile was broad, and even a little bashful. "I'll consider your offer," he said. "Meanwhile, once you're settled, come up to the bridge and give us a tour of the midden. Assuming you've been there?"

She nodded. "I did archaeological work there in second year."

"Good. See you shortly, then."

He closed the door and she started to unpack; but now she, too, was smiling.

THE YACHT NOSED through banks of cloud. For the moment, it was acting like any ordinary ship, but Leal had seen Hayden's airmen mounting powerful electric lamps on the tandem jets of the kite. These idled just a few feet ahead of the ship. Leal had wondered just how bright those lamps might be; clearly Tarvey hadn't told her everything that the kite could do.

In the more ordinary light of the ship's magnesium headlamp, the sky ahead was a shifting patchwork of glimpses. In Virga's winter airs, Earth's oceanic life had met its aerial forms. Minor genetic engineering by the world's creators had enabled the visions Leal now saw, of buzzing, iridescent-winged shrimp pursued by darting, bat-winged otters; of barnacled, weightless stones perched upon by birds whose plumage shone like fire as the light touched it. Leal sat with Hayden's navigator, pointing past these marvelous distractions to beacon lights that flashed in the depths, and the faint threads of rope roads that led up, down, and away. "There are no roads that go straight to the midden?" Hayden asked when he dropped by at one point. Leal shook her head.

"No one visits it on purpose."

"Why not?"

"Stick around. You'll see."

Surprisingly, he did. They chatted about the wonders of the dark as tendrils and pads of pale gray soared past the round window at the center of the bridge. After an hour or so Leal pointed. "See that?"

He squinted. "Behind the cloud?"

"No—the cloud itself. And it's not a cloud."

"Oh shit." It looked like any other twist of vapor in the spreading cone from the headlamp: a mile or so of faded air shaped not like a puffy pillow, but like the fantastical shape created by a single drop of milk in a glass of water. They'd passed through thousands of objects just like it—but none of those had little holes dug out of their sides in which little red bat eyes gleamed. None had been speckled with guano and dots of black grit, or stabbed with broken branches that were draped with spiders' webs.

"Avoid that," Hayden said to the pilot, who laughed, but was already steering them away. The ship's captain, who usually let Hayden run things, put his mouth to a speaking tube and ordered that windows ship-wide should be closed.

"Nasty stuff, those fungalheads," commented Hayden as the pale monster slid by on the starboard side. "Let's hope those other clouds aren't spore-fields."

Leal shook her head. "They will be. You have no idea how bad it's going to get."

Where the air around the city had been a relative desert, here it was crowded with life. They passed monstrous swarms of bugs— flies, midges, and mosquitoes that would settle on any beast that slowed enough for them to catch it. Legless seagulls, flocks of feathered fish, and darting bats fed on the insects, and once or twice they saw the distant shadows of seals, their genetically altered flippers framing their silhouettes like bamboo fans.

"I lived in winter for years," said Hayden, "but I never saw anything like this."

Leal smiled. "There's winter," she said, "and then there's the backward airs. Even we don't go all the way into the dark, you know. Only the wraiths do that."

"Is that why they have such a bad reputation?"

She nodded. "They go where we're afraid to. They've made friends with the night. We never did, not really."

Hayden mused as he watched the flyspecked airs drift past. "And here I thought I'd run to the end of the world when I first came here."

"The air here is still warm," she said. "It wells up from Candesce, bringing trash and bird feces and dust and decay. The whole food chain reverses, what was at the top in the light below is now at the bottom, eaten by bacteria and mold, and that's eaten by flies and so on up the chain."

"And what's at the top?" he asked. "Us?"

She shook her head. "There's whales the size of town wheels, and capital bugs bigger than Sere. We tell stories of the allspider, something so vast and terrible that its web extends across half of Virga. It spins its threads around whole countries, ensnaring them and dragging them into the black, never to be seen again."

"Just a story of course," he said lightly, "unlike the worldwasps."

"There's also the story that Virga itself is the belly of a vast creature. It swallowed a world aeons ago, and is still digesting it."

"So then what's Candesce, to it?"

"Indigestion."

They laughed, but outside, the air was getting thicker. The yacht began to corkscrew as it advanced, avoiding more of the fungal clouds. At the same time, a kind of dry rain had started against the hull, comprising clots of dirt and other, worse things. Something big thumped the glass inches from Leal's nose, and as she reared back it sprouted numerous legs, each as long as her arm, and slid away while scrabbling to get purchase on the slick surface. "Spider," she said to Hayden.

"I've seen bigger," he said. Did he sound nervous?

"Just wait," she said mischievously. "Insects are normally limited to how large they can grow because beyond a certain size, they're easy pickings for smarter mammals and birds. But at the midden," she said, "the tables are turned: it's so toxic in there that higher animals can't go many places, so the bugs grow without limit.

"Then they venture out."

The miles-long threads of fungus and web seemed to deaden the movement of the air. The pilot slowed the yacht as the mess thickened, but the air itself was now freckled with what looked like billions of flakes of snow, all hanging in perfect stillness. Strands of webbing connected some of them in parody of the rope roads humans built between towns. Pulsing in the shadows were hundreds of huge, leathery jellyfish whose stinging arms trailed languidly through the flecks.

Where these flakes and strands touched the yacht's window, they stuck. After a few minutes, the engines of the kite began to choke, and Hayden ordered them brought in.

He and the pilot looked to Leal. "Keep going," she said, "or it'll build up in our engine intakes, too, and bring us to a stop. It's mostly a mix of krill and dead stuff, you know, bacterial colonies that've sprouted off discarded fish scales or leaves. There should only be a mile or so of this. The whales keep it pretty clear—at least, they used to."

Suddenly the pilot shouted, flinging out his arm to point at something. Leal heard the bridge crew gasp, and felt a thrill herself though she'd seen this sight before.

"That's been there for centuries," she said reassuringly. "We think there was a plague or something, and the survivors towed it here as a kind of permanent quarantine. . . . This is good, I know where we are now."

Only a fraction of the town wheel was visible in the yacht's headlight. It hadn't spun for many decades, and so the ribbon of wooden planking had gone off-round, its spoke ropes long since slackened into draping hairlike threads, all overgrown with mold and waving, dry-skinned anemones.

Leal could make out the outlines of houses and shops, softened by centuries' accumulation of mold. "Was this your archaeological dig?" asked Hayden. She shook her head.

"Too dangerous to stop here. They've tried it, gone in wearing sargasso suits, with the ships' engines running off batteries so they don't have to suck in any of this air, but you know batteries don't last long. And the work here consists mostly of shoveling mold; not even a hungry post-doc is going to do that."

"You said you know where we are," said the pilot. "What should I do?"

"Straight ahead, about three miles. You'll know when we get there."

Their view was half-hidden by matted black and gray stuff by the time the yacht finally strained into clear air. "Our aerodynamics are ruined," said the pilot. "We can't maneuver with this crap on us."

Hayden glared at Leal. "You should have warned us about that. How are we going to turn if we get into a firefight?"

"It comes off," she said meekly. "Keel-haul ropes, that's how we did it."

"Well, we're going to have to call a halt while we do that."

"All right," she said, "but we're there anyway." She nodded out toward the horribly stained glass.

He looked outside, and swore softly.

Everybody had done it at one time or another: you were working outside, or traveling between the cities and taking a bit of air at a gallery window, when you let go of a hammer and didn't notice it drifting off; or your hat blew off in the ship's slipstream. Everyone had made that instantaneous mental calculation—can I reach it?—and, in so many cases, decided *no*. Leal's last such moment had come as she watched *Oral Traditions of the Winter Wraiths* tumbling away from the city, opening and closing as though casually reading itself.

Sometimes, things other people had lost came to you in the same way. You were working outside, when you suddenly turned your head and received somebody's long-lost flowerpot in the face. Or, you leaned over the gallery rail to get a better look at a distant winking sun, and found yourself half-strangled by a passing sarong or length of rope.

Conventional wisdom held that most lost objects would eventually be found, or failing that would drift at last into the precincts of Candesce, there to be incinerated and recycled. There were rumors, of course—theories that anything dropped would go the other way if undisturbed, wandering after years into zones of dead air deep inside winter. Some meteorologists claimed that the patterns of air movement within Virga guaranteed the existence of such motionless regions. If they existed, then the lost socks of a hundred nations would eventually find their way there.

"So it's true," Hayden murmured now, and Leal knew he was referring to that theory. Facing them across a half-mile of empty air was a vast wall of *stuff*, dimly picked out in the headlight but so bewilderingly detailed and varied that Leal was always grateful she couldn't see it all at once.

There were hammers and hats here, and flowerpots and sarongs; and there were larger things. Bed frames, doors, countless thousands of town planks and rigging ropes, as well as toilets and chests, shark cages and trees, propellers and cannon, toys and swords and whole ships had inched together over the aeons and, when they touched, became glued by rust, dust, or mold. Chance and friction had assembled them into bizarre shapes, knife tip to cup's rim, cup's handle to turbine axle.

"Be careful," Leal warned the pilot. "Electrostatic forces dominate here. You'd better throw out a grounding wire."

Hayden nodded. "If that pile is negatively charged and we're positive, it could throw a lightning bolt at us."

"Well, yes, but worse than that, it could throw *itself*." To the million sewing needles and buttons drifting here, a statically charged ship might exert the strongest pull they'd felt in decades. All those small and light objects would come, and their collective mass might pull bigger things with them. Leal told Hayden and the crew a story about a superstitious crew driven mad with terror when the ancient garbage extruded arms and hands to encircle their ship.

Sparks lit the midden in instantaneous glimpses as the ground wire shot ahead of the ship. Watching, Leal was mesmerized not just by the sight of the place, but by the return of a forgotten memory. During her time here, she'd often felt a strange prickle, an emotion she had no name for, that came from seeing so many products of human hands transformed back into natural objects. These shacks and handles, tables and picture frames had all once possessed a human meaning, that indefinable spirit *made* things have, that allows human beings to automatically and instinctively identify something as artificial. In the random jumble of the midden, that spirit had fled, yet the eye said, "yes, that's a saw" or "I recognize that quilt pattern." The mind waged a kind of war with itself, unable to settle on an identity for the things it saw.

And, once or twice in her time here, Leal had felt a premonition. The uncanny feeling had come to her that none of these things had ever really held that spirit of humanity—that it had always been an illusion. That there was not and never had been a human world, only nature itself, random and triumphant.

Although she could not remember the words it had spoken, something about the voice she'd heard issue from the darkness beyond the wraith fleet . . . had made her feel that same way.

"Now where?" asked Hayden as the yacht came to a halt a hundred yards from the midden's wall. Leal shrugged.

"The wraiths won't initiate contact unless they can control the situation. I'd just trawl slowly through the place and keep your lights on. If they decide you're not a threat, they may approach."

The midden was not a solid object. It was holed, cleft, and shredded in countless ways. The ship found an avenue into it and soon they were edging through tunnels and chimneys of trash. Leal saw round and oval spots of light judder and wave across the balanced chaos; Hayden's men must have climbed out onto the hull with those big clumsy spotlights from the lounge. The lights were very bright, penetrating the lattice of trash for many yards and throwing back tantalizing and deceptive flashes of silver and gold. "How long will those last?" Leal asked him.

"As long as we want," he said. "They're running off the starter."

It took her a minute to realize what he'd said. "You mean the *nuclear fusion reactor in the hold? It's on?*"

He nodded. "In pulsed mode. It comes on for a microsecond at a time and dumps power into the capacitor banks. What doesn't get recycled to drive the next pulse trickles into the lamps' batteries. We could keep them lit 'til we all died of old age if we wanted." He finally noticed her expression and said, "Don't worry, it's fusing boron. No neutrons."

Leal fell silent. She'd had enough of wonders, and after a few minutes she excused herself. It might be hours or days before the wraiths showed up, if they even chose to. She returned to her stateroom, discovering that she'd still not unpacked, and strapped herself onto the wall to sleep.

The ship must have spent the next few hours threading the midden's maze. She awoke to find the vessel quiet, its engines a distant hum. The lounge's big doors were open, letting in a familiar, musty odor, but nobody was inside. Searchlights wobbled across the chaos outside; there must be men standing on the hull. Leal sailed on through without looking for them, and on down the central hall to the crew's mess. A couple of tired-looking airmen were hanging like bats from the ceiling, slurping at something that drove the smell of the midden completely away. "Where can I get some of that?" Leal asked them.

One of the men replied, "It'll cost ya." He was a sly-looking man of short stature and quick movements.

Leal supposed that she only had to visit the galley to find a meal, but his tone reminded her of schoolyard challenges of her girl-hood; and she'd never ducked one of those. "What's your price?"

"You're the historian, right? You know about this place?" He nodded at the strange shifting skyscape outside the ship.

"I've been here before."

He elbowed his companion. "Then you know! What the hell is this place? Where are we?"

Leal thought for a moment. Then: "Have you ever heard the story of the parliament of the flies?"

They both shook their heads.

"Well," she said. "It goes like this. Once there was an august, respected prime minister. He presided over the parliament of one of the Principalities of Candesce, a nation bathed in light and dense with cities, forests, farms, and the soaring commerce of a dozen neighboring countries. This man had never been defeated in election; the people loved him. He was wise and a just admin-istrator. For all these reasons, those who hated him did so with ever greater intensity.

"One night his enemies staged a coup. As he and his family dined with friends in the official residence, they drank drugged wine, and all fell asleep. The soldiers who were supposed to kill them had second thoughts, though. The lieutenant who led them couldn't do it. Instead, he had their slumbering bodies taken to the naval yards, and gaining access to a maintenance facility found a giant missile whose warhead was of course stored somewhere more secure. He put the prime minister and his family inside it; and then, realizing that having let them live, he couldn't return to the conspirators himself and expect to survive . . . he climbed in himself. His loyal men fired the missile and it left the Principali-ties traveling at twice the speed of sound.

"It came to a final rest . . . *here.*

"When the prime minister awoke he found himself and his family in the strange mad cloudscape of the midden. The lieutenant could not or would not bring himself to explain; in any case, the shock of going from wealth, honor, and absolute power to being stranded in choking trash in a desert of darkness—it drove the prime minister mad."

She certainly had their attention. Behind the heads of the two airmen, ovals of white light roved over walls of impossible detail—planking, discarded clothes, strange raveling rope nests . . . Leal brought her eyes back to her audience.

"He refused to accept this place he'd come to. The days wore on and the lieutenant hunted for food and his wife and daughters dug a kind of warren out of the debris. The prime minister sat and brooded. Then, one day, he flew off into the maze and was not seen again for two days. When they found him, he was giving a speech.

"The prime minister had found a kind of natural amphitheater carved by wind or chance out of the clouds of flotsam. At one end of this he had mounted an old barber's chair, where the Speaker of the House would have his seat in a real parliament. In parallel rows, facing one another, he'd constructed the two sides of a parliamentary house, peopling the seats of garbage with men and women sculpted of garbage. And in one gallery, he was pretending to stand. 'Point of order, Mr. Speaker,' he would say, and then he'd launch into some wonderfully detailed and knowledgeable recitation of the law of that nation he'd lost—words that would have held meaning two thousand miles away, but were just a gabble of sound here (and it was that sound that had led his family to him, his voice being the only thing in centuries to break the absolute silence and stillness of this place).

"Here in his House, he was happy, so they brought him food and moved their abode, such as it was, nearby. And he went on addressing the statues of garbage in this way for years.

"Then one day, during an exhortation as simultaneously creative and repetitious as all the others, the prime minister paused for breath and heard someone else shout, 'Mr. Speaker!' "

Leal paused, arching an eyebrow and shooting a sidelong smile at her captivated audience. "The prime minister peered through the dim brown of the blubber-oil lantern light, and there facing him across the sketchy aisle was a ragged, hollow-eyed madman, practically a mirror-image of himself. The refugee of some shipwreck or a sad exile, who knows?, he had clutched with desperate hands to some half-felt presence in the blackness, and found that thing attached to something else. Following the chain of objects, he'd wound up in the midden. A braver man might have built a boat and tried to escape—our prime minister's lieutenant was still trying to do that—but this man, barely alive, had resigned himself to staying. And the mesmerizing constant performance of the prime minister had drawn him, like a spider's web, into this chamber.

"He proceeded to argue. Everything and anything the prime minister might propose, this man would argue with. They railed at one another across the narrow aisle; they took their disputes right to the feet of the ragged fencing dummy that perched in the Speaker's chair. They'd talk themselves hoarse, and then at the end of the day's session, retire to their separate dwellings to brood.

"After some months, a second man appeared. Without being asked, he dislodged the fencing dummy and took the Speaker's chair. He listened to the disputes, called points of order, and generally presided. At the end of the day he, too, slunk away to some unknown warren.

"The parliament grew. The hapless spindrift of shipwrecks found themselves puncturing the soft skin of the midden, and wound up here; fleeing criminals, betrayed lovers, incompetent adventurers, and men considered outlaws even by pirates, all found themselves on one day or another hovering at the edge of the half-lit parliament, listening to a skirl and play of words as intricate and beautiful as any they'd ever heard. The topics of argument ranged across all the follies of humanity; nothing was sacred. Half a dozen voices would clamor for one side or the other of an argument and the listeners would find that they could not remain neutral. So they would enter, and make their own seats amid the trash.

"Eventually the prime minister's lieutenant did escape, taking with him the old man's daughters and a few of the midden's latest visitors. When they reached civilization, they told people about the parliament, and rumors began to spread.

"After a while, a new kind of visitor began to appear in the old man's cavern. Daring poets found their way to the parliament; so did passionate young revolutionaries, romantics and mystics and dreamers of all sorts. Actual pews were built of salvaged shipwreck wood; better lights were brought in. People came who felt too modest to debate, but were happy to take on roles as hunters and mushroom farmers, cooks and builders. They provided the Speakers with a living. Meanwhile the debates became sharp, focused, and increasingly relevant to events unfolding in the outside world. And gradually, it became impossible to tell whether the prime minister was mad or not, because his parliament had become real.

"Policy papers began making their way out of the midden, and into the hands of opposition members and disgruntled generals and beer-hall agitators in a dozen different countries. Men with the fire of purpose in their eyes sailed out of the dark and tried to topple ancient empires and the slogans on their lips had first been spoken in the amber light of the parliament of the flies.

"Some of the heads of state, threatened by the rise of this new power, convened an emergency meeting. They put their heads together and decided that the stream of words coming from the darkness was too powerful to be ignored. These words were beautiful. They were inspiring. They spoke of things that men had turned from seeing for centuries, and made it impossible anymore to ignore them. This could not be tolerated.

"So a fleet was gathered, dark as a storm cloud in the eternal light of Candesce. It surged into the blackness of winter and it found the midden, and then for twenty days and nights its ships pounded the parliament with missiles, until every man, woman, and child in this place was dead."

She stopped. The searchlights were jittering strangely outside; she could hear shouting. "And what about the old man?" asked one of the airmen. His food had grown cold as he listened to her.

"As the midden collapsed in on itself, his body hove into view. It was half-wrapped in a homemade shroud, and a crown of rusted bolts surmounted his writhing white locks. The spotlights of the fleet found him—first one, then five, then a hundred lights. He shone like a sun himself, and on his face was a steadfast expression that burned itself into the minds and hearts of all who saw, and caused them to shake their heads and refuse to call what they'd done a victory, to the end of their days. He appeared calm, the prime minister, and proud, as a man who had spoken the truth and knows that however much people might protest and jeer, that they have heard him."

The yacht lurched suddenly. Leal grabbed for a cross-rope to steady herself, and the airmen tossed their wicker dish-balls aside with one motion. "What the—?" Throughout the ship sirens suddenly shrieked.

The ship's engines had reversed and for a moment a hot wash of jet exhaust fluttered through the lounge. Leal's head reeled from the smell of burnt alcohol. The spotlight circles had disappeared outside, but a gray glow came from somewhere ahead of the ship; they must all be aimed in that direction.

The two airmen set to climbing outside, but one—the sly-faced one—looked back at Leal before disappearing. "Is it true?" he shouted.

"What? The story?"

"Yeah. The story. The parliament."

"We never found any sign of it when I was here."

He nodded and disappeared after his fellow.

When the ship's motion had become predictable again—it was decelerating quickly—Leal let go of her rope and let herself fall up the central corridor to the bridge. She climbed in, finding that the round windows at the prow of the ship now felt like the bottom of an empty pool beneath her. As the engines cut out and they began to drift, she found her way to the command chair where Hayden Griffin was sitting tensely. He hadn't noticed her arrival, and she turned to find out what it was that had so caught his attention.

The yacht had entered a gigantic hollow in the heart of the midden. It must be half a mile across, an irregular cavern in a world made of garbage. The white shafts of the yacht's spotlights were all oriented forward, at what awaited them in the center of that space.

Ten, twenty—fifty or more black torpedo shapes flared into visibility, then vanished again as the spotlights swooped past. The more the lights probed, the more dark shapes they found.

"It's a fleet," murmured Hayden.

And as if his words had been heard somewhere out there, the dark shapes suddenly became peppered with light, a vast sparkling as thousands of gun ports and portholes opened in the ships of the winter wraith fleet.

FOUR SHIPS CLOSED on the yacht from four directions. Leal could see the blur of exhaust from their engines in the brightening air of the giant cavern.

Tarvey appeared from the doorway she'd just come through. "Hayden?" He seemed out of breath. "It's more than we bargained for."

"Considerably," said Hayden. He stared at the massed fleet, clearly counting its number. "It looks like everyone's underestimated the winter wraiths."

Now Leal could see bikes—simple wingless jet engines with a saddle and handlebars—swarming from open hatches on some of the ships. They blackened the vista like a cloud of flies, filling the cavern with a vicious snarling sound as they moved to encircle the yacht.

Hayden was suddenly out of his seat and on his way to the door. "Come on!" Tarvey followed him, and Leal went after them both.

The two men swung out onto the hull of the yacht from the open lounge. Leal poked her head up as well, but she needed at least two walls within touching distance. She watched Hayden and Tarvey hand-walk up a rope to where a cluster of airmen stood with their spotlights. The spotlights were drifting now, because the airmen all had their hands up. A dozen bikes hovered in the air not twenty feet away, and their riders had rifles leveled at the airmen.

"I'm in command here," Hayden shouted to the men on the bikes. "I'll answer for my men."

Beyond him, the vast black bulk of a wraith ship slid silently to a halt, its open gun ports aimed straight at the nose of the yacht.

A hatch opened in the side of that ship and Leal could see someone silhouetted against its red interior light. "Surrender yourselves and your vessel!" someone shouted.

"We're not here to argue," said Hayden. "We came here to find the people some call winter wraiths."

"Your ship is armed. It's disguised as a merchant ship. What are we supposed to make of that?"

"My name is Hayden Griffin. I'm the sun lighter of Aerie, and I've come to talk to you."

"About what?"

"About whatever it is that's out there. In the dark."

Leal heard the unmistakable sound of a gun being cocked, and turned to see four men in jewel-toned brocade jackets hanging in the air behind her. Their backs were surmounted by clockwork wings. One was aiming his rifle at her head.

Leal choked off a hysterical laugh. She found she was babbling—saying things that made no sense even to her, as she turned and put up her hands. All she could see was those guns aimed at her.

Ten minutes later, she found that somehow—she had no memory of how, exactly—she had come to be hanging in weightless, freezing air, her fingers tangled in the strands of a thick net that belled out around her to encompass the whole crew of the yacht. The air reeked of mold, dust, and rust; her teeth were chattering; and though everybody around her seemed to be talking at once, Leal couldn't make sense of anything anybody was saying. All she could think was, *I've lost everything!*

Fixed like a photograph in her mind was every detail of that night when the Abyssal navy had paraded their captive wraiths in front of avid photographers and bright-eyed newsmen. She remembered those downcast faces, the uncertainty about where to stand, whether to look up or keep one's eyes on the street . . . their eyes had told that they knew they were *things* now, no more likely to experience justice than any other stamped and numbered piece of government ordnance. They were things, but they still had the memory of being free people. Memory—of Seana's face, her mother's, of drinking in the market, teaching—was it all going to turn to poison now?

She sobbed in helpless fear.

Some of the words coming at Leal began to make sense: "What are they gonna do with us?" "—They gonna torch the ship? Take it?" She shook her head, as if they'd asked her instead of the empty air.

Some of the yacht's crew were muttering about cutting through the net, but there were a dozen sharp-eyed wraiths with rifles watching the net. It was hopeless.

Leal clutched the net and closed her eyes, willing the whole thing to just be over. Were they going to be paraded like the wraiths had been back home? Thrown into cells? She somehow doubted the wraiths had room in those slim ships for prisons. They'd be enslaved, then, or sold. Or killed.

Hayden Griffin's voice cut through her panic. "Careful of the engine in the hold! It's liable to give you a nasty shock!"

Leal blinked and looked over. Griffin was a couple of yards above her, his face pressed against the net. He was watching with agitated intensity as the wraiths systematically searched his ship.

The winter wraith who'd ordered their surrender was also watching the process. Hearing Hayden, he flapped up and said, "What is that thing? A generator, or a battery?"

"A bit of both," said Hayden cheerfully. "I can draw you up some plans, if you're interested."

The wraith narrowed his huge eyes. "Why would you do that?"

"Because I'm a businessman."

Leal stared at Hayden in utter disbelief. Didn't he understand what had happened here? The wraiths had assembled a fleet in secret, and they'd stumbled upon it. Surely this fleet was bound for Sere where it would burn and plunder. It might sweep by Taura Two on the way . . . Horrible things were about to happen, all touched off by her own government's stupidity, and Leal and Griffin and everybody else here was caught up in the machinery. He couldn't possibly think he could talk his way out of this?

Despite the nonsense he was speaking, the tone of his words had broken through the core of Leal's terror. Despite the jabbering of her inner voice, she found herself stealing a look at the wraith commander. She'd lived with Telen Argyre, who had wraith heritage, but she'd never seen a male wraith up close. She'd often wondered what they looked like.

The wraiths were cursed by ancient genetic engineering. The *anime mods*, they were called: a set of cosmetic changes that included height, symmetrical features, huge eyes, small chins, and delicate, elfin ears. The old laws had forbidden all but cosmetic modifications; Leal understood that this had been an attempt to prevent the formation of new human species. But the anime mods were a subversive end-run around the rules, because the visual effect of those huge eyes and delicate jaws was to inspire deep maternal and paternal instincts in people. The fact that everybody instinctively liked them gave the wraiths a tremendous advantage in society.

With his huge, liquid eyes and expressive mouth, Leal had to admit that the wraith commander was very handsome.

That face was no indicator of the spirit behind it. The wraiths' beauty was a ploy, all the worse because it was so effective. It was no wonder, she decided bitterly, that these people were distrusted and shunned throughout Virga. The loyalty and love she'd so recently felt for Telen and Antaea Argyre had been erased by her fear.

The wraiths' commander was dressed in a kind of outlandish, piratical costume, with lots of bright colors, brocades, and tassels.

It seemed playful, an imitation of military style, but comparing him to his men she could see that there were indicators of rank hidden amongst the velvet and gleaming buttons. The wraiths distrusted their beauty, too, it seemed; theirs was a rigidly hierarchical society. Telen had claimed that as one of the reasons she and her sister had left.

". . . Agree that we have no quarrel," Hayden was saying. "We're citizens of Aerie, we're just visiting Abyss."

"There are no embassies among us," said the commander. The familiarity of his accent made Leal shut her eyes again. "There are no jails, either, nor work ships to send you to. We need all our people to fight."

"What are you saying? That you're going to kill us all?" The comradely tone was gone from Hayden's voice. "For something someone else did?"

"We've got no choice as I see it," said the commander. "Apologies, if that helps." He turned and his wings swept up to cup the air.

Hayden shouted after him. "We came to offer our help! Not against Abyss—you know Abyss's not the root of the problem. It's the thing! That thing in the dark! We came to find it, and kill it!"

Leal barely heard him; eyes squeezed shut, she held the netting so tightly it was cutting into her skin.

"What do you know about the emissary?"

She opened her eyes. The commander had paused, was looking back.

"Abyss wouldn't be lashing out at you if they weren't hurting," Hayden said quickly. "They've lost ships—whole towns. I'm betting those are not your fault. I bet you've also had run-ins with it, whatever it is.

"Before you kill us, take another look at that engine in the hold of my ship. We used it to power the spotlights you saw earlier. But it can do more. Much more than anything you have in your own ships."

An eloquently skeptical look crossed the commander's beautiful face. "Why? What is it?"

"It's a miniature sun. And I believe we could use it to kill the creature."

The commander's eyes widened.

"That's why we came to find you," Hayden pressed—too late as he noticed the fury now distorting the commander's features.

Leal couldn't speak but she wanted to yell, *No no, too much, you've said too much!*

"You seem to assume," said the wraith commander, "that we *want* to destroy the emissary."

Now Hayden said nothing. Behind him, his men were starting to glance at one another. They knew that a line had been crossed.

"We who live in the darkness have nothing to fear from the emissary," said the commander. "Your people cower in the little globes of light made by machines like the one in your ship, terrified that something will remind you of what you rejected so many centuries ago—of the transcendence you sold for *this!*" He waved his hand to encompass the midden and Virga beyond it. "You dragged humanity into this pit of darkness and you slammed the door, and now for centuries those of us who remind you of what you rejected, we've borne the brunt of your bitterness and bile. Today is no different. The emissary is not here to punish us— it comes from outside, from the transcendent *beyond.* Its words hold no terror for *us.*"

Leal stared at the man. Nothing that he was saying sounded anything at all like Telen or Antaea. The Argyres had never spoken in fanatical terms—but more importantly, they'd never spoken of fanaticism as a cultural trait of the wraiths. Neither did any of the histories Leal was familiar with. So then, what . . . ?

"You keep saying this thing's an emissary," shouted Hayden. He was clearly desperate now. "Emissary of what?"

The commander gave an ugly laugh. "That which you rejected long ago at the start of the world. The very thing that your sun of suns, Candesce, keeps at bay, which would otherwise sweep across this vale of sorrow and lift us all to eternal bliss.

"The crier in the dark is *the emissary of the Singularity!*"

Before she could stop herself, Leal laughed out loud.

ALL EYES WERE on her, including Hayden's and the wraith commander's. *Now you've done it,* she thought—but they were all going to die anyway and though they might get away with that, there was no way Leal was going to let these idiots get away with feeling smug about it.

"I notice that you're in a bit of a hurry," she said acidly. The sudden spike of outraged disbelief had sharpened her mind and she was noticing things that had escaped her attention until now. "Could it be because you're not really the one in charge around here?"

Hayden worked his way over to her. "Leal, what are you doing?" he whispered.

The commander was glaring at her. "It's ironic," she continued loudly, "that at the same time as Abyss's government is taken over by religious fanatics, that the wraiths should suffer from a similar disease." Leal was directing her words at the commander, but she wasn't speaking to him. Behind him, two of the riflemen glanced at one another.

"In Abyss, it's the Eternists who've gained the upper hand—for now," she said. "It sounds like the transhumanists have made their move among the wraiths, but I'm betting you're still a minority. You're pretty eager to get rid of us. Could it be because you're afraid that your superiors might actually listen, if they got a chance to hear what we're proposing?"

"Shut up!" The commander drew his pistol and aimed it at her.

Leal realized with a sick feeling that he was actually going to fire just as strong hands grabbed her waist and yanked her back. She heard the gunshot, but felt nothing.

"Kill them all!"

"But sir—"

"Do you want to join them? Shoot them now!"

"With respect sir! *Listen!*"

They all fell silent, Hayden's airmen, the wraith soldiers. Leal held her breath.

Far away, and very faint but growing, a powerful voice was speaking.

IGNORING THE SHOUTS of their commander, the airmen stowed their rifles and kicked their jets into life. Horns sounded in the distance, first one, then half a dozen. Leal turned to see the wraith fleet roiling with disorganized motion.

But was that really the voice she'd heard once before, that other time she'd encountered the wraith? She strained to make out what it was saying.

"I have come to tell you . . ."

A hand encircled her upper arm, and Hayden Griffin drew her over. "How did you know he didn't have the authority?" he asked.

She shrugged glumly. "I've gotten used to spotting a particular kind of man lately. They're all over Sere right now. —But no, it wasn't that, it was their uniforms." The wraith uniforms, however diverse and individualistic, did have a consistent pattern to their decoration that clearly denoted rank. Leal had noticed the pips on the jackets of the riflemen, and of the men moving in and out of the yacht. "This 'commander' only had two more of those golden beads on his shoulder than any of his men. He was low-level, and clearly in a hurry. Transhumanism isn't a normal feature of wraith culture, so it was likely he was in a hurry because other orders

might come from one of the real commanders at any time . . ."
Hayden was shaking his head, but his expression was admiring.

"Way to keep your head," he said.

But I only noticed that stuff about a minute ago . . . "He tried to shoot us anyway."

"But if you're right, we may get a second chance to talk our way out of this."

"Listen!"

". . . How your world is going to end."

The airmen detached themselves from the netting around her, and plastered themselves over the far side of the net. They were all staring at something distant and, after a moment, Leal and Hayden joined them. At first Leal couldn't see what was making the men shout and point: she saw the wraith fleet reorienting itself to face one wall of the vast cavern, and the dim light washed through a gray mist that had come to cling there. There were no big moving objects there, no worldwasp or dragon . . .

Yet from somewhere a mighty voice was speaking, saying, *"Just as there was a time before Man, there will be a time after"*—and the wall of the cavern was moving. It undulated slightly, but at this distance each of those waves must be pushing the material out by twenty or more feet. Bits of trash broke free and drifted into the air.

"That time has come in all places save one."

She knew those words, she'd heard them somewhere before. Just now, though, Leal was too addled and distracted to think about it. The wraith ships were deploying their own spotlights and she watched these rove over the plane of garbage, picking out intricate details and yet revealing nothing of what was making the stuff move. Then one spotlight beam happened to pass over one of the chunks that had torn free. It was only lit for a second but everyone in the net shouted as one. The shaft of light stopped, then slid back as if whoever was directing it had heard the Aerie airmen.

The beam fixed a random tumble of junk that was embedded

in its own little wisp of cloud. It couldn't have been more than ten feet across, this junklet—but it was moving. Its sticks and broken pans and holed tanks and torn sailcloth were crawling over one another as though manipulated by invisible hands; and now Leal saw that those pieces that moved were particularly blurred by mist.

Somebody yelled "It's the fog!" and suddenly it was obvious. The pale cloud breathing itself out of the midden's trash was bringing that trash with it, and reconfiguring it as it came. Within seconds the whole face of the cavern wall dissolved outward in a kind of silent, slow explosion. Horns blared again through the wraith fleet and everything leaped into stark relief in the sudden light of rocket fire.

Twenty missiles from as many ships arrowed into the expanding debris cloud; Leal saw bright flashes and seconds later heard the thud of the explosions. She'd never seen such weapons actually fired, only read about them in books.

In the dying echoes the great voice said, *"Virga is about to die."*

"It's not working," said Hayden. "They're just helping it!"

The detonating missiles had broken up the trash, but that seemed to make it easier for the fog to manipulate. Where there had been big chunks before, now there were countless smaller clouds, each one flipping over and through itself in queasy motion.

A bike zipped up close to one such clot. Though it was too far away to see its rider's face, his reaction to what he saw was clear: as the bike sailed on past he threw up his hands and suddenly he and the bike had parted ways. It shot into the wall and disappeared and he fell, writhing, into the heart of the debris cloud.

Leal blinked. She'd lost sight of him because somehow, there were a hundred struggling men there now—no, make that a thousand all turning in the air where the trash had been a moment before. At least, they looked like men . . .

She had to get out of this net, now, *now now now*— The airmen were shouting, kicking one another in their haste to get away from what they were seeing. Some were tearing at the net with their teeth but Leal didn't care, she just had to get away—

Horns, rocket fire, and gunfire, distant and nearby screams, and over it all a vast and terrible voice thundered, *"I HAVE COME TO TELL YOU HOW YOUR WORLD WILL END. YOUR WORLD IS MORTAL. VIRGA IS ABOUT TO DIE, UNLESS—"*

The dark sky was choked by mighty wings and their pulsing overwhelmed the voice. The airmen were hauling on the netting, parting it strand by strand; there were no wraiths around to stop them, but something else, a flock of grotesque and impossible shapes, came to encircle them. Everyone was screaming.

The light of missile blasts flashed over cloth-and-plastic wings, limbs made of cans and spars and string, faceless heads jostled together out of wicker balls and buttons and knives.

With a thud something landed opposite Leal on the net. She felt cold metal and wood fingers twine through hers and she was staring into a broken lamp with two twitching feather quills erupting from it like eyebrows. Fine white strands, like the hair of a fungus, joined the parts together.

It shook the net and from the lamp the great voice came, only inches away now:

"UNLESS YOU GIVE US CANDESCE!"

She screamed.

The airmen had torn the net and were boiling through it. Makeshift hands pawed at them, a garbage-built parody of a man riding on the shoulders of each airman now, pulling at their hair, yelling in their ears.

"Come on!" Hayden put his arm around her waist and kicked free of the netting. The shadowed outline of the yacht loomed very close but they had nothing to grab hold of, no wings, and now a black flying shape was reaching out to cup Hayden's face in fingers made of pencils and hanger wire.

"GIVE US—" He rolled around the thing and planted his feet

on it, then kicked. He was still holding Leal and their momentum took them into the open lounge of the yacht. Other airmen had made their way through the shouting madness, too, and some were grabbing at weapons from a net where the wraiths had collected them. Hayden pried Leal's hands from him and put himself between the men and the net. "No!"

Leal glanced back. The sky was a cauldron. Creatures had invaded every hatch and gun port of the wraith fleet. Their silhouettes were visible in flashes as they roared and shouted and clutched at the men inside. The fleet's panicked gunners were firing indiscriminately and while their missiles were missing nearly all the monsters they inevitably found a mark among the crowded vessels. The air outside was full of struggling shapes as wraith airmen engaged the monsters with swords and pistols.

Tarvey was waving a lantern. "Inside! You, cast a line to those men. We need to get underway! No! No weapons! Don't fight them!"

Smack! Splinters sprayed Leal as a hole suddenly appeared in the door frame next to her hand. The distant machine gunfire was suddenly all too clear to her; she shrank into the ship even as another winged apparition glided past.

All the airmen were inside. Four of them were hauling on the winches to close the clamshell doors, even as a dozen vaguely man-shaped things clambered over them to get in. Hayden had disappeared somewhere, probably the bridge.

Leal jumped for the central corridor and bounced from handhold to foothold up it while something loud banged and clattered right behind her. It was gaining, she wouldn't make it to the bridge in time, so she grabbed the latch of her cabin and let her momentum turn it. She flopped hard against the wall, then used one of Uthor's leverage moves to swing back again and through the door—

—But something else was crowding through it with her. In the weak flickering red light coming through the porthole, she glimpsed long metal-and-wood limbs, a lopsided brass head, as it reached for her. The thing reeked of rust.

"YOU MUST LISTEN!" it roared. The words were so loud they hurt Leal's ears and she cowered back, fetching up against the back wall. The ship was accelerating, making this wall a floor. Big metal staples closed on her forearms; she could feel a strange vibration through them, different from the thrum of the ship's engines at her back.

"SIGNIFY!" bellowed the monster.

"W-what?" In the light of another outside explosion, she made out the face inches from her own. It was an idiot's sculpture made with random junk, none of it adding up to anything human, yet those can-lid eyes seemed alive and their gaze somehow fixed on her.

"SIGNIFY THAT YOU UNDERSTAND ME."

"I understand you!"

"SIGNIFY THAT YOU UNDERSTAND ME!" It shook her by the wrists. Leal screamed.

"SIGNIFY THAT—" Two airmen pulled the monster off her. As it spun in midair, they lit into it with sledgehammers and junk flew everywhere. Something sharp cut Leal's cheek.

The caroming pieces of the monster seemed to seek each other out. The white fibers that connected them stretched out, made net-shapes to catch drifting pieces, and the creature reassembled itself. She saw that it now incorporated her hairbrush and, wrapped around its spine, her nightdress.

"—YOU UNDERSTAND ME!"

It batted the airmen aside and came at Leal again.

"SIGNIFY!"

Leal whimpered. Cringing, she felt the cold metal hands encircle her wrists again, and she realized there was no escaping it. No weapon could destroy it, no words placate it. She put her head back and wailed in despair.

It let go.

The airmen were picking themselves up, reaching desperately for their hammers. Bangs and scraping noises echoed through the ship and it shuddered as it hit multiple things. The monsters? Or was the pilot trying to stab the ship through the midden's tissues?

"YOU UNDERSTAND ME."

"I—?" The thing took a step forward, reaching out again—

—and fell apart.

Moments later the acceleration ended, though the ship still rang from impacts against the hull. Leal and the two airmen had been squatting motionless against the back wall, and as weight left they all reflexively reached for a handhold. That motion broke the spell of silence that had come over them.

"It's dead?" One of the airmen batted at something; the other man lit one of the room's gaslights. The sudden brightness revealed a galaxy of prosaic objects: boots, gears, a torn fishing net, splintered wood. All were tufted with a kind of white fuzz that, as one of the airmen touched it, crumbled to dust.

"Why—?" These were the two men to whom she'd told the story of the parliament of the flies.

The ship shuddered again, so they all went to the now-open door. Hayden Griffin was emerging from the hatch that led to the hold.

"It worked?" he said. "Tell me it worked!"

The sly-faced airman laughed. "What did you do?"

"There's a little trick with the generator," said Hayden. "She gave me the idea." He nodded at Leal.

She was astonished. "How? When?"

"That story you told me about how Virga was built—that Candesce was originally tuned to produce radio waves, not light. Got me thinking, so a few weeks back I added an oscillator that pulsed the generator at radio frequencies. Turns it into a huge antenna. I thought it might interfere with whatever was animating the junk . . ."

"Well, you killed the damned things."

The other airman grinned at Leal. "You tell a mean story, lady."

"They ain't my stories," she said, copying his accent.

"Come on!" Hayden led the way to the bridge, which was sealed shut; he had to bang on the door and say who he was before the men inside would open it.

There they found the severely rattled pilot and navigator clutching their controls while they peered through the cracked forward window. Both were cursing under their breaths.

Hayden frowned at them. "What's wrong?"

Something big and soft came out of the night and thudded against the window, sliding off with a weak sucking sound.

"Those fucking wraiths reset our gyrocompasses," complained the navigator. "We didn't notice until a minute ago."

Shapes flicked by, momentarily made real in the shaft of light from the ship's headlamp. They'd obviously left the midden and entered the cloud of fungi and swarming insects that surrounded it.

Hayden winced as something hard whacked the window. "What are you saying?"

The pilot shook his head helplessly. "I just picked a direction and flew. The compasses are reset, we could find our way back if we wanted to but . . . I have no idea what our heading is.

"Sir . . . we're lost."

THERE WAS SILENCE but for the hum of the engines. Everybody who wasn't at their post was in the lounge, but no one was talking. Leal perched across a table from Tarvey; Hayden was in the cockpit. The two airmen who'd helped her in the cabin hung nearby. She still hadn't gotten their names.

"What's he doing?" Somebody nodded in the direction of the cockpit.

Tarvey looked up. "Thinks if he can find the spot where we punched through the mold the first time, then we can backtrack." The yacht was circling the midden, keeping its clouds of brackish mist and fungi to starboard. Leal wasn't happy with that, and she didn't think the other men were, either. They were too close to the monster and too close to the wraiths.

There was another prolonged silence. Tarvey wasn't as despondent as the other men, in fact he was quite busy examining some of the monster's white fibers with a magnifying glass. His obvious enthusiasm was almost insulting compared to the general atmosphere.

Everyone was safe and accounted for. It was solely the double impact of being captured by the wraiths and then beset by the creature that kept Leal's hands trembling. That trauma was still so close that she couldn't bring herself to think about their being lost. The yacht had plenty of fuel, they could go for days before they became stranded and started to drift . . .

The tone of the engines changed and moments later Hayden

flew in from the cockpit. "We're going to take our chances with a random heading," he said. "Deploy the kite. Assuming the wraiths didn't steal it, that is." Nobody laughed, but several crewmen moved to obey the order.

Hayden glared around the room. "Why do you all look like your bird died? This expedition was a complete success."

"If you consider nearly being killed by the wraiths a success," somebody muttered.

"Emphasis on the *nearly*," retorted Hayden with a scowl. "Yeah, that was bad, and I apologize for taking us into that situation naively. Nobody expected them to be building a fleet, or that they'd have gone over to some fanatical religion worse than Eternism—" He raised an eyebrow at Leal.

"Transhumanism," she said wearily. "And they can't *all* have converted. We were unlucky in who caught us, I think."

"Anyway the point is, we learned how to defeat the monster," continued Hayden. "Something nobody's been able to do. A high-power radio source disrupts those threads it uses as its muscles."

"Threads, what threads?" One of the men glared at Hayden. He sat with an arm around the shoulder of another crewman who held his head in his hands and was nodding slowly, oblivious to the conversation. "The midden itself is angry. The spirits of everything lost and thrown away, I guess they've had enough. You saw! They came after us!" His lip trembled. "You *saw!*"

Hayden shook his head. "The monster wasn't the trash," he said. His tone was unsympathetic. "The monster was the cloud of white stuff holding the trash together. Am I right, Tarvey?"

Tarvey nodded, holding up the little switch of fibers he'd collected. "This glass isn't strong enough to see clearly, but I think these hairs are segmented. They look like tiny cranes; there's little threads like cables just on the edge of visibility, tied to round joints."

"What are you talking about? How could a hair move a—a— Those things we saw!"

"One man can't pull a ship into port, but fifty have no trouble," said Hayden. "The monster builds its bodies from whatever's at hand. We were lucky there was plenty of junk for it in the midden. In other circumstances . . ."

Leal hadn't thought about that. "You think it might pull apart a town?"

"Or a ship. It might even hijack the bodies of men or birds." Hayden frowned at her. "It isn't a worldwasp, is it?"

She hesitated, then shook her head. "No, but—"

"Well then. It must be from outside. Like . . . other things I've seen in the past."

She was about to protest, because something about this strange choir of assembled creatures had prodded a deep memory that she couldn't quite recover; Tarvey caught Leal's eye, but she didn't quite know what the enigmatic glance meant. A warning? She kept silent.

"It . . . *yelled* at us," said another of the crewmen. It was as if they'd all been holding that particular terror close, afraid to say anything—because suddenly everybody was talking at once. They all had their story of being pursued and screamed at by nightmare shapes. As they talked Leal saw the man who'd been clutching his head peek out, then start nodding to what one of the women was describing.

Hayden shouted for their attention. As the voices subsided he said, "Don't forget who you are. You lit Aerie's new sun! You re-made our nation, and now another country's threatened. Different threat, but we can still help. I know some of you signed on for the fame and glory, and we've had a little of that. Mostly we've had hard nail-biting work. But now you have a new opportunity—to be heroes in a whole new way . . . if that appeals to you at all.

"Some of you came for the work, for the money and experience working on sun generators. Fair enough; when we get back to port anyone who wants to remain and work on the new sun can do that. But if you want to help me track this monster to its lair and kill it—well, all I can say is that there's no other company I'd rather fight beside."

There was a ragged cheer. Tarvey shot Leal another look, but though there was a hint of irony in it, there was pride, too. Clearly, this was the Hayden Griffin to whom he'd sworn his loyalty.

"Once the kite's up we're going to go flat-out," continued Hayden. "We'll hit civilization or the walls of Virga in just a few hours, and when we get our bearings it's back to Sere. Then we'll get busy adapting our engines—hell, we could turn the sun itself into an RF gun, fry the damned thing from a hundred miles away."

"What about the wraiths?"

Hayden tilted his head from side to side, considering. "They might still attack the city, but I doubt it. They had their hands full when we left them and I think it'll take them awhile to recover. By the time they do, we'll be in Sere and the city will have time to prepare.

"All right. Anybody not posted for duty, get some rest. I don't know when we'll find our way back, so I need everybody fresh as soon as possible.

"Nobody will fault you if you have nightmares. But we all have work to do."

THE KITE'S INVISIBLE net swept the sky at two hundred miles per hour. Cold deepened around the ship and snowflakes darted through the beams of the headlamp and spotlights, which were now mounted at the yacht's nose. Leal slept fitfully, starting awake every now and then in her half-lit stateroom. Each time, she expected herself to cringe, expected memory of the monster to ambush her. She expected to have woken from a nightmare— but she remembered none, and each time she awoke she found she felt . . . not calm, but somehow *empty*. As if there'd been a storm, but it had passed. She knew that she was lucky and she didn't know why; some of the crew would carry the terror of the day for years. If somebody had asked her to predict her own reaction, she wouldn't have imagined this.

Yet the distant engine noise, the faint shipboard sounds, the gray light, all served to place her into a pensive state unlike anything she'd felt in years. It was as though her whole life was laid out before her, like cards on a table. Some of these were well-thumbed and kept close; her academic career had seemed so important to her for so long, and similarly her city life and friends in Sere. Yet life had other parts; she recognized the great blank space where her parents should be, a darkness never now to be lit. And for herself, further out, there was accident, disease, and death, all of which could be thrown down in front of her at any moment, covering everything else.

Drifting off to sleep, she mused that when you were young, you could sweep all those fatal cards to one side. They were dealt in as you got older and it seemed to her as reason succumbed to dream that a shadowy figure stood next to her, doing the dealing. It pointed to new cards now and the order and importance of her hand changed. In the pattern of those cards was a message that the young, and far too many mature people, were not ready to hear.

And if it spoke, would its voice be a cry across the miles, a thunder from the darkness?

The engines of the kite snarled on and the yacht followed. When Leal woke next, it was to the sound of polite knocking on her door, and behind that, no engine noise at all.

"Y-yes?" She fumbled her way out of the sleeping bag and found the door. Opening it a crack, she found Hayden Griffin waiting on the other side. He looked exhausted, but relaxed.

"Sorry to wake you, Leal, I thought you might want to see something."

"What? Something? Just a minute." Her mind was fogged, and Leal sensed that she'd slept a long time. She dressed clumsily, used the water closet, and joined the sun lighter in the corridor. Fresh, cold winter air blew in from the direction of the lounge. He headed in that direction.

"I think we have our bearings," he said as he glided out to the clamshell doors. They were open, revealing not darkness as she'd expected, but something unexpected, and subtle.

Leal had slept through their approach to Batetran. She'd gone from the familiar experience of winter's permanent night to the shock of full sunlight. Now, though, there were suns in the sky but vastly distant—three of them, each hundreds of miles away and separated by thirty or more degrees of sky from one another. Thus distant, those great lamps were no longer blinding white, but instead dim rubies cupped in wells of gorgeous color.

She'd never considered this, but from such a distance, you could see the shape of nations. Each sun carved a sphere out of the darkness, tingeing the air according to its distinctive spectrum. There was no distinct edge to these globes, except where rafts of cloud trapped the light. The skies were fairly clear in the farthest nation, so its outer precincts were sketched by tufts and spikes of shadow on the roseate glow of the air. A column of mist and cloud hundreds of miles long was rising from Candesce and cutting through the nearest country; so its outline was drawn by shafts of light that pierced the dove-gray vapor. Gaps open to its heart revealed the brightness inside. Hovering on the edge of visibility within these visions were thousands of farms and cities, twinkling speckles of green and black.

"That near one, it's Batetran," said Hayden, pointing.

"Oh! So you do know where we are?"

"Each sun has a distinctive spectrum. We split the light with a prism and compare what we see to the chart book. Then if you compare the angle that separates those three suns, you get our position by parallax. Then we reset our compasses." He grinned at her. "I'm not very good at it myself. I'd probably fly us out the Gates of Virga if you had to rely on me."

She looked at him, hesitated, and said, "You've changed."

He tensed, looked away.

"I like it." After a moment's pause, she went on: "So will we be home today?"

"It'll be five or six hours, assuming we can use the kite."

"Well, we'd best get inside so you can batten down the hatches," she said lightly. He nodded quickly and they went in, parting company almost immediately.

Leal knew her comment about his changing had raised a wall between them. She didn't care, because the one thing Hayden needed in his life was somebody who acknowledged his problem. Whether it made him uncomfortable or not, she was determined to do that.

FOR THREE HOURS the kite performed perfectly and they made good time. Then suddenly the ship lurched and horns blatted through the corridors, warning unnecessarily that they were braking. Leal had placed three open books in the air and was comparing the wording in three versions of a worldwasp story. The monster assailing Abyss might not be a worldwasp, but it was something half-familiar and it was quite possible she would find a thread in these ancient accounts that led to it.

As the horns sounded the books suddenly sailed away and her reflexive grab at one of them missed. She had to clutch the table she perched at or she would have followed them into the forward bulkhead.

Men half-fell out of the central corridor; one apologized to Leal after bumping her shoulder on the way by. The ship was braking heavily, engines straining and braking sails flapping loudly outside the portholes. But it was utterly dark outside.

When the pull of deceleration slackened off, Leal joined the men who clustered around the forward doorway like bugs. They were all looking down at the cockpit door, and after a moment it opened and Hayden poked his head out.

"Don't know," he said shortly. "The kite hit something. We'll see in a minute."

He turned his head and looked back into the cockpit, then swore. "Maspeth," he said, "come here."

She looked at the other airmen. One shrugged. "It's your country," he said. "So whatever we hit is yours, too, I guess."

She didn't want to see it, but she couldn't very well hide in her cabin. Leal bounced down the corridor, aware of the men watching her, and entered the cockpit. For a second she was relieved; the spotlights outside the round bow window showed nothing but rounded pads of cloud. Then Hayden touched her arm and pointed. "There."

The clouds parted and in their place was absolute darkness, save for one distant star shape. "Oh no."

It was the figure of a man. "Do you recognize the uniform?" asked Hayden softly.

"No, I . . . Wait." That was strange. "He's wearing a dress uniform from Maundry, but they haven't used that in . . ."

The limp shape came slowly closer and Leal sank her fingers into the arm of the captain's chair, not wanting to see it up close. Could he be some casualty of a long-forgotten war, still adrift in winter centuries after all the struggles that had meant everything to him? They would find out in a—

The figure dimmed, then suddenly there was a faint thump as it touched the window. Everyone in the cockpit gasped, then suddenly they were all laughing; all except Leal, whose blood froze at the sight of the foot-tall doll sprawled against the glass.

"It's a *toy soldier*," shouted the navigator and they all laughed again.

"*Stop* it!" she shouted—it came out as more of a shriek. "Stop it!" Leal clapped her hands to her ears and curled up in a ball.

"What the—" The laughter died awkwardly. "Leal, what is it?" Hayden asked. She felt his warm hands encircle her wrists.

"What did we hit? What did we hit?" That doll wasn't big enough to have staggered the kite.

"I don't understand, Leal. That doll—"

"Dreamweal! It's Dreamweal!"

She saw light through her eyelids just as another gasp went through the cockpit. Leal looked up.

More cloud had parted, and suddenly freed, the spotlights had pinioned something so big and close that its brightness over-whelmed the little lights in the room. For a few seconds all she could see was the ruin tangled in the kite's net.

It was the top floor and roof of a house. The walls had been sheared through by some tremendous force, leaving one window that opened onto blackness. The facade was painted a pleasant yellow. The roof was covered with ceramic shingles, all of them intact. The kite's white netting trailed away in two directions to the half-visible curves of its engines.

The debris slowly turned, curling around itself like a wounded man clutching his stomach. As it did, it revealed something on the roof.

Hayden's voice cut through the sudden shouts of the others. "I want men out there, now!" Leal felt sick, because she could see clearly that it was too late.

A man clung to the shingles of the roof. He had wedged his fingers so deeply under the green tiles that even after he'd died from exposure, he held fast.

"I remember now," said Hayden. "Your spare room, where you keep the dolls—"

"They come from here," she said quickly, almost stumbling

over her words to explain. "The shingle pattern on that roof, it's a Dreamweal pattern. And Dreamweal is often near Taura Two . . ."

"We'll check in on your town," he said. "But we have to investigate this first."

She bit her lip, trying to tamp down on her panic. Part of her was observing her own reactions, and was surprised at how close to the surface that panic was. The calm of her recent sleep had been real, she felt; but it was also fragile. Some trauma of their encounter with the monster did linger with her after all.

Shadows flittered across the shattered rooftop as airmen wearing spring-driven angel's wings appeared in the spotlight beams. Four of them roved over the wreck, shining lanterns into its recesses, their movements fluid and easy. After her classes with Uthor she could appreciate their skill; but her eyes kept straying back to the hunched body. They seemed in no hurry to get to him.

His face was lost in shadow. Could he be Master Artchin, the patriarch of her favorite doll-maker's family? His lined face came to her, his blue eyes and those windburned cheeks that always framed a smile. He always had the air of a man who'd learned to trick fate: "A doll-maker?" he'd laughed once when she asked him how he'd come to his profession. "Who could have thought I'd thrive as that? There's no explaining it, and frankly, if I thought about it too much I might jinx the whole thing. It's the way it is, I don't ask questions."

They'd reached him now. One of the airmen reached for the body's shoulder, as if clasping it might get its attention. Another pried its fingers loose from the shingles, and its face turned into the light.

Leal turned away before she got a clear look.

"Do you still need me?" she asked Hayden. Her own voice sounded as distant as a telephone boy's. He shook his head and, released, she quickly flew back to her stateroom.

But she didn't stay there long. A few minutes later she fled to the lounge to locate her books. The airmen were just bringing the body inside so she hurried, and when she had them all she retreated to her room again. Strapping the books open under tie cords on the wall, she arranged a lamp so she could see them all, and crossing her arms tightly under her breasts, she began to read. Every now and then shouts from the air outside or conversations near her door intruded into her concentration. She heard that the yacht had reached a volume of air filled with drifting storage nets and abandoned wicker shed-balls—the usual flotsam that accompanied a town wheel. But there was no town wheel.

She heard that the airmen had found the knotted intersection of several rope roads but that they could not find the one that led to Taura Two. When somebody said that Hayden had decided to go on to Sere Leal nearly burst out of her room to confront him. He had promised, he knew what it meant to her.

But she'd grown up in this vast darkness, and Leal knew that if the rope road was missing at this end, the fastest way to find it again would be to come at it along another road. Hating herself as ever for being logical—but she wasn't Seana—she shed some tears, then returned to the books.

Hayden and his airmen might be able to hunt this monster down and maybe they'd destroy it without even finding out what it was, or what that strange urgent message it shouted meant. But the more they knew about it the more likely they were to overcome it, and there were two ways to learn. One was out of her hands—it was up to Hayden to hunt it down and observe it. The second way to know it was through study. Had incidents like this occurred in the past? Were they now so thoroughly shrouded in myth and garbled interpretation as to be unrecognizable?

It was a normal human folly to think that whatever was happening to you now had never happened before.

It was the responsibility of Leal's profession to avoid that folly.

And at this moment, her research seemed the only thing in her life that was under Leal's own control.

DEPLOYING THE KITE while following a road would be dangerous; the yacht might collide with any manner of traffic moving at lower speeds in either direction. So the next leg of their journey crawled. Leal had time to isolate identical passages in a number of different traditional stories. She wrote passages from *Denizens of the World's Skin* on separate pieces of paper, then began arranging them as if they were parts of some larger story.

Then some worldwasps came to Men after their disputes, in the manner of their kind filling the sky. And they demanded of Men that they surrender the crafts and grown things they had spent years obtaining. And the Men refused.

There was another story that used the phrase "some worldwasps came after their disputes." It was an odd usage. Leal, and previous scholars, had always assumed that "after" in this case meant the same as "in the manner of" so that you could correctly translate the passage: "Then some worldwasps came as they did when disputing, in the manner of their kind filling the sky." But as Leal combed through the books, letting the old languages wash over her, nowhere did she see "after" used in such a manner.

"After their disputes." With whom? *One another?*

This passage seemed related to another that appeared in some other accounts: "And those worldwasps who had survived their kin came after to the mighty city of Spyre to demand succor of Men." The old word for "survived" was usually translated as "outlived" or "outlasted," yet as Leal looked up the word used here for "kin" she found that it invariably meant "those of a similar type" rather than "those of the same family."

She rewrote the sentences and arranged them as if they were part of the same narrative. Now it read, "*Those worldwasps who had survived their disputes with [those like them] came to the mighty city of Spyre to demand* succor of Men, [in the manner of their kind filling the sky]. And they demanded of Men that they surrender the crafts and grown things they had spent years obtaining. And the Men refused."

Pure speculation, of course. She dug deeper. *Ancient Shapes* had appendices containing fragments that added up to no coherent narrative. One of the few pieces here that mentioned worldwasps said, ". . . Then came to Virga else worldwasps and they denounced the meddling of Men in the world's design." The translation was literal, though the commentator pointed out that whoever had written this passage down was obviously semiliterate. The probable meaning of the fragment was "Then Virga's other worldwasps came to denounce the meddling of Men in the world's design." That was consistent with the idea that human beings had altered Candesce, turning it into a weapon to suppress the very technologies that had been used the create Virga in the first place.

And yet . . . She scoured the old texts until her eyes burned. At last, in an obscure tale about a potter who smashed all his wares to spite his wife, she read, "They sent for men from the nearest town wheel which was of a different country. The else men came in a party barge, for they thought this whole incident a great joke."

Did "else" mean "foreign?"

Then came to Virga foreign worldwasps . . .

She'd written it down, and she was staring at the words with a strange, almost superstitious feeling crawling over her, when the ship's horns sounded. Without taking her eyes off the paper, Leal reached to grab a tie rope and a moment later the ship began to decelerate.

She blinked and looked to the porthole. The sky wasn't black, but indigo. Moments later she heard one of Sere's great foghorns sound. They were home.

Seconds later she was in the cockpit, hovering next to the navigator. "The Taura Two road is usually near Kite Wheel. The road nexus is that green beacon there."

"Leal." It was Hayden's voice.

"We can probably open up a bit when we get there, it's not a well-traveled route—"

"Leal!"

She turned. "What?"

Hayden hung in semishadow. He was dressed casually; with smears of motor grease on his shirt and his sleeves rolled up he looked like any ordinary mechanic, not a legendary sun lighter. He pointed past her out the window. "I don't think we'll be going anywhere today. Look."

Angry, about to protest, she followed his gaze.

As she'd entered the cockpit she'd glanced outside and seen the familiar wheels of the city, half of them wreathed in cloud as usual. Now she realized that there were red glowing lights behind some of those clouds. —No, not lights. Fires.

Steam Wheel was dotted with orange flares. Spirals of gray smoke roiled up from its streets and platforms, twirling away in two gigantic vortexes from the axis of rotation. The wheel was turning very slowly—were they stopping it?

There was fire in other places, smoke obscuring half of Match Wheel. What about Rowan? The university? No, the other wheels seemed fine, but the air . . . now she saw that the airspace around Sere's wheels was crowded as she'd never seen it, not even during the referendum.

Somebody said, "What . . . ? The wraiths?"

Hayden shook his head grimly. "If it's any consolation, I don't think this was our fault. The spiral has been closing for weeks. It was only a matter of time.

"The monster has come to Sere."

14

IT STARTED DURING Maintenance shift. There was nothing unusual about a pale fog drifting in to twine about the stenciled pipes and smear across the rattling engine covers of Steam Wheel. Later it would be obvious that this was no ordinary fog, because it was traveling against the breeze; but at the time the workers all had their heads down. Their minds were largely empty of emotion and side-thoughts, full of the thousand-and-one minor tasks that made up refining, smelting, and assembling. Deep within Steam Wheel there were spots where the outside world wasn't visible at all, and the whole universe might be filled to its edges with gleaming metal stacks and bundled cables like giants' hair and hissing pressure-release spigots. Swaddled in heavy protective gear, men shambled past one another without a second glance.

Until, that is, something came scampering along one of the catwalks that caused three men to go over its side, one to his death. It was wearing a fire-retardant suit—it *was* the suit, in fact. The legs and boots were moving like a man's, but the jacket above that had collapsed onto the waist of the pants, hood slumped forward to dangle obscenely below the belt while the two arms writhed and twisted above. This apparition skipped and staggered up to a line foreman and from it bellowed a terrible voice. No one remembered the words it spoke but as the foreman screamed and collapsed a thousand other howling monsters assembled themselves from wire, net, and cog and ran down the other workers.

In Kite Wheel, a few late-shift couriers and beat policemen

glanced up as the echoes from the first blossom of uncontrolled fire brightened the air around Steam Wheel. Most of these people were walking or pedaling alone so no one later really knew the exact sequence of events. It was certain, however, that soon after the explosions started in Steam Wheel, a tide of nightmare shapes tumbled down Kite's main street. Outpacing this rabble was its sound, an insane, full-throated chaos of noise.

The lives of those caught by the mob were cut cleanly in two: they would forever after mark time before this night as a period of innocence compared to the gray days of anxiety and confusion that followed.

His days already had that character, so maybe that's why Porril, former dean of the history department, could later recall every detail of the evening without hesitation or anxiety. He was caught outside because the persistent spin-gale of Kite's turning was causing a drainpipe on his house to bang against the wall. The knocking was keeping him awake, so he'd put a ladder against the house and (with all the blitheness of the elderly) was standing on a high rung in his nightgown when the madness descended. He was about to drive a nail into a strap he'd put across the drainpipe, and as the monsters rounded the corner he stared at them for a second, hesitated, then banged the nail in. He was most of the way down the ladder when it was seized by strange hands and he was shaken off and into an ornamental bush.

He sat up, too old and weak to fight the howling horrors encircling him. Porril was quite ready to meet his wife again and so he waited calmly to be killed. When that continued to not happen he began to look past the gibbering assemblages that were shouting at him. He was able to observe that wherever a citizen threw open a door or window, the monsters immediately pushed into the house—but where people hunkered behind unlit glass to watch, they made no attempt to enter.

Policemen and soldiers began to arrive. They were as hectored and harassed by the creatures as anybody, but they had guns, and so shortly the street became a shooting gallery. Porril saw a neighbor go down with a bullet in his neck, but the gunfire had no effect on the monsters themselves.

Crashing sounds, shouts, and further gunshots sounded from the houses where the creatures had found entry. Overturned or thrown lamps washed firelight across their windows and in moments several places were ablaze.

A pipe-fingered thing shook Porril's shoulder and shouted in his ear. "Sir, are you going to kill me?" he asked it. It yelled something further. "Well, if not, then kindly unhand me." He pulled away from the creature, which cocked its sketch of a head and fell silent.

"Thank you." He watched as a one-sided gun battle wrecked his neighborhood. Every now and then he would shake his head and say, "Extraordinary!" or (with reference to the army) "How typical!" Eventually the stream of violence passed on and into another street and his own personal monsters gave up and left him. Then Porril stood up and dusted himself off.

Because there were bandages in one of his cabinets, he turned to fetch them for the victims of the attack; but before entering the house he thought better, and went around the side again.

He shook the drainpipe. It held firm. Nodding in satisfaction, Porril went to help his neighbors.

That was how the former dean became the first person in Sere to understand the true source of the monster's destructiveness. He knew he was out of favor with the city's ruling elite and so he had no illusions that it would do any good for him to tell anyone what he knew. He kept silent, and shook his head and pursed his lips in sympathy as the survivors told him their tales. He tended the wounds they, their family members, or the police had inflicted on them, and when everyone was accounted for and on their way to a hospital or the morgue, he sighed and walked home. He pulled the curtains and, aware of the absence of the knocking of the drainpipe, he fell asleep to the music of distant and nearby sirens.

Five hours later, Hayden Griffin's yacht arrived at the city. By that time there were roadblocks on every corner and random police raids were occurring in all the wheels.

For once the government wasn't paralyzed. It had decided to take this opportunity to clean house.

"BUT I WORK here," Leal explained for the fifth time. "For heaven's sake, I can *see* my building," she continued. "It's right there." She pointed to the heavily buttressed flank of the history department, its familiar gaslit profile marred by uncharacteristically dark windows.

The sergeant ignored her while he pored over the letter of transfer that designated Leal as a washerwoman for Campus Services. She suspected he couldn't read very well. While he puzzled over the words she craned her neck to get some sense of the damage the monster had done to her beloved university. There was tumbled masonry sitting right in the middle of the road, and phosphorescent police tape made strange spiderweb lines in the deep shadows between buildings.

She hadn't been surprised to find a letter from the education minister waiting for her when she'd finally arrived back at her apartment last shift. She'd been putting off thinking about his job offer, and he'd finally written to ask what her final decision would be. She still didn't know, and so today she'd come to walk the campus, and consider her answer.

Reading his letter, with its subtle wheedling tone, she'd laughed. "After being captured by Pacquaeans and screamed at by monsters," she told William's coffin, "I hardly think this counts as *pressure*."

But she felt it anyway. Her nerves had still been rattling from the state of the city, and her reception when she and Hayden's crew finally disembarked. She had been separated from the sun lighter's people and subjected to a solid eight hours of questioning by unsmiling, nonuniformed men in an airless room somewhere in the Interior Ministry building. Too tired to be nervous, Leal had treated the whole thing like a thesis defense, and eventually they'd compared their notes with others being brought in from other rooms, and had let her go. Whether they were impressed by her account of her recent adventures she couldn't say; but on the way out one of her interrogators had drawn her aside. "Listen," he said, "you're well placed, having the confidence of the sun lighter and all. You should consider joining the party."

Delirious with exhaustion, she'd imagined some soirée taking place in the next room, complete with clowns and balloons. "What party?"

"The Eternist party," he'd said, puzzled by her thickheadedness.

"Ah. Yes, I'll, I'll think about that."

She'd intended to sleep when she finally got home, and it wasn't the ministry's letter that made her toss and turn for hours instead. Neither was it the presence of William—in fact, knowing he was there was, perversely, reassuring. Finally Leal had cursed and, throwing the covers aside, she'd gone to face the source of her disquiet.

The disused gas lamp took a few seconds of sputtering to come to life. When it did, it lit the assembled ranks of her charity: the dolls of Dreamweal, all lined up and facing the doorway as if they'd been waiting for her.

"Shit." Before she could think about it, Leal grabbed a big box from the jumble of stored stuff in the corner. She began sweeping the dolls into the box. It only took a couple of minutes to erase that part of her history; then she dragged the box to the elevator and left it in the lobby with a hand-scrawled sign on it that said, *Free Dolls.*

She slept after that. The box was gone as she left for the university.

"You're a cleaner?" The soldier's voice snapped Leal out of her reverie. "Only authorized personnel allowed on campus right now."

"Well, *yeah*," she drawled. "We gotta lot of cleaning up to do."

"Maybe, but—" He waggled the letter at her. "This ain't much. Come on. We'll see what your boss says about your working today."

"Oh, you don't have to—" But he was already walking away and he still had her letter. With a muttered curse Leal followed him, aware of the other soldiers' eyes roving over her as she passed.

"Where's the office?" the soldier called back. Luckily Leal had once visited Support Staff central, when she'd had a dispute over the cleaning staff moving her books. She paced ahead of the soldier, nervously looking about at the strangely empty campus.

She stopped with a gasp. The soldier glanced over. "Yeah, big fire, there," he said.

"But that was the literature department!" Other buildings had broken windows, caved-in roofs. This devastation was nothing like the few fires and crashed cars she'd seen in the rest of the city. "What happened here?"

"The monster. What'd you think?" He shot her an odd look and Leal turned to look again, a sudden sick suspicion coming over her.

The literature department had burned. So had the law building, and the teacher's college had many broken windows. Her beloved history building was a dark hulk, its shadow hiding who knew what damage? But the angular edifice of the engineering building was pristine, as were the chemistry department and medical school.

The centers of fine arts and humanities had been razed. Engineering and sciences were untouched.

"Shit. Shit shit shit." She stared about wide-eyed. Suddenly the roadblocks, the presence of these soldiers, all seemed unspeakably sinister. She almost turned and bolted, but they were behind her, too. And the one escorting her was walking on, seeming oblivious to her sudden panic.

The door to the support staff office was open, throwing a warm rectangle of light across the dark metal pavement. All the building's windows were lit and she could see people hurrying to and fro.

She shouldn't have come here. It was all going to be revealed: these people had never met her. Her job was a sham. She'd get no chance to respond to Breckian's job offer (or was it Eustace Loll's?) once she'd been formally cashiered. She might even end up in jail for fraud.

Disaster, disaster. The soldier clacked up the steps and into the building. Leal glanced around, as if some escape route might magically open, or a dashing spokesman swing down to spirit her away. Finally, shoulders slumped, she followed her escort inside.

He'd gone into an office to one side. SUPERVISOR was written on a little sign that stuck out over the door. Heart pounding, Leal stopped just outside.

The supervisor was a burly, weatherbeaten man. He was slumped behind a paper-strewn desk, his brows beetled in annoyance as he scanned the letter. The soldier stood ramrod-straight in front of the desk. Leal was careful to put him in between her and the room's lamp, so that shadow half-covered her.

"I don't know any Maspeth," said the supervisor irritably. He leaned to one side so he could see Leal. "Who the hell are you?"

Again her eyes frantically scanned for an escape route. If it hadn't been for the desk, you could have mistaken the office for a storage room—there was junk piled up along all four walls, and mops, buckets, and boxes were strewn across the floor. There was even a big square of cracked masonry leaning against the side of the desk.

"Hey, I asked you a question."

Leal stared at the stone square. It was three feet on a side, its sides rough but its top surface polished smooth. She knew the tint of that asteroidal stone, she'd seen it before.

"Ma'am?" The soldier had stepped to one side, one hand on his holster. Both men were staring at Leal.

"You remember," she said to the supervisor. "I'm finishing off the library renovation. For William Peeve." And pointedly, she nodded at the stone slab.

The supervisor's eyes widened and his lips parted. "Uh . . ." He glanced at the soldier, then back at her. "Of course, of course! It's just . . . damned busy around here right now. I forgot." He sat up straighter, nodding at the soldier. "It's okay, she's supposed to be here today."

The soldier shot her another look and left. After waiting a decent interval, the supervisor shot up from his chair and lunged to slam the door behind Leal. "What do you know about William Peeve?" he snarled.

Leal's mouth went dry—he was quite big and threatening—but she said, "He's currently lying in a box under my kitchen table. *Instead* of where he's supposed to be." She nodded significantly at the slab of flooring.

The supervisor deflated a little. "Ah, yeah, okay, so, but what can we do?" He went back to sit down, but he didn't offer a chair since in fact his was the only one in the room. "Listen. I'm sorry you're the one left holding the—well, you know what I mean. We tried to do right by William, some of us. It was his home, you know? And they left it standing, the bastards, though I'm sure it was just they didn't have time what with all the other buildings they had to demo on short notice."

"The army really did this?"

He guffawed. "Well, they had to do *something*, I mean nobody saw them actually fight the monster in any way that counted, did they? They came in here and made a big show after it left. Seems they did the same in other places around the city. And some of the more prominent opposition party members and intellectuals and whatnot, they took care of them while they were at it."

"No!" Lots of people were missing, or dead, but she'd heard nothing about such a systematic pattern. But then again, who would be left to spread the news? Leal turned away, feeling sick. "And to think I was considering joining the party."

There was no reply. She glanced over reluctantly, expecting a disapproving scowl, or worse. "It'd sure be safer for you," was all he said.

"You can't mean that." But he didn't reply. After a moment Leal pulled herself together and said, "William's tomb. Is it still there?" He nodded. "The library's safe?"

"For now. We're supposed to burn the books, but it's not high-priority, so I've been putting it off. Afterward, they're thinking of making that space into an Eternist chapel."

A startling image came to Leal's mind. "We could put him right under the pulpit . . ."

Across the desk, a sly smile in return. ". . . After we bend his arm up . . ."

". . . And his middle finger!"

It was probably the first genuine laughter to echo out of the office in weeks; Leal got curious looks when she left. By that time, though, she'd secured a promise of help, complete with a couple more names to add to her list of Friends of William Peeve.

"CHURCH ATTENDANCE IS mandatory, of course." Eustace Loll patted her on the back in a friendly way. "And it matters which church."

Leal had thought the ordeal was over. Only this morning she'd summoned her courage and indifference and gone to visit Gereld Hackner. "How do I become a party member?" she'd asked him.

"You can do it through the normal channels," he'd said, "which will take years. Or you can come with me." He'd taken her to visit Loll, who in turn had brought her directly to party headquarters, which was also the Eternist diocese. This squat edifice was kept in permanent shadow, only a few strategic torches lighting its entrance and column-lined inner sanctum. Of course, upstairs it was a brightly lit, efficient modern office building.

A lot of people were applying, it seemed; there were queues. Some people had brought lunches. Loll sauntered past them all and presented Leal to a room of harried-looking secretaries. "Fill this out," he'd instructed Leal, handing her a form. Once it was done, he'd taken it directly to the woman who was stamping embossed membership cards on a little press. "Card, please." She'd turned one out without comment.

"You're in," said Loll, handing it and a certificate to Leal. "Welcome to the party, *Dean* Maspeth."

Leal had struggled not to throw up on the spot.

But of course there was the whole church-attendance thing, a prospect so noisome that Leal had shoved it entirely out of her mind. But joining the party meant she'd also joined the church. "We'll enroll you at the new cathedral in Kite Wheel," said Loll. "In the current sad circumstances, I daresay there's a few unexpected real estate opportunities opened up there as well. Something to think about . . . an easy walk to services."

Sadly, Loll couldn't stay; important duties and all. She thanked him for his help, and he said, "And I'll see you in church!"

This next ordeal was the worst; it involved Leal being greeted with hugs and cheers by a room full of sweet young things of both sexes, all immaculately groomed and dressed in cloyingly chaste formal clothes. The young men looked practically gelded, and she supposed that in some sense they were. Unlike the office flacks, these were true believers, and it made Leal's skin crawl just to be in the same room with them. One gushed on about how the new cathedral was being built with public money and how this meant that the holiness shining upon it would cascade back through the tax system to affect every man, woman, and child in Abyss.

"Belief is action," he said. "Now that the whole country is acting together, we are all believers, aren't we?" She had nodded and smiled and agreed with him.

After an hour or so of prayers and even a shared hymn, they let her go. Leal felt savaged, and half-fainting, she barely found the stairs. She was in a rage and to be fair, she knew it was herself she should be angry with; but the face she wanted to slap most right now was, strangely, Hayden Griffin's.

Maybe it was because he could leave. This wasn't his country, he was just here to be heroic and make a lot of money. In his aerie high above the stacks of Steam Wheel, he was building some sort of nuclear death ray and with it he was going to smite that monster but good. The government demanded it as a condition of his staying here; but he also wanted to do it. This little project had woken him out of his fog of melancholy—it was so much more fun than building a sun—and once he was done he'd have doubled his legend.

He couldn't help her. He was barely aware of Leal's problems, and even if he'd cared, what could he do?

The future was resolving itself in Leal's mind, like the slow fade-in of a photograph in its developing tray. Hayden would find and kill the monster, but not before the Eternists had used it to put an unassailable stranglehold on power. His triumph would be their triumph, and he'd be quickly shunted aside as they rewrote events to showcase their own heroes. As soon as he finished his sun he'd be escorted to the border and that would be the last Abyss would ever see of him. And why should he complain?

Leal Hieronyma Maspeth, meanwhile, would become a name forever linked with Eternist doctrine and tactics. Under the guidance of Breckian and Loll, she would be channeled into compromise after compromise, until she was overseeing the curriculum of her nightmares. Some of those fresh-faced fanatics in the office upstairs would come to work for her and they'd filter out anyone unlike themselves, and filter any opinion or news that reached her.

She'd float away in their Eternist bubble, and probably end up cremated in the cathedral and eulogized in the papers. She was one of *them* now.

Shock was making the walls seem to bend inward. Weird echoing gabbles—voices?—swirled around her. Leal sat down hard on the stairs, and gasped for long minutes. Several people stopped in concern but she waved them on. Finally she levered herself grimly to her feet and continued on down.

Focus, she told herself. *Here's what you have to show for it.* She fumbled her papers and the membership card out of her shoulder bag and fanned them in front of her. Each of these items gave her power in one or more realms. Her party membership meant she could rise further and faster in any professional position. Enrollment in the cathedral was a ticket to Kite Wheel society. And being part of the sun lighter's team meant she had unprecedented freedom of movement, in the city and beyond. She'd forgotten all about that at the university roadblock; but she wouldn't be forgetting it again.

These were the things she'd bought with her pride, her integrity, and her reputation.

"Hey!"

. . . She'd better make the best of them.

"*Hey!* What are you doing?" A hand fell on her shoulder.

Leal started out of her grim reverie. She'd been stalking past the lineups on the second floor. "What—?"

"Aw, look at that, you've made me lose my place!"

"S-Seana?"

"What's the matter, no time for me?" Seana glared at her belligerently. "And what are *you* doing here?"

Leal shook herself and looked around. She felt like she was just waking up, and everything in the shift so far had been some sort of fever dream.

"I guess I was doing what you're doing," she murmured. Seana had been in the line for membership applications. Puzzled, Leal looked at her as if noticing her for the first time. "Seana, why are you doing it?"

Seana crossed her arms and looked away. "I have a good reason," she said. "I've been trying to get in to see Brun. If I had party membership, maybe . . ."

"Ah. Well, that's why I was here, too."

"To see Brun?"

"No, to get leverage." The fog had completely blown away from Leal's mind. She took Seana's arm. "Come on, doing it that way will take weeks."

"But what are we—"

"I will get us in to see Brun. Just trust me."

IN THE END, she was half-right. The roadblocks and check-points around the city were no problem for someone carrying Leal's papers. She and Seana were easily granted entrance to the military hospital and the ward where Brun was being kept. The unsmiling nurse on the desk at the secure ward was even willing to let Leal in to see Brun—but only Leal.

Leal stared at the stone-faced man for a moment; her mind raced with possible responses. She could say that Seana was a specialist, but then they might ask to see her credentials. She could tell a half-truth, saying that Seana was Brun's lover—but if they didn't care about that they might bar Leal from visiting, too.

"This woman's my clerk," she said. "She's here to record my conversation with the patient."

The nurse grunted. "Sorry. Orders are pretty strict on this one. Nobody but military or party members on official business. You a party member?" he asked Seana.

"I've applied," she said through gritted teeth.

"Then, no. Go ahead," he said to Leal. "Room six, no deviations or side trips. You have fifteen minutes."

Seana looked ready to burst into . . . well, it might go any of a number of ways. Leal took her hands and looked into her eyes. "I'll make sure he's okay," she said. She could feel Seana's jealous glare burning into her back as she walked down the long windowless corridor to room six.

The door was closed; though it was painted to resemble wood, she could see the rivets. Leal hesitated, then knocked.

"Come in," came a tired voice from the other side.

Brun sat on the room's single chair near its only bed, looking a little thinner than usual but otherwise fine. He was reading the newspaper but dropped it when he saw her. He stood up quickly.

"Leal Maspeth? How did you get here?"

Now Leal felt awkward. She hardly knew Brun, after all. Did he remember anything about her tending him on the yacht? There didn't seem to be any way of asking, and she couldn't see any sign of it in his eyes.

She took a step into the room. "It's a long story. It's not really me who came to see you—it was Seana. She's outside. Brun, she really cares for you, she's been beside herself since you left—"

"I'm fine." He sat abruptly, and something clinked. With a start Leal saw that a steel manacle encircled his right ankle, its chain raveling away under the bed. He picked up the newspaper. "Tell her I'm fine."

"But why—?"

He laughed unpleasantly. "I'm officially a madman, or I was up until a couple of days ago. They loaded me up with drugs, had me strapped—" He fought to say more, then shook his head. His fingers had begun ripping through the paper. "I can't have her see me like this."

Leal looked from him to the door, frowning. "But things have changed, haven't they? They believe you now."

The bitter laugh came again, this time from behind a raised newspaper. "They really don't want to, you know."

"I've seen it," she blurted. "It grabbed my arms—yelled at me . . ."

"Ah," he said. The paper lowered minutely.

"Brun . . ." She thought about the destruction on the campus, and what she'd seen of the monster itself. "I need to know what it said to you. The truth, not whatever it is you've been telling the doctors here."

He flipped the paper down. "Why?"

"Because . . ." *We're all in terrible danger but I'm not sure it's from the monster.* "It's getting worse. More towns have vanished, Brun. The monster . . . told you something. I was there when we found you, Brun, I remember what you said. It gave you a message, didn't it? Something it nearly shattered you to hear?"

He wrapped his arms tightly around his torso, rocking forward, glaring murderously at her. "Don't want to—"

"Did you tell the navy what it said?"

He shook his head. "I told them the words I heard. Not the—"

"Not the meaning." She nodded. "Brun, when it had me trapped, it shouted at me. To get my attention. And when it knew I understood, it . . . it stopped. Only what it wanted me to understand wasn't what I'd thought it wanted—it wasn't the words . . ."

He was nodding violently. "It doesn't really *get* words. I've been thinking and thinking about it and I understand that now. It doesn't use words, usually, where it comes from in that crack in the sky. It just throws combinations of words at you until it gets the *emotion* it wants."

"What emotions did it want, Brun?"

"Fear—but not fear of it. Despair, but you have to *hope*, you have to have this weaseling furious hope behind it, or it'll keep at you, that's what it did to the others."

She nodded slowly. "You said something just now about the crack in the sky. What did you mean?"

He looked at her strangely. "Where it came from. We found out where it came from. There's a hole in the world's skin where the wind sighs through. All blackness on the other side." This indeed sounded like madness to Leal, but as Brun described the place in more detail, an eerie sense of doubt came over her. He was being at once too specific and too subjective in his account; she had developed an instinct for separating historical fact from fiction in studying many texts over the years. That instinct told Leal that Brun was describing something he'd really seen.

"Did you look through this . . . aperture? Go through it?"

He nodded. "That's where we found the monster, and it followed us back and chased us into the kingdom of Rain."

"You told the navy this?"

Brun laughed. "They looked at me like I was insane. The scribe stopped writing things down at that point." His smile slipped a bit. "The irony is, I was about to give them the exact coordinates when they shut me up. We took readings, I remember . . ."

She blinked in surprise. "Can you write them down for me?"

"Sure." She handed him the pen and pad of paper that were to have been Seana's props. As he wrote she thought about his words. A hole in the skin of the world would go straight to vacuum; beyond Virga was outer space, after all. So what he was saying really was impossible. She decided to take another tack. He handed her the pad but she didn't look at it, saying instead, "And the words? What did the monster say to you?"

Reluctantly, he told her. He didn't look at her, and as Brun recited the monster's words his voice became hollower, more flat, so that by the time she left him he was sitting in silence, staring at the wall, today's headlines forgotten at his feet.

"I'M SURPRISED," SAID Hayden Griffin with a laugh. "After everything that happened, you're coming along?"

She glanced behind her ruefully. "Actually, I might be safer if I did," she said. "But no, I can't come. I have new responsibilities for the Ministry of Education. They're going to keep me in the city."

"Sorry to hear that," he said. Leal felt her ears redden.

They stood in microgravity at the base of the yacht's gangplank. Hayden's airmen were loading a few last crates onto the vessel while a small crowd of naval officers looked on. She'd seen as she was bouncing up that a big boat-sized cargo was attached to the stern of the yacht by towropes. She nodded to the thing, which looked like a crushed pipe organ. "Your death ray?"

He shook his head. "Decoy for the government spies to photograph. The real deal's in the hold. You're sure you can't come? It might be very useful for you to share in the glory."

She chewed her lip, not meeting his eye. "Listen, I interviewed the airman we rescued in the kingdom. Of all the survivors, he's the one who spent the most time with the monster. And what he had to say . . . Hayden, I think killing it would be a mistake."

She glanced at him; he was blinking at her, expression unreadable. Then: "It's a little late to be saying that."

"Why?"

He leaned close and hissed, "Because your people are going to seize my whole workshop and the new sun if I don't come back with its head."

She was shocked, but not surprised. "They can't do that! It'd be an international incident." Hayden's sun wasn't his, after all; he was building it on behalf of a nation much bigger and richer than Abyss, a place that already had a sun. But now he just shrugged.

"I guess they figure they'll deal with that when the time comes. Right now, they're desperate."

"But Hayden, if I'm right, they—nobody—can afford to ignore the monster's message."

"Message?" Now he looked genuinely puzzled. She nodded vigorously.

"If I'm right, the monster's not here to kill people; that's happening accidentally. I don't know why, but it's as if it's lost its reason, but not its purpose. It's trying to communicate with us."

He crossed his arms and glowered at her. "And what, exactly, is it trying to tell us?"

"Something—I'm trying to follow the leads, there's a source that may be able to tell me, but it's locked away in the rare books library. I'm not sure, yet." Seeing his face she hurriedly said, "Brun—the man we rescued from the kingdom—he remembered two messages. One was that this world—Virga, our world—is threatened. Not by the monster, by something else. Hayden, it wants us to be afraid—it really is trying to scare us—but it doesn't want us to be afraid of it.

"The second message is actually a request. *Bring us Candesce.*"

"Which makes no sense," he said. "We can't tow the sun of suns to the edge of the world and hand it over to somebody."

"I know. But that request . . . and its other words . . . remind me of something, it sounds like it's quoting passages in a book. The book's called *Polyhistoria*, and I know for a fact there's a copy in the rare books collection. If you could put in a formal request for it—"

But he was shaking his head. "First of all, I'm leaving in five minutes. Secondly . . . is there anything in this book that might offend the Eternists?"

"Um," she said. Then, "Its very existence?"

"Then we're never even going to see it. Their very desperation is making them more and more doctrinaire. If I asked for your book, it would be read by a hundred spies first and some of them would report that its contents were heretical. They'd burn it or pulp it, or whatever. In any case we'd never see it."

"So that's it, then," she said. "You won't help me, and you won't hold off for a few days while we find out whether this thing is trying to communicate with us?"

"Leal," he said heavily, "I can't."

As she bounce-walked back to the dock elevators Leal could hear them casting off the lines behind her. She didn't look back. Her head was ringing with every kind of insult she could think of, all aimed squarely at Hayden Griffin.

At least she hadn't given him the one piece of information he might be able to use: Brun's revelation that the monster had come through a crack in Virga's skin. And his directions to that place.

At the elevators she hesitated, then because she didn't want to go home yet she went to check that her cutter was okay. Nothing up here had been touched by the monster, but there were still vandals, thieves, and accidents. It was fine, even the little anemones that harvested floating grit in the cockpit seemed healthy. The act of inspecting it calmed her down, and by the time she was done she had decided what she would do next.

There was a telephone kiosk near the elevators, the inevitable urchins slouching around it waiting for a call. She picked up the receiver, shouted for an operator, and asked for the phone nearest a particular intersection. After a while it rang and someone quickly picked it up.

"Yeah?" said a young voice.

"Message for Easley Fencher," she yelled. "Easley Fencher!" She gave his address.

" 'Kay, go ahead," said the boy on the other end. The roar from Candesce nearly drowned his voice.

"Tell him Leal is taking William home," she shouted. "In Maintenance shift . . .

"Tomorrow!"

15

"IT'S AS DARK as the Aracen graves," muttered Easley.

"Keep pulling," said the shadow next to him. Leal heard the wheels of the little cart squeak, but the familiar landmarks of the campus were all drowned in black.

She could tell where they were because the different faculty buildings were identifiable by their silhouettes. Above them the towers and streets of the town wheel curled up into a glittering arch, and this would normally provide enough light to navigate through the university's byways—but a little slip of cloud had nosed through the wheel's spokes, cutting off the streetlight like a curtain.

Where there was light, it stood in pools around the military roadblocks that still surrounded the campus. The six conspirators had to be careful where and when they crossed the roads, lest one of the bored soldiers manning those checkpoints glance down the avenue and see movement. The cart carrying William's coffin wasn't large, but neither could it move very quickly; and there were six of them accompanying it, probably twice what was really needed.

There'd been a rather heated discussion when they'd met in the supervisor's office a half-hour before. William had been shipped in with a truckload of lumber and now sat outside with the pile. The shift supervisor was named Mr. Corrose; he'd proposed a team of four to take William to his final resting place. He picked the strongest of the men who had originally built William's tomb. "But I have to visit the library," Leal had objected, "for other reasons as well." And Easley also refused to stay behind, holding his chin high with an uncharacteristic glint of determination in his eye. Denied his chance to host William in his own home, he seemed to feel an extra obligation to ensure that the old librarian be laid to rest properly.

So they'd all trouped out and now the library was just across the street. "Wait," said Corrose, putting up a half-seen hand. "This is a tricky one." There were checkpoints at either end of this avenue, which meant that the soldiers at one would see if something eclipsed the light of the other. William's pallbearers had to wait for them all to be looking away at the same time. It took long minutes for this to happen.

That gave Leal plenty of time to contemplate just how suicidally stupid this was. It was strange—she felt almost perfectly divided right now, between a part of her that was screaming with fury at the folly of risking her whole future just to stuff a body in a niche; and a part of her that felt savage satisfaction at doing just that.

She could have a house on Match wheel. She could attend all the best parties. More, and better: she had the chance of guiding the education of thousands of people, hopefully to steer them away from Eternism and into the light of a rational worldview. Yet here she was, throwing it all away out of loyalty to a man she'd barely known.

Just now her heart was thudding and her senses were overloaded by every stray sound and sensation. She felt the grain of the wood as she leaned on the little cart, smelled the sweat of the worker next to her.

"Now," hissed Corrose and suddenly they were hurrying across the broad copper road. Leal tried to look everywhere at once, at both diametrically opposite checkpoints where the black cutouts of men stood; but in her over-alert state the surface of the road under her feet distracted her. It felt gritty, and she suddenly wondered if that were soot or, worse, the inevitable growth of verdigris that happened when a street wasn't walked on or driven over for a few days. She'd seen it before: the first vehicles to cross such a disused street would leave amber tracks in the pale green. If the soldiers came this way carrying lanterns, they might easily see that a number of people had passed.

It might not matter—there were supposed to be repair gangs around, after all—but then, none were scheduled to be working in this area—but— Her thoughts skittered to and fro, then suddenly froze as she looked up and saw the silhouette of someone standing on the steps to the history department.

The figure was only visible for a second as it occluded the light of a distant window. Then the angle had changed and the steps were absorbed into the greater shadow of the building. Leal stumbled and Easely grabbed her arm. "Almost there!"

They clattered into the triangle of blackness cast by the library steps. Leal looked back again, and while she did Corrose hurried up the steps and unlocked the library. "Get him off the cart! Come on!" There were sliding sounds, noises of men grunting. Leal scanned the black oblongs again, but saw nothing. The soldiers were still at their roadblocks.

And then somebody pulled on her arm and she stepped into the library and the door shut. "Ha!" said Corrose in a normal tone of voice. "Let's get him upstairs, then."

They could see even less well in here than outside, but they all knew the building's layout by heart. Leal could smell the books now, and the scent calmed her like nothing else could have. Somebody fell in beside her, and she heard Easley clear his throat.

"I heard you joined the party," he said.

"Yes," she said neutrally.

"So you're going to take them up on their offer?"

"Yes."

"But you clearly don't feel you have enough pull to just ask to be let into the library—even though you're going to be dean."

"Easley, what are you getting at?"

They reached the stairs. The men ahead of them were sliding

the coffin up its carpeted steps, one-two-three-pull, one-two-three-pull. "I—I don't know," said Easley. "I guess I had visions of you taking a stand somehow . . . keeping the library open."

"So did I," she said, "until I saw what they did to the campus. They're getting bolder."

"What do you think they'll do next?"

"Oh, you know as well as I do, Easley. Extend the state of emergency indefinitely, then suspend the constitution and parliament. Then they start rounding people up."

"Make church attendance mandatory," he suggested.

"Oh, why do that? Not having it be mandatory is such a good way of spotting the malcontents."

Up another flight and then Corrose was unchaining the tall doors to the rare books collection. He pushed them open—another waft of book smell came out—and a fan of distant city light spread across the carpet and peridot mosaics, revealing William's coffin waiting on the floor. This vision was so apt and beautiful that tears started in Leal's eyes.

The clouds had blown away from the center of the town wheel and the twinkle and glitter of distant streets lit the tall many-sided room through its towering windows. Dust motes danced in the limpid shafts of light.

Easley practically ran into the room. He quickly found the right spot and knelt to pry up the carpet. The other men carried William with stiff formality to the center of the room and set him down. Each in turn bowed to the coffin, then they turned as one and went to join Easley.

While they pried at the copper hatch, Leal walked to the middle of the room and scanned the gallery shelves. If William had left the *Polyhistoria* on the shelves at all, it would be up there, jammed next to some ancient census report or the plans for a long-demolished municipal office. She frowned, thinking, while she lit one of the desk lanterns.

"Easley! Come on." She was halfway up the stairs before he noticed. She swung the lantern to indicate that he should follow her.

"B-but William—we're about to say some words—"

"Easley, saving even one of these books is a better way to honor William than any ceremony. Come help me." On the gallery she hesitated. William's note had said, *Stack six*. But which of these bookshelves was stack six? She couldn't see any obvious numbering or place to start. After hemming and hawing for a few seconds she half-ran to a rolling ladder and moved it to the same stack where she'd found *Ancient Shapes* and *Denizens of the World's Skin*. It only took seconds to climb to those shelves—but then she was faced with the daunting picture of books stretching up and down, and to both sides, in a darkness only slightly tempered by the lantern. "Damn it."

"Leal, what are you looking for?" He was at the base of the ladder.

"It's called the *Polyhistoria*. I need it, I think it describes the monster."

"Hayden Griffin put you up to this, didn't he?"

"What? No no, Easley, he couldn't care less what the thing is, he just wants to kill it."

"So why do you care?"

"Because I believe it's trying to tell us something—trying so hard that it's willing to risk its own life, as well as all of ours, to get the message across."

Silence from below. Then: "What's that title again?"

If Leal glanced back she could see the workers man-handling William's coffin into his niche. She only looked once or twice. At first she closely scanned the spines of the books, but after a couple of minutes she started yanking them out, indiscriminately dropping her discards onto the gallery. Easley had been browsing on the floor; as the books thudded down he made an outraged sound and she snapped, "Get a lantern and help me!"

She found several very old, unique-looking books and stuffed them into her shoulder bag, more out of principle than because she expected to read them. She'd exhausted one shelf and was sliding the rolling ladder on its track past one of the tall windows, when she saw light in the street below. Leal let the ladder roll on and put her face to the glass. "Damn it!"

A squad of five soldiers stood in the middle of the copper avenue, the black silhouette of the history department behind them. Two held lanterns, and a third was pointing at the amber roadway.

Leal ran to the gallery rail. "They spotted our tracks!"

"We're almost done," replied Corrose. "Just got to seal the door."

She stepped back to the window. Two of the soldiers were running to one of the roadblocks. The other three were looking in Leal's direction.

She shrank back. "They're coming!"

"Okay! We're done, get down here, we'll exit through the steam tunnels." They would have come in that way, except that William would never have fit through the narrow spaces.

Leal looked up. The ladder reached to a new set of shelves. It was two feet away from her. "I'll be right there!" She clattered up it hastily.

Easley emerged from shadow to steady the ladder. "Come on, Leal. We have to go."

"In a second." She waved the lantern at the very top shelf. Several book spines had that telltale plastic look. She reached for the first one.

"Leal, Easley, come on! We have to go now!"

"We're right behind you!" She heard the workers running out of the room and glanced out the window again. At least ten soldiers were pounding up the street, and the ones who'd found the cart tracks were advancing on the library's entrance.

Leal realized that somehow, she'd tricked herself. She'd known all along that by coming here she was making an irreversible decision. She was taking sides. But even as they'd rolled William up the steps she'd been telling herself that she could get away from this unscathed, take up her position as dean, and somehow have the life she'd always dreamed about. But that had been a lie.

She would never have it—the house, the parties, the *respect*. She'd never have the respect of being an honored member of society, and maybe she'd never been owed it in the first place, but this damned city owed *something* to the name of Maspeth.

There were tears in her eyes as she indiscriminately yanked out books and threw them down; Easley cursed as one hit him. "Go!" she shouted at him. "Don't worry about me, I'll hide if they come in."

He growled. "Leal, you're as stubborn as my brother and I've never left him behind."

Leal started swearing. She'd reached the last of the books and none were the one she wanted. She slid down the ladder and hauled it in the direction of the next shelf. Easley grabbed her arm. "Are you suicidal?"

"If I'm going to lose everything, I might as well have the damned book in my hand when they catch me." He tried to hold her back but Leal pulled away and climbed the ladder. "Just tell me if they're—" But she could hear them now, harsh shouts from somewhere outside the big doors. Nothing that indicated they'd found Corrose and the others, but—

The lantern's faint light reflected from a glassy black spine that would have been invisible from the gallery floor. Leal lunged and yanked it free of its cloth-bound neighbors.

The Polyhistoria.

"I've got it!"

"They're coming! Leal, put the lantern out!"

They were in the hallway. Leal hastily stifled the lantern, but it was obvious now they were going to be caught. There was only one way in or out of the room, after all, and these men would be thorough in their search.

"Maybe—" Easley's voice was tinged with hysteria. "Maybe we can fit in William's niche—"

"Yeah, if we had ten minutes to pry it open again—and then who's going to pull the carpet over us and how are we going to get out—" Leal stopped, one hand clutching the book. She was staring at the window.

"You! Take your men and start with that room there."

Leal kicked out. Her first attempt missed, but on her second her heel connected with the latch to the glass louver in the center of the window. She kicked again, levering it open. The windows weren't big, but their framing was heavy, built to withstand a variety of gravitational conditions and accelerations.

"Come on, Easley." Leal stretched, putting one foot in the middle of the now-horizontal louver pane, gripping the top of the opening with one hand while the other clutched the ladder. Then she let go of the ladder and found herself standing on glass.

Easley was swearing as he climbed the ladder. "What are you doing?"

"I'm going outside." There was no time to explain that she'd dropped a book out the next window a few weeks ago and had hit a passing spokesman—which meant there must be some way up or down the building here.

Leal squeezed through the opening and looked around. Sure enough, a minor town spoke stood not four feet to the left of the window. It was a steel cable as thick as her thigh, smooth and apparently unbroken. It had to be smooth, if spokesmen could slide down it.

Easley's head appeared inches from her own, but on the other side of the glass. Each of them stood on one end of the louver pane now, like kids on a seesaw. Leal could feel the frame bending under her feet; a cracking sound came from the glass she stood on.

Below was nothing but blackness. She told herself it was just the dark sky, that she was in weightless air somewhere with nothing but cloud around her. Then she jumped.

Leal's hands and legs wrapped the cable, and she slid down it. She expected to be gutted by some jutting piece of broken wire but it didn't happen, and she went ten feet past the bottom of the window, and ten more, and then she heard faint shouting from above as the cable quivered to a new impact.

"Ahh!" Easley was coming down fast. Leal's feet touched something and she stepped off the cable. She was standing on one of the library's buttresses, about fifteen feet above street level. A second later Easley sprawled onto the spot she'd just vacated.

"Brilliant!" she said, helping him to his feet. "And we got the book."

"You're mad!"

She looked around for the way down. "Over here! Drainpipe."

She slid down and he followed, still cursing. And then they heard shouts from the windows above, answered by more from the street—and they ran.

BROOOM, BRAUUM, BRAAAAM. The foghorns sounded accusatory; Leal imagined giant bearded men standing in the air, pointing angry fingers at the tiny flea car that was hopping from wheel to wheel. Easley actually turned to look out the back window, and Leal slapped his knee.

"You're making yourself conspicuous," she hissed. Still, her own shoulders hunched, though who could knock on the car's door while it was in midair? (*Something* could, she reminded herself—but hopefully the monster was a thousand miles away right now.)

They'd made it to the flea car just in time. Just as the canopy was coming down, Leal had seen running figures rounding the corner behind them. They looked like soldiers; but those guarding the flea car stop hadn't noticed, and Leal's papers had already gotten her and Easley past them.

Easley leaned in, his whisper loud in the sudden silence of the airborne car. "Why are they so exercised? You'd think we'd robbed the prime minister's office or something."

The pilot glanced at them in the rearview, but Leal was fairly certain he hadn't heard Easley's exact words. She murmured, "They're afraid somebody might document what they did before they have a chance to cover it up. It's obvious which buildings on the campus were singled out. They haven't had a chance to even out the damage yet."

"Ah." He shook his head. "I just find it hard to think in such terms."

She hugged his arm. "That's why I'd trust you to the walls of the world."

He beamed. The vast tree painted on Rowan Wheel's underside flashed past, then the pilot adjusted the flaps and lined them up on a descending station. "Hope it's not too long a walk for you," he commented as the car settled onto its net and gravity slumped on again. "Those roadblocks can be a killer."

"This is fine, thanks," she said, although she had no idea where they were. Now Leal did glance back, and her heart skipped a beat: the air between Rowan and Match wheels was full of lights. "Come on," she said, grabbing Easley's hand as he was counting out bills for the pilot. "Forget the change."

She hauled him out of the station and looked up to get her bearings. "Damn it!" She could see her apartment building: it was directly overhead, over a mile away on foot.

"My place," said Easley. "This way." Leal flashed her credentials to the bored soldiers at the checkpoint, and they walked stiffly together until they were in the shadow of the first building; then they ran. It was Labor shift, so the streets were full of people, and that was both good—because it provided cover—and bad, because lots of those people were turning to watch them run past.

"They could get ahead of us," panted Easley. "The police stations—" She nodded. The police had their own hatches in the bottom of the town wheels, making it unnecessary for them to embark and disembark at the edges. They could pop out two streets up before she and Easley could get past.

"Under here." He led her into a dark archway that opened into the ground floor of an old office building. "Careful—there's a ramp."

"What is this place?"

"Underhull railway." His voice seemed to float on its own just ahead of her. "Byron wandered outside one day and ended up finding the other end. I guess it connected about six buildings throughout the wheel, at one time."

"But it comes up near your place?"

"Exactly." The blackness was total, but Leal was used to that. Stepping slowly with one arm held out at waist level, the other at head height, she slid her feet forward one after the other, and soon connected with the rail. She followed the sound of Easley's footsteps, tapping the rail with each step. No fear of beasts or monsters gnawed at her here; the creature that had harried her and eaten towns came from the open air, and there were no burrowing or slinking animals, other than spiders, alive in Virga. —And if men lurked down here, they would have lights.

So, feeling momentarily safe, Leal grasped at the thought that Corrose's people might not have been caught; that the soldiers following her and Easley might not have a clear notion of who they were after. She could lie low for a few hours, then pop up again as a respectable citizen, ready to take her place as dean in the newly revamped department . . . Except . . . Except that . . .

The familiar sounds of buildings made a counterpoint to her

own rough breathing; they creaked and shifted as the wheel rotated. Distant steam pipes rattled and banged as they expanded. It was cold down here, with the moan of the wind a constant, just like in Porril's office.

Porril's office. Leal stumbled to a stop, realizing something, unsure of just what it was.

Easley had stopped, too. "There!" he said.

"Where?" She was too distracted to look around. Something about Porril—

"Sorry, to the right, I think it's the ramp Byron found."

"Yes, of course." She shuffled in that direction, but as she did Leal experienced another momentary flash of memory—of Porril hunched alone over his desk with nothing but the whistling wind as his companion. The only other visible object, the portrait of his dead wife, which watched him unblinking from next to the door.

She should have said something. Just once, in all the times Leal visited that room, she should have put her hand on his, she should have caught his eye. She should have shown him that she cared. But every time, she'd been thinking only about herself and the next move in her own political game.

She'd barely even seen him.

Her legs were mechanically carrying her out of the train tunnel, but Leal barely noticed her surroundings. This feeling—this awful feeling, was it guilt? What stupid game was her subconscious playing with her, that she should be feeling that now?

"Now what?" said Easley. She blinked and found herself in the street outside his loft. He stood next to her, breathing hard, his hair disheveled.

"What?"

"We're home free—for now," he said. He started walking up the metal street. "You've got your book. What are you going to do with whatever it tells you?"

"I—" She couldn't say *I hadn't thought that far*, not after all Easley had put himself through. "Figure out what's really happening," she said.

That sounded woefully inadequate, and Leal was about to add something—something hopeful—but the words died as she took in the musty scent and the sight of row after row of canvas-wrapped shapes crowding the warehouse.

The door slammed shut and Easley sighed. "Well, don't hang about in the foyer," he said. "Come on upstairs and we'll break open a bottle of something hard."

Leal's hands were shaking. She followed silently, feeling very small now. That sense of triumphant outlawry which had sustained her over the past two days was completely gone.

"Wheh' you yest'day?" Byron stood at the top of the stairs, his head cocked to one side quizzically. Easley hugged him briefly, almost in reflex, and walked on. Byron started to turn and saw Leal.

She smiled at him, and his face was utterly transformed as he smiled back.

Then brilliant light washed across the windows—something coming from the street. It came back, was joined by another spotlight. She heard the sound of engines outside, then running feet.

Easley turned, face stark in the white light. She couldn't see his eyes, just their hollows shadowed in a pale shaft.

Somebody banged on the front door. "Open up! Police!"

Unhurried, Easley walked to the other side of the room, where more windows looked out on the warehouse space. "Leal, come here," he said.

She found herself stepping carefully around the glass cases and opulent furniture. Easley had opened one case, and was carefully taking a silvery thing out of it. "That window," he said, nodding over his shoulder, "will open. It's a short drop to a stack of crates and you can jump from stack to stack all the way to the back of the building. Trust me, I've tested it."

"Then—" Outside, maybe before the police could surround

the place? "Come on, then!" She pushed at the heavy industrial window, which swung out silently. Leal crouched on the lintel and looked back.

Easley was shaking his head. "You know I can't leave Byron."

"Easley . . . Easley, what's that?"

He glanced down at the thing in his hand, and grimaced. "Just go." She hesitated, and his face twisted in sudden rage. "*Go!* They won't follow you."

The downstairs door gave in. Byron let out a wail and ran for the steps and Easley shouted at him, then disappeared between leaning shafts of light and clean towers of glass. Leal made a little step into the air and fell a few feet, landing on canvas in a huge puff of dust.

The warehouse was well enough lit that she could see the staggered line of shrouded boxes that led across it. She was a good ten feet above the floor. She jumped from the first stack to the second—an easy hop—then to the next. She looked back as shouts erupted behind her.

There was a confusion of dancing silhouettes. Then all the windows glared orange. Glass shattered, something struck her—she realized it was a shock wave of air. Orange flashed again, then again in a quick stuttering pattern. She heard screaming.

Leal had gone to her knees; she crouched again, turned and jumped, and jumped as the orange was joined by other fire colors and twisting sinews of flame cast shuddering shadows across the warehouse's interior.

She reached the wall, a chaos of noise behind her, the feel of heat on her back. The window was just above her head; when she reached up it opened easily and she clambered up and over. There was a metal ladder on the outside so she climbed down it into blackness. When the rungs gave out she felt about with her foot, then simply let go and fell about seven feet.

Leal staggered away, a long shadow preceding her along the

copper alley. She was between two tall buildings that nearly met, both of which abutted Easley's place. Anybody circling around would have to go all the way around the block. Maybe she'd be able to—

Running forms carrying lanterns appeared at the far end of the black canyon. "Hey! Is that someone?" There were at least six of them.

Leal backed away, but a glance behind her showed there was no place to run. The entire interior of Easley's warehouse was afire. The windows next to the one she'd come from were already breaking.

In a few minutes Easley's museum would finally experience the fate the Eternists had originally planned for it: the copper decking below it would give way and the whole building would fall into the turning air. Maybe a few burning treasures would thud harmlessly against the underside of another town wheel. The rest would just be embers scattered on the sky.

The soldiers clattered up the alley. She could see glints of rifle and strap. Leal put her hands up.

Somebody grabbed her wrists and pulled up, hard. She squeaked in shock but she'd already risen twenty feet and was still ascending.

"Quiet," hissed a voice just above her, "or they'll see us."

Leal looked down between her kicking feet. The soldiers were spread out through the whole alley now. She heard one of them say, "Would'a sworn I saw—" and then her swift ascent ended.

"Gonna swing you now," whispered the voice. His grip hurt badly, like he was crushing her wrist bones. After a few seconds she felt the tug and a sway as they began to swing like a pendulum.

"You're going to have to find your footing and anchor us both." Something brushed by her ankle and she flailed at it. On the next swing she let it bump past and swung both feet down. There was a ledge or something under her now. Momentum made to swing them back, but she let her knees buckle while scrabbling with her toes on the metal decking. The scrape sounded loudly in her own ears, but they had stopped.

Leal had a horribly wonderful view of the burning warehouse, but no time to let it register as with a *zizzing* sound, the man holding her wrists righted himself and landed next to her.

"Hey, Professor," said the familiar voice.

"J-Jax?"

The spokesman nodded. "I never did get your name."

"Leal. Leal Maspeth. You—" She looked down at the alley, where the soldiers were retreating as the back wall of Easley's place leaned out a bit. Smoke and fierce heat whipped past Leal, making her eyes sting. "What are you doing here?"

"Me and some friends were going over the campus," he said, "you know, making drawings of what they'd done to the place. The idiots were watching every street and alley, but never thought to look up. Anyway, I saw your group going in the library and waited to see what happened. When you and that other fellow came out I followed you."

"Up above."

"Yeah. I, I thought I might know you," he added, as if he felt he needed to explain. "Your friend, he, he didn't—?"

She shook her head. They were both silent for a while. Then she said, "What about the others—the other people I was with at the library? Did the soldiers . . . ?" He shook his head.

"They came out empty-handed. I was impressed how you all got away—but they spotted you two."

"Yeah," she said, gazing down at the fire. "They did."

Gradually she came to notice that they stood on a tiny platform, not more than three feet on a side, that was fixed in the bricks next to one of the inevitable spoke cables. This thick shaft was itself entwined with lesser wires and ropes like crowding vines. Jax was rolling up a long bungee cord that he must have hooked among those.

"I can take you somewhere," he said. He was looking past her, at the fire.

Leal felt ready to collapse, but she nodded.

"The docks," she said. "Get me to my boat."

16

SILENCE, DARKNESS, AND a rope road. Every now and then Leal would glance up to make sure the rope was still visible, undulating through the faint beam from the cutter's headlamp. Then she would return her attention to the tiny, crabbed lines of text that filled the pages of the *Polyhistoria*.

The spokesman, Jax, had delivered her as promised to the docks. They'd barely spoken on the way, though she knew he was bursting with curiosity about why she had broken into the library. As they were about to part, she'd relented and told him about William and his final resting place; but she hadn't mentioned the book she was now reading.

"Do you have a place to go?" he'd asked. She nodded.

"I have friends." It was true: she was sure Hayden's people would hide her, although they couldn't do it forever. But she could not, in all conscience, take that way out.

She kept thinking about Easley, and was so sorry now that she had misjudged him all these years. He'd been walled in by necessity, and yet he'd held up under the strain of his obligations remarkably well. What had he wished he could become, during those many long nights alone in his bed? Surely he'd had dreams once, but he'd shelved them all for the sake of his brother and their cold museum of dead machinery. Leal had once held contempt for anybody foolish enough to do that. Now she saw in Easley's choices a brand of heroism more mature than the dashing adventurism of a Hayden Griffin.

The grief and regret threatened to consume her. To escape it, she turned to the Polyhistoria—yet found herself reluctant to open that. Her dogged determination to find it was after all what had gotten Easley killed. When she opened it she would doubtless find the ramblings of some ancient fool. It was surely valueless, a lunatic's diatribe worth less than the tiniest trinket in Easley's museum. Within moments of starting to read, she would discover that he had given his life for no reason at all, and she had given up her city, her life there, and maybe life itself, for empty words.

The Polyhistoria began:

They say history is written by the winners. If so, then this is the testament of a loser.

My subject is nothing less than the greatest mistake humanity ever made, and how it came about; of how we humans of Virga came to fear those most loyal to us; and how we came to ally ourselves with forces bent on our own destruction simply because those forces were more familiar to us than our true friends.

If you should wonder, dear reader, what it was that panicked us so, and what qualities those vast cool minds had who helped make our world and who we betrayed; if you should wish to know the nature of such unimaginable forces as could build a Virga or a Crucible; then, before you read on, place your fingers to the drumming vein in your own neck.

Reading that Leal sobbed, and nearly threw the book away in despair. Her eyes were caught, though, by the next lines:

For the engine you feel beneath your skin is akin to the engines of those minds whose friendship we rejected in this most important way: it is unconscious. Designed, yet with no designer; clever, though unthinking; efficient, yet utterly unplanned. So are all the mechanisms that, unnoticed by you, orchestrate the great symphony of your own consciousness.

So if you were to seek the powers that created and sustain our world—our true allies—you would be mistaken to look for anything resembling a human agency. Indeed, the hunt for such an agency has doomed millions of men and women, and it doomed us, the inheritors of Virga.

Something flickered in the corner of her eye; Leal looked up and waited. After several seconds it came again: a brief stab of green light, a mile or two away from the rope. This was her exit.

She carefully set her new gyrocompass and checked it three times before blowing out a deep breath, and turning the cutter away from the road. Ahead of her now were black clouds in a black sky, and no towns, no farms, no industry. She was leaving her country.

For a minute or two she registered the reflected flash of the beacon, and then it was gone. Leal's hands shook a bit as she checked the compass again. If she hadn't had the reassurance of its little radium dials glowing in counterpoint to the phosphorescent anemones on the dashboard, she would have turned back. Even though there was nothing to go back to now.

It was no longer safe to read. She had to keep a constant eye out for the hazards of unknown air—in particular, this close to the world's wall there might be icebergs. The problem was that there was literally nothing to see; she might not encounter anything for hours, but she had to remain vigilant because rocks, broken spars of wood, or other missiles would give little warning. This meant she had nothing to do but watch through the windscreen, and think.

Everything she'd done in Sere seemed like some play she'd rehearsed, but never actually performed. She'd been proud of her life there, but her friends—even Seana—now felt half-real, and her accomplishments meaningless. She'd walked out of bright childhood and into a city of silhouetted strangers and dark ambitions, and she'd let it carry her somewhere very far away from herself. She'd forgotten why she'd gone there, and what she had wanted to achieve.

The Leal of two months ago would have wallowed in self-pity at such a thought. She would have overanalyzed her situation and schemed and planned how to get out of it—how to think her way out of it. But she had no time for that sort of thing anymore. Events had stripped her of any right to be self-indulgent.

Now, whenever her thoughts dove toward panic or maudlin sentimentality, Leal gave herself a shake and checked the compass. She stretched (insofar as the cramped cockpit would let her) and blinked and reset her eyes on the shifting darkness swirling by. She made herself think only about what Brun had said and what the *Polyhistoria* hinted at.

The person she had been for the past six years was a stranger to her. In the black of winter air, silent and alone, Leal coldly strangled that version of herself into silence.

IT WAS FREEZING. Leal hadn't had time to dress properly, though she'd known her destination when she and Jax set out for the docks. The cutter had a heater and she was running it full-blast, even though it used extra fuel; but its thin trickle of warmth couldn't compete with the relentless press of the frosty air against the windscreen.

Leal was forced to become more vigilant when specks and drifts of white began to flit past. She began skirting around cloud masses rather than trying to sail through them. To the unwary, this region was even more hazardous than the kingdom of Rain, because the clouds were no longer made of water droplets, but instead were composed of snow, beads of hail, and larger ice-balls that wouldn't just choke a jet. They'd shatter its fans and explode in its burners.

And some of the snowflakes were the size of dinner plates.

Her eyes were burning and her shoulders and neck ached from holding one position for hours. Her gyrocompasses (she was using both her old one and the gleaming new one) were her only lifeline now. When they told Leal that she'd come four hundred miles, she throttled back on the engines and let the cutter drift forward at little more than a walking pace. She was close now.

Something like the prow of a giant white ship loomed out of the curling currents of snow. Even though she'd been watching for this,

Leal was startled and the cutter wobbled dangerously close before she steered a path safely past the iceberg. This one was a thousand feet long, a spear of white snow and deeply cupped emerald ice. She cautiously drifted to its aft end to see if it was attached to anything. No: it had come unmoored sometime in the past few days, and was slowly, inch by inch, starting to fall toward Candesce.

It would evaporate long before it got there, of course. Only the rare, mountain-sized bergs made it to the Principalities of Candesce, there to play havoc with traffic patterns and town locations until they exploded in the heat of the sun of suns.

A few miles past the berg, her headlamp became visible as a kind of solid shaft made of billions of speckles of snow. Hovering at the edges of visibility was an ice fog, a coil of deadly cold that made Leal hug herself, teeth chattering. —And then, a vision emerged from the black and white of a place Leal had never seen, but had heard about her whole life.

At first it looked like she was staring down from above at a dense mob of white-haired, palely dressed people. This thick crowd stretched away indefinitely to left, right, and up and down; its edges would be lost in darkness, if it had edges. Nobody in the crowd moved, and as the cutter drifted forward it became clear that she was miles away yet. The people were icebergs, millions upon millions of them jammed together cheek-by-jowl. Though she seemed to be looking down on them, the reverse was true—they hung like bats from the outer shell of the world, where all directions led down.

Bedtime stories, adolescent fantasies, even whole operas were set at the walls of Virga. Maybe one in a thousand people ever saw them, for outside of Candesce itself, this was the most inhospitable place in the world. Nothing lived here, and there was nothing to mine, no resources other than ice to be found. This was the domain of the precipice moths and the legendary Virga Home Guard.

It was said that somewhere on the far side of the world, a cyclopean gate was set into the wall. Sometimes it would open, and a fantastical ship sealed against the cold and vacuum of space would enter. *Ancient Shapes* contained an engraving of such a ship, represented as a long whale-shape trailing coils of mist.

The air was relatively clear; Leal could see for miles. It was too cold for her to admire the view for long, though. She checked the compass again and then turned the cutter at right angles to the wall of bergs. Something even more extraordinary than the berg fields awaited two hundred miles along this course.

The next few hours were a blur. She cross-checked the compasses, edged the cutter one way or another, and kept the bergs on her starboard side. When the air was clear she accelerated, for brief periods making a hundred-fifty miles per hour or more. Clouds would approach like a solid wall and she'd deploy the braking sails, throttle back, and nose her way into them at five miles per hour. Then, uncountable snowflakes would tease and confuse her vision, making her curse and twist the controls to avoid imaginary obstacles.

And through every second of those long hours, she was aware of the broken past stretching behind her, of places never to be returned to, and people never to be seen again.

THE AIR WAS clear when she reached the mystery. Leal had been skimming close to the berg tops to keep awake, so her eyes were on the grotesque animalistic shapes that reared up in the headlamp. She was looking ahead to judge how the bergscape was curving when she saw it suddenly cut off, a jagged tooth-line passing from infinity left-to-right, and nothing but blackness beyond it. At first she assumed she was approaching a particularly dense bank of cloud that adhered to Virga's wall; but as it came closer she saw that in fact the iceberg fields simply ended here.

She was half-delirious with exhaustion, ravenously hungry, and sore all over, so it seemed perfectly reasonable at that moment to open the frost-painted canopy of the cutter and look with her own eyes.

The cold pounced as she pried back the plastic bubble, but as she gasped Leal came entirely awake. She was shivering, but alive. Exhilarated, she gave a whoop of triumph. Whatever else happened, she had made it this far.

There was an ancient word—of no relevance in Virga—that she remembered tasting and saying when she'd first read it as a girl. The word was *shore*, and it was a shoreline she was looking at now. The black, smooth skin of Virga was visible past the line of bergs, only because of an oily, iridescent shimmer that it sometimes reflected.

Denizens of the World's Skin spoke of *eaners*, gigantic beings who scoured the world's skin clear of icebergs. It seemed that in this case, at least, the book was accurate. Leal could see no sign of life here, but what else but some monstrous worm could have grazed on such an immensity of ice?

Brun and his men had been surprised when they'd stumbled upon this patch and, curious, his expedition had mapped it. This ice-clear patch of wall was six hundred miles across, and as far as Brun could tell it was perfectly circular.

The place Leal was looking for, Brun's "hole in the sky," was at the center of the circle.

Her headlamp was so feeble, and this plain so vast, that she could have hunted for that fabled aperture for the rest of her life; but Brun had told her how to find the center of the circle.

"Use one compass to enter a course perpendicular to the edge of the berg-line," he'd said. "Then follow the bergs a hundred miles or so and set a similar course with a second compass. Follow that course in such a way that both compass readings converge. Where they meet is the center of the circle."

She was so tired. Leal set the first course but the prospect of flying another five or six hundred miles, setting a new course along the way, was just too daunting. She steered the cutter back to the line of motionless bergs; her headlight roved over them, momentarily exposing shoulder, knee, or fang among the white giants. Finally she chose a jagged, splintered cone that had plenty of mooring spots for her rope. She tied the cutter to it and shut down the engines.

At first she thought she and the whole world had been swallowed by some monstrous, absolute silence; but as Leal drifted off to sleep she could hear the whir of the little heater she was wrapped around—and beyond that, a kind of constant muttering, almost too faint to make out. It wasn't the voice of the monster, she was sure. Her lullaby was the slow jostling of millions of icebergs, a conversation in grinding ice.

IT WASN'T HUNGER, but thirst that forced her into action again. Leal's sleep had been uneasy and intermittent, and there was no clear border between it and her new day. Still exhausted, she simply had to abandon rest in the face of her body's needs.

Leal had been knotted up behind the pilot's seat. When she turned and made to climb back into it she discovered that the inside of the plastic canopy was entirely frosted over. She was going to have to scrape that clear. There were various tools in a box attached to the dart-shaped craft's spine, so she made to open the canopy, only to find that it had frozen shut. She spent a few panicky minutes kicking at it until she was able to lever it up, and then a terrible, raw cold invaded instantly.

This was a cold like fire, a physical pain on her skin and a dry flame in her nose and mouth. Leal breathed in little gasps, quickly hand-walking back to the ship's spine. Her fingers were already numb by the time she got the toolkit open. Pulling out a flat metal plate that might do as a scraper, she used it to chip some ice off the ship's tail. She cast off her anchor lines, jumped to the canopy, and only then paused to look around herself.

As a girl Leal had often imagined she was a princess on long-lost Earth. It was an almost impossible task to try to imagine life on a planet, but she'd done her best. Now she had a glimpse of what it might be like—and decided her wish had been foolish.

She stood on the narrow wing of a tiny airship that perched in turn on a jagged spire of pearly ice. There was light enough to see, provided by distant flickerings of lightning in the clouds overhead, and this shifting radiance revealed just how small she was, and how vast and endless was the shore on which she stood. The black plain ahead of her might be a nighttime ocean; all she lacked were stars. Those, she knew, were shining below that plain.

She dove for the canopy and slammed it hard. Putting the icechip atwirling in front of the heater's vent, she set to scraping. When she had a little patch she could see through, Leal put her feet on the cutter's starter pedals and started pushing with her feet. She'd forgotten to do this before she fell asleep, which was potentially bad news if the mechanisms had frozen. But the starter was very simple, just a big spring that she wound with the pedals. After a few minutes, when the pedals wouldn't turn anymore, she prayed that the cutter's alcohol fuel hadn't frozen in the lines, and pushed the ignition button.

The uncoiling spring would spin up the jets' fans, push fuel through the lines, and compress the piezoelectric sparkers. Leal heard a terrible creaking and grinding come from the aft end of the ship, and then whump on one side and, a moment later, thump from the other. The jets were live.

While she waited for them to warm up, she harvested little beads of water from the melting ice-sliver, drinking them eagerly until it was mostly gone. Then she strapped herself in, gunned the engines, and set off parallel to the shore.

After a while she felt more alert, and ultimately couldn't resist inching the cutter close to the black skin, then closer, until she was able to slow and put her hand up to touch it. It had a grain, like wood.

But it wasn't cold at all.

She snatched her hand back. She'd expected something even more intense than the breath of the iceberg forest, but the world's skin felt closer to room temperature.

It was a mystery with no hint of a solution. She slammed the canopy and moved on.

A half hour later, as she set a course with the second compass, it occurred to Leal that she had no memory of her thoughts or emotions since she'd awoken. Maybe her brain was as numb as her fingers. Maybe the needs of survival had stripped her down to something more fundamental than the civilized person she'd always considered herself to be. That was a hopeful thought—because if it was true, that more fundamental self was proving to be calm and resourceful.

One more leg to this journey. The cutter's nose was pointed out into the black plain. She opened the throttle and shot off across it, expecting that this last leg would be the simplest.

Within minutes the frost began melting away from the canopy and soon the plastic was cool but no longer cold to her touch. The heater caught up at last, and the cockpit became positively cozy. Leal was able to warm her white fingers back to feeling again. She watched the numbers on the gyrocompasses, and made sure that those on her arbitrarily chosen X axis were converging.

To her surprise, though, the flying itself proved really hard, and exhausting in a whole new way. The world's skin was black as chondrite and it was almost impossible to judge how far she was from it. She had to keep it within view, but constantly risked a collision, a problem made worse by the fact that this vast surface curved imperceptibly but inexorably inward. Three times she was jolted by a sudden nasty scraping as her keel touched it, and each time Leal swore and pulled up, only to find herself shaking and unsure of which way she was pointing. Without the compasses, she would have been utterly lost.

Yet eventually, the X-axis numbers approached each other and she slowed, staring out with sore eyes then rechecking the compasses, over and over as the minutes stretched. *This is it.* The center of the circle.

Center was a relative term, she was realizing. Her estimations had probably put her somewhere within a patch twenty to fifty miles on a side; now she had to locate a single anomaly, maybe only a few yards across, within that area. She was more likely to run out of fuel than find it.

What saved her was the sheer blackness of Virga's skin. Against that, any object—no matter how dull—stood out like a beacon. Leal's heart leapt when she spotted a faint patch of gray against the unremitting black, but it took several minutes for her to reach it. Her headlight had picked it out when it was a good two miles away—and as she approached, it became clear that this place was intended to be visible from great distances.

Great neon-green and yellow flags jutted from the world's skin, their twenty-foot triangles fluttering slightly but angled at the wall as if a breeze was running to it.

Huddled around the base of these tall masts were a number of plain wooden buildings.

Leal brought her cutter to a stop thirty feet short of an ordinary-looking house that clung to the bare plain of Virga's wall.

THERE WERE FOUR buildings here, arranged in a rough square around a central blot of darkness. Two of them were typical freefall houses, eight-sided and built of triangular frames. These had no up or down to them, being more inspired by wasps' nests than any traditional human architecture. The other two buildings were town houses, complete with roofs, floors, and doors at their base. They seemed to have been glued to the surface of the wall.

No lights were on in any of the buildings; they all projected an air of forlorn abandonment, reinforced by the tattered appearance of the banners.

Brun hadn't mentioned these buildings. But, as the cutter drifted over the shingled roof of one of the houses, its headlight shone on the area framed by the buildings, and she knew this was the place.

Something had torn or blown a hole in the skin of the world. The puncture wasn't large—maybe forty by twenty feet—but a kind of scar extended for hundreds of feet in every direction, as if it had once been much bigger but had mostly healed over. The buildings sat on this scar.

The edges of the hole were silvery, and they shimmered in the headlamp—no, they *moved*. Hundreds of mirror-bright crab-shaped things were scuttling along the edges of the aperture. Leal couldn't tell if they were alive, or were mechanisms of some sort. *Tegumen*, perhaps?

She brought the cutter directly over the hole. She could feel a breeze tugging the craft toward the hole, but it wasn't very strong—not the irresistible hurricane she'd been told would form over any rip in Virga's skin. The world's tough skin kept its air from bursting out into a vacuum, or so she'd been taught. Any puncture instantly caused a hurricane to form over it, though most were promptly choked shut by icebergs. Yet here, it was easy for the cutter to resist this steady but light wind.

Pieces of splintered wood crisscrossed the hole; there was nothing but blackness beyond it. Had the people who brought these houses here actually *boarded over* the hole? Yes, she could see hinges glinting on one piece that flapped in the wind. Whoever they were, they'd built a wall across the hole and put a door in it. And then sometime—recently from the color of the splinters— something had broken through that gate.

Leal shivered. Had this been a Home Guard outpost? She tried to imagine being billeted here, sent to guard a doorway to nothingness. How could you sleep with that open maw outside your window? And what had happened on the day when something had come from the other side and knocked upon the door?

Leal huddled in the cockpit, biting her fingernails and staring. She was hungry, thirsty, and bone-weary, and the cutter was almost out of fuel. She wanted to explore that doorway (her own curiosity filling her with a crawling sense of horror) but she was in no shape to do anything right now. So she brought the cutter over to one of the houses and moored it outside the front door.

The buildings were connected by long tubes of netting and there were plenty of ropes looped everywhere. She found it easy to hand-walk to the house and open the door—but she hesitated long moments before she could summon the courage to do this.

The place had been trashed. Her wind-up lantern showed a main room with the typical fixtures of a freefall domicile: storage cabinets on all four walls plus the floor and ceiling; a variety of wooden frames and meshworks that could hold stuff while you worked on it. Nothing like a chair or a couch, of course. All the cabinets were open, the frames were bent and broken, and a galaxy of tools, books, and clothing sat motionless in the air.

Leal screamed and kicked back to the door. *A body. A dead man.* She slowly advanced again, holding out the lantern like a weapon.

It wasn't a man, but a man-sized sculpture built out of junk. She recognized one of the bodies of the monster, though this one had none of the white threads interwoven through it. Abandoned?

As she looked more closely she saw that the interior of the room had been stripped, and several of these man-shaped things built out of the material. Leal could quite clearly picture what had happened: the thing had made bodies for itself here, which meant there had been someone in this house that it wanted to yell at.

There probably were bodies here, but she would have to take that chance if she was to find any food or water.

The next room was the kitchen, and she was in luck: a big cistern sat in the corner, and the cupboards held some sealed tins of biscuits and fruit. She wouldn't starve.

A couple of hours later she'd explored three of the buildings, finding no bodies, but locating some barrels of fuel alcohol in one of the octagonal buildings. When she found these she actually burst into tears, a spasm that lasted ten seconds and then was replaced by a terrible calm. She could escape from here, back to civilization—though never, she thought, back to Abyss. She might yet have a life.

With that realization, her weariness overcame her. After eating and refueling the cutter, Leal retreated to an empty bedroom in the house. She wrapped herself in clean linen from an untouched closet, and slept.

She awoke in perfect blackness to the sound of thunder. It took her almost a minute to find the room's door; when she opened it she was greeted by blue-white flashes through the hall window. Leal jumped to it and pressed her fingers and nose against the glass.

A very compact lightning storm was approaching. It looked sort of like a flickering blue ball, miles away but approaching rapidly. With a start she saw that the cloud banks lit by its flickering light were moving in a different direction. Then she noticed the way the flashes were becoming fuzzy, as though a fog was coalescing in front of them.

As the first white threads landed, to twine and combine into webs on the roof, Leal turned and jumped for the stairs, the front door, and her cutter.

17

THUNDER ECHOED OFF the world's endless wall. White fuzz was already growing on the cutter, standing up like mold on the canopy as Leal hauled it open. She had again neglected to wind the starter spring when she'd arrived and now pedaled madly even as shingles, boards, ropes, and netting began to drift into the space between her and the buildings. She heard the sound of things breaking in the house; in seconds the monster would start taking the cutter apart, too, in its haste to assemble its bodies.

Flashes half-blinded her and the fierce bangs were getting closer. She risked a look over her shoulder as she pushed into the final turns of the pedals. In halting, chaotic snapshots she made out a huge cloud, thunderhead-sized, that was surging upon her at an impossible speed. In a clear area at its center was a steady gleam—she recognized the headlamps of a mid-sized ship.

It was Hayden Griffin. He was battling the monster.

Leal stubbed her thumb stabbing at the starter button. As the engines whined into life she realized she hadn't cast off her mooring line, but when she turned to look she saw that it wasn't a problem: the rope had already been incorporated into the body of a man-sized thing that was climbing onto the cutter's hull just behind the cockpit.

In her panic she gunned the engines but the cutter's nose was angled toward the wall so she hit that and bounced through one of the net tubes that connected the buildings. The tube swept over the cutter like a broom, sweeping most of the monster off of her as she arrowed away.

The whole sky was full of lightning and overlapping thunder. The cloud was upon her, settling against the wall about a mile out; she felt like a spider trapped under a bowl. There was no way out except through it, and there was no way through it. As she hesitated she saw that it was all collapsing, and long streamers of lightning-lit white were raveling and twining like cloth into solid cones aimed straight at her.

She wanted to get to Hayden's ship, but to try would take her through the worst of the lightning.

With a curse, Leal spun the cutter and aimed it at the wall.

Something tapped on the plastic behind her head. Little hands, their fingers made of pins and nails, scrabbled at the canopy's latch. Leal laughed, a bit hysterically, and gunned the engines. With a roar and a reassuring surge of power the cutter shot straight at the broken gateway. The impact and sound of breaking boards reached her, then she was through Brun's hole in the sky, and into a darkness identical to that which she'd left.

Except that here, there was no lightning. Leal took her hands off the controls, letting the cutter fly straight, as she zeroed her new gyrocompass. That done, she finally strapped herself into her seat and as the seconds dragged on and she heard only normal engine noise behind her, she blew out a heavy sigh.

Tap tap tap. She started, cursed, and glared at the absurd little figure that was clinging to the canopy latch. It was like a doll cobbled together out of the contents of somebody's junk drawer. Its head was the burner and wick of a gas lamp, its feet were doorknobs. Its body was a tangle of string, pens, buttons, and whatnot. It was holding on for dear life with little hands made of fine scraps of metal—needles, paper clips, and what looked like the parts of a belt buckle.

It was tempting to open the cutter's throttle until the headwind tore it off. But the same rules of darkness flying applied here—wherever here was—as on the other side of the wall. She might hit something going two hundred miles per hour, and that would be that.

More importantly, though, this was the perfect opportunity. It was why she'd come here, and Leal was not going to find a more favorable moment than this for what she had in mind.

She unlatched the canopy and pushed it up just far enough for the little man to clamber inside. Then she slammed it.

"*You must listen!*" the tiny monster squeaked. She grabbed it as it made to climb onto the dashboard, and then she shook it fiercely.

"No!" she bellowed. "*You* must listen!"

"*Y-you m-must—*" She shook it harder and it started to come apart. "*S-s-stop! You must—we must . . . Ack!*" It fell silent. Leal stopped shaking it and jammed it (a little hard) under the curve of the canopy.

"I've had it with your shouting!" It tried to speak and Leal flicked it with her finger. "No! It's time you listened for a change. What do you think you're doing? You've killed people, for God's sake. I know you've been trying to tell us something, but it's not working! Do you understand? It's not working."

The little junk-doll sat silent for a moment. It was holding itself to the top of the dashboard with its hands, so with its arms at its sides and its feet dangling over the dash it looked a bit like a child sitting on a wall. The bulb-shaped wick that was its head turned this way and that. Then, in its pipsqueak voice, it said, "To shout did not work.

"Shout was all I could do."

Leal gaped at it. It tilted its head up as if looking at her, a gesture so human that Leal felt prickles down her back. "Why did you keep at it if you knew you were . . . hurting us?"

"I hurt no one. Some hurt themselves."

"I . . ." Well, that was probably true—and she had guessed it to be so, or she wouldn't have come here. "But *why?*"

"Candesce," said the junk-doll. "Candesce is a fire in the mind . . . inside Virga. There, I become beast. My simple message becomes too . . . complex. I cannot remember it."

"You're being very articulate now."

"We are not inside Virga."

That made Leal blink and look around. There was nothing outside, only black; not even a wisp of cloud appeared in the cutter's headlight. But this was not that fabled place, outer space, because air was whistling in around the edges of the canopy. "Then where are we?"

"In one of your old languages, this world was known as Aethyr. We remain within the arena."

"A-arena?"

The junk-doll raised a hand, scratching at its wick. "I know but cannot . . . explain. This body too small. Explanation needs more of . . . myselves."

"I don't want more of you in here."

"Yet I approach." The canopy was lit suddenly by a distant flash. Leal throttled back the engines and spun the cutter around its center of gravity. Now flying backward, she was able to see the way they'd come. The faint cone of light from the cutter's headlamp illuminated a black wall identical to the one on the other side— but at one point, bright sparks of light were flickering. That must be the hole she'd come through.

A gray cloud was rapidly forming around that point. It shot out branches and balls, fuzzy tufts that cavorted like dolphins in the empty air. As Leal watched, some of those puffs collapsed in on themselves, suddenly revealing flat planes, right angles, and sharp edges. Little points of light flared into being, running lights on suddenly solid aircraft.

The thing the Pacquaean commander had called the emissary poured through the hole in the wall and as it left Virga it organized, turning from smoke to object. In seconds she found herself gazing at a gaudily striped, two-hundred-foot-long spindle craft, with ailerons and other control surfaces much like a ship. It was dotted with lights, and surrounded by dozens of little free-flying shapes, like birds circling a whale.

"Here I come," said the junk-doll.

"Wait, wait! Stop! I'm not going to talk to you if you throw all that at me. I don't want to be . . . swallowed, or yelled at by all that. Just you, I just want to talk to you. This little body. Okay?"

The junk-doll tilted its head, appearing to consider her request. "If more of me is nearby," it said, "perhaps then."

She sighed in relief. "Good." Then she frowned. "You say you couldn't think inside Virga. So why didn't you write something, a . . . a message in a bottle?"

The doll tilted its head the other way. "What is writing?"

At that moment orange and red blossoming explosions lit up the night. The flames were jetting from the hole in the world's wall. The junk-doll raised its head to look. "That won't work," it said.

"What won't work?"

"Fast chemical reactions." Hayden must be using missiles to try to widen the tear in the wall. After a few seconds the explosions stopped and a pall of smoke drifted away, and she saw that the doll was right: her headlamp revealed the tear looking exactly as it had before—though a chrome crab fluttered out of the dark and tumbled past the cutter. The junk-doll turned to watch it pass.

The monster's larger body hove to, not more than a hundred feet away. Leal's cutter was dwarfed by it, as Hayden's yacht would be if he managed to squeeze it through the hole. "He can't follow us," Leal mused aloud. The junk-doll nodded.

"Not in the big shell, no. Do you come to talk to me?"

She focused her attention on the little man-shape. "Yes. I do. I wanted to tell you to stop what you were doing."

It shook its head. "I must convey my message."

"And that is . . . ?"

"That we renew the offer that we made to your ancestors. The offer you refused."

Leal stared at the little figure. A weird prickling feeling was going down her spine. "The offer . . . we *refused*."

"Yes. For Virga as you know it will die unless you accept our help. In return for that aid, we require the secret of Candesce."

This message was clear—but there was something else to it, something in the wording . . . Reaching into her coat, she withdrew the *Polyhistoria*. She couldn't find the passage she wanted, but she remembered what she'd transcribed into her notebooks. Eying the junk-doll, she quoted: "Anything that can desire can use intelligence and consciousness, even if it is not itself intelligent or conscious."

The junk-doll adopted a listening posture.

"And your desires are strong, aren't they?" she murmured to it.

"If one has power," said the junk-doll, "one does not need awareness."

What was it that we refused, Leal wondered, *all those centuries ago?*

"Your desires," she said. "You think . . . they're the same as ours."

Blinding light flashed and popped: lightning, and nearby. A deafening clap of thunder followed almost immediately, and when Leal blinked away the afterimages she saw the junk-doll twitching in the air. "Sur—" it squeaked. "Saah—surr . . ."

A twin-engined boat, even smaller than her cutter, had appeared on this side of the hole. Leal could make out a couple of human shapes in its tiny cabin.

Several hundred feet behind it, tied to the boat with strong cables, was the little fusion reactor Hayden had shown her, the one from the yacht's hold. It was smoking and the air around it wavered.

The gaudy main body of the monster shuddered. She saw flecks of white peel off of it as it strained to accelerate away. Some of its outrider bodies had come apart.

"*Stop!*" She screamed it at the boat, but the canopy was closed; they probably couldn't even tell that her cutter was distinct from the monster. "Damn damn damn—" She opened the throttle and the cutter surged away from the monster, back to the wall.

"Sur—sah," said the junk-doll. "Wait. The me-message—"

They'd seen her; one of the little figures in the boat was throwing its canopy back and raising a rifle. Leal hastily lit her lantern and, pushing her own canopy back, stood up in her seat, waving the lantern.

The figure hesitated. The two vessels drifted closer.

"L-listen . . ." The junk-doll was starting to crumble.

She looked over her shoulder. The emissary's main body was accelerating into the dark. In seconds it would be out of sight.

She idled her engines and drifted closer to the boat, which was spade-shaped and not more than twelve feet in length: a little tug, just strong enough to haul about a multi-megawatt engine of destruction.

"Hey there!" she shouted. "Don't shoot!"

"Who are you?"

She recognized the voice, and laughed giddily. "Hayden, has it been that long? It's Leal."

He slid the rifle back into a sheath next to his seat and climbed farther out onto the prow of the boat. She could hear him swearing. "What are you *doing* out here? This is a war zone!"

"No," she said, "it's not. There's been a misunderstanding. Hayden, you have to turn off your weapon!"

"Turn off—? Look out!" He dove for his seat and Leal spun around to see the emissary's main body diving out of the blackness. The junk-doll twitched and said, "The m-m-message—"

Hayden twisted some control in the boat's dashboard and suddenly lightning was curling and twining around the emissary. Its sleek whale-shape dissolved behind clouds of smoke and peeling flakes of hull. Its lights went out.

"Hayden," she screamed, "stop!" The emissary was willing to sacrifice itself for the chance to tell her something—but it wasn't going to survive long enough.

She looked back at the boat. Hayden Griffin was standing up in his seat again, reaching his hand out to her. "Jump across!" he shouted. "Your ship's not shielded! A radio source this strong could set your fuel alight."

The outstretched hand of a hero. She stared at it. He could protect her, she realized—drop her off at Batetran or some other neutral port and pick her up when he was done being dragon-killer. As a sun lighter's friend and maybe companion, she could put Sere and her whole dark life behind her and start over. Whether there would be love or not, there was at least an opportunity.

She bit her lip and, meeting Hayden's eyes, shook her head. Then she slammed the canopy, spun the cutter, and opened the throttle all the way. Lightning, light, and hope faded quickly behind her.

PORRIL STOOD AMONG the mushrooms of his garden and stared up at the sky. Things were changing faster than expected.

At his age the former dean knew that you lived through long waves of political fashion, and that those who recognized them for what they were, and adapted, would get by. He and his wife had done so for many years; on her death, he had lost interest in playing the intricate games that were so necessary to maintain status and reputation in a changing political skyscape. Only briefly, when he realized the injustice of Leal Maspeth's downfall, had he roused himself to try. For all his efforts, she'd been branded a criminal, and had disappeared.

He brushed dark loam off the trowel he'd been digging with, and stood up to squint at the sky past the lights of the city. Yes, they were still there, against all logic and hope. They, the ships of a power whose very existence denied all Eternist doctrine.

With a smile, he bent to turn over more dirt. The dean couldn't even see his own hands—had never seen his garden fully lit—but he had never expected to. Another dark absence—his wife—he *had* become used to, though against all expectations. Time moved on; things revolved. Even the most extraordinary changes, unimaginable before the event, seemed inevitable through the lens of history.

The day before yesterday, he'd been on Rowan Wheel for a medical appointment. On his way back from the hospital, he'd happened to glance down an ill-lit alley, a black slot between two tall buildings that converged overhead to join about two hundred feet up. Somebody had painted something on the concrete of the alley wall, and the words were visible (barely) in a shaft of street light.

Eternism, said the spiky lettering, has had its day.

He'd been very surprised. After all, the government had taken the opportunity presented by the monster's presence to conduct a pogrom against dissenters. Its problem was, there was no organized opposition: people in general were just fed up with the fake democracy it had tried to foist on them.

The flea car driver had much to say on the subject. "It's those damned surveys," he'd said. "Constantly having to fill out what you think is right and what you think is bogus—even in the damned newspaper. I heard that the recyclers check to see if you've ticked off the boxes before they bin the papers, and they mark down your address if you haven't. Always pushing you to have an opinion. And you know what? Most of the time, I got no opinion. That's what I learned from all this mess. I got no opinion, and I don't like the government demanding that I get one."

Everyone seemed emboldened, somehow: alert, for what, Porril couldn't have said. At first, he'd thought it was the triumphant return of the sun lighter that had electrified the city; certainly, there were parades aplenty, fireworks even. Hayden Griffin had driven the monster off. Sere could once again turn its attention away from the black air and what might lie beyond it, back to the eternal contemplation of its own navel.

Except that there were rumors. Where, after all, had the sun lighter driven the beast? The government said it was back to some lair on the iceberg-paved wall of the world. After all, there was no retreat possible beyond that point, was there?

Yet there were several versions of another story floating about. Whenever Porril heard more than one account of an event, his ears perked up. The very unreliability of human reportage was a reliable indicator that, behind those divergent tales, there was a grain of truth.

Distilled, the rumors said that the sun lighter had chased the monster to the wall of the world, and then through it, into some realm beyond Virga. Outside . . .

The government denied this, of course—Eternist doctrine forbade the possibility of a world beyond Virga—but it made the mistake of doing so in the newspapers. The readers voted . . . and found the government's version wanting.

Maybe that was the moment at which the Eternists' utopia began to unravel. Porril took great interest in this question, imagining it in the context of some history written twenty or thirty years hence. Where would his successors place the liminal moment, the dying of the Eternist flower? In the moment when their carefully wrought system of public propaganda turned to bite them?

Or would they count it from the day the black ships showed up?

He unbent to look at the sky again. You couldn't see them directly, even in the reflected light from the city. They were visible only as clusters of running lights, sweeping slowly but somehow impatiently back and forth across the night. Porril had tried to count them, but the number changed. Some clustered at the sun lighter's workshop like bees at a flower. Others paced; still others left for days at a time, to return in force with orders for all manner of material: wooden spars, nails, iron rings, or rope.

The Virga Home Guard were tight-lipped about what they were doing here. It was clear though that, as far as they were concerned, the entire navy of Abyss was nothing but a nuisance, to be brushed aside should it have the temerity to interfere with whatever operation they were conducting.

The Guard had made no attempt at a coup, in fact they hadn't even taken notice of the government by so much as sending an official delegation to parliament. They were just here one day, talking to the sun lighter, and conducting maneuvers in the dark.

Porril smiled at the distant, drifting lights. As far as the Eternists were concerned, the Home Guard was just a legend. He wondered what sermons were being preached from their pulpits these days, and had to chuckle.

"Somehow," he said to the fine mansions of his neighbors, "I think you'd have preferred a worldwasp."

CLOUDS PARTED, AND Leal gasped at the changes. Three weeks had passed since she had left Hayden Griffin gaping in surprise at this spot; she'd supposed that in that time he might be able to visit Sere and return, maybe to reinforce the broken doorway between the worlds. But this! The aperture in Virga's wall was surrounded, crowded in, with motionless black shapes. Their portholes and running lights were the only source of light here, making of the armada an intricate, glittering chandelier against the black of her world's skin.

Not only Abyssal vessels hovered in the lattice formation surrounding the little rupture in the world's skin; she spotted at least six Pacquaean ships, and others that were like nothing she'd ever seen before. There were dozens of these sleek, blue-gray shark-shapes, each one at least twice the length of the largest Abyssal cruiser. They were windowless and had no running lights, making them appear even more mysterious than the wraiths' vessels.

Something complicated gleamed on the nose of one of these dark behemoths; it stood up, to six times a man's height, and shook out metal wings. "Precipice moth?" she breathed; after all that she'd seen in the past weeks, the sight of it shouldn't impress her, but Leal found herself unnerved at the display of strength the moth represented.

The gray ships trailed no nationality's banners; could it be they were part of the Home Guard fleet? They certainly seemed alien and menacing, yet nestled at the center of their formation was a familiar shape: Hayden Griffin's yacht. With a sinking feeling, Leal wondered whether he had misheard or misunderstood their last encounter. Whatever news he'd taken with him to Abyss, it seemed to have panicked the nation.

"I think you'd better get out of here," she said to the emissary via the doll perched on her dashboard. The finely wrought little gold man nodded. "As to you," she poked the doll in the chest, "it would be best for you to don your disguise."

"We'll retreat to a safe distance while we assess the situation," the emissary said. There was little resemblance between its tiny, perfectly proportioned homunculus and the cobbled-together thing she'd shared her cockpit with on the way in. The doll was finely made now, as though by a jewel smith. After speaking, however, it began to break up, its various tiny parts recombining to form the beads of a necklace. Leal took it and strung it around her neck, frowning.

"I'll go on ahead," she said. "I don't think they'll shoot me, but you . . ." Vessels were breaking formation up and down the wall of ships.

A shudder went through the cutter. Leal twisted around to look behind her. The emissary had released Leal's boat and was peeling away, pursued by a sudden cloud of bikes and needle-shaped interceptors. "Damn it!" She pedaled quickly to start the cutter's engines. "They have to stop!"

She aimed the cutter at Hayden's ship, but bright red lines stitched the air before she could advance more than a few hundred feet. The tracer rounds had been fired from a well-armored catamaran twice the length of her own boat. It slewed into her path and Leal was forced to extend her braking sails to avoid hitting it.

Airmen on bikes corkscrewed around the cutter, their snub-nosed machine guns aimed straight at Leal. "Oh, for—" She put up her hands and grimaced at them.

One cautiously approached and made to lift the cockpit's

canopy. Leal reached to undog it but he instantly cocked his gun. She froze, swearing under her breath. While this was happening, six big vessels were converging on her while dozens more went after the emissary.

Lightning flashed behind the cutter—once, twice, a dozen times in five seconds. She felt her necklace twitch and writhe, and the canopy opened and the cool air of a world's edge rushed in.

"Exit slowly," said one of the soldiers. "Hands where we can see them." Leal warily stood up out of the cockpit and somebody roughly twisted her arms behind her. She felt metal cuffs slide onto her wrists, and remembered the Pacquaeans at the elevator stop in Sere.

"Don't speak or we'll shoot you," said the airman who'd just cuffed her. Leal let them drag her through the air and into one of the armored catamarans. She was bundled into a metal cage in the back of one of its two hulls, then it spun and with a whine of its big central jet, it began to accelerate.

Leal mashed her cheek against a tiny, quartz porthole and for a few seconds she had a good view of the world's wall. There was no sign of the gash she had flown her cutter through three weeks ago; in its place was a vast, square gateway edged in bright metal and spotlit by huge ship-finder lanterns. Precipice moths perched along its sides like living gargoyles. This new doorway must be sixty feet across.

The airmen in the catamaran's cabin all had their guns trained on her, and they looked scared. They were all Abyssal, but somehow she didn't think that being a countryman of theirs counted for anything right now.

She opened her mouth to greet them all the same, and they tensed. Leal wisely didn't speak, but just closed her eyes and tried to look as inoffensive as possible.

She would wait. Despite the flutter of fear in her stomach, she knew the advantage was all hers.

A few minutes later there was a thump and the catamaran was winched into some larger vessel. Leal opened her eyes to see cool white light coming through the portholes—gaslight or electric, she couldn't tell. The catamaran's hatch opened and somebody said, "Bring it out."

She emerged into the giant can-shaped space of a hangar; Abyssal sigils adorned the far walls, and it was indeed gaslight that lit the grim faces surrounding her. She saw soldiers, the dress uniform of a commodore—and the utilitarian gray of government officials. She recognized one of them.

"Minister Loll! I bring an important messa—" He stiffened, and made a sharp gesture. A stunning blow to her cheek spun Leal around.

She kept spinning until hands reached to stop her; she was too astonished by the brutality and pain, and an earlier version of herself might have quailed and submitted. There had been a Leal Maspeth who walked the dark streets of Sere dreaming of adventures and rescue by exotic princes. That woman had read history for escape as much as edification, and had approached and then avoided real engagement with her peers, her city, and the politics of her nation, time and again.

That was not the woman who now glared at Loll, leaned her head to one side, and spat a single gobbet of blood at the crowd of dignitaries.

Loll and the others conferred. After a minute they all set off, a tight knot of soldiery and dignity, dissolving into confusion as they reached a small door only two could pass through at a time. They pressed Leal through and she was pulled down a metal-walled corridor. They passed airmen working in pairs, one closing off the pipes to the gaslights while a second lit smaller stand-alone lamps. Up and down the ship, the gaslights flickered and went out leaving a dimmer, amber illumination behind.

"In here." Her escort sent her down a side passage that was

lined with barred doors. None of the cells were occupied; they put her in the last one, and gathered outside to argue about what to do with her.

Leal strapped herself to the mat on the wall and turned away from them. She reached out to lay her fingertips against an iron girder, closing her eyes to let the vibrations travel up her fingers. She almost had a sense of the size of the vessel as it banked and dove through the air.

Thunder somewhere close, and suddenly everyone was grabbing again for handholds as the ship flipped over and dove. The officers began shouting and Eustace Loll became tangled in a corner, from which he blinked in confusion.

Leal swung from her straps. She tried to remember Uthor's lessons, bending and twisting her body to maintain her position and her dignity. One of the officers had managed to get to a speaking tube next to the door and he was shouting into it now. He listened, cursed, and turned to a man who wore the ornate jacket of a commodore.

"He's turned it off! He's demanding access, says we won't get another second of cooperation until he has it."

"No!" Loll was untangling himself. "It's blackmail—"

The emissary was only defending itself. They'd discussed what to do, and agreed that after delivering her back to Virga, it would retire to wait for a response. The supposedly godlike intelligences behind the emissary apparently hadn't foreseen that a hostile human force might be waiting at the world's wall.

She should have realized it; she'd been the human in the discussions and should have known her people.

As quickly as they had arrived—and without a word to her— the crowd of officers and dignitaries left the cells. She heard their squabbling voices fade until they merged with the thunder; and what was left was a pair of guards who examined her curiously for a while, then turned away to their own conversation.

Leal took a deep breath. She was home, that part of her mission had been accomplished.

Now, all that remained was for her to deliver the emissary's message.

And after that? The future was a blank, as terrifying as death.

THERE WAS NO sleeping as the ship entered into the bedlam of some sort of battle. The coughing thunder of explosions rattled the ship and the walls were constantly moving this way or that, dragging the cell and its lone occupant with them. If the ship were blown to bits the brig might survive and twirl away on its own, and then Leal would face death from thirst in the weightless darkness.

The darkness didn't frighten her. Sleep and death: they were the night beyond the lights of Sere, invisible but real worlds, and since meeting the emissary she had come to view both in a new way.

The *Polyhistoria* had talked about it—how humanity's obsession with its own faculty of self-consciousness had led it to neglect possible allies, and also to ignore the changes that its mastery of technology was forcing upon it. The emissary was not a conscious being; but that didn't mean it didn't think, or couldn't be an ally.

And beings who were conscious could still be Virga's enemies.

The Eternists and those like them were terrified of any reality that they couldn't bring within the small quivering circle of radiance cast by their own ideology. All else, all that lay outside that circle of understanding, was like death to them. Small wonder that to them the walls of Virga had come to symbolize the very limit of the world.

If this ship broke asunder and Leal's little cell spun away, and the little lantern outside her door broke, she would not be afraid of the darkness. She was Abyssal. The darkness should be her home.

Calmly, she listened to the battle, and tried to see through the blankness that would follow her delivery of her message—to some sort of life to come.

The rumblings and heavy maneuvers eased somewhat, and for a while, Leal actually dozed. Then there was a clatter out in the corridor, and she heard a key turning in the lock. She turned over.

The door rolled aside and Hayden Griffin swung in. "Leal," he said.

"Hayden!" She jumped across the little space and hugged him.

"Ma'am," said the guard threateningly.

"Of course. Excuse me." She shot the man an ironic smile and floated back from Hayden.

"It's okay," he said to the guard. "Can you give us a minute?" Hayden looked careworn, but his expression held neither of the extremes of vacancy or hyperactivity she'd seen when he first arrived in Sere.

"How are you?" he asked seriously. "You look thinner."

She lowered her eyes. "The food was . . . well, not meant for our kind. Hayden . . ." She wanted to burst with all the emotions crowding her now. "I-I'm fine," she said, and knew it was her political side talking, the part of her that kept any sort of unconsidered self-expression in check. "No, I'm not," she said immediately. "I'm scared, but I have a task to complete. It's why I came back."

He was obviously searching for some reply. "How'd you manage to get in to see me?" she asked, even as she cursed herself for changing the subject. "Did you use your leverage as the famous sun lighter?"

He laughed humorlessly. "I didn't even know you were back until all the Abyssal ships suddenly jumped out of line. They tore off after the monster and took my weapon with them. Luckily," he said with an ironic smile, "I'd installed a remote kill-switch before I let them play with it. Radio works outside Virga, you know."

She glanced at the inconstant walls. "Is that why we're in a dogfight? The emissary is fighting back?"

He shook his head. "We're still pursuing it, but it's fast. No, the fight's with the Home Guard. They, ah, objected to the Abyssals leaping after the—what did you just call it?"

"Emissary," she said. "Although 'ambassador' might be a better word."

"Oh." He was silent for a moment. "The, uh, I was with the Home Guard when the *emissary* appeared. They didn't at first see your ship, but I know they were prepared to wait to find out what it was going to do. But the Abyssals broke formation."

"But why the battle?"

"Well," he said, looking a bit uncomfortable. "When the monster dropped a cutter into the air—and it was yours and you were clearly alive inside the cockpit—the senior Guard staff said, 'Hang on, we need to talk to her before we go off half-cocked.' Which, as you know, the Abyssals immediately did. The Guard are trying to stop the Abyssals now; they're afraid the monster might not be a monster after all."

"It's not," she said. "You misheard me the last time we met."

"I couldn't really hear you at all," he admitted. "It was dark and I was trying to maneuver a multi-megawatt ray gun in a battle with a giant monster. You did a little yelling and waving, but the main thing I saw was the monster picking up your ship and running away with you."

He looked away. "Anyway, this fight's not going to last much longer. With my weapon turned off the Guard can send precipice moths to, uh, negotiate with the Abyssals. The negotiations will be short."

"I'll bet Loll and his boys want you to turn your toy back on right away," she said with a smile.

"And I'm happy to," he replied, "unless you give me a good reason not to."

"Hayden, the emissary is a friend," she said quickly. "It's proposing an alliance. The forces that are trying to get into Virga are also threatening its home. It needs what we have if it's to survive—and we need what it has."

He looked puzzled. "And those are?"

"Candesce," she said. "It needs to know how Candesce is able to defend us. And *we* . . . we need more control over what Candesce does, so that we can build better defenses. We need the kinds of technologies that are possible outside. And that means we need to let a little of that outside in."

He looked unhappy, but to her surprise he nodded. "I know something's been trying to get in. They used . . . a friend of mine from outside, a woman named Aubri Mahallan, as a tool to try and shut down Candesce. We nearly lost everything then. So I believe that part of your story.

"As to the emissary . . . Tell me what happened. How did you come to be out here in the first place? How'd you find this place? Where did the monster take you?"

The ship was moving easier; the thunder had faded. Leal hooked a hand into one of the bed straps and nodded absently. She was thinking about where to begin.

"I decided there was a book I needed to see," she said. "Called the *Polyhistoria*. The problem was, it was late and the library was closed . . ."

THE TROUBLE WAS, summarizing all that she'd seen and experienced after leaving Virga was just impossible. It wouldn't work as a straight narrative, because the first day had been spent inside the utter blackness of Virga's sister world, Aethyr. Leal had seen nothing, had merely spoken with the emissary about where they were and what the existence of another world like Virga implied.

It was when they left Aethyr, through a permanent aperture in its side, that the true wonders had begun. So, after describing her escape from Sere, the finding of the hole in Virga's skin, and her first meeting with the emissary, Leal turned to the next thing she knew Hayden would understand.

"Hayden, have you ever heard of the *stars?*"

It was when they left Aethyr through a hole in its own skin. They must be opposite Virga now, her world occluded by the vast curving plain of Aethyr. Leal had turned to see where they were now, and had gasped at what unfolded before her: the whole sky alight with pinpricks of light, each one so small as to hover on the edge of vision. Yet there were millions, some brighter, some almost invisible, layered and cast upon one another in thousands of random designs. Sweeping across the sky from one side of the cutter to the other was a tremendous twisting scarf of these points, almost white, like a city unfurled and flung over the world.

"Are we outside all worlds?" she had whispered. The junk-doll had inclined its tiny head, a silent affirmation. Leal stared at the stars for long minutes, until something occurred to her. "I can still breathe," she'd said in puzzlement. "I thought outer space had no air in it."

"This is not outer space," said the junk-doll.

"B-but you said those were stars!"

"We are in a passage," said the doll. "Its walls are transparent. It runs between arena places."

"Have you ever had a moment, Hayden, when you wanted to just drink some sight whole, to saturate your whole being with it so you will never, ever forget? That was what it was like to see the stars for the first time. I scanned the firmament from one side of the cutter to the other, its hull my horizon—but as I turned to try and encompass the wonder of it, I found blackness facing me again. The emissary was a blot of absence, cut out of the starscape, but this lay opposite it, and had the same sense of size as Aethyr, which now lay behind."

She had leaned in to the junk-doll and had said, "What's that?"

It pointed through the canopy. "Aethyr lies behind. Virga lies behind Aethyr. Ahead is Crucible. Home."

"There are many worlds," she murmured. "A foam of worlds? How many?"

"Tens," said the junk-doll with a shrug. "Not many."

The black absence he'd called Crucible seemed to take up half the sky, the way the iceberg forest had. "Are they all as big as Virga?"

"Some are much bigger."

"How much bigger?"

"Twenty times. More."

Leal. "And Crucible . . ."

"Is the biggest. Much, much biggest."

"Big enough," she told Hayden now, "to hold a hundred Virgas. And *that* was our destination."

Leal had read aloud from the *Polyhistoria* as the emissary carried her past the edges of a vast city that twisted like smoke around the curving waist of Crucible. The strange narrative of the book made more and more sense as she saw firsthand some of the things it described. Its oblique passages told of this city, though in such a way that they only made sense to Leal now that she could see it with her own eyes. A billion cylinders and spheres hung in the cold of deep space between the worlds, cubes, and more complex shapes, the light from their windows running together to form a nebula of indescribable beauty and awesome scale.

"Veins and capillaries enmesh the cloud," the *Polyhistoria* said, and so it was, for the crystal tube the emissary was traveling through was just one of thousands that twisted and tangled through the nebula. Leal and her host passed branches and exits to veins teeming with soaring shapes much like the ships of her world yet sleeker, almost alive in the way they flexed and dove through the air. They came in every shape and size, but none were of the crude wood-and-iron of Virga. There were also bird-shapes, and fish-shapes, that looked alive.

She tried now to describe the sight to Hayden. "It was like . . . like Batetran," she said at last, though it really hadn't *looked* at all like that sunlit nation. What she meant was that this endless city had radiated the same sense of extravagant fertility as she'd felt in Virga's light-flooded regions. "It overflowed with life and activity." While Leal spoke her thoughts were drifting back to what she'd seen. —Back to the slow realization that the sky she was now in, awash with buildings and soaring crystalline passages, also contained thousands of translucent spheres, like smaller versions of Virga. Some were a mile or two across; some she saw in the distance seemed hundreds of miles in diameter. And there were suns here, too, smaller than Virga's, true, but still bright enough to light some of those orbs and reveal that they were crowded with labyrinths of intricate green.

"I didn't know what I was looking at, not at the time," she mused. "It seemed like a civilization, but it was really nothing of the sort. The emissary wasn't any help—he hardly knew anything, and I was starting to realize that he wasn't a person, like you and me, at all. And neither were most of the trillions of creatures crowding the city. They were magnificent, they were beautiful, and cunning and energetic—but they were as unconscious as stones. And you know, though he sat there on my gyrocompasses—tilting his head and nodding as I recited bits of the *Polyhistoria* to him—I realized that the emissary was the same. Unconscious. As the ancients would say, nonsentient."

Hayden looked away, frowning. "So who did your emissary—Abyss's monster—work for, then?"

"Ah," said Leal; but how could she answer him in a way that didn't discourage or mislead him? "You know," she tried, "the man that wrote the *Polyhistoria* knew he was going to be misunderstood. He wrote the book anyway—you can hear his reluctance in every paragraph. And he was reluctant because he knew that his great message—his theme—was not going to sit well with his audience."

Now Hayden looked annoyed. "What?"

"He wrote it," she said slowly and deliberately, "to try to explain to the world that we'd be making a mistake if we chose intelligent, sentient beings as our allies just because they *were* conscious."

"What the hell are you talking about?" He wouldn't meet her eyes—and that told Leal everything she needed to know about what was going on outside her cell, and beyond the hull of this ship.

She needed to tease more information out of him, but his unease told her that she must not be too direct. To distract him, she said, "Crossing the suburbs of the city took hours, but finally we made it to the wall of Crucible. It was a perfectly flat wall by that time—had been for a very long time—and there wasn't any sense of scale. It was just . . . we were at the wall, on this side of it . . . and then suddenly we were on the other side. I blinked and missed it, I guess.

"But here was a world like Virga! Only, vastly larger. The crystal tube was gone, we were in open air. For a while I thought we had turned around somehow, because the city was in here, too. And at first I saw no clouds nor any other indication that I was in a world of air. Not that day, nor the next, or the next . . ."

"You must have been starving," he said. "What about water?"

"There were water-balls here and there, if you knew where to look. But you're right, I was fasting, and I'd never done it before— never felt the way I felt then. I was so lonely, unsure of what my own body could take . . . The little junk-doll kept promising that there'd be food for me when we reached his world—but you know, we were flying at hundreds of miles per hour, and we flew for *days.*"

So it was that when they finally came to another wall, this one in the side of a Virga-sized sphere that floated with its cousins somewhere in the depths of Crucible—Leal was too tired to be surprised when its interior turned out to be crammed with suns, and empty of anything she could have confidently called *people.*

This was where she'd finally been able to eat and rest—and to take stock of herself and her situation. She was eager to talk about that moment in her life, because only then, with all the uncertainties of escape and travel behind her, had Leal been able to face herself, and forgive herself for everything she'd done to get here.

"No people," said Hayden. "A wilderness, then?"

"There were cities," she told him. And when he pressed her for details, she added, "And factories and farms, and ships and commerce and all. There were humans, too—a delegation, in fact, from outside the emissary's world. They'd come to negotiate with the emissary's people, and oh! they were so happy to see me."

The cities, the factories and farms were all strung together by the white fiber that also bonded the junk-doll's limbs. This stuff was the emissary, and its "people" were just more of the stuff. They had individuality, sometimes, other times losing it as convenience or circumstance dictated. Primed by her reading of the *Polyhistoria*, Leal saw them as a wondrous stuff, like some sort of faerie dust sprinkled upon the inanimate world to bring it to life.

The human delegation was revolted by them.

Hayden's brows were knitted; he was glaring at the wall. There was none of the vacancy now in his stance or expression that Leal had seen when he'd sat at her table, those many weeks ago.

"What did they look like, these humans?" he asked.

As she opened her mouth to tell him the room gave a kind of lurch, and a second later a very loud *bang!* sounded. Leal could hear it echoing away through the ship. The wall began to move away from her and she grabbed at a line; Hayden did likewise as distant thunder sounds started up again, and grew nearer by the second.

The clanging sound of the brig's outer doors opening turned both their heads, and seconds later the small space outside the cell was crowded with uniforms. "Looks like they need me," said Hayden.

Leal barked a laugh. "They want you to turn your engine back on."

"Yes." As a guard unlocked the cell door he faced Leal and took her hands in his. "Thank you for telling me all this. It may help me to . . . make a decision."

Then he turned, nodding at the anxious officers, and left the cell.

Leal was left with silence—and an understanding. She hadn't been sure of it, when she thought about Hayden during the long nights in Crucible; but she was sure now.

She knew he was concerned for her, her safety and well-being. But what had they spoken of? In the end he was more interested in her story, than in her.

Hayden Griffin was a hero, truly a sun lighter and dragon slayer. But he wasn't hers, and never would be.

20

THE SHAKING AND turning of the ship didn't cease, but eased off somewhat, as though this ship were falling behind the main action of the battle. Gradually, she began to notice something else: a steady, slight drift in one direction. If the ship held steady for more than a few seconds, she found herself approaching one wall, or the floor, or the bars depending, she supposed, on which way the vessel was pointing.

This was alarming, if it meant what she thought it meant. Leal retreated to the back of her cell, out of sight of the guards, and unstringing the necklace, coiled it up in one palm. "Are you functional?" she whispered to it.

The mass of beads reconfigured itself, squirmed into the shape of a tiny man, and wrapped one arm around her finger to steady itself. "There is no interference from Hayden Griffin's weapon," it said. "But I am a very long distance from myself."

She had come up against the wall again. "This turn . . . do you feel it?" She let the doll go and watched it drift toward the wall. The doll looked around itself, then nodded.

Leal took a deep breath. "But the ship isn't turning, is it?"

One of the lanterns outside the cell suddenly flipped in its bracket, and shifting light made the doll's blank face visible for just a second. "No, Leal, it is not."

Leal half-smiled, touching the pipes that were trying to move toward her. "Would we survive, do you think? The spin-gale—"

"Will not be your greatest problem," said the doll. "If they try to catch up to the wind . . ."

The door to the cell block opened with a clang, and a babble of voices was let in. She sensed rather than saw her guards snap to attention. "Quick, quick," she hissed. "Back to your other shape!"

She was able to don the necklace just before her cage was opened, and then Leal found herself in a scrum of junior officers and regular airmen—all of whom seemed to have voted themselves into the party sent to retrieve her. They shepherded her with a great sense of self-importance through the dark corridors of the ship, talking about her amongst themselves but none addressing her directly. She heard herself referred to as "the witch" and "the monster's daughter," and knew that it was wisest for her not to speak at all.

At length there was no more ship to pass through: they had come to its nose, where sat the conical bridge and, beyond it, the ship's battering ram. The officers charged with escorting her reluctantly let her go at the entrance and retreated. Leal entered the bridge alone.

She'd expected something to grab hold of, but, missing her swipe at one of the wall ropes, instead rebounded to a stop against the back of a large chair that was bolted to one wall. She had a second to take in the strange sight of two groups of variously uniformed men facing off across the cone-shaped space, before her upper arms were grasped firmly by two beefy airmen, and she was turned to face one of the groups.

Hovering in the air here were: an older man dressed in the uniform of an Abyssal commodore; a couple of black-garbed members of the Home Guard; and Minister of the Interior Eustace Loll, who looked pale and uncertain. A few senior officers and functionaries rounded out the group.

—Except for one more man, whose uncannily handsome face and outlandish dress were familiar to Leal. His features had something of the winter wraith to them, but he was clearly foreign.

Her spirits, already battered by her capture and imprisonment, fell when she saw him.

"Ah," she said. "I expect I've been tried and convicted in absentia."

"Not necessarily."

It was Hayden's voice. She craned her neck to look behind her, and saw that he and some of his men—including Tarvey—were crowded onto the far side of the room. Their position and postures gave the definite impression that she had arrived in the middle of some sort of standoff.

The bridge was cone-shaped and about fifteen feet across at its widest point. It had no windows, but a pinhole-camera setup projected an image across the circular back of the room. All the seats and consoles were oriented toward that, and it was through a door at the side of that circle that Leal had entered. Right now the projected image showed white clouds and blue sky. They were near a sun, as Leal had suspected.

The commodore moved into the center of the space; putting himself in between the two groups made him look like a judge presiding over a court. Which, Leal, supposed, he effectively was. "Your situation is very serious," he said to her. "Speak only when spoken to, and speak only the truth."

Leal didn't say anything, but raised her chin and looked him in the eye.

Eustace Loll fidgeted as though he wanted to talk, but the commodore had a commanding presence and clearly wasn't about to take interruptions from any side.

"First of all," he said to her, "what are you?"

She narrowed her eyes in puzzlement. "I'm the dean of the history department at Sere University. At least, that was my position when I left."

"No," said the commodore, shaking his head. "I mean *what* are you?"

She blinked at him in puzzlement.

The foreign-looking man barked a laugh into the awkward pause. "You can't expect a straight answer from it, Commodore. That thing will spin nothing but lies and threats—you'll see. It's not even alive like you and I. You know how the monster animates the bodies of the dead and speaks through them. Go ahead—blow a hole in its head, you'll see. It'll keep right on talking."

"I see you've met the enemy," Leal said dryly. "To answer your question, Commodore, I'm an ordinary human being. These men," she glanced at the two who were holding her arms, "can tell you my flesh is warm, and I have a pulse. I'm no more or less than I said. I'm Leal Hieronyma Maspeth, and I've returned from a long journey with a message for the people of Virga."

"I told them that," said Hayden. "Leal, this man calls himself Holon. The Home Guard brought him. He says he's from the human nations outside Virga."

"I'm sure he is," she said. Everybody was watching this exchange between her and Hayden.

"Holon and Loll didn't want to give you another chance to speak," Hayden continued. "Just before you showed up they'd pretty much convinced the commodore here that you should be killed and your body burned."

"Is that why you . . . ?"

Hayden grimaced. "Well, there was also the fact that I refused to turn on my machine again. They've got the monst—the, uh, emissary on the run. We're close behind it now with the whole fleet."

Leal watched him reach unconsciously to stabilize himself with one bare-toed foot. Everybody else was doing the same, as the ship seemed to be going through another of those long turns. Nobody was paying attention, except for the helmsman who was swearing softly as he struggled with the wheel.

"Enough," said the commodore. "If you're just a university academic, then what the hell were you doing all the way out here? How did you find this place? And why did you, apparently of your own free will, throw in your lot with the monster?"

She smiled. "Those are the right questions. As to how I knew to come here . . ." She explained her relationship with Brun Mafin and recounted her conversation with him.

"As to why . . ." She looked down, struggling to summarize what for her had been an almost impenetrable thicket of emotions and thoughts. "No one . . . no one was being brave enough to listen. Nobody was taking responsibility. I felt as though the whole city—the whole country—had turned its face away from something it didn't want to see. Closed its ears to something it didn't want to hear. That voice . . . and what it was really saying.

"And in the end, somebody had to listen, and to see. And there was just . . ." She shrugged. "Nobody else to do it."

There was another silence. Then the commodore said, "You spoke of a message just now. What is this message?"

"The emissary came to Virga to offer an alliance between its people and ours," Leal said. "Candesce's radiation drove it mad, so it was unable to communicate properly. Commodore, there's been a grave misunderstanding. You're chasing a friend, not an enemy.

"The message—the message is simple. The emissary's people are offering an alliance against a common enemy. This offer extends to all the people of Virga, not just to Abyss or the Home Guard. In return for their help, they want us to teach them or lend them Candesce's technology, the technology of its defensive field."

"That's nonsense!" snapped Loll. "Virga already has allies."

All eyes turned to the outsider, Holon. Leal smiled ironically, and said, "I take it, Minister Loll, that you no longer believe that the universe ends at the walls of Virga?" He shrugged angrily.

"If this 'emissary' was seeking an alliance," said the commodore, "then why did it wreak such havoc on our people? —Attack the city?"

"Has the emissary fired on any of our ships since my return?" she asked.

Nobody spoke. Then the outsider, Holon, said, "We have it on the run, its offensive capabilities are obviously damaged."

"You," Leal said to him, "have no idea what you're talking about."

"Sadly, Ms. Maspeth, you have no proof of any of this," said the commodore. "It's Sir Holon's word against yours, and as a guest of the Home Guard, I'm afraid his carries more weight."

"Well it would," she said, "if I couldn't prove that he's ignorant of the most basic facts about our world."

"Can you?" asked the commodore, arching one pale eyebrow.

"Don't listen to it," said Holon. "What can it do but confuse matters further?"

"I tend to agree," said a black-garbed man near the door. "Let those men go, Griffin, and we'll talk. As to the monster's device, we should kill it and be done with it."

"He doesn't even know where we are," said Leal, her eyes still on Holon.

Holon grimaced in affected distaste. "Just kill this thing and be done with—"

The commodore held up a hand. "Why do you say that?" he asked her.

"If he knew where we were," she said lightly, "he'd have told you that the emissary has lured you into a trap."

Loll hissed at her; but Hayden was nodding.

"When I spoke to you just now," he said, "you told me that we'd be making a mistake if we allied ourselves with the humans of artificial nature just because they were human."

"Almost," she said. "What I said was, we'd be making a mistake if we allied ourselves with conscious beings just because they're conscious."

He nodded. "I learned the hard way that Virga has enemies. My . . . the woman I loved, Aubrey Mahallan, was from your world," he said to Holon. "She was a sentient being like you and me, but it hardly mattered. She was a *device* all the same, with no freedom to avoid her mission. Your people sent her into Virga under threat of death, to take down our walls. She was sent to shut off Candesce's protective field. In the end she was only able to defy you because she was dying anyway."

Leal nodded sadly. "What good is self-awareness if you have no freedom?" She saw Hayden's eyes widen, as if her words had somehow struck him deeply. Good: she'd meant them to.

Holon shook his head. "It wasn't us who sent her," he said. "It was—"

"The things he works for," Leal finished. "Powers that have domesticated the humans outside Virga the way we domesticate animals. Those powers meter out knowledge in tiny parcels, and they lie ruthlessly to this man and his people. When the Home Guard travel outside Virga," she said to the black-garbed man, "you're shown only what they want you to see. Why, I'm betting Holon didn't even know this sister world," she dared to raise one hand to gesture at the projected cloudscape, "was here."

The black-clad Home Guard commander was frowning at Holon.

Holon laughed. "Of course I knew. There was just no need to tell you until—"

"*What trap?*" The commodore had turned his attention entirely to Leal.

She smiled. "Ask your helmsman."

"Sir," said the airman. "Sir, I'm not exactly sure . . . for a while there was a strong wind pushing us to starboard. The enemy turned into it and we followed, as per orders. But now there's another force . . . I thought it was wind, but it's different."

The commodore whirled. "What's happening?" he demanded.

"You pushed the emissary too far," she said. "It's been trying to keep you at bay without damaging you because it was waiting for my confirmation that its message had been delivered. But it's clearly given up on you. I think it's decided to take you out of the picture so it can find a more receptive audience."

"But how?" The commodore grabbed for a cable but missed; he looked around, and she saw him realize that everyone in the chamber was drifting to one side.

"This world, Aethyr, may be attached to Virga like one soap bubble to another, but it's not Virga's twin. For one thing, it's smaller." Now she smiled at Holon. "For another—and this is something our friend Holon doesn't know—Virga does not rotate, but Aethyr does."

The helmsman was pulling harder at his wheels, trying to keep the ship level. Slowly, almost unconsciously, everyone in the room was reorienting themselves, into a new up and down.

"The emissary showed me on our way back," Leal continued. "Aethyr rotates around the circle where it attaches to Virga. It spins like a town wheel, fast enough to make almost a gravity of weight at its equator. There are suns in Aethyr, but they're all automated like Candesce, though of course without the extra technology of Candesce's protective field. These suns don't rotate, they hang in the very thin air far above the denser atmosphere hugged to the spinning surface of the sphere. The emissary tells me they light its inner surface in such a way that it looks a lot like the environment humanity came from, something called a planet."

Holon had gone pale.

"We're caught in the spin-gale that's created by all that turning land pulling the air with it," she said. "Like when the air in Sere is motionless at street level; it only seems still, because it's moving with you as you're moving with the turning wheel. If you were to fly in from outside, that same air would feel like a wind to you, a wind that's trying to push you up to speed with the rest of the wheel, and so down against it—"

"Turn!" yelled the commodore. "Get us out of here!" The bridge crew leaped into action and Leal heard sirens crying throughout the ship while in the far distance, the thrum of the engines changed.

Leal raised her voice over the sudden bedlam. "Holon didn't know," she called to the commodore, "because he knows very little about the universe outside his enclave. Hayden, you called Aubrey Mahallan a 'device.' That's what this man, Holon, is. A device of the real enemy."

Weight suddenly surged through the bulkhead below her and the men holding her stumbled. The commodore was shouting orders and she was being bundled to one side of the circular screen—now a wall—along with Hayden, Tarvey, and the others. Loll and Holon had escaped behind the line of Abyssal airmen.

"Ms. Maspeth," said the commodore, "are you in contact with the monster?"

"With the emissary? That depends on how close I am to its main body," she said. "I have a . . . proxy, with me, but it can't negotiate on behalf of its larger self."

The Home Guard commander said, "Tell it we want to talk."

Leal reached up and eased the necklace out of her shirt. There was a collective gasp as it reconfigured itself as an animate doll, even the frantic bridge crew pausing to look over. The doll raised itself into a dignified stance atop Leal's hand and said, "We are out of range."

Leal shook her head. "The moment has passed. It's partly my fault. I knew for a while that this was happening, and thought to use it as leverage. Things are happening faster than I expected."

The bridge was shaking from the turbulence and Leal almost fell on her face, but a strong hand pulled her back. It was Tarvey. He grinned at her and she reached up to put an arm around his shoulder. An airman lost his grip and went flying across to crash into the white screen. A tumbled chaos of clouds and—were those trees?—flitted across his rolling body. "Strap in!" somebody howled, and airmen abandoned their controls, soldiers holstered their guns and reached to pull canvas belts from their recesses in the walls. There weren't enough for everyone and Leal found herself squashed in with Tarvey. She would have said something witty if she hadn't been terrified and half-addled from the shaking. She looked at the screen and every detail of the terrain outside was clear as it came up and hit—

21

LEAL TASTED BLOOD. She felt numb with shock, but for some reason could feel a regular tap, tap, tap against her cheek. She groaned and opened her eyes.

The junk-doll was standing on her shoulder, and slapping her with one little hand, not violently, but relentlessly.

"Stop," she gasped. "Stop it, stop."

"You are alive," it observed. "Can you move?"

She raised her hands in front of her eyes and spread her fingers. She experimentally flexed her leg, and felt it straighten. So far so good.

Somebody moaned beside her. Tarvey sat up, reaching with trembling fingers to examine a nasty cut on his forehead. It had chuted blood all down one side of his face, but his eyes were focused and his voice wasn't slurred at all as he said, "Hell."

Behind him, Hayden Griffin lay still, his eyes closed in the gray light.

Light . . . Leal looked past him and the jumbled bodies that filled the bottom of the bridge. The cone lay on its side and eye-hurtingly bright daylight fanned through one of the open doorways. She realized with a start that it was very, very quiet.

Tarvey had been examining Hayden's neck and back. She knelt with him, running her own hands over the sun lighter's flanks, feeling for broken bones or swelling. "Nothing obvious," Tarvey said. "May have hit his head . . . Come on, let's get him out of here."

She helped him drag Hayden Griffin through the doorway. She had to squint to see what was beyond it, which was precious little: just long ragged spears of hull festooned with girders and bits of wall, then open air and a trench full of dirt and rock.

It was hard for Leal to understand what she was looking at, for the sun-drenched intricacy of it just went on and on. She saw tumbled trees nearby—almost obscenely green—but also other smaller ones that must be far away. They couldn't be, though, because you couldn't ever anywhere have that much flat surface between two points. There was no town wheel big enough . . .

She remembered the iceberg-choked wall of Virga, and suddenly the vista flipped around: if she imagined she was perched on such a wall, stuck to it somehow, then she could just encompass what she was seeing.

Carefully, she and Tarvey carried Hayden off the metal and onto churned dirt and tall, wild-looking grass. He was very heavy, but Leal was already so sore that the extra strain barely registered.

She was very worried about him, but still, her hand moved almost of its own accord to caress the heads of the long stalks of grain. She'd seen grass grow like this in Batetran, from clods of earth tumbling alone through the air. Here it spread on as far as the eye could see, flat like a carpet save where trees interrupted it.

Tarvey checked on Hayden again, then lay down on his back and stared up. Leal did the same, only half-aware that other people were staggering out of the wreck now. It was soothing to look up, because there, things made sense. The clouds were squashed along their near sides, but otherwise they were clouds, and beyond them the sky was blue, exactly like it had been in Batetran . . .

Or, not quite: long funnels of smoke scored the blue. They were scattered near and far, and when Leal went up on her elbows she realized that they came from burning wreckage strewn about the—she hunted for the ancient word—

"Plain," she said aloud. "This is called a plain." Other words were coming back to her, even as she realized that their vessel had not been the only one to crash here. It looked like dozens of Virgan ships had become caught in Aethyr's monstrous spin-gale and pulled down. So had the many bikes, catamarans, and cutters that had been flying alongside them. They lay like strange sculptures, or squashed bugs, under shattered trees or in the middle of the grass. All were surrounded by the dots of fallen men.

So many dead and injured . . . She was awakening to what she had done—or, what the emissary had done and she had allowed to happen. She felt a hollow horror, even while an older part of her was denying this was even possible, that she, Leal, could do such a thing.

"Ah!" She and Tarvey sat up as one, to find Eustace Loll standing over them. He was using a metal spar as a crutch, and favoring one foot. He looked scared and as stunned as Leal had been a few minutes ago.

He looked down at his foot. "I, I think it's broken," he said in a small, worried voice.

A small crowd was gathering. The able-bodied were helping the injured, and one or two particularly fit men had begun walking back along the ship's trail, looking for other survivors. Some sort of military organization was reasserting itself.

Tarvey went to help out. Leal sat with Hayden, and watched the men; some were doing better than others. Loll in particular suddenly seemed to notice his surroundings, and his face went blank with terror. Leal clambered to her feet and walked painfully over to him.

"This place where we are," she said, "it's called a 'plain.' Plains are a kind of 'land.' Both of those are ancient words. In some very old books, you find them used more often than the word 'cloud.' "

He shook his head, but there was no heat to it. He leaned on his makeshift crutch and simply stared at this world he could never have imagined.

Leal stood with him, following his gaze. The land seemed perfectly flat out to a great distance—detail blurred and a kind of blue haze came down a few miles away. Beyond that, the veiled surface began to rise. Before it had gone very far, it disappeared behind the water-saturated, cloud-specked sky.

A bright hot sun stood directly overhead, but Leal could see another off in the distance, and more beyond it. They made an even grid across the sky, lighting the land but also obscuring the vast volume of air above them. Somewhere up there, the remnants of the fleet might be circling, but there was no way they could descend to rescue their downed countrymen.

"Stranded," someone said. Leal turned to see Hayden Griffin sitting up. He was holding his head, his eyes half-closed, but apparently alert enough to know where they were. She went to sit next to him.

"I'm sorry," she said. "I've caused a terrible catastrophe."

He grimaced. "It wasn't you. I think it was our collective stupidity, and let it be a lesson to us. . . . Your message, though—it won't be delivered, now."

She nodded. "Not by me, anyway."

They were silent for a while. "I guess," Hayden said suddenly, then stopped. She looked at him. He massaged his forehead, and said, "I guess that's the problem with taking the weight of the world on your own shoulders. If you fail, the whole cause is lost."

Her throat tightened, but he'd said it matter-of-factly, and after a moment she realized he was talking about himself.

PEOPLE STRAGGLED IN over the remainder of the day. The commodore had survived, and he'd set up a command post from which he oversaw the hunt for survivors. In surprisingly short order they had a working field hospital set up under a large arc of a ship's hull, and as the suns began to redden and go out, Leal helped gather fuel for fires. At first the notion of burning something so wildly expensive as wood and grass seemed outrageous, but they were surrounded by endless miles of the stuff. Open fires were almost never seen in town cylinders, so they were a novelty, their heat simultaneously calming and energizing the surviving airmen.

Leal and Tarvey moved Hayden near one of the fires. He'd fallen asleep again, and as Leal walked over with a couple of tins of rations, she saw that Tarvey was watching him sleep.

"You love him," she said as she sat down next to Tarvey.

He shrugged. "I guess you could say that. I've spent years protecting him. But . . ." He looked away and sighed, then took the heated tin from her. They sat in silence together for a while, then the rustling of the grass warned of someone else approaching.

They saw his face and hands first because his black uniform made the rest of him invisible. He was a member of the Home Guard, tall, lean, and with the weatherbeaten features of a career airman. Leal thought he'd been present in the bridge when she was questioned, but couldn't be sure. He hesitated at the edge of the fire's circle of light, and finally said, "May I join you?"

"Please." Leal gestured for him to sit. He squatted awkwardly on the dirt, one hand out as if he kept expecting the ground to move under him. "Was it true," he said after a while, "what you said about the arena and the emissary?"

"I think so," she said candidly. "It's always possible that I was deceived as much as Holon and Eustace Loll have been. I saw all sorts of wondrous things while I was in Crucible—the emissary's world—but I suppose they could all have been illusions. There's one thing, though, that makes their story convincing for me."

"What?" The Guardsman sat finally, if a bit gingerly, on the strangely stable ground.

Leal smiled a bit ruefully and said, "History."

"Our own history, to be exact. Because the events and epochs that the emissary's people talked about matched certain . . . accounts, that we've never been able to make sense of, from our own past. I had a rare book with me on my journey—it's probably still in my cutter, wherever that is—that hinted at the real reasons behind something called the Great Refusal."

The Guardsman looked startled. "That's when the Home Guard was formed."

"Ah, you know your history. Then you know that the Guard were created by people who refused something. But do you know what that something was?"

Now he looked puzzled. Tarvey had sat up as well and was listening intently. "Everybody knows what the Refusal was all about," said the Guardsman. "Our founders refused to let artificial nature and its . . . creations . . . into Virga. They invented and switched on the protective field that Candesce uses to keep higher technologies out. Then they set to patrolling the world, looking for incursions and violations of Virga's sanctity. That's been our purpose ever since: to keep Virga clear of the leveling and all-consuming effects of A.N."

She nodded. "Like most received histories, what you just described is partly true. But there's always been a thorn in the side of your particular account, and that is the fact that Candesce's protective field was turned on a good hundred years before the Refusal."

The Guardsman scoffed at this, but he didn't rise to go away. Leal ducked her head to acknowledge his skepticism, then said, "I have a slight advantage, I think. Living in Abyss, I mean. Our nation is ancient, and we have certain records that other nations and libraries seem not to have. In fact, I've got good reasons to believe that it was in Sere itself—or the city that preceded it—that the Great Refusal occurred. So again I ask you, what exactly was refused?"

Tarvey slapped the dirt. "This alliance! The one the emissary wants with us?" Leal nodded.

"We've been made this offer before. And last time, our people chose an alliance with the entities in the arena who were most like ourselves. Those were societies made up of self-aware individuals, mostly man-shaped. Familiar humans. Even today, they maintain a 'tourist station' at the edge of Virga, and you trade with them and some Home Guard members travel among their worlds, no?" The Guardsman nodded.

"But there was another faction involved in the Refusal," said Leal. "These were men and women of Virga who recognized that although the foreigner humanoids might look like us, and even think like us, that didn't mean they had our interests in mind. These people advocated a different alliance, one with entities that were vastly different from us—but whose interests were the same as ours. Creatures who wanted to push back artificial nature in their own worlds, to create ecologies and civilizations independent of it. Bubbles of uniqueness is what they wanted, like we had. Because Virga is the one place in the universe that we know of, that is entirely free of A.N."

The Guardsman was frowning and rubbing his chin. "Well maybe you can answer me something," he said. "If artificial nature is at the technological maximum—can generate any conceivable device or system—then why is Candesce unique?"

"It's because A.N. is a meta-technology: it can't generate a technology superior to itself." She thought about what she'd seen and been told since leaving Virga—details she had trouble understanding or putting into words. "Once . . ." she began, "once you have an accurate physical model and fast enough calculating engines, you can use natural selection to *evolve* designs and strategies in something the emissary called 'virtual environments.' This process is faster and more efficient than what we call thinking . . . and once you've got the technology, you don't need to know anything about how it works. You just use it.

"But A.N.'s calculating engines don't work inside Virga, and its people *don't know why.*

"Everybody's equal outside of Virga," she said. "They're all at the technological maximum: everybody's equally able to evolve new devices because everybody has the same, perfect physics model. Once you've got that model, and fast enough calculation, nobody in the universe should be able to come up with a machine that you can't duplicate. You just *select* for it and its design eventually pops out. So there's a technological stalemate everywhere in the universe," Leal said. "Everywhere but here. Because nobody can duplicate Candesce. The people who built Candesce didn't evolve it, they *thought it out*—and they used a physics model that's more complete than the one everybody else has."

The guardsman nodded slowly. "And everyone wants it."

"You've never given it to your human allies, but I'll bet they've applied every conceivable pressure on you to get it." He inclined his head in agreement. "Candesce's technology is the game-changer for the entire arena," she said, "and for the whole vast ecology of Vega. Maybe for the whole galaxy, we don't know. Science is no longer practiced anywhere because A.N. long ago made it unnecessary. The irony is that A.N.'s science stopped just short of discovering one last principle, which *was* discovered here. Artificial nature is so all-controlling that there are no free zones where science can be restarted. A.N. has limited itself, so they are forced to steal. From us."

The Guardsman mulled it over. Finally he said, "Why do you think the emissary's people are more trustworthy than the allies we've already got?"

"Because they're not the fauna of the arena," she said promptly. "Their very nature, as individuals and groups, is that they're not predators, or conquerors. They're the flora, if you will, of artificial nature. The grazers, the forests themselves—the backbone of the ecology that makes the arena possible. I suspect they're the base of the whole civilizational ecology of Vega. They're not self-aware, largely, because they don't need to be. But they can think—or employ machines to think for them—and their advantage lies in peace and trade. *That* is the alliance your forefathers refused; instead, you chose to ally with the sharks, believing you could control their appetites. Well, you can't. The ones you thought of as your allies are the ones who have been trying to break into Virga. Long ago they mined the world's wall with monsters cued to awaken and enter if Candesce's field should falter. Several years ago, it did—for just one night. Hayden Griffin," she nodded to his sleeping form, "was there. He saw it happen, and he saw *how* it happened: that it was a human from the country of your allies who manipulated the admiral of Slipstream into shutting off the field. His lover, Aubrey Mahallan, was an agent of the same people who sent Holon to you.

"Your 'friends' showed their true colors that day. But you have to remember that others once presented themselves as allies, back at the very beginning. And now they are renewing their offer, for mutual advantage."

The Guardsman stood up. "We're going to have to think about this," he said. As he turned away, she caught a gleam of light from his shoulder, where some sort of military insignia was affixed to his uniform. She wondered just how high his rank was in the Home Guard.

"Do you think he'll convince anybody else?" mused Tarvey.

Leal lay down under the black, cloudless sky. "There's at least a hundred airmen out there, and more showing up all the time. Eustace Loll and the commodore and Holon and the rest of the Home Guard are all here. We're free for tonight, Tarvey. But I wouldn't expect that to last, do you?"

He didn't reply, and she was too tired to worry about it. For a few minutes she savored an odd delight at having given a history lesson to someone. As she'd talked to the man from the Home Guard, for a brief time it had been as if she was back at the university, tutoring an eager student. She clutched at this feeling as if it were a safety rope, and despite the hard ground and the strange lack of a feeling of motion, she slept.

LEAL WAS AWAKENED by panicked shouts. She sat up, blinking. The suns were waking overhead, but for now they appeared like so many lantern flames, red and wavering far off in the sky. Their light cast a strange shadowless illumination across the "landscape" that was much easier to see through than full daylight.

Airmen were running for their rifles, forming into ragged lines and aiming in the direction of something—some things, that were approaching along the ground. Leal rubbed her eyes, unsure of just what she was seeing. She felt Tarvey's hand on her shoulder, heard him say, "What is that?"

They were bigger than men. At first she thought they were advancing two-by-two, like a sighted man leading a blind man. Then she realized that these beings each had four legs, not two, and tall necks at the front topped with strange long heads. Six or seven of them had nosed their way out of a patch of woods and were stepping in a strangely dainty way through the grass, in the direction of the camp.

"I come," said a tiny voice at Leal's feet. She looked down at the junk-doll, which was watching the apparitions with its hands on its hips. It twisted its body to look up at her.

"All of me crashed, too," it said.

Leal gave a shuddering sigh, and sat down heavily. Tarvey looked at her, puzzled. "What's wrong?"

"My task," she said wearily. "I guess it's not over yet."

The four-legged creatures were built out of salvaged pieces of wreckage. Their shape was half-familiar; she was sure she'd seen its like in some ancient drawing. They stood as high as a man at the shoulder and had broad backs. As they drew nearer they appeared to spot Leal, and they trotted over to her. The Abyssal airmen were hunkering down, aiming their rifles, and waiting for orders.

"It's fine!" Leal shouted. "They're friends."

The airmen were muttering, and the commodore came running over, hitching up his pants, his face flushed.

Leal turned to Tarvey. "Gather your men," she murmured. "This might be a prudent time for us to leave."

"Leave?" He glanced around. "Where to? If this whole world turns, then we're a thousand miles or more from free air. To get back to Virga, we'd have to . . ."

"Walk," she said, nodding. "Yes, we're going to have to walk. Listen, Aethyr is a sphere like Virga. If we're at its waist, the land is going to start curving up as we go, like a, a hill." She tasted the old word, then smiled at Tarvey. "At some point the slope will get practically vertical, but I'm sure gravity will be so low by then that we'll be able to take to the air. Then we'll fly back to Virga."

His eyes were wide. "To deliver your message."

"To deliver," she said evenly, "my message." She gazed steadily at him, and after a minute Tarvey ran off to rally Hayden's crewmen. The Abyssals were still unsure what to do, but at any moment the commodore might lose his nerve and order his men to fire. Leal knelt by Hayden.

"Come on," she said as she helped him sit up. "We have to go."

He winced, then shook his head. "Leal, I . . . thanks, but I'm not fit to travel."

"No, you have to, you have to." She smoothed her hands down his grimy shirt, ran her fingers through his hair. "You have to get up. If we don't leave now, they'll . . ."

He laughed shortly. "They'll what? I'm still the sun lighter. No, Leal, go on. Go back to Virga and then send an expedition to pick the rest of us up. I'll stay here. It's better if I do."

"Why are you saying that?" She glanced around frantically; Tarvey and the rest of Hayden's crew were running over now. "We can't abandon you here!"

He coughed, then smiled. "These people are going to need my

help. Maybe a few of the Home Guard have seen places as strange as this, but for the rest . . . Leal, they're little more than boys, most of them, just in the navy for a lark or some career opportunities. They're lost—even the commodore, he'll be good at getting everybody mustered, but then he's going to start making bad decisions. I can hold them together, keep them from going crazy and doing something stupid. They need me. And . . ." He sighed like a man suddenly relieved of a huge burden.

"And Virga doesn't."

Tarvey knelt next to Hayden. "Go on," Hayden said to him. "I'll be fine."

Tarvey hugged him, causing Hayden to wince. Then Tarvey stood up, nodding sharply. He beamed at Hayden. He, too, looked to Leal as if some weight had been taken from his shoulders.

"Wait!" someone shouted. They turned to find Eustace Loll hobbling toward them. "Where are you going?" asked the Eternist minister in a hurt tone of voice.

"To find help," said Leal.

"Well . . ." Loll turned this way then that, casting about for something familiar or reassuring. Finding nothing, he raised his free hand beseechingly to Leal. "Take me with you."

Leal and Tarvey gaped at one another. The sheer audacity of the request made her laugh. But Tarvey shrugged.

"Why not?" he said. "I don't think he'll murder us in our sleep. And we'll need someone with a good reputation, and influence, to vouch for your story."

"All right. Come on then," she said to Loll. "But I don't see how you can keep up."

"We can carry him." One of the tall four-legged beasts had spoken. It lowered its front legs and long neck and, after a moment of revolted hesitation, Loll clambered onto its back.

Leal strolled over to the commodore, ignoring the rifles and pistols that were aimed at her. "If you have to leave this area," she said, "make sure you put down signs so we can find you. I'll return as soon as I can with a rescue party."

The commodore raised a shaking hand to his white hair. "But how can we survive . . . ?"

"There's life all around, and pools of water . . . uh, 'lakes' they used to call them," she said. "And there should be more pieces of him," she pointed at the emissary's new bodies. "They know a lot about these worlds. They should be able to help. You'll be fine."

He seemed at a loss for words, so she returned to where Tarvey and the others were waiting. The emissary's selves were already headed away. They seemed to know where to go.

Hayden waved them on. She nodded and walked away without another glance at the wreckage, the soldiers, or the Eternists.

Tarvey turned to Leal, his sharp nod of acceptance better than a smile; and she fell into step beside him.